The Sean O'Rourke Series
Book 2

A Killer For The Common Good
LAWMAN

by

Michael E. Cook

TELEMACHUS PRESS

This book is a work of fiction. Names, characters, places and incidents are either the product of the author's imagination or are used fictitiously. Any resemblance to actual persons, living or dead, or to actual events or locales is entirely coincidental.

Cover design by Tad Gallaugher and Telemachus Press, LLC

Published by Telemachus Press, LLC
http://www.telemachuspress.com

Contact the author at mailto:cookorourkeseries@gmail.com

ISBN: 978-1-942899-08-2 (eBook)
ISBN: 978-1-942899-09-9 (Paperback)

Version: 2015.05.27

10 9 8 7 6 5 4 3 2 1

Table of Contents

PROLOGUE

Sean O'Rourke, has a learned a lot in the short time he has been a Federal Marshal. It will take every skill he has ever acquired to stay alive. There are more outlaws than there are lawmen, and it will take time to clean them out. It seems that the more he kills, the more of them there are.

Now with several deputies, it is time to pursue the Hawks, and then the Anderson bunch. But how many lives will it cost? How many more times will he and Michael have their toast, "Here's to not getting killed."? Will his woman, Maggie, be in constant danger? Will these outlaws use her to get to him? Do these outlaws have eyes and ears everywhere? Who runs the Hawk clan?

The Sean O'Rourke Series
Book 2

A Killer For The Common Good
LAWMAN

CHAPTER ONE

Sean handed the note he had written for Michael to Ike and told him one more time. "Make sure he gets this note. I have told Michael what's going on and I want you to swear him in as a Deputy Federal Marshal. I know that is not legal, but I won't be here to do it, so I'm giving you the authority. Ike, you are now a Deputy Federal Marshal. Consider yourself sworn in."

"Hey, I never said I would do this," said Ike. "I'm leaving afore too long anyway."

"Don't worry about it Ike," started Sean. "Things will not be different for you. Just swear Michael in when he gets here, and as soon as your leg heals, go ahead and resign and take off. Tell him I'll get him a badge later when I get back, unless you got a badge laying around that says Deputy on it."

"Actually, I do have a Deputy's badge," responded Ike. "I'll give it to him, and if he wears it, it's up to him."

"Thanks Ike, I'll be goin' now. Best of luck to you, and tell Michael I'll be back as soon as I can," said Sean.

"Don't go gettin' yerself killed," said Ike. "You are very out-numbered this time."

~~~~

Sean went to the General Store where Jonathan was waiting. "Got all you need?" asked Sean. "Do I owe anything?"

"No, I'm well supplied," answered Jonathan. "Let's get movin'."

They took off at a trot heading south. After maybe a mile out of town, Sean asked Jonathan. "What do you like to be called? Do you want to be called Jon, Jonathan, or maybe even Reb?"

"Well, most folks call me Jonny. Where did you think they got the name Jonny Reb? Just kiddin' there yank. Call me Jon, and I'll call you Sean if that suits you," said Jonathan.

"It's a good thing you got a sense a humor, there Jon," said Sean. "You'll need it where we're goin'. You got plenty of ammunition for that Henry?"

"Believe it or not, that yank had over two hundred rounds on him when I took his rifle," answered Jon. "Never knew there was that many bullets for just one man. I've fired it several times, and it's a honey."

"That's good," said Sean. "Now what's that pistol you got in that flap holster?"

"It's just an army Colt, cap and ball," said Jon, "but it's in good shape."

"Well if we don't get ourselves killed shortly, I'll get you a new pistol," said Sean. "One of those new conversions to metal cartridges. I got a gunsmith in St. Louis who can do conversions. I carry three of them, plus my Sharps, a Henry, and a ten gauge. I bought that Spencer for a friend of mine down in the nations. He was badly wounded by the Anderson bunch. I hope he's still alive when we get there."

"I reckon you don't want to get killed for lack of shootin' back, do you?" asked Jon.

"No, I do not," answered Sean. "This is a rough bunch we're after. Are you ever gonna ask me what this job pays?"

"I wasn't worried about it," said Jon, "but since you brought it up, tell me."

"I'm the Marshal, and I get fifty a month," said Sean. "You're a deputy, so you'll get forty. Plus, we can collect any reward money offered. You cannot make that much money anywhere, but it's a dangerous business. I'm savin' my money for a good saloon. If we don't get killed, you can think about spending your share."

~~~~

In a few days, they arrived in the Nations. They had not seen a living soul on the entire trip. As they moved deeper and deeper into the Nations, they still saw no one, but almost every house or shack or barn of any kind had been burned or shot to pieces.

"Who does this Anderson fella think he is, Sherman marchin' to the sea?" exclaimed Jon as they neared another burned house.

"I told you this was a rough bunch," said Sean. "When I was down here a while back, he wasn't here, but I found his hideout and burned it to the ground. I left notes all over the place so he'd know who did it. That man's hated me since we were boys back in Tennessee. He joined the reb army at the beginning, but got kicked out for shooting prisoners. Then he joined Quantrill. After the war, he didn't slow down one bit. He might be goin' around killin' and burnin' to find out if anyone gave me a hand when I was here."

"Well did anyone help you when you were here?" asked Jon.

"Yes, a man named John Littletree," said Sean. "I came to know him because his son tried to steal my horse one day, but that's another story. Telegram from the Judge said his place is maybe being watched. We'll be there shortly. When we get closer, I'll slip over that way and have a look-see. Then we'll figure out how to move. I hope you're good at slippin' up on folks."

"Don't forget," exclaimed Jon, "I'm half Cherokee. Remember, I slipped up on you, and I've learned a lot more since then. You shot me when I was too busy talkin' and didn't have my hammer cocked. I shot the yank who shot me when he didn't have his hammer cocked. I don't intend to get shot again."

~~~~

When they neared the small village where John Littletree lived, they dismounted, and tied the horses in a small thicket of trees. Jon stayed while Sean slipped in to see what, if anything was going on. As he got closer, he spotted some horses. There were two of them hobbled about five hundred yards north of the village, and two more were hobbled about four hundred yards to the south. Sean had his spyglass and was careful to make sure it didn't glare in the sunlight. About two hundred yards from the horses to the north, he spotted two men. One appeared to be sleeping while the other was keeping watch. To the south, there were also two men. One of them appeared to be sleeping also. Sean could see their rifles, but could not make out what they were. He worked his way back to where Jon was.

"Well, there's four of them watching the place," started Sean. "When it's closer to dark, we'll get closer and I'll show you where they are. After dark, we'll slip up on them. Try to take one of them alive if you can. If you can't, try to not fire any shots if possible.

Don't hesitate. I don't wanna bury you yet. I assume you have a good knife, right?"

"Yep," answered Jon, "I got a good knife and it's sharp enough to shave with."

~~~~

The small village was down in a small valley with woods on the north and south sides. The woods were not thick as they had probably been harvested for the building of the village. Right before dark, they made their approach, and Sean showed Jon the layout and the location of the men watching. "I'll take the two on the north side, and you get the two on the south side," Sean began. "Remember, try to take at least one alive if possible, and no shooting unless there's no other way. If I were you, I wouldn't use that Henry for a club. They're good shootin' rifles, but they weren't made for cracking someone's skull."

"I'll get it done," responded Jon. "Now let's get movin'."

~~~~

Both men started their move. There was a half moon, so there was some light, so they'd have to be very careful. Sean moved like a cat. His years with the Cheyenne taught him well. He moved to within ten yards of the two men, and they had no idea he was around. Jon had moved well too and was close to his two. On the north side, one of the men was still sleeping. He was snoring something awful. The other man keeping watch, was chewing on a piece of jerky. With all that noise from the snoring, Sean easily crept up behind the one who was awake and cracked the back of his head with the butt of his Sharps. The man asleep woke up at the sound of the crack and started yelling, "What the—?" Before he could finish, Sean cracked his head with the Sharps also.

It was very quiet that night, and the sound really traveled. Jon had heard the crack when Sean had hit the first man, and then heard the second man start to talk, and then the crack when Sean hit him. The man awake on Jon's side had heard it also. He had his rifle up and was going to shoot when Jon came from behind and stuck his knife upward, just under his ribs on his right side and practically gutted him. The man was thrashing some, and it woke up the second man. Before he could do anything, Jon had his pistol stuck on the man's forehead. "I wouldn't move if I were you. I never miss at this range," said Jon. The man must not have believed that Jon would shoot him, and reached for a pistol that was laying beside him. As soon as his hand touched it, Jon squeezed the trigger and the man's head practically exploded. Then there was total quiet.

Lamps were being lit down in the village. People were coming outside to see if they could see what had happened. Sean waited a good fifteen minutes, then let out a yell. "Are you still with me Jon?"

Jon answered back, "I am, but these two are not. Had no choice."

"Let's get their horses and take them down to the village," said Sean. "I got my two tied and gagged."

~~~~

When they got down to the village, young John Littletree was standing in front of his family's cabin. "Hey young man," said Sean, "is your Pa healing up alright?"

"Yes he is," answered young John. "We have been waiting for you and are glad you are here."

"Glad to be here," said Sean. "This here is my Deputy, also named Jon, Jon O'Brien. I want you to round up any elders you can find or any of your tribal police and bring them here. I'll go check on your Pa while you're gone."

Young John did as instructed, and Sean went inside to see his friend. Jon stayed out and kept watch. "I see you're getting better, my friend," said Sean. "I hope you'll be up shortly. What we're gonna do here may get rough. I brought you a repeatin' rifle also, a Spencer, seven shots without reloading, and fifty rounds."

"It is good to see you, my friend and I thank you for the rifle," John said. "I hope to be better before it gets too rough. Our people have put up with those outlaws for too long, and we will not do it anymore. They have killed too many, and now they will bleed."

"My new deputy and I just took care of four of them," said Sean. "Two are dead, and two are tied up outside. I figured to see what your tribal police wants to do with them after I try to get them to talk."

"I'll tell you right now, my friend," said John. "We will do it the white man's way. We will hang them."

"That's alright by me," said Sean. "I do hope we get some information out of them first." Sean heard some talking outside, and he knew the police or some elders were outside. "I'm goin' out to talk with your people, John," said Sean. "Be back in when we're done."

Sean went back outside, and there were four men standing beside young John. John introduced them as tribal police. One spoke. "I am Tom Redshirt," he started. " I became the Chief of

Police after these men killed our Chief, Sam Eagle. We will hang these men in the morning. If you want to question them, do it before then. I will look for a good tree right now."

"Alright," said Sean, "see you in the morning. Jon, see if you can get any information outta those two, like where's Anderson, how many more are there, name's and such. Try to make them think we'll go easy on them if they talk."

~~~~

Jon pulled the two from their horses and tied them to a hitching rail and began questioning them. They must have been loyal to Anderson, because Jon couldn't get anything out of them. He stopped after a good while. He thought about doing some nasty things to them, but decided it didn't matter. They were going to hang in the morning anyway.

Sean came back out after talking with John for a while. "Well, any information?" he asked.

"Nothin'," answered Jon. "I guess they don't believe in snitchin' even if they know they're gonna die."

"Well anyway, you and I will take turns keeping watch, two hours at a time," started Sean. "Won't be long and they'll know somethin's wrong when those men are missin' or don't show up back at their camp. I'll take first watch. You bed down over by that big oak so you won't be far away if somethin' happens."

~~~~

Nothing happened that night. Right at daylight, the tribal police came and put the two outlaws on some horses with their hands tied behind their backs. They moved to the far end of town. There was another huge oak tree with a big limb that looked like it was perfect for the job. John and Sean stayed by John Littletree's cabin. They wanted to let the tribal police take care of things.

Just as Tom Redshirt was about to swat the horses on the rump, Sean heard the thump as a bullet struck Tom in the back, then tear through his body. Then he heard the shot. When the blood splattered from his body, the horses bolted, and the two outlaws were hanged. "Take cover," Sean yelled. "They got a man up there somewhere and he knows how to shoot."

~~~~

Just as Sean finished yelling for everyone to take cover, there was another thump and a split second later, the shot was heard. Another tribal policeman fell dead. By this time, everyone had taken cover. Sean had his pistols on him, but he needed the Sharps. Jon had his Henry and his pistol on him. Sean yelled to Jon, "I saw his smoke that time. Gotta get the Sharps, and work my way up around him. He's way up near the top of the ridge to the south, four, maybe five hundred yards out. When I yell, take that Henry and fire as many rounds as fast as you can up there. It's outta range, but should make him keep his head down for a bit. That should give me time to get the Sharps and move into the trees. He's probably not alone either. Could be several of them to the north and south. After you see me in the trees and working my way around, you work your way up behind me. Stay maybe fifty yards back. I'll get that shooter. You watch my back."

"Whenever you're ready," replied Jon. "I'll make this Henry sing like it's never sung before."

Sean let out a yell and Jon opened up with the Henry. Young John Littletree saw what was going on and grabbed the Spencer and opened up too. Other tribe members joined in also with whatever weapons they had. Sean worked his way to his horse and grabbed the Sharps from the scabbard and some shells and was soon in the trees. Jon reloaded the Henry and began to work his way into the trees. As he was running and almost to the trees, he heard a shot, and then it felt like his belt was being torn off. He looked down and saw that the bullet had ripped the flap off his holster. He grabbed his hip and went down pretending to be hit. This shot had come from a different direction than the sniper's, and was very close. Jon lay there hoping this shooter would get careless and come over to see his victim.

It didn't take long. In a few minutes, Jon could hear someone coming towards him. Then he heard talking. There were two of them. Jon slipped his hand onto his pistol. He was laying on his belly with his head turned to the right. They were coming from his right. As they got closer, Jon could see that one had a Spencer and the other, a Sharps carbine. They must have been confident because neither of them had their rifle pointed at him, plus neither of them had their hammer cocked. When they were maybe ten yards away, Jon went from his belly onto his left side, pulled his pistol, and shot both men in the chest. They hit the ground dead. Both of them were also packing pistols, army Colts, so Jon stuffed them into his belt and went back to following Sean.

Sean had heard the first shot and turned around to see Jon go down, and when he did, he saw another outlaw to his left. The outlaw and Sean both saw Jon shoot the other two outlaws. Sean was only about fifty yards from the outlaw, so he decided he would try to close in on him if possible before he would take a shot at Jon. If he couldn't get close enough in time, he would just shoot him. The outlaw was so intent on getting a good shot at Jon that he wasn't concerned about anything else and was taking his time. He knew that Jon had not seen him, so he just stood where he was, right beside a big oak tree. Sean was right behind him when the outlaw began his squeeze on the trigger of his rifle. When Sean cracked the back of his skull with the Sharps, the outlaw's rifle fired as he fell, the bullet striking the ground just in front of him.

Jon had not seen the other outlaw. When he heard the shot, and then saw Sean, he waved to Sean to let him know that he was alright, and they again started working their way around the shooter. They had moved several hundred yards without seeing any more outlaws. As they were moving, the shooter was still firing toward the village. By the way he was firing, Sean could tell that he was methodically picking his targets and making each shot count. Sean figured that he must have been a Sharpshooter during the war, but he was making a mistake, he wasn't changing positions.

Sean worked his way up a small knoll and got behind a huge tree stump. As he peered over the top of the stump, he could now see the shooter. He was behind a down tree. He was over five hundred yards away, but Sean could see that he was using a Sharps with a telescopic sight. Beside him was another man with a spy glass. This man was being a spotter for the shooter and was probably supposed to be watching his back also. Sean signaled Jon to move up to his position. When Jon got there, Sean showed him the shooter's position. "There's two of them," started Sean. "I'll take out the shooter first. Then we'll get the other one. You watch our backs."

The shooter was in the kneeling position with his rifle across the down tree for a rest. Sean was on the shooter's right side and could only see the shooter from his shoulder up. The other man was on the shooter's left, right beside him. Sean would try for a head shot. He took a quick check of the wind, sighted in, and began his squeeze on the trigger. A split second after the Sharps roared, Sean heard a loud scream, and then a moan. Then it was quiet. Sean and Jon waited a good ten minutes, then slowly worked their way to the shooter's position. Both men lay there dead. "Just how in the hell?" said Jon. "You only fired one shot."

When Sean had fired, the shooter had apparently been taking aim on another target when the bullet struck. It went through his right hand, through the grip on the stock of the rifle, through both sides of his face, and into the side of the second man. There was a big splinter sticking out of the right eye of the shooter.

"I seen a lot of strange things in the war," said Jon, "but nothing like this. I'd never believe this if someone told me. No sir, I wouldn't believe it. Do you reckon that splinter went into his brain and killed him, or do you think maybe a piece of the bullet broke off and went in through his eye too? Too much blood to tell. This guy was shootin' with his mouth open. The bullet missed his teeth."

"Don't matter how it happened," replied Sean. "We would have killed them anyway. Now let's set tight for a spell and make sure there's no more of them around." It was still quiet after fifteen minutes, so Sean and Jon worked their way back down to the village. As they entered the village, the people came out from cover to meet them.

"Did you get the shooter?" asked John Littletree.

"Yes," answered Sean. "We killed four more too. Did we lose any more down here?"

"Two more were hit after the two tribal police were killed, but they should live," answered Littletree. "We have killed nine of them so far. How many more do you think they have?"

"Well the telegram I got from the Judge, said there were fifteen to twenty of them," answered Sean. "That telegram was based on information from you, John. Just how did you get a telegram sent anyway?"

"When that gang first came back, I was getting a visit from a Cherokee friend of mine. He was a scout for the Union Army when they were at Vicksburg," replied Littletree. "He volunteered to get the word out for us. I wrote the message and gave him some money. I have no idea where he went to get the telegram sent. We're glad he got through, and you are here. When we first saw them, and they started burning and shooting, there were fifteen to twenty that we saw. Anyway, we have cut them down some."

"Yes," said Sean, "we have cut them down some, but a gang like that has no problem finding more scum to fill their ranks. Now we have the advantage. Anderson's not used to tanglin' with people who can fight back. He's used to ambushin' and killin' folks who are defenseless and not ready for him. We will be ready now. Jon, take young John and a couple others and go out and round up the weapons and horses of the ones we just killed. Go careful like, more of them may have heard all the shootin' and come to see. I doubt if Anderson himself would come. I believe he sees himself as a great commander and would send others to report back."

~~~~

Jon and the others rounded up the weapons and horses and got back without incident. Each of the outlaws had a rifle and at least one pistol. Some of them had two pistols. All of them had been packing plenty of ammunition. The shooter with the Sharps with the telescopic sight had at least seventy five rounds. The stock of the rifle was in bad shape after the bullet had passed through, but it had not broken off and John Littletree believed he could wrap rawhide around it and make it strong enough to shoot. If that didn't work, he would carve a new stock.

"Let's get the dead buried and the wounded patched up," said Sean. "Then we're goin' after them. Are the men here ready for this?" Sean asked Littletree.

"Yes, my friend," answered Littletree. "We will make them bleed and finish what they have started."

CHAPTER TWO

Michael O'Connor arrived in Abilene four days after Sean and Jon had left for the Nations. Ike was setting out in front of his office with his leg propped up when the stage arrived. He knew right away that the big man getting off the stage was Michael and called to him. "Michael O'Connor, I have a message for you from your friend Sean O'Rourke. Please come over and get it. As you can see, I don't get around too well yet." Michael got his bag from the stage driver and walked over to Ike.

"And who might you be sir?" asked Michael.

"Name's Ike Coleton," answered Ike. "I was a part time town Marshal here till your friend swore me in as a Federal Deputy. You better go ahead and read this message so you'll know what's goin' on."

Michael read the message, and without any questions or complaints, he looked at Ike and said, "Swear me in." After the swearing in, he asked Ike to point him in the direction of Maggie's Place.

"Just down the street a bit," said Ike. "You can't miss it. It's the only saloon in town." Michael thanked Ike, shook his hand, and started for Maggie's Place.

As he entered the saloon, his eyes went straight to the painting on the wall. "Jesus, Joseph, and Mary," Michael said out loud to himself, "if that's Maggie, my young friend has the most beautiful creature on God's green earth for his woman." Michael could not take his eyes off the painting. He was totally mesmerized and would have stayed that way for some time, but after several minutes, he thought he heard a voice, a woman's voice. "No, it can't be," he thought to himself, "pictures can't talk." Then he heard it again. This time he turned around, and there she was.

"Hello, you must be Michael O'Connor, Sean's friend," she started, "I'm Maggie and I'm very pleased to finally meet you."

Michael could not speak. Was it even possible? This woman was even more beautiful than the painting. After a few more minutes, he was finally able to speak. "Apologies, ma'am," he started, "I have never been near such beauty and I am speechless."

"You're a big handsome man yourself," replied Maggie. "My ladies will be after you if you're not careful."

"And just what would they want with an old war horse like me ma'am?" asked Michael.

"Some women know a good man when they see one," said Maggie. "I would know that you are a good man even if Sean hadn't told me all about you."

"You're embarrassing me ma'am," said Michael.

"I didn't mean to," replied Maggie, "But you are a good man. I can tell, and now, please call me Maggie. That's my name."

"Yes ma'—, I mean Maggie," said Michael.

"Now that we're acquainted, grab your bag and I'll show you where you'll be staying," began Maggie. "There's a room out back, and it has everything you will need. It even has a big bed which is a good thing since you're a big man." Then Maggie led him to the room and showed him where everything was.

"This is more than I'll need Maggie," said Michael. "It's more than I've had the last twenty plus years."

"Glad you appreciate it Michael," said Maggie. "Take some time and get yourself settled, then come out to the bar and we'll show you how we do things here."

It didn't take Michael long to get settled. After being in the army over half of his life, he didn't have much in the way of possessions, just old uniforms, two new sets of clothes, one of which he was wearing, a jacket, and a Colt army revolver. He laid on the bed for a few minutes just to give it a try, and was amazed at how comfortable it was. "I better get up and get to the bar before I fall asleep on this thing," he said to himself.

Michael made his way to the bar, and Maggie was there with Tom. Tom had been the regular bartender ever since Maggie opened the place. Maggie introduced them to each other. "I'll be glad to have the help," Tom said. "Business has really picked up lately ever since your friend Sean showed up around here."

"I can imagine so," said Michael. "My young friend has never looked for trouble in his life, but sooner or later, it seems to show up around him. Anyway, this'll be a big change for me."

"What do you mean?" asked Tom.

"Because I've never been on this side of the bar before, my friend," answered Michael. "And Maggie, if it's all the same to you, I won't be wearin' that Deputy badge in here while I'm working, not unless a situation arises. Don't want to scare away customers."

"That'll be fine, Michael," said Maggie. "This is usually a quiet place, but whenever you have liquor and women, there's always a chance for trouble. As time goes on, you'll learn who the potential troublemakers are. There's a man named McCoy who wants to build huge cattle pens and bring the railroad here, so the Texas boys can drive their herds up here to ship. If that happens, this place will boom. There will be more saloons and gambling houses and lewd women than you can count. Let's enjoy the easy times while we can. Tom, show Michael where everything is and how much we charge for drinks. Michael, I have one more thing before I give you to Tom. I know you have a pistol. You may wear it if you feel the need. If you are comfortable without it, that's all right too. I keep two shotguns behind the bar, double barrels. There's one near each end. We've never had to use them, but I know that sooner or later, something will happen."

"Maggie," Michael began, "I'll do everything in my power to keep from using guns. I'm a pretty good talker and I'm pretty good with my fists."

"Thank you Michael," said Maggie, "I know you'll do your best. There's one more thing. Sean tells me you can hold your liquor."

"Yes Maggie," replied Michael, "indeed I can, but I'll tell you right now. I will not drink on the job, and I'll be there when you need me."

"Thank you Michael. I was going to say that I wouldn't care if you had a shot once in a while on the job, just don't abuse it," said Maggie. "I know you're an honest man and I will be able to count on you. Now Tom, show Michael all he needs to know."

~~~~

Tom took Michael to the storage room and showed him where everything was. "The whiskey comes in those barrels and we have to put it in the bottles," Tom began. "We take every precaution so we don't spill any. At this place, we do not water down the liquor like most places do. We figure if you give someone a good drink at a decent price, they'll be back. We don't have ice, so our beer is warm, but we're hoping to get an ice house built so that at least some of the time, we can serve cold beer. We do not have wine or champagne, maybe someday when we have the clientele. Things don't pick up around here till late afternoon, so I always come in late morning and get everything ready. We have a darn good cook here too. We just call him Cookie. He comes in mid morning and gets his stuff ready. He'll stay till about seven in the evening. His wife helps out when we get really busy. Maggie let's us eat for free. Maggie's girls don't live here. She let's them use the rooms upstairs. They keep all the money they earn. Maggie figures we make enough money off the liquor their customers drink. Have you got any questions, Michael?"

"No, I'm ready to get started," answered Michael.

"Alright, now there's only one more thing," said Tom. "We do not take credit. When a man gets a drink, he pays. Maggie will not let anyone run a tab, and I mean no one. If someone doesn't pay, out they go, and I mean quickly. And, they will still owe for the drink they didn't pay for."

"I do have one question, Tom," said Michael. "Just how can any man concentrate on what he's doing when that gorgeous woman is around?"

"I'm tellin' you, Michael," answered Tom, "when I first started working for Maggie, it was tough. It still is. I think my wife likes it that I work here. She thinks it keeps me all worked up for when I come home to her. Maggie's girls are very beautiful too. They may be working girls, but they are not tramps or trash. You'll find that out when you meet them."

~~~~

The first two days working at the saloon went really well. Most of the townspeople were warming up to Michael very well also. He had gone around and introduced himself to everyone he saw and everyone he met seemed very nice. There was a young business-man who was starting a bank, and Michael was one of his first customers. After a week at Maggie's, Michael knew for sure that he wanted to own a saloon. There had been a few men drink a little too much and had gotten loud, but there had been no serious issues. One of Maggie's girls, Betty, who was maybe a little older than the other girls, but still very attractive, was taking an interest in Michael. Michael thought that she might get into trouble with Maggie because it seemed she was up at the bar a lot talking to him and maybe not paying attention to customers. The customers must have been drinking enough, because Maggie never showed any signs of being upset.

~~~~

Halfway into the second week, things changed. Ethan Hawk came into Maggie's Place looking for trouble. One night right after dark, he came tearing through the front doors of the saloon and started yelling. "Where's that mick bartender who's s'posed to be friends with that no count lawman O'Rourke? I'm gonna beat the hell outta him."

"Over here," said Michael from behind the bar. "Now come over here and we'll discuss this like gentlemen." Michael could see that Hawk wasn't armed.

"Are you stupid or what?" said Ethan as walked up to the bar. "I came here to whoop ya, not talk to ya."

Michael could smell the whiskey on his breath, but could tell that he wasn't drunk yet. He could also tell that this man smelled bad, really bad. Michael looked him straight in the eyes and said, "Kind sir, if we're goin' to have a fight, you need to bathe first. You smell bad. I mean really bad. I don't want to be gaggin' from the smell as we're fightin'. Now go get a bath and come back. I'll be here waitin'."

"Why you stupid mick," Ethan shouted as he took a swing across the bar at Michael with his right hand and missed. When he missed, it threw him off balance a little, and Michael reached out, grabbed his hair, and slammed his face into the bar, breaking his nose. Blood went everywhere. When Ethan finally got his wits back and the blood wiped off some, he stood there cussing across the bar, but Michael was not there. "Where you at, you son of a bitch? Now yer gonna pay!" he said. There was a tap on Ethan's shoulder from behind, and he turned to see Michael standing toe to toe with him. Ethan reared back to throw a right hand, but as he did, Michael gave him a good jab in the gut bending him over. As he was going down, Michael put his two hands together, put them back over his head, and then slammed down as hard as he could driving Hawk the rest of the way to the floor.

"Maggie darlin'," began Michael, "if you'll excuse me for a few minutes, this gentlemen needs escorted to jail. I'll return shortly. Would someone see if we can find this man some medical attention?"

Michael practically carried Hawk to the jail. Ike was there and hobbled over and opened the cell for him. "Just what I need," said Ike. "I'm trying to get healed up and get outta here, and now we got trouble with the Hawks again. Just what I need."

"Now don't go gettin' yourself all worked up," said Michael. "I'll come over and have a nice talk with this gentlemen in the morning, and see what we can work out. I'm sure he'll be reasonable."

"Yeh, he'll be real reasonable alright," said Ike. "He'll want you reasonably dead."

"The whole reb army couldn't get me killed, so I don't believe this gentleman can do it," said Michael. "Now good evening to you."

~~~~

When Michael got back to the saloon, he was an instant celebrity. The short fight gave the customers something else to talk about, and while they were talking, they were drinking. When the excitement died down some, Betty let Michael know that he was spending the night with her. He did not object.

The next morning, Betty made him the best breakfast he'd had in years. "You're a good woman and a good cook," Michael said. "I hope that we can have breakfast again sometime soon."

"You can count on it," Betty replied. "Been a long time since I wanted to cook for a man. You're a good man, Michael O'Connor. You're a good man. Any woman would be proud to cook for you."

"You're not just saying all these things because I bested that Hawk fella, are you?" asked Michael.

"No Michael, I am not," Betty replied. "I'm saying it because you are a true gentleman, and they are very rare around here."

"Betty, you are a gem," said Michael. "Now I better finish my coffee and get down to the jail and have a talk with Mr. Hawk. I'll see you this evening at work." He gave her a long passionate kiss and then left for the jail.

~~~~

Michael opened the door to the jail and found Ike asleep on a cot behind his desk. Ethan Hawk was still asleep too. Michael gave Ike a nudge in the ribs to wake him and then grabbed a metal cup off Ike's desk and banged it on the bars to wake Hawk. "What in the hell do you want, you stupid mick?" said Hawk. Then Ike mumbled something about someone making coffee.

Michael grabbed Ike's chair and sat down in front of the cell. "Allow me to introduce myself," began Michael. "I am Michael O'Connor, Deputy Federal Marshal Michael O'Connor, and you sir, attempted to assault a Federal Officer. I'm gonna leave you in there for ten days and see if it improves your manners any. After ten days, if I see no improvement, you'll be in there for ten more days."

"So yer a lawman too," started Hawk. "Don't matter, sooner or later, I'll git outta here and your life won't be worth spit. We'll git you and that other no count lawman. Like I told him, and I'm tellin' you, there's more of us than there is a you. Some a my kin might just pay you a visit anyway before I get outta here."

"Well, Mr. Hawk," Michael began, "if any of your relatives come to town causin' any kind of trouble before you get out of here, I will come here and personally put a bullet in your brain. Now you think about that while you're in here. Whatever will happen, you'll be first to die."

CHAPTER THREE

The wounded were patched up as best could be done. Their wounds were not mortal. Then Sean told what was left of the tribal police to round up the elders. It wasn't long and all the elders were present. They were meeting at Littletree's cabin. "I want you to round up all of your people who are fighting age," Sean started. "I want them and their families here. Then I need a count on weapons."

"That may take a couple days," said Littletree. "There are several families who live way out in the hills and on small farms. We do not know how many have been burned out or killed by the gang."

"When we came this way from the north, every building of any kind was either shot to pieces or burned or both," said Sean. "So we won't waste time looking to the north. If there were any survivors, they would probably have come to the village thinking it would be safer. Now let's get people out looking. While your people are out, make sure they keep a good look-out for that bunch. I don't want anyone getting ambushed. You people are supposed to be good at this kind of stuff anyway."

"At one time," started Littletree, "our people were the best trackers and could sneak up on any living creature. Living like a white man has made us soft, but we are still good trackers, and all of us can still shoot a bow. That will come in handy when we want to keep things quiet."

"That's good to know," said Sean. "Now I want four lookouts posted, two on the north ridge several hundred yards apart, and two on the south ridge several hundred yards apart. Figure out some kinda signal that we will all understand in case we get more visitors. After the men get back from bringing in the others, we'll send out scouts in every direction until we find their hideout. Then we'll come up with a plan to attack them. It's fall now. I figure they'll head down to Texas or even Mexico for the winter where it's warmer, so we want to get them taken care of before then."

~~~~

It took a full two days to round up everyone and get them to the village. Most of them were worried about leaving their homes empty and unprotected. Sean assured them that dead men could not rebuild a house after it was burned down, and that they were safer in the village where they had greater numbers. After the people were settled, Sean had the elders get everyone together for a meeting. Sean counted thirty men and boys who were of fighting age. All of the men had some type of rifle. Some of them were even flintlock, but they assured Sean that they were reliable. The weapons that were from the outlaws were distributed among them, and anyone who was not familiar with the weapon they received, was given instruction.

"We're gonna start sending scouts out now. They will go in all four directions and be out all day." Sean began. "If one or two men are spotted, do not kill them unless you have to. Try to follow them if possible. Maybe they'll lead us to the main bunch. Maybe they'll just be scouts keeping an eye out for us. Use your judgment and be careful. Once the main bunch is located, get back here as quickly and as quietly as possible, and we'll figure out a plan of attack. Once we do attack them, we do not want any prisoners. Anyone of them left alive is gonna hang anyway. Now you elders pick your first four scouts and get them moving. We will still keep four lookouts posted at all times."

~~~~

Two days went by with no sightings, but on the third day, a scout who had gone to the west, returned and said that he had located the main bunch. "My name is Charlie Redhorse," he said as he started giving Sean the information. "About eight miles west of here, I came upon two men. They appeared to be scouts. After watching them for maybe two hours, they started moving to the west. I followed them for two more miles. They led me right to the main bunch. There were no lookouts posted that I saw. I got off my horse, and was able to get maybe fifty yards from them. I counted twenty men and horses. There were several shacks and a big corral for the horses. The whole place is on a small rise sur-rounded by woods and there's a small creek just to the south."

"That means they'll have the high ground," said Sean. "Did you see Anderson, or anyone you thought might be Anderson?"

"Yes, I saw him," answered Redhorse. "I heard several men call him by name, and there's no mistakin' him. He's wearin' a fancy reb coat, and a cavalry hat with a big plume on it. He's wearin' a cavalry saber, and has a pistol strapped to each side. The one on his right side looked like a LeMat."

"You did good, Redhorse," said Sean. "Looks like they've already picked up a few more men since they were first spotted. We need to get after them before they get more. When the scouts all get in today, we won't send any more out. We'll keep the lookouts posted just in case. We're goin' after them tomorrow mornin'. Be leavin' right before daylight. Now I want to have a talk with all the elders over at Littletree's cabin."

~~~~

"We're headin' out with twenty men." Sean started. "We'll leave ten men here to protect the village just in case. They will keep the lookouts posted. I want two of your best horse thieves to go with us. When we get there, they'll be responsible for runnin' off their horses. I intend to surround the place and get as close as possible. We will not go chargin' in like some troop of cavalry. We'll fight on foot, staying low and under cover. Don't be in any hurry. Take your time, pick your target, and make it count. Maybe they'll have some kind of meetin' or somethin', and we can get a bunch of them outside all at once. After the first volley, they'll head to the shacks. We'll let them stay in there a while and waste their ammunition while we stay low. Then we'll burn them out. Now make sure your men have plenty of food, water, and ammunition, and get as much rest as they can. See you all before daylight."

"You got it all figured out, don't you Sean?" said Jon.

"Yep," Sean replied, "all but the part where we don't get killed. Now get some rest. We'll sure as hell be busy tomorrow."

~~~~

Twenty men headed out the next morning before daylight as planned, leaving ten behind to protect the village. Sean had them move in a single column with Charlie Redhorse way out front and a flanker on each side maybe a hundred yards out. Sean did not want any surprises. They could smell the smoke from the hideout well before they got close. When they got closer, Sean sent out two scouts to make sure they didn't have any lookouts posted, or anyone on guard duty. Both returned without seeing any lookouts or guards. "That bunch is overconfident or just plain stupid," said Sean. "They are not used to bein' the ones getting shot to pieces. Just a bunch of ambushers and backshooters."

They moved to within one hundred yards of the hideout without detection. "We'll tie the horses here and fan out around the place," said Sean. "Nobody shoot till I do unless you absolutely have to. You two horse thieves work your way to the corral and start easing out the horses if you can. If you can't, run em off soon as the shootin' starts. I don't see anyone outside yet, so let's ease in closer." They got within fifty yards and waited. Finally, men started coming out of the shacks to relieve themselves, but only one or two at a time. After about a half hour, someone in one of the shacks yelled, "Come and get it while it's hot." This bunch apparently had their own cook.

Sean had his Henry with him this time. He wouldn't need the Sharps for this close range. Several men lined up at the shack, got their food and headed out and sat around one of the several campfires that were still smoking from the night before. When Sean counted ten men, he decided to open fire. As soon as he fired, Jon and the Osage opened up, and the rest of the horses were stampeded. Men were falling like flies. Some of the ones not hit, lay flat, hoping to not get hit, while a few others ran to their shacks. Most of them were cut down before they made it. Then the ones laying flat panicked, and got up and ran to their shacks. Only one of them made it. By now, what was left of the outlaws had armed themselves, and were firing back from inside the shacks. Sean was proud of the Osage. They were taking their time, picking their targets, and making them count. The outlaws were firing away like they had plenty of ammunition and were not worried about wasting any. Sean could tell that at least two of them had Henrys, and another two had Spencers. After about an hour, the shooting slowed way down. Sean could tell now that there were only four of them left. There were two in one shack and two in another. He decided it was time to let them know who he was and that they didn't have a chance.

"This is Marshal Sean O'Rourke," he shouted. "You are sur-rounded and have no chance. You have two minutes to come out, or we'll burn you out. Throw out your guns and come out." The door of each shack came open and rifles and some pistols were thrown out. "Now raise your hands well above your head and come out," said Sean.

The outlaws came out of the shacks, but only two had their hands above their heads. One of them had been hit in the chest and had his left hand over the wound. Blood was coming out of his mouth. Another man had been hit in his right leg above the knee and was bleeding terribly. He fell dead right after he cleared the door of the shack. Then the one shot in the chest died. The two remaining, stood there with their hands up awaiting their fate. The one on the right had a hateful look on his face and stared at Sean without a blink. "I know you, lawman," he said. "Yer that son of a bitch that killed some a my kin up in Kansas."

"You must be related to them Hawks," replied Sean. "I see you haven't learned anything since then, have you?"

"You son of a bitch," the outlaw yelled. Then he pulled a pistol that he had stuffed in the back of his pants.

Before he got the pistol around to fire at Sean, Sean had one of his pistols out and put a hole in the outlaw's forehead. Then Sean said to the other outlaw. "Are you gonna try something stupid too, or do you wannna live long enough to hang?"

"You can't hang me out here with no trial, lawman. You're no judge and jury," the outlaw said.

"I'm not gonna hang you, mister," replied Sean. "They are. This is their land, and it's their law. You came down here killin' and such, and now you're gonna pay up. Jon, take this fella and tie him good while we have a look-see around here and see what, and who we got."

The body count was fifteen killed with only one left alive. Anderson was not among the dead. If Redhorse was right and counted twenty men yesterday, then four of them left before they got here. Not one of the Osage, or Jon and Sean, had even been wounded. Sean decided it was time to question the lone survivor, although he doubted if he would get any information out of him.

"Got any idea where Anderson went or what he was doing?" Sean asked.

"Go to Hell, lawman," he replied. "Them Injuns'r gonna hang me anyway, so why should I tell you anything?"

"You probably don't know anything anyway," said Sean. "Why would he tell some dumb peckerwood like you anything? You're so dumb, it's a wonder you can even walk and talk at the same time."

"Keep talkin', lawman," he said. "You won't be talkin' so much when he gits back here in a few days with more men."

"Well," started Sean, "I see that I was wrong. You did know something. Now get yourself ready to meet your maker."

The outlaw didn't say one word after that. The Osage had a good tree picked out and had the rope and the horse ready. The outlaw didn't make one sound as the horse was swatted. He was lucky. The rope must have been placed perfectly, and his neck broken, because there was no movement or kicking as he swung.

"Will we wait here for a few days and see if Anderson returns?" Charlie Redhorse asked Sean.

"We could," answered Sean, "but it's not far to the village. I think we should go back to the village and wait there. We have better food and shelter there. We'll keep scouts and lookouts posted for several days, but I really don't think Anderson will be back for a while. They had no extra horses, and why would he round up more men right before winter? That's just more men to keep busy and feed. I figure this bunch we killed today was about to head out too. I still think Anderson left for a warm place for winter, Texas or Mexico. Probly come back in the spring with a vengeance. Anyway, we can't let our guard down. If you people want to bury these fellas, it's up to you. I don't think they deserve it. Get all the horses, food, guns, and ammunition rounded up and we'll head back."

The Osage didn't bother with burying the dead outlaws, but one of them did let down the outlaw who was hanged. "That's a good rope." he said. "I need it at home. If someone happens along, they'll know that this fella got hung anyway."

~~~~

When they got back to the village, everything they had taken from the outlaws was divided among the families. "There's enough ammunition here now to hold off the whole Yankee army for a week," said Jon.

"That's good," said Sean. "Come spring, it'll probably be needed."

That night, the Osage celebrated their great victory and danced well into the night. It reminded Sean of the time that he, Braddock, Black Wolf and the scout, had whipped the thirty Comanche. He also remembered that he took an arrow in his side then too, and how Katie cared for him. It seemed centuries ago. He would turn twenty two in a few days. "I have lived and seen enough for ten lifetimes," he said to himself. "I fully intend to live a few more."

~~~~

A full week went by without incident. Scouts and lookouts had been posted. Sean decided that it was safe for the families to move back out to their farms and places, and they didn't need scouts out every day. He also decided it was time for him to get back to Abilene. "I'll be leavin' in the mornin'," he told the elders. "Don't get careless while I'm gone. Your people should always keep a weapon nearby, and you should keep sending scouts out every few days. Send out the best men who can read sign, and keep lookouts posted once in a while. If Anderson does come back, he'll want blood and lots of it. He'll want me, but he'll take it out on you. Him and I will meet someday, and I'll send him to hell where he belongs." After Sean was done speaking, Jon asked if he could speak with him for a bit. "Sure Jon," Sean started, "what can I do for you?"

"Well, do you remember when I said I was goin' down to the Nations and try to find some of my Pa's kin?" said Jon. "Well, I'd like to take some time and go over to the Cherokee territory and see if I can find any of them. I'll get up to Abilene shortly after that."

"That's fine by me," said Sean. "I want to spend some time with that woman of mine and not play lawman for a short spell."

"I can't blame you there," said Jon. "That woman a yers has gotta be one of the most beautiful creatures I ever did see, and I only saw that painting."

"She surely is," said Sean. "She surely is. I been with some beautiful women, but she makes a man wonder why he hasn't had a heart attack after he sees her. Let's talk about somethin' else. I won't get much sleep as it is thinking about her."

"That friend a yers, Michael, he should be in Abilene by now, shouldn't he?" asked Jon.

"Yeh, he was s'posed to get there within a week of us leavin'," said Sean. "I hope it's goin' well for him there. Ike's leg should be healin' good by now. He may be gone before I get up there. Let's get somethin' to eat and then get some rest. I wanna head out right at daylight."

~~~~

The next morning, right after a quick breakfast, Sean and Jon were ready to head out. John Littletree came out to see them off. "You two are always welcome here," he started. "We will always be in your debt. May the wind always be at your back."

"You are a good friend," said Sean. "Keep yourself safe, and remember to get ahold of me when you need me. Judge Simmons will always be able to track me down. Good bye, my good friend."

Then Sean and Jon went their different ways, Sean north to Abilene, and Jon east to Cherokee territory.

CHAPTER FOUR

The ride north through the Nations was uneventful. Sean didn't see a living soul. When he crossed into Kansas, it was the same the first day. On the morning of the second day, he came upon a huge cattle trail. Someone was taking a herd somewhere to the northeast. Sean decided to follow the trail as it wasn't more than two days old. About noon, the direction of the trail changed to straight north. Tracks were all over as if maybe the herd had been stampeded. Sean followed what looked to be the main trail for a short distance, then in the distance, he saw the buzzards. When he got closer to where the buzzards were circling, he saw one man and one horse. The man appeared to be digging for some reason. Then Sean spotted the bodies. There were six of them. Four of them were laid out together, and the other two were maybe fifty yards to the right. The man digging had not see Sean yet, so Sean decided it would be a good idea to yell out and identify himself so this man wouldn't take a shot at him.

"Hello," Sean yelled, "I'm Federal Marshal Sean O'Rourke and I'm comin' in." As Sean got closer, he recognized the man right away. It was that Texas Ranger, Captain Wallace. He was the man who tried to get him to join the Rangers before he joined the Army. He also shot that Marshal who was trying to back shoot him. "What went on here, Captain?" Sean asked.

"Sons a bitchin rustlers," the Captain started. "Jumped us yesterday mornin' just after we started the herd movin'. I guess we got careless and wasn't payin' attention. Hadn't had any trouble and wasn't spectn' any. I see you finally put on a badge."

"Yep, I did," replied Sean. "I met up with a man who had been a Federal Judge before the war. I had killed some deserters who had killed some civilians and the Judge was there when I was taking the bodies to headquarters to explain what I had done. Then he did some checking up on me and found out about my shootin' skills and how good I was with my fists. He asked me to look him up after the war and he'd appoint me a Federal Marshal. I told him I'd take the job on one condition."

"I already know what that was, don't I," the Captain said. "You won't hunt or kill Indians unless they're tryin' to kill you. I bet you were one of them Sharpshooters too, weren't you? I heard about them Sharpshooters that were shooting just sergeants and corporals. Men coming back to Texas after the war told a lot of stories about their sergeants and corporals getting killed right and left. They said there was a price on your head."

"Well I was one of them Sharpshooters, and I did hear there was a price on our heads," started Sean. "Now how'd you end up out here pushin' cows?"

"I quit the Rangers not too long after the war," he started. "Texas was just a plain mess. Carpetbaggers started coming in. No work to be had for most folks. Seems like every one of those fellas that rode with Quantrill and Bloody Bill, came down to Texas to keep doing what they'd been doing during the war. There was even some talk about disbandin' the Rangers and creating a special State Police Force. Probly be all Yankees and carpetbaggers. They didn't think us Rangers would enforce the law on our southern boys. So I quit. Most of the men in my company did too. I had heard that some of those meat packers up in Chicago would pay as much as thirty to forty dollars a head for longhorns. There's longhorns everywhere in Texas. They just ran wild during the war. Whoever can round them up and get a brand on them, can say they belong to them. Me and four men from my Ranger Company decided to round some up and see if we could get them up to Chicago. We got us a cook with a wagon. He was a good cook too. We had five hundred head and ten extra horses when we started. We was gonna get the herd to St. Louis and find a buyer. If we'd done it, we wouldn't need to work another day of our lives. I guess we was dreamin'."

"So how'd the rustlers start out?" asked Sean. "Were they tryin' to kill you and your men right off, or were they just tryin' to stampede the herd?"

"I don't know if they were shootin' to stampede the herd, or if they were shootin' at us," answered the Captain, "but the herd stampeded soon as the shootin' started. My four men were killed pretty quick. They were shot; then run over by the herd. Don't know what happened to the cook. Those other two dead ones were part of the gang. I killed them myself. I was about to shoot another one, when my horse bucked and I went flyin'. I banged my head on a rock or something cause when I came to, them and the herd was gone. They musta seen the blood on my head and thought I was dead. That horse a mine musta got loose from em and come back. Been ridin' that mare for five years. She can be a cantankerous bitch for other folks, but she seems to like me. They must notta been worried bout just one horse."

"How many of them were there?" asked Sean. "I would guess maybe twelve or so by the tracks I can make out, and did you recognize any of them?"

"I'd say maybe twelve or so too," replied the Captain. "And I didn't recognize any of the ones I saw up close, but there was one of them that I will not forget. He was wearin' a fancy reb coat, and had on a reb cavalry hat with a big plume on it. He also had a cavalry saber on him. I'd know that son of a bitch anywhere if I ever see him again."

"I know who that son of a bitch is," said Sean. "His name is Anderson, George Anderson. He's been robbing, burning, and killing ever since the war ended. He rode with Quantrill after they kicked him outta the reb army for shootin' prisoners. He must have his own private army now. Me and a Deputy of mine and some Osage just had a big gun battle with a bunch of his men in the Nations just a week or so ago. We killed fifteen in that fight, and hung another one. A few days before that, my Deputy and I killed seven of them and the Osage hung two others. The two that were hung by the Osage were taken alive, but we couldn't even get their names outta them. I did find out that one of the outlaws in the big gun battle was named Hawk. There were four of them left after the gun battle. They surrendered, but two of them died of their wounds pretty quick. The one named Hawk recognized me from when I killed some of his kin in Abilene. He tried for a pistol he had stuffed in the back of his pants, and I killed him. We hung the other one. Couldn't get any information outta him either."

"Well after I get these men in the ground," the Captain started, "I'm goin' after 'em. They won't be movin' that fast, and my brand is easy to recognize. It's a circle with TR in it."

"Why don't you set and rest for a spell," said Sean. "I'll get your men buried for you. I won't bury them other two. They don't deserve it. They're downwind anyway. Once we make sure you're all right to ride, we'll get after them. I got a pretty good idea where they're headed, and if I'm right, you'll need to be in good shape when we find them. Now before anything else, just what is your first name? I don't wanna be callin' you the Captain, or Ranger, or Wallace."

"My first name is Robert, and everyone calls me Bob," he answered. "Now just where do you think those rustlers are headed?"

"Do you remember when I told you about that fella named Hawk and how he recognized me from when I killed some of his kin in Abilene?" exclaimed Sean. "Well there's a big clan of Hawks that live not too far from Abilene. Seems their herd always gets a little bigger when no one else's does. When I first took this job, I had a warrant for Ezra Hawk. After I killed him and another outlaw, I took their bodies into a new little town. I didn't know at the time that it was Abilene. Some of Ezra Hawk's kin were in town when I got there, and I had to kill three more of them and beat the hell out of another one. Ethan Hawk was the one I beat up. I threw him in jail for a short time, and we had a nice talk before I let him out. I told him that if I ever had any more trouble with any of the Hawks, or seen paper on them, that I would go out to their place and wipe them out. Ethan swore that there was more of them than there was me, and sooner or later, they would get me. Anyway, I think that Anderson is in business with the Hawks, and has been for some time. As far as I know, no one has ever bothered the Hawks around Abilene because they have never been a problem there. Plus there's been no real law in that area and probably hasn't been since before the war started."

"Sounds like a good place for a bunch like that to live," said Bob. "So do you think that after they get my herd to the Hawk place, they'll change the brands and try to move them?"

"Somehow, I doubt if they try and change brands," answered Sean. "If they want to ship them, and someone asks about the brand, they'll probably come up with a phony bill of sale, and say they bought them. No one could say otherwise, except you, and they think you're dead. Now let's stay here the rest of the day and camp here tonight. We'll get after them in the morning if you're fit enough. Now you just rest some while I get these men in the ground."

The ground was very hard and rocky, but Sean made the graves as deep as he could. After he got the bodies in the graves and covered, he would gather as many rocks as he could to help cover the graves. That would make it harder for any critters to dig them up. The four bodies were really beat up, and some of their arms were all but torn off. Sean was very careful as he dragged them to their graves. When he was done, Bob said a few words about each man, and then at the end, he made a promise to them. "I will get those sons a bitches for you, I promise," he said.

It was getting late now, so Sean started a fire and got some coffee going. Then he made biscuits, bacon, and beans for supper. Neither one of them talked much at all during the meal, and as soon as it was over, Bob got out his bedroll and was asleep in no time. Sean cleaned up everything, but kept the coffee going for a while. He didn't want to sleep yet. He wanted to think about Anderson and the Hawks, but Maggie kept creeping into his mind. Was she all right? Did she miss him as much as he missed her? Was Michael in Abilene keeping an eye on her? Would the Hawks try anything with Maggie? After he convinced himself that Maggie could take care of herself, and she missed him as much as he missed her, and that Michael was there, and very capable, he hobbled the horses, put out the fire, and went to sleep.

~~~~

After a breakfast of coffee and biscuits, they saddled up and headed out following the cattle trail. Bob said he was good enough to ride, and Sean wasn't gonna stop him. After about five minutes, Bob asked Sean. "Whatever happened to that big Walker pistol you was carryin' when we first met? I see you still got a Sharps."

"I lost that pistol and my Sharps over around Atlanta," answered Sean. "They kinda got blowed up, and me along with them. That Sharps I got now is a new one, uses metallic cartridges. All my pistols I carry now have been converted to metallic cartridges."

"Just why are you packin' so much iron?" asked Bob. "You got them three pistols, the Sharps and the Henry on your saddle, and I seen that ten gauge on your pack horse. I reckon you're ready for about anything."

"Like I always tell folks, I don't intend to get killed for lack of shootin' back," Sean answered. "I been lucky so far. I see you got a Spencer. Hope you got plenty of ammunition for it."

"Yeh, I got a hundred rounds in my saddle bags," replied Bob. "Had a bunch more on the cook wagon. My men all had Spencers, even the cook. We were all carryin' army Colts too, cap and ball.

But they was in good shape. I can't remember ever havin' a miss fire with mine because somethin' wasn't workin'. Course I always keep my powder dry, and keep it freshly loaded. Got a lot of use chasin' Mexican bandits. Say, just when did you join the boys in blue anyway? Did that big mick Sergeant you were with when I met you, talk you into it?"

"That Sergeant's Commanding Officer found out about me being with the Cheyenne, and he asked me to scout for them through Indian land when they were ordered back east for the war," answered Sean. "I joined the army on the way to Cairo, which is where we were ordered to go. They let me stay in the same cavalry unit as that Sergeant. His name is Michael O'Connor, and we are very good friends. We decided that we were gonna be partners and own a saloon after the war. He should be in Abilene right now, and he should be a deputy of mine too."

"How can he be a deputy without you to swear him in?" asked Bob.

"Well there's this part time town Marshal there. He got shot in the leg when some men robbed the General Store," started Sean. "He said he was headin' to California soon as his leg was good enough to ride. I got a telegram right before I left to go down to the Nations saying Michael would arrive within the week. I made that Town Marshal a Deputy Federal Marshal, and he was s'posed to swear in Michael when he got to Abilene. He really didn't wanna be a Federal Deputy, but I told him that after he swore in Michael, and his leg was good, he could just resign and take off. I hope Michael is there when we get there. I could use some help. Speakin' a which, how'd you like to be a Federal Deputy?"

"Tell you what, Sean," Bob answered. "I'll be a deputy until we get those men killed and my cows back. Then I'm gonna retire from the law."

"That's all right with me," said Sean. "Consider yourself sworn in."

They rode a while longer without talking, then Bob spoke. "Just what was it like back east in the war?" he asked. "I heard stories from men coming back home."

"You and I seen death and been in scrapes," started Sean, "but nothing like what went on in the war. Anytime you got into it with bandits or Comanche, it was maybe no more than thirty or forty. Just try to imagine thirty or forty thousand men tryin' to kill each other, artillery blowin' the hell outta everything. People and horses getting ripped to pieces. Stacks of arms and legs that were amputated layin' in piles outside the field hospitals. Men bleedin' to death waiting their turn with the surgeon. Men screamin' in pain while gettin' a leg cut off cause there's no more drugs."

"Yep," replied Bob, "I'm glad I missed it. There were a few battles in Texas, but I was way over to the west chasin' Apaches. Don't miss that either. So when did you get in with the Sharpshooters?"

"Before we were even in our first engagement," began Sean. "Some Captain came to our unit and said they were forming a new unit of Sharpshooters. Anyone could volunteer, but they had to qualify. We had to put ten holes in a ten inch circle at two hundred yards without missing once. Anyway, I did good and they made me a Corporal and a shooting instructor. Seems like I was always gettin' promoted."

"Well gettin' promoted couldn't be a bad thing, could it?" asked Bob.

"Depends on how much more responsibility they give you," answered Sean. "After I made Sergeant, I was second in command of our unit. You shoulda been there for that promotion. General Sherman himself promoted me at Shiloh when I was about to give some Quartermaster my rifle butt because he wouldn't give me some ammunition for my Sharps. I was second in command because our sergeant got killed. Later on, our Captain was badly wounded, and they made me a Captain. After one of General Sherman's aides was wounded on the way to Atlanta, the General made me his aide, and I was promoted to Major. I was wounded down around Atlanta, and after I healed up at some fancy hospital in Pennsylvania, they sent me to Washington D.C. I spent the last few months of the war doing nothing."

"Sounds like someone was lookin' out for you near the end of the war," said Bob.

"Some folks thought Sherman was lookin' out for me, but who knows," said Sean. "I resigned my commission soon as I heard Lee surrendered and headed to St. Louis. I was learnin' the saloon business at a place called "The Palace" while I was waiting for Judge Simmons to get back from the war. He's the judge who made me a Federal Marshal."

"I've heard about that saloon," said Bob. "I hear it's a really nice place and has the most beautiful girls."

"It surely is a nice place," said Sean, "and the women are very beautiful.

The owner is a man named Sam Draper. He's a good man. I lived there while I was waiting for Judge Simmons. I think I learned enough about the saloon business that Michael and I can have our own place without goin' bust."

~~~~

They didn't talked for a while, then both of them spoke at almost the same time. "Buzzards," they both said. As they neared the place where the buzzards were circling, Sean spotted a body just off the trail to the right. As they neared it, Bob recognized him right away. "That's our cook," Bob said as he dismounted and went to examine the body. There was dried blood everywhere. The body was face down, and as Bob was turning the body over, he started yelling at the top of his lungs. "Just who in the hell would do somethin' like this!" As Sean neared the body, he knew what had happened. The cook had been slashed twice. One slash went from his left shoulder to his right hip, and the other one from his right shoulder to his left hip. The cuts went clear to the spine.

"Anderson did this with that cavalry saber you saw," said Sean. "Couldn't just shoot the man. He had to play toy soldier with his toy sword. I'm tellin' you Bob, he is about as low as they come. I had a man tell me back in Kansas City that he thought Anderson would shoot his own mother if he didn't like what she made for dinner. We gotta get this son of a bitch."

"You know him, don't you," said Bob. "You know Anderson."

"Yes," started Sean, "I know him. We both grew up in Tennessee. He was a year older than me. He was always startin' trouble. I had to beat him up every once in a while. His sister was my first love. When I hooked back up with her during the war while we fighting around Chattanooga, she told me the last thing her brother said when he left was that he was gonna shoot me some day. She told me about him gettin' kicked out of the reb army for shootin' prisoners, and then he joined Quantrill. He got a taste for killin' and pillagin' and such, and he hasn't quit since the war ended."

"Whatever happened to that girl, his sister?" asked Bob.

"Do you remember me tellin' you about killin' some deserters who had killed some civilians?" said Sean.

"Yeh, I recollect that," Bob replied.

"Well those deserters killed her folks, and then killed her, and raped her after she was dead," explained Sean. "Me and another man had been out scoutin' when we heard shots and went to investigate. We found them there and saw what they were doin', and I killed them. We were gonna get married after the war. Took a long time to get over that. Well let's get this man in the ground and get after them again. We'll be in Abilene in about a day and a half. Won't be any trouble finding the Hawks. Their spread is only about two miles from town. We'll stop in town first before we take on the Hawks."

"Is your friend Michael any good with a gun?" asked Bob.

"He's not quick," answered Sean, "but he hits what he shoots at. He's pretty good with a pistol when he's on horseback. I never told you about my other deputy did I?"

"No, you didn't," said Bob. "You just mentioned that you had a deputy with you down in the Nations."

"Well, he was a reb Major that I shot at Chattanooga," explained Sean. "He thought he had me dead to rights, but I shot him through the shoulder with my Walker. Then I took him to get patched up and then helped him escape. He was half Cherokee. After the fightin' down in the Nations seemed over, he asked if he could go to the Cherokee territory and find his Pa's kin. His folks had died of the fever during the war. I let him go, and he said he'd meet me in Abilene soon as he could."

"Well just why would that man wanna be your deputy after you shot him?" asked Bob.

"I ran into him in Abilene after I found out the Anderson bunch was back down in the Nations," said Sean. "I was intendin' to buy a Henry rifle from him, but he said he would take his Henry and go with me as a deputy. He figured I had saved his life by not gettin' him sent to some prison camp."

"Well I hope he shows up too," said Bob. "Anderson may take a lotta killin'."

~~~~

They were less than a day's ride from Abilene now. They stopped for a few minutes to rest the horses. Sean decided they should walk the horses for awhile. As they started walking, Sean spotted what looked like some tracks heading to the west. "Bob, you stay here," Sean said. " I'm gonna follow these tracks and see what I can make of them. Can't tell much till I get away from all these cow tracks." Sean followed the tracks for maybe a mile. Five riders had broken away from the main bunch and had turned southwest. When he got back to Bob, he told him what he thought was going on. "Five riders broke away from the main bunch," he started. "I'll bet it was Anderson and some of his men. He left the herd with the Hawks. Either they paid him off, or he'll settle up later. I still say he's headed to warmer weather for the winter, Texas or Mexico. We'll stay after the main bunch. I know where they're goin' for sure."

"Let's get goin'," said Bob.

The trail was leading a little to the west of town. Sean figured they were keeping way out of sight of the town. When they were a half day's ride from town, they saw buzzards circling again. "Just who or what in the hell is dead now?" said Sean. As they got closer, Sean knew who it was. Ike Coleton lay there. He had been shot in the back and in the back of the head. "That's Ike Coleton," spoke Sean. "He was that part time town Marshal that I was telling you about. No doubt in my mind that the Hawks killed him. Probly for lettin' me put Ethan Hawk in his jail, or maybe somethin' else happened while I was in the Nations. Let's hurry up and get him in the ground and get to town."

They dug the grave as quickly as they could, said a few words, and were off toward town. "Do you think there's any chanca us gettin' bushwacked on our way to town?" asked Bob.

"You know as well as I do that there's always a chanca that," answered Sean. "You were a Ranger. I'd say it wasn't always you doin' the bushwackin'. The ground all the way to town is flat with a few low rises. Anyone could be layin' in the high grass just waitin' to take a shot at us. Specially if they knew we were comin'. Anderson may be low down scum, but he's not totally stupid when it comes to stayin' alive, same for the Hawks. Now let's keep our eyes peeled as best we can."

CHAPTER FIVE

When Jim O'Rourke rode into Abilene, the few people who were on the street just stood and stared. More people came out of their houses or shops to see what the other people were watching. Some of them looked as if they had never seen a colored man, especially one wearing a Yankee cavalry hat, and carrying a Henry rifle across his saddle. There was also a cavalry saber strapped to his saddle and he had an army Colt on his right side. The holster for the Colt was not an army holster with a flap, but was the type used by individuals who wanted to pull their pistol quickly, and it was tied down. Jim rode until he came to the Marshal's office, then dismounted and tied his horse. "There's nobody in there," came a voice from across the street. It was the young boy who worked at the livery.

"Thank you, young man," Jim said. "Could you tell me where I might find the Marshal?"

"This town don't have no Marshal no more," the boy said. "He up and quit just the other day. There is a man that's a Federal Deputy, and you can find him in the saloon. It's the only saloon in town."

"Thank you, young man," said Jim, and then he headed to the saloon. He carried his Henry with him.

As he neared the doors of the saloon, a voice came from behind him. "Yer not goin' in there, nigger."

When Jim turned around, there were two rough looking men staring at him. They were standing side by side. Without saying a word, Jim stepped up to the one on the right, got right in his face, and before the man could say or do anything, Jim gave him a left hook to the gut as he held the Henry with his right hand. When the men buckled over, Jim brought up his right knee and caught him in the face sending him flat on his back. The other man was getting ready to take a swing at Jim when Jim took the butt of the Henry and smashed it into the man's forehead sending him flat on his back. "Now is there anyone else who wants to keep me outta there?" Jim said.

Two more men came forward, both of them were packing pistols. One man had a Colt stuffed in his belt, and the other man already had a pistol in his hand. Jim didn't know it, but the one with the pistol in his hand was Ethan Hawk The other man was a cousin of his. "We don't allow niggers in this town. There's only one thing I hate worse than Injuns, and that's niggers, specially uppity niggers." said Hawk. "Just cause you wore that blue, don't mean shit ta us. We're gonna shoot you some, then we're gonna hang you."

"Mister," started Jim, "I don't know you, and I don't wanna have to kill you, so why don't you just leave me alone?"

Hawk never said another word. He just started raising his pistol. Before he had the pistol up to shoot and the hammer cocked, Jim had his Colt out and put a hole in Hawk's chest. Then Jim pointed the Colt at the other man. The other man had just started to clear his holster as Jim spoke. "If you wanna die mister, you go ahead and pull that pistol. Don't matter to me," said Jim. "I can kill you now or I can kill you later, and that's what I'll do if you cross my path again. Now make up your mind."

The man never said a word as he slid his pistol back down in his holster. Then two other men helped him drag Hawk over to a buckboard and load him on it. Not a word was said as he drove out of town. The crowd was in total disbelief. That colored man knew how to fight, and how to shoot.

As Jim turned around to head into the saloon, he found a big man standing in his way. Then he noticed the star on the man's chest. Michael had been watching almost the whole time. "I'm Deputy Federal Marshal Michael O'Connor," Michael started. "Who might you be, and is there something that I can help you with, young man?"

"My name is Jim O'Rourke," Jim began, "and I'm tryin' to find Sean O'Rourke."

"Funny," Michael said, "you don't look Irish. Just funnin' there, young man. I believe I know who you are. You're the young Jim that Sean told me about from back in Tennessee. If you're him, I'm pleased to meet you."

"Yes, I'm that Jim from Tennessee," said Jim, "and I'm also pleased to meet you."

"Well let's go inside and you can tell me all about yourself over a drink. You are a drinkin' man, aren't you?" asked Sean.

"I've been known to take a sip once in a while," said Jim as they went through the saloon doors and found a table.

There were no other people in the saloon as it was still early in the day. Jim spotted the painting of Maggie on the wall before he got to his seat, shook his head one time, then sat down. "That woman in the painting is Maggie," Michael said. "This is her place. She's young Sean's woman. She's the most beautiful thing I've ever seen. By the look on your face, I'd say you think so too."

"You're right, she is," said Jim. "I just didn't say anything with her being a white woman and all. Don't want to start another fight."

"Don't you worry, Jim," Michael said. "You're among friends here. If you're young Sean's friend, then you're my friend too. You sit tight. I'll go get a bottle and some glasses. As Michael was on his way back to the table, Tom came out from the back room. "Hey Tom," Michael said, "come over here. I want you to meet a friend of Sean's from back in Tennessee."

"Pleased to meet you, young man," Tom said. "Any friend of Sean's is a friend of mine. Is there anything else I can get for you? The cook will be here shortly. I can have him fix you up something soon as he gets set up."

"That'll be fine, Tom," Jim said. "I'll have whatever he's fixin' today. I haven't had a good meal for a spell."

"I'll have the same thing," said Michael. "I'll pay for Jim's meal. Now, young Jim, just how did you know that Sean was out here."

"Everybody's heard about the new Marshal out here," started Jim. "I heard about him way back east before I mustered out. When I heard the name O'Rourke, I knew it was him. I figured I'd see him again while I can."

"Young Sean told me all about the shootout back in Tennessee where your Pa was killed and you got wounded," said Michael. "What happened after that?"

"After I got healed up," began Jim, "I asked Sean's Pa to take me up north. He took me up to Cincinnati, and that was the last I saw of the O'Rourkes. Sean's Pa, said that I should have a last name and that he'd be pleased if I took his, so I been calling my-self Jim O'Rourke ever since."

"Just how was it up north for you?" asked Michael.

"Well I was free, but most folks didn't treat folks like me that way," Jim started. "Sean's Pa had taught me all about horses and smithin', so I got a job as a smithy, but they treated me bad and paid me just about enough to starve on. I moved all over the place takin' jobs wherever I could find them. Findin' them wasn't hard, but gettin' paid right was always a problem. More than once, I had to force my boss to pay me right, then get out of there before the law came."

"Us Irish were treated like that by the British," said Michael. "I know what you're talkin' about. How'd you end up in the army?"

"The war had been going on for a while, when I heard they were forming an all black regiment up in Massachusetts, the 54th," said Jim. "I worked my way up there and signed up. I was with them when they tried to take Fort Wagner. Got shot up some. Towards the end of the war, I got myself in the cavalry. Mustered out not long ago. I came out here to find Sean, and I also heard that before too long, they're gonna form two colored cavalry regiments out west, so I figure I'll already be out west when they do decide to form up."

"You must not mind fightin', my friend, if you're goin' back in the cavalry," said Michael.

"I kinda liked the army," said Jim. "It was like my home. I felt I belonged. I'm not big on the killin', but it sometimes goes with the job."

"You might just get some more killin' right here before you get back in the army," began Michael. "That man you just killed, well him and his clan already had a good feud goin' with young Sean before I ever got here. I had a fight myself with Ethan Hawk not long ago. He's the Hawk you just killed. I had him in jail and had just let him out a few days ago. The town Marshal quit, and I couldn't spend a lot of time constantly checking on Hawk, so I let him out. I had him in jail for attempted assault on a Federal Officer. He was a big man, but he wasn't any good with his fists."

"So how'd this feud with the Hawks get started?" asked Jim.

"I'm not really sure," answered Michael. "Young Sean just told me that he had to kill some of them and beat the hell out of another one, and that they had sworn to get him. Ethan Hawk was the one Sean beat the hell out of. When I got here, Ethan found out I was a friend of Sean's and thought he was gonna beat the hell outta me. I took care of him and gave him ten days in jail. I told him if his manners didn't improve, I'd give him ten more days. He said I might get a visit from some of his kin before he got out, but that didn't happen. I hear that there's a whole bunch of them out at their spread. I hear it's only about two miles from town. I'd say that we should not let our guard down. Sooner or later, they'll come."

~~~~

Their food was ready and the cook brought it to them. "Let me know what you think of it," he said. "I tried a new recipe. I'll tell you what I call it after you let me know if you like it or not." Then he went back to the kitchen.

"Looks good to me," said Jim. "I've been eatin' beans and salt pork for the last month. Anything's gotta be better than that." Jim took a bite. "Oh my, don't recognize the meat, but it sure is good." Michael took a taste.

"I know what this is," Michael said. "It's Irish stew. It's not like momma used to make. It's better. It'll be interesting to see what the cook calls it."

Then there was no talking as they both tore into their food. After several bites, they started talking again, but before they had said much, a stranger walked into the saloon. He was carrying a Henry rifle and had an army Colt at his side. "I'm lookin' for a Michael O'Connor," he said as stood just inside the doors.

"And who might you be, my good man?" asked Michael.

"My name is Jon O'Brien, and I'm Sean O'Rourke's Deputy," Jon said.

"Well I am Michael O'Connor," Michael said as he stood up and extended his hand to Jon, "and I am very pleased to meet you." They shook hands and then Michael introduced Jon to Jim. "This man here is Jim O'Rourke," said Michael. "He's a friend of Sean's from back in Tennessee." Jim stood and extended his hand to Jon, not knowing if Jon would accept it or not, but Jon extended his hand and they shook.

"You look like you weren't sure if I'd shake your hand there, Jim," said Jon.

"That's right, I wasn't sure," said Jim.

"Well I'm half Cherokee and half Irish," said Jon. "I been in a few fights cause someone called me a breed. If you're a friend of Sean's, you're a friend of mine. Now can I have some of whatever that is you're eatin'. It looks mighty good."

"You surely can, my friend," answered Michael as he headed to the kitchen and asked the cook for another plate.

"Well, what's the verdict?" asked the cook. " Do you like it?"

"You've outdone yourself again," said Michael. "You would make someone a good wife if you didn't have a wife yourself already. Now what are you gonna call this stuff? I know it's an Irish type stew."

"Nothin' fancy," the cook said. "I'm just gonna call it Cookie's Abilene stew."

"I'd think about changin' the meat if this town becomes a cow town," said Michael. "Texas cow men might not think too much of eatin' lamb."

"I'll worry about that when that happens next year or the year after," said Cookie. "I bet those cow men wouldn't know what lamb tastes like anyway. They'd probably think it was just some young tender steer."

~~~~

Michael took the plate from the kitchen out to the table and handed it to Jon. Then they all got into some serious eating. "Excuse my manners," Michael said. "I'll get you a glass Jon. You are a drinkin' man, aren't you?"

"I've been known to have a few from time to time," said Jon. "It's been a good while since I've had a drink. It will go good with this good food we're eatin'."

They had all just finished their food, when Maggie came down the stairs and made her way to their table. "Michael," she started, "would you please introduce your friends to me?"

"It would be a pleasure," said Michael as he stood. "This fella here is Jim O'Rourke. He's a friend of young Sean's from back in Tennessee."

"Pleasure, ma'am," said Jim as he stood.

"This other fella is Jon O'Brien," began Michael. "Sean knew him from the war, and he's Sean's deputy."

"It's an honor to meet such beauty," said Jon.

"Thank you Jon, and I'm very pleased to meet both of you," Maggie said. "Hopefully Sean will be back before too much longer. I'm sure he'll be glad to see all of you. Michael, you make sure these men are taken care of and have a place to stay. Whatever you do is all right with me. I've got to get to the bank now. I'll see you all again shortly."

"That woman has got to be the most beautiful creature I've ever seen," said Jon. "Just lookin' at her makes me hurt. Sean is one lucky man."

"He surely is," said Michael. "Now when do you think we can expect young Sean back?"

"We left the Nations at the same time," Jon began. "I went over to Cherokee territory tryin' to find my Pa's kin, and he was headed straight back. I knew he wasn't here when I put my horse over at the livery and his horses weren't there. He must've got into somethin' on his way here. I hope he's all right."

"Young Sean can handle just about anything, so let's try to not worry about him," said Michael. "Now if you two don't mind, I have a room out back that you can share. There's only one bed, but I'll get another cot in there if that's all right with you two."

"You don't need to be givin' up your place for us," both Jon and Jim said.

"It's not a problem," said Michael. "I've been spending my nights with Betty. She's one of Maggie's girls. You two can figure out who gets the bed and who gets the cot." Then Michael showed them the room. "You two get your gear and get settled, and Jim, you probably want to get your horse over to the livery. In about an hour or so, we'll get together, and I'll let you know what's goin' on around here. Jim already knows most of it, but Jon, I need to fill you in. So we can meet in the saloon in about an hour."

Jim and Jon got themselves settled and went to the saloon to meet with Michael. It was late in the day now, and the saloon was starting to get busy. Michael assured Tom he would get to work as soon as they were done with their meeting. Michael picked a table close to the bar and it was positioned so he could still keep a good eye on the place, and no one could get behind him unless they went in front of him first. "All right Jon," Michael started, "this is what I know and some I've already told Jim. When Sean first came to Abilene, he had a run in with some Hawks and had to kill some of them and beat up another one. They have sworn to get him. Not long ago, I had a run in with Ethan Hawk. He thought he was gonna beat me, but he ended up in jail after I got done with him. He told me I should expect a visit from his kin before he got out of jail. I assured him that if the Hawks came to town for trouble, I would put a bullet in his brain. Well, that never happened. I let him back out of jail when the town Marshal quit. There's no town law now. Then Jim here killed Ethan Hawk in a gunfight earlier today. The Hawks have a spread not far from town. The whole clan lives there. They normally don't cause trouble in town, and no one messes with them. I guess that changed when Sean had to kill some of them, and now Jim is on their hate list. I figure we should be ready for anything at all times. I'm sure Sean will be back any time now, so we need to make sure he won't ride into an ambush. Now that's all I know."

"I think I know why they haven't come right back to town after Jim killed Ethan Hawk this morning," started Jon. "We had a big gun battle down in the Nations with the Anderson gang before we left. One of the men we killed was a Hawk. Could be that a bunch of them are ridin' with the Anderson gang and are not at the spread right now."

"You might be right, Jon," said Michael. "Starting tomorrow morning, we'll take turns scouting outside of town. The ground's pretty flat around town, so we won't need to go far to see anything coming. The Hawk place is to the west, so we should only have to scout to the west. When one of us is out scouting, the rest of us will keep alert in town. So if you two have nothing to add, I need to get to work."

~~~~

Jim and Jon stayed at the table and Jon got a bottle and a couple of glasses. Several of the patrons kind of stared at Jim when they came into the saloon, but after they heard the gossip about the shootout in the morning, the stares stopped. One of the patrons came up to Jim, introduced himself, and thanked him for killing Ethan Hawk. "I guess he won't be missed by some of these folks," said Jim.

"No, I don't guess so," said Jon. About that time, Maggie's girls showed up for work. Two of them went right to Jon and Jim's table.

"Evenin', boys," said one of the girls, "I'm Sally, and this is Martha. Mind if we sit down."

"No ladies," said Jon. "I'm Jon and I don't mind, and I'm sure Jim doesn't mind."

"Are you sure you don't mind settin' with a colored man?" asked Jim.

The girl called Martha spoke. "Jim, they call me Martha, but my real name is Fox Woman. I am three quarters Creek Indian. I'm sure you noticed my skin is darker than most white folks. My hair is lighter than most Indians. I don't know how that happened. Anyway, setting here will be a pleasure."

"Both of you ladies are beautiful," said Jon. "Now let's have some drinks while you tell us all about yourselves." After a few drinks, Sally escorted Jon up to one of the rooms upstairs and Jim took Martha to his room. He and Jon had decided to take turns on the bed, and tonight was his turn.

After they had finished, Martha gave Jim a passionate kiss and a hug and said, "I will not charge you Jim. You are a gentleman and a good lover. It's very seldom that I get both at the same time."

"Thank you, Martha," said Jim, "maybe we can get together again sometime."

"I hope so too," said Martha as she went out the door.

~~~~

Jon was enjoying himself with Sally too. "Haven't you had enough," said Sally, "I need to get back downstairs. You know what I do for a living, but Maggie also relies on us to get the men drinking." After looking at Jon's sorrowful eyes, she said, "Alright, just one more time." When they were finished, Jon paid her, gave her a pat on the butt, and then kissed her on the neck. When he gave her that kiss on the neck, she came close to having him again, but finally changed her mine. "We'll get together again," she said as she went out the door.

Jon got himself dressed and came back down to the saloon. There was a good crowd now. Most of the tables were occupied, and on one, there was a high stakes poker game. Jon decided he would get a drink at the bar and watch the poker game for a few hands. There were four men playing. Two of them were dressed nicely, but one of them definitely looked like a gambler, and the other two looked like ranch hands. The gambler was winning most of the hands. The other three men were starting to grumble a bit, but they kept playing. The pot seemed to get bigger each hand. "Seems like awful high stakes for those two fellas who look like plain old cow hands," Jon said to himself. He waved at Michael who was behind the bar to come over for a minute.

"What is it?" asked Michael.

"Well, first off, I think that there's some cheatin' goin' on in that poker game over there, but I haven't spotted it yet," said Jon. "And it seems odd to me that those two men who look like plain old ranch hands would be in a high stakes game like that. Those pots have been more than they could make in three months. They're packin' new iron too. I think we better keep an eye on that table for a spell."

"Sounds like maybe we should," said Michael. "I'll try to watch as best I can back here, and you let me know if you see something. There's a shotgun at each end of the bar too if the need arises."

~~~~

When it came time for the man who was winning to deal, Jon paid close attention. He finally spotted it. He was dealing off the bottom at times. He was good at it too. Most people wouldn't spot it. Then Jon spotted something else. There were cards up his sleeve too. Jon was about to tell Michael what he had seen when one of the ranch hands stood up and yelled across the table. "I finally caught you, you son of a bitch," he said.

"Just what are you saying?" said the gambler.

"Yer a cheat," said the ranch hand, "and I'm gonna kill you." Then he started to draw his pistol. Before he had his pistol up to fire, the gambler had reached into his jacket and pulled out a small revolver and fired. The bullet struck the man dead center and he fell to the floor, but he was not dead yet. He lay there bleeding from his mouth for what seemed like fifteen minutes. Then he finally died. The shooter was standing now with the pistol still in his hand, but had lowered it to his side. The other ranch hand must have been friends with the dead man. He was down on his knees beside the dead man. He didn't believe that the man was dead and was shaking him. All of a sudden he stood up and had his pistol out and took a shot at the gambler, but missed. Before he could get off another shot, the gambler raised his pistol and shot the other ranch hand in the chest. He was dead when he hit the floor. There was total quiet. No one in the whole place even whispered. After what seemed an eternity, the gambler placed his pistol back in his jacket, started raking up the money off the table, and said, "I imagine that this game is over with gentlemen. I'll take my leave now."

Jon had his pistol out as he walked toward the table. When he was right beside the table, he raised his pistol and pointed it at the gambler's head and said, "The money stays, and you will keep both your hands out where I can see them."

"Just what do you think you are doing?" the gambler said. "I had to shoot those men in self defense. Almost everyone here is a witness."

"You are a card cheat mister," Jon said, "I spotted you the same time the first fella you shot did. Now, hold your left arm straight out to your left side and hold your right arm straight out to your right." The gambler was hesitant. "Do it now, mister, this hammer is cocked." The gambler did as instructed. "Now, with your left hand, reach into your jacket and pull out that pistol by the butt, with your thumb and first finger. Keep that right arm out straight." The gambler did as instructed. When he pulled out the pistol, he dropped it. He was hoping Jon wasn't paying attention to his right arm, because he reached into a pocket low on the right side of the jacket and was pulling a derringer. Jon was not fooled one bit. As soon as he saw the man's hand go into the pocket, he shot the man in the face. Blood splattered all over. The other well dressed man at the table had blood all over his fine clothes. Jon holstered his pistol and turned around and said to Michael, "I guess we better get this place cleaned up. Gimme a hand and we'll get these bodies out of here." Michael and Jon took out the bodies, and Tom grabbed a mop and a bucket and did his best to get the blood off the floor. They took the bodies over beside the barber shop. "I'm gonna go through their pockets and see if we can find out who these men are," said Jon. "There may be somethin' on them with a name or somethin'."

There was nothing on the ranch hands that could help identify them, but they both had a large amount of money on them. "Whoa," said Jon, "there must be two thousand dollars here between the two of them. I'd say these two are not what they seem. Tomorrow morning we should go over to the Marshal's office and see if there are any wanted posters. Maybe these two are wanted. Who does the undertakin' in this town?"

"The barber," answered Michael. "We won't bother him till the morning. Better check this gambler's pockets too." There was nothing in the gambler's pockets to help identify him. He did have a couple of marked decks, the derringer, a shoulder holster, and several cards up both sleeves. "Well let's get back to the saloon. We'll take this money and keep it locked up tonight. We'll use some of it to pay the barber to get these men buried. Tomorrow, I'll take it over to the bank and have them hold it. Maybe it's from a hold up somewhere."

When they got back, Michael could see that Maggie was not happy. "Maggie darlin'," started Michael, "it's a shame that this had to happen. In the future, I'll do better to make sure it doesn't happen again. Would you do something for me, Maggie darlin'?"

"Sure, what can I do for you?" asked Maggie.

"While you're mixin' with the customers, could you ask around and see if anybody knew any of those men?" asked Michael.

"Yes, I'll ask around, and I'll have the girls ask too. I don't believe there was anything you could have done, Michael," Maggie said. "I'm just upset some. This is our first shooting. I surely hope it will be our last. Maybe someone may know one of those men." Then Maggie put a smile back on her face and started mixing with the customers. Jim was at the bar when Jon approached the bar.

"I guess you didn't need my help," said Jim. "Glad you didn't get hurt."

"Me to," said Jon. Then he walked over to the table where the poker game had been. The money was still on the table. The other well dressed man was still there. "I'm sorry about your clothes, mister," said Jon, "I guess I shoulda shot him in the chest. Wouldn't a been so messy. Are you an honest man, mister?"

"I like to think that I am," he answered.

"Well you go ahead and get what you think is your money off the table," said Jon. "The rest gets locked up. We think those other two men who were dressed like ranch hands were playing with stolen money. We found two thousand dollars on them after we took them outside. The man grabbed his money from the table and thanked Jon.

"My name is Bill Thompson," the man began. "I'm a cattle buyer and a speculator. I came here to see this town and what it could look like if McCoy gets those pens built and the railroad here. I also fancy myself a good poker player, but I'm ashamed. I shoulda spotted that man cheating."

"I watched for a long time before I caught him," said Jon. "We can both be ashamed. By the way, my name's Jon O'Brien. I'm a Deputy Federal Marshal. It's good to meet you."

"Good to meet you too, young man," Bill said. "Don't worry about my clothes. I got plenty more. We got a Chinese laundry back home, and those people can clean anything."

"So do you really think Abilene will become a cow town?" asked Jon.

"I'd bet on it," said Bill. "Once I know the railroad's coming, I'm gonna put up two hotels myself. Those boys up from Texas will want to sleep in a bed after that long trail. I might build some saloons too. This one's nice, but it won't be enough once the herds start coming here to ship. Well, it's been good talkin' to you. Think I'll turn in. A family down the street let me have a room for the night. Maybe I'll see you tomorrow."

Jon said goodbye to Bill, then went up to the bar. Jim was still there. "I think I'll have one more drink, then turn in," Jon said. "I got a good feelin'. I think Sean will be here tomorrow."

"I'll have one more myself, then turn in too," said Jim. "Sean's gonna be surprised to see me. It's been over ten years since we've seen each other."

~~~~

When the last customers finally left the place, Maggie looked at Michael, and gave a sigh of relief. "It's been a long day," said Maggie. "It seemed a lot longer than usual with all that happened here."

"That's because it was longer, Maggie darlin'," said Michael. "It'll be daylight in about an hour. I guess anytime there's a shootin' somewhere, it gives people something' to talk about. Now did you find out anything about those men?"

"No, I didn't, and the girls didn't either," answered Maggie. "I hope Sean gets here soon. I really miss him."

"You and me both Maggie, darling. You and me both." added Michael. "Now Tom and me'll straighten up a bit, and then we'll all get some rest. I have a good feelin'. Young Sean'll be here sometime tomorrow."

CHAPTER SIX

S ean and Bob made it into Abilene the next day without incident. It was still early morning, and there was almost no one
out on the streets yet. "Let's get our horses over to the livery and
get them some rest and feed," said Sean. "Then we'll find Michael
and find out what if anything has been goin' on here." As they
were entering the livery, the young boy who worked there spotted
them and came running to them.

"Marshal, Marshal," he started, "three men got shot last night
at the saloon. Two of them got shot by a gambler, and your
deputy shot the gambler. Yesterday mornin', some colored man
killed Ethan Hawk in a gunfight. I saw that. That colored man was
fast. Ethan Hawk already had his gun in his hand, and that
colored man drew and shot him dead. Mr. O'Connor seemed to
know who that colored man was. I think that him and your deputy are stayin' at Maggie's place."

"Slow down boy," said Sean. "You just said a mouthful. Now
you said three men got shot at the saloon last night. Two got shot
by a gambler, and my deputy shot the gambler. Then you say
some colored man killed Ethan Hawk yesterday mornin' in a
gunfight, and you think Mr. O'Connor knew him."

"That's right, Marshal," said the boy.

"Well thanks boy," said Sean. "See to our horses. Give'm good rub down and feed. We may be needin' them soon."

As Sean and Bob started walking to Maggie's Place, Bob looked at Sean and said, "This town's not that big yet to have that many shootins'. I recollect you tellin' me that you already killed some Hawks here, and now that colored man killed another Hawk, and those other three at the saloon. That's way too much killin'. What'll it be like when this place grows?"

"Well if you really want to count all the shootins'," replied Sean, "add in those two I shot that had robbed the General Store." Bob didn't say a word, he just shook his head as they walked into the saloon. Then he saw the painting on the wall.

"Oh lord," Bob said, "that can't be a real woman. Can't be possible, no way."

"It is possible," said Sean. "That's Maggie, and you'll meet her today. Bob stood there staring at the painting and Sean, seeing that no one was in the saloon, went to the back room. Tom was there starting to get ready for another day of business. "Hey Tom," said Sean, "I hear you had some excitement in here last night."

"Yes, we surely did Sean, and I'm glad you are back," Tom replied. "And Maggie's missed you somethin' terrible. Everyone is probably still asleep. It was a long day with the shootins' and all."

"Do you know where Michael and my other deputy are now?" asked Sean

"Michael has been staying with Betty, one of Maggie's girls," answered Tom. "Your other deputy and that colored man, Jim he calls himself, are sharing a room out back."

"Thanks Tom," said Sean. "Come out here a minute and I'll introduce you to another deputy of mine. That is if we can get him away from Maggie's painting. Bob, come over here. Tom, this is Bob Wallace. He used to be a Texas ranger. Bob, this is Tom. He tends bar here." They shook hands and Tom said, "Pleased to meet you Bob. Any friend of Sean's is a friend of mine."

"Same fer me," said Bob.

"Tom, would you get Bob a drink or whatever he wants?" said Sean. "I got to get to the telegraph office. I'll get that outta the way while everyone is still sleepin'."

"Just give me a shot of rye, Tom," Bob said, "I'll just stay here lookin' at this painting if no one objects. You go on about yer business."

~~~~

As Sean was walking to the telegraph office, he kept wondering who Jim was. "I'll find out soon enough," he said to himself. When he walked into the telegraph office, he told the operator, "get your finger ready cause I gotta long one this time. All right, here we go,"

St. Louis
Federal Court House
Judge David Simmons

Back from Nations <stop> twenty five outlaws killed in gunfights <stop> names unknown except one Hawk <stop> Anderson still at large <stop> Anderson and Hawks rustled Texas herd <stop> five Texas men murdered <stop> herd headed to Hawk spread <stop> believe Anderson headed south for winter <stop> former town marshal murdered by Hawks <stop> have three deputies

<stop> another one possible <stop> Hawks closest <stop> will pursue them first <stop> Anderson has many more men than thought <stop> will not stop till Anderson dead <stop> send any reward money here <stop>

O'Rourke

"I'll be in town for a while," Sean told the operator. "So if there's a reply, get it to me."

"Sure will Marshal, and good luck gettin' that bunch," said the operator.

"Thanks," Sean said as he headed back to Maggie's place. As he neared the saloon, the colored man was standing in the doorway. Sean knew who he was right off. He ran up to him, gave him a hug, and shook his hand. "Jim, I never thought I'd ever see you again," said Sean. "No I never did. Just how did you end up out here and where have you been in the meantime?"

"It's good to see you, Sean," Jim began. "I never thought I'd see you again either. When your Pa took me up north, I learned real quick that most folks didn't care for colored folks. I bounced around takin' smithin' jobs wherever I could. Had a few problems gettin' paid right and had to make trouble for the boss once in a while, and move on before the law came. I joined the 54th Massachusetts after the war started. Got shot up some. I spend the last part of the war in the cavalry. Mustered out not long ago. I came out here to see you. Your reputation is known way back east. I knew it was you everyone was talkin' about when I heard the name O'Rourke. Oh, I took your last name too. Your Pa thought I should have a last name and said he'd be proud if I took his. I heard they might form two colored cavalry regiments out west, and I thought that if and when they do, I'll already be out west."

"Well I don't know about any colored cavalry regiments, but I got a job for you right now if you're willin'." said Sean.

"What would that be?" asked Jim.

"Well I know you can use your fists, and everyone in town knows you can use that pistol," said Sean. "How bout bein' a Federal Deputy Marshal while you're waitin' on the cavalry to form up?"

"That'll be fine," answered Jim. "May as well get paid for killin' folks."

"That sounds bad," said Sean, "but that's the truth. That's just what we do. It's what we have to do. Someday maybe they'll be courts, judges, and such out here, but right now there isn't, and if we don't kill outlaws, they'll sure as hell kill us. Consider yourself sworn in." When Sean had just finished talking, Jon walked into the saloon. "How was your trip Sean?" Jon said, "You shoulda beat me here unless there was some kinda trouble."

"Yeh, I came across this man here," started Sean. "Jon O'Brien and Jim O'Rourke, this fella here is Bob Wallace. He's a former Texas Ranger." Jon and Jim shook hands with Bob. "I came across Bob when I was just into Kansas. Him and some Texas boys were drivin' some cows when they were ambushed by Anderson and the Hawks. The other men were killed. Bob's a deputy now too. I knew Bob from before I joined the army. Anyway, we'll be goin' after the Hawks soon. The stolen herd was headed right for the Hawk spread. Hey Tom, is there any coffee on? I could sure use some coffee."

"I'll put some on," said Tom. "Won't be long. Cookie's got the fire goin' already."

"So Jon, did you find any of your Pa's kin down there?" asked Sean.

"No, what was left of them got killed in the war," said Jon. "They fought for the south. I did meet a beautiful Cherokee woman I intend to look up again some day. Need to get back there before she gets herself married off."

Michael was coming in the front doors now. "You made it back, my young friend," said Michael. "We'll be havin' a toast after we get business over with." Michael then went up to Sean and gave him a firm hand shake. " I've met these other fellas already," said Michael. "Now who might this other fella be?"

"Don't you remember that Texas Ranger who wanted me to join the Rangers?" asked Sean. "Well this is him. Michael O'Connor, this is Bob Wallace."

"I'm pleased to meet you, again," said Michael. "Sorry I didn't remember you. As I recall, you shot that lawman who was tryin' to back shoot young Sean."

"Yep, I did," said Bob. "He was a low life. He wasn't missed by anyone."

"Ike Coleton's dead." said Sean. "We found his body not far from town, shot in the back and in the back of the head. It had to been the Hawks. We buried him out there."

"They killed him right after he left town," said Michael. "It couldn't have been Ethan Hawk. He wasn't out of jail very long before Jim shot him. That's a shame. All Ike
   wanted to do was get out of here."

"We'll make 'em pay," said Sean.

~~~~

The coffee was ready now and Tom brought a cup out to Sean. "Anyone else want anything?" asked Tom. They all shook their head no.

"Well let's all sit down, and I'll tell you how we're gonna get started," said Sean. "None of us have ever been to or even seen the Hawk place. I want two of you to go out and do some scouting. Get the layout of everything, how many houses, barns, buildings and such. How many people? Are there any women or children there? Where are the cattle? The ground all around is mostly flat with low rises. Whoever goes, needs to be careful. There is not much cover out there in places except the high grass. Jon, how about you and Bob goin' out. Take my spyglass too. Just make sure you don't let it glare in the sun. When you get back, we'll figure out the best way to get after them. Now if nobody objects, I'm goin' to the barber shop. Gonna get a shave and a bath, then see Maggie." No one objected and Sean left for the barber shop, and Jon and Bob went to the livery to get their horses ready.

~~~~

When Sean got to the barber shop, someone was already in the chair getting a shave. "Almost done," said the barber. "You be next."

"You're Marshal O'Rourke, aren't you?" said the man in the chair. "I'm Bill Thompson. I met your deputy Jon yesterday after the shooting. He's a good man."

"Pleased to meet you, and Jon is a good man," replied Sean. "Just what brings you out here,?"

"I'm a cattle buyer and a speculator," answered Bill. "Soon as I know for sure the railroad is coming to town, I'm gonna build some hotels and maybe some saloons and such. This place will need everything if McCoy gets those pens built and the railroad comes here."

"Well if you're a cattle buyer like you say, Bill, I may have some business for you shortly," said Sean.

"You got a herd somewhere?" asked Bill.

"I don't, but one of my deputies was with some Texas boys, and they had a herd rustled a few days ago, and we're gonna get 'em back," answered Sean.

"So you know where they are?" asked Bill.

"Yep, they're not far from town right now," answered Sean. "I got two deputies out scoutin' the place right now. After they get back, we'll figure out the best way to take them on."

"Well I'll buy the whole herd if you can get them. How many head is there?" asked Bill.

"He had five hundred when he started," answered Sean. "Don't know if any were lost when the rustlers stampeded the herd or not."

"Well if you all can get them back, I'll pay top dollar," said Bill. "If you can drive them to Kansas City, we can get them by rail up to Chicago. I'll pay thirty five dollars a head, and I'll pay the shipping as long as the herd is healthy. Sound all right?"

"Sounds all right to me," said Sean. "I'm sure it'll be all right with my Texas man. Now if you'll excuse me, I'll grab a quick bath while you're gettin' shaved. I don't wanna smell like a horse when I see Maggie."

"So Maggie's your woman, huh," said Bill. "I met her at the saloon last night. I was wondering why I hadn't had a heart attack when I saw her. That woman is uncommonly beautiful."

"Yes she is," said Sean. "A man would have be to dead for ten years to not know how beautiful she is. Nice meetin' you Bill. I'll be seeing you later."

Sean finished up at the barber and was headed back to Maggie's place, when the telegraph operator approached him. "Got you a reply, Marshal," he said. "Just came in." Sean opened it up to read. It started:

O'Rourke

One hundred dollar reward for each gang member <stop> money being sent <stop> one hundred dollar reward for each Hawk <stop> two thousand dollar reward for Anderson <stop> hang Anderson when caught <stop> God speed good luck <stop>

Judge David Simmons

Sean folded up the telegram and stuffed it into a pocket. He went into the saloon and had just started up the stairs for Maggie's room when she was starting out her door. Not a word was spoken. They ran to each other and hugged and kissed till they were out of breath. Then Maggie pulled him into her room. They were not seen for five hours. As they were getting dressed, Sean grabbed her again and kissed her passionately. Then he held her at arms length and said, "Maggie darlin', I have a question for you," said Sean.

"Yes, what is it?" said Maggie.

"Just what is your last name, darlin'?" Sean asked. "I've never heard anyone say your last name."

"That's because no one here knows my last name, except the bank," Maggie answered. "It never seemed important, but if you really want to know, it's O'Sullivan. You knew I was Irish with this red hair. I dropped my husband's name when he was killed. His name was Cooke."

"We're some bunch, aren't we?" said Sean. "I'm Irish, two of my deputies are Irish, one uses an Irish name, and the other is Scotch. And of course, there's you, my beautiful red haired Irish beauty. Some folks'll probably come up with a good name for us all, like the Irish Brigade or something."

"The only people who will call you any names, are the ones you'll be after," said Maggie. "From what I hear, there's plenty of them who want you dead. Will you please make sure that doesn't happen? I believe I need you with me. I hope you feel the same."

"Oh Maggie, I do feel the same," said Sean. "I will keep myself alive for you no matter what it takes." Sean pulled her to him and began kissing her again. They made love for another hour. They finally got control of their passion and got dressed, but not without distraction. Maggie went to work and Sean went to find Michael. Michael was in the back room getting ready for the evening's work.

"Michael," began Sean, "it's high time we drank our toast."

"Yes, it is," said Michael. "Get us a table and I'll get a bottle and some glasses. Michael came back with what must have been the best bourbon in the house. He sat down and filled both glasses and said, "Here's to not getting killed." They touched glasses and Sean repeated, "Here's to not getting killed."

They finished the glass slowly. Both men knew how to enjoy good liquor. Sean took the bottle and filled the glasses again and then said, "Here's to hoping that we can always make our toast." Michael repeated the words, and they again slowly enjoyed the bourbon. "Any word yet from Jon and Bob?" Sean asked Michael.

"Not yet," answered Michael. "I would think they'd be back any time now. Let's have another glass while we're waiting. I won't be needed at the bar for a while yet. Did you want to get something to eat? Cookie's a mighty fine cook as you probably already know."

"Sounds good," said Sean. "I need to keep up my strength. I'll have whatever he's got on." Michael went to the kitchen and returned with two plates. It was pork chops, potatoes, and beans. Sean took one bite and said, "That man'll make someone a good wife someday. Best pork chop I ever had. It is so tender."

"I understand you're spending time with Betty, one of the girls," Sean said to Michael.

"Yes I am," said Michael. "She took a liking to me not long after I got here. She's a gem of a woman."

"That's great, Michael," said Sean. "Let's have another toast. May our women always love us, and may we always love them." They touched glasses again and Michael repeated the words. Just when they had finished their meal, Jon and Bob walked into the saloon. "Did you find out what we need to know?" Sean asked them.

"We got everything," answered Jon. "I mean everything."

"Well you two get some food in you then we'll all get together and make plans," said Sean, "Michael, let's find Jim and let him know we're about ready to make plans."

"I think he's still in the back room," said Michael. "I'll go get him."

~~~~

After they all were done eating, they went to a table in one of the corners where they wouldn't be bothered, and no one could hear them. Not many men were in the saloon as it was early, and the girls hadn't started work yet. "So what did you find out?" Sean asked.

Bob spoke up first. "They got some place out there, I'm tellin' ya," started Bob. "There's a main house and it's huge, and there's ten smaller houses surrounding it. There's two big barns and several other buildings. There's also a huge corral. There's very few trees and brush for cover, just high grass. We saw women and children at some of the smaller houses. The houses are arranged so almost everything can be seen from every house. The smaller houses are about fifty yards from the main house and surround the main house, but they kept an opening so the trail from town can be seen clearly from the main house. There was an old ugly woman sitting in a rocking chair on the front porch of the big house. I swear she had a shotgun across her lap. We saw two men in the corral and a few horses. The cattle are about two miles to the west. We saw my brand and I saw brands that I recognized from back in Texas. We saw three men watching the herd. There could have been more. The herd was spread out pretty good. There might have been as many as two thousand head there. That's what we know."

"It sounds to me like if we rode in there without knowing where most of the people are," started Sean, "we could get shot to pieces. If there's that many houses and buildings, that's a lot of cover. I really don't wanna get into a big gun battle there and get women and children killed. I think I'll slip back out there tonight and see if I can tell how many are in the houses. There's a full moon tonight so I should be able to move good. It gets dark earlier now too, so after I see who's at the houses, I'll slip over and check out the cattle. Maybe they won't have a nighthawk out. If they don't, I got an idea already. I'll tell you all about it when I get back. Bob, I got a buyer for your cattle already. Talked to him this mornin' and told him what was goin' on. Bill Thompson's his name. Jon met him last night. He's gonna stick around and see if we get the herd back, and he'll pay top dollar. I wouldn't discuss this with anyone tonight, especially if you're in the saloon while I'm gone. We don't know all the Hawks, and any of them, or even a cousin could be in there and over hear you. Jon, you find Bill and tell him not to mention this to anyone. I'll be goin' out shortly. Stay alert. Them Hawks might try somethin'. They know Michael, and they know Jim. Watch your back, and keep your eyes on Maggie. I'll be tellin' Maggie goodbye now."

~~~~

Maggie was busy mixing with customers when Sean asked to speak with her for a few minutes. "Maggie darlin', I gotta go do some scoutin'. Could be gone most of the night." Sean said. "Keep a pistol on you and keep alert. Michael and the boys will be alert too. I'll be back before you know it."

"Just where are you going?" asked Maggie. "And why does it have to be tonight? You only got here this morning."

"I'm sorry darlin'," Sean said, "but I can't tell you anything. That way, if you were taken, you wouldn't know, so you couldn't tell."

"So if I got taken, they could work me over or abuse me, and I couldn't tell them cause I don't know," Maggie said. "Seems to me I could get abused whether I knew or not."

"Well let's hope nothin' happens," said Sean. "I gotta get goin' now. I love you Maggie."

"I love you too, Sean O'Rourke," replied Maggie. "Hurry up and get back."

~~~~

There was a full moon so Sean could see very well. He rode to within five hundred yards of the Hawk place, tied his horse to a scrub bush, then proceeded on foot. As he was working his way closer, he hoped that the Hawks didn't have any dogs, but that was unlikely. Almost everyone who lived away from any town had at least one dog. Sean had a good supply of jerky with him and figured he could bribe any dog unless they were trained to attack. When he got about a hundred yards from the place, several dogs started barking. They weren't tied and they were coming after him. When they got closer, he could see that there were four of them, and they were big mutts. As they got closer, Sean started talking to them. When they were close enough to see clearly, they had quit barking and were wagging their tales. Sean sat on the ground, started petting them, and gave each of them a good chunk of jerky. Sean then got up and continued his approach. The dogs followed along as if they belonged to Sean. Sean spent time checking out each small house and then the big house. Seven of the smaller houses were occupied and Sean could tell that there was a man in each of them. Sean counted four men in the big house. As he moved from house to house, he kept giving the dogs more jerky. They followed him back to his horse, and went with him when he went to check out the herd. When he neared the herd, he again dismounted and tied his horse to some brush, and proceeded cautiously on foot. The dogs went right along with him. Sean was worried that the dogs might spook the cattle, but the dogs didn't seem to mind the cattle and cattle didn't mind the dogs. As long as he moved easy like, the cattle didn't mind him either. After an hour or so, Sean had still not spotted a nighthawk, so he went back and got his horse. He could cover more ground, and maybe there'd be less of a chance of spooking the cattle. Sean circled the whole herd and no nighthawk was spotted. He dismounted to relieve himself. When he did, he spotted a few head away from the main bunch. He mounted and started in that direction, but when he started, the dogs took off and drove the cows back to the main bunch. "Well I'll be," Sean said to himself. "Those are cow dogs. They trained them to be cow dogs." Sean decided he'd seen enough and headed back to town. The dogs went right along with him. Sean also decided that the Hawks didn't treat their dogs very well, or they wouldn't have went with him.

It was almost daylight when Sean got back to town. He took his horse to the livery and the dogs went right along. The young boy from the livery was already there. "Hey Marshal, are these your dogs?" he asked. "I sure could use me a dog if you want to get rid of any of them."

"Tell you what, son," Sean said. "You look after 'em today and I'll see what I can do. I'll be needin' them tonight. Make sure they get somethin' to eat. You can probably get some scraps from Cookie."

~~~~

Everyone was still asleep at Maggie's Place. Sean cleaned himself up as much as he could without taking a full bath, then climbed into bed with Maggie. He was going to give her a little kiss on the cheek and get to sleep, but when he did, she woke up. "I'll get some sleep later," Sean said as they became tangled together.

It was past noon before Sean woke up. Maggie had already dressed and gone. He was sure his deputies were getting impatient waiting to hear from him. He got himself dressed and made his way down the stairs to the saloon below. Michael and his other deputies were at a table drinking coffee. "Can I get Cookie to make me some breakfast?" Sean asked. Tom was there and he went into the kitchen, said something to Cookie, and brought Sean a cup of coffee. "Cookie'll have you somethin' shortly," Tom said to Sean.

Michael spoke first. "Well, what did you find out last night, and do you have a plan yet?" Michael asked.

"Seven of the ten small houses were occupied last night. There was a man in each one," Sean began. "There were four men in the big house. There was no nighthawk out last night. I also made friends with their dogs. There's four of 'em and they got 'em trained to be cow dogs. I watched em round up a few cows that had scattered from the main bunch. They followed me back here. The livery boy's watchin' em for me. Anyway, I have two ideas. One is that we can slip out there after dark and move the whole herd. The next day when they come to check on them, they'll think they was rustled, and a bunch of em will come after 'em. We can set up and pick em off. That way we won't have any gun battle near the houses where there's women and children."

"That sounds good," said Bob. "Now what's the other plan?"

"We can slip out there after dark and when they come out to check on the herd the next day, probably two or three at the most'll come out, we can grab em," said Sean. "Can probably do it without firin' a shot. When they don't get back, they're bound to send out someone else to see what's goin' on. Then we grab them too. After that, I couldn't be sure what they would do. Maybe send out the rest. If they did that, we'd have 'em cut down some, and we'd still be away from the houses. So, anyone got a better idea, or any idea at all?"

"I like the first idea better," said Jon. "That way we can get it over with quicker. The other way could take a few days."

"I go along with Jon," said Bob.

"Sounds good to me," added Jim.

"I have a question," said Michael. "Should we have someone here to look out for Maggie just in case? You never know for sure what the Hawks might try."

"Yes, Michael," Sean said, "I think we should and it should probably be you. Everyone's used to seeing you in the saloon now. If you weren't there, it might look suspicious. So we're in agreement. We'll slip out tonight after dark and move the herd. You men make sure you get any rest you might need. We could be up all night."

"I talked to Bill and he's takin' the next stage outta here," said Bob. "He's going to Kansas City and said to send him a telegram when things get sorted out."

"That's good," said Sean. "That'll give us time to figure out how we're gonna move the herd after we take care of the Hawks. We should take the whole herd and not worry about cutting out other brands. We can try to get the money to the rightful owners later."

"Those other brands from Texas that I saw belong to people that I know to be dead," said Bob. "Some were killed during the war, and some were killed when their cows got rustled."

"We'll still do our best to find out if any owners are alive or have kin that are alive," said Sean. "It's only fair. We'll meet at the livery an hour before dark. Make sure you got plenty of ammunition and some food and water. See you all this evening."

~~~~

Sean spent the rest of the day with Maggie. She was not happy about him going out again so soon. "Maggie," began Sean, "if things work out tonight, we might get rid of the Hawk problem once and for all. It's gotta be done."

"And after the Hawks, it'll be the Anderson bunch, then someone else," said Maggie. "I may as well get used to it. I don't have to like it though. You know that when this town gets growing, they're gonna need a town Marshal. Maybe you could do that."

"No, I won't do that," Sean began. "Lookin' after a bunch of drunk and horny Texas boys is not somethin' I will do. That's somethin' that you need to think about too. Those Texas boys all carry guns. They get to drinkin' and carryin' on, anything can happen. You just had that shootin' in here the other day. That kind of thing can happen on a regular basis whenever a herd comes to town. You do a good business now, but it'll go crazy if this place becomes a cow town. Will you really want that? Anyway, we both got things to think about. Right now, I'm tellin' you that I love you, and I always will. Now if you don't mind, I feel like kissin' you."

"I don't mind at all," said Maggie. "Kiss me and then kiss me some more."

CHAPTER SEVEN

It finally came time to meet at the livery. As the men showed up, Sean told them to make sure they had plenty of ammunition and some food and water. Then Sean talked to the boy from the livery to make sure that he had fed the dogs. Then he said to the boy. "So you want one of these dogs, huh boy?" Sean said. "I bet you got one picked out already."

"No, not really," the boy said. "I like 'em all and they seem to like me."

"Well I'll get you one of these dogs after we get done with 'em," Sean said. "You gotta promise to do somethin' for me, all right."

"Sure Marshal," the boy said, "you just name it."

"You cannot, no matter what, tell anyone that you seen me and my deputies ride out this evening," said Sean. "People could get hurt or killed if you do. Do you understand, son?"

"Yes sir, not a living soul no matter what," he answered.

"That's good, son. Just what is your name anyway?" Sean asked.

"It's Billy, Billy Thornton," he answered.

"All right, Billy, you think about these dogs. I'll get you one," Sean said.

~~~~

As they were riding out of town, Sean gave them some more instructions. "When we get close to the herd, two of us will circle the herd and make sure there are no nighthawks," Sean began. "Just because they didn't have one last night, doesn't mean they won't tonight. If there are any, we will take them without shooting. Shooting could stampede the herd, and it's possible that shots could be heard back at the Hawk place. There's good moonlight so we should be able to move the herd easily. We want to move them to the north a few miles, and find a good place to set up when they come after us. Bob, I don't think anyone but you has moved a herd of cattle before, so we'll need some tips from you."

"The main thing about moving a herd is go easy like," said Bob. "Talk gentle like to them. There's four of us and the dogs. First, we'll bunch 'em up a little tighter. I'll pick out a cow that looks like a leader, and get her up front. I'll give her a push and see who follows. Younger cows should follow. Once a few get movin', the rest will follow. I'll stay in the lead. We'll need one of you on each side as they stretch out, and a man in the rear ridin' drag. If these are cow dogs, they should help us keep them movin' and from strayin' without bein' told. Remember, go easy like. Sing or sweet talk 'em. They won't care if yer outta tune or not, as long as it's easy like."

"All right, Bob, we'll be as sweet as we can," said Sean.

~~~~

As they neared the herd, they stopped, and Sean and Jon went to circle the herd looking for nighthawks. As he was leaving, Sean told Jim and Bob. "Remember now, no shootin'. If someone would happen on you, try to take 'em without shootin'."

Sean went to the east side of the herd and Jon went to the west. They met each other at the other end of the herd, and neither of them had spotted a nighthawk. The dogs must have known what was going to happen because they had already started bunching up the herd. Sean and Jon went back to where Jim and Bob were, and then they started getting ready to move the herd. Bob picked out a likely looking cow, put her in the lead and got her moving. It was just like he said. First, some of the young ones followed. Then they all followed. There was a few that couldn't make up their minds, but the dogs took care of that. Sean took the drag as he wanted to be in the rear and make sure they weren't being followed yet. They moved along at a good slow pace.

After several hours, they came to a big rise. There were a few trees at the top and some scrub brush. Sean decided this would be a good place to set up. "We'll get the herd on the other side of this rise where they can't be seen," Sean began. "We'll drive them over the top so hopefully, the Hawks will follow the trail up too. We'll get the herd settled down as best we can. Maybe they'll want to rest after us keeping them up all night. Those cow dogs should help keep them bunched. We'll go ahead and get some breakfast, and then we'll pick some positions."

It was still dark, but daylight wasn't far away. They made a fire, and Jim made bacon, biscuits, and coffee for breakfast. "You make good biscuits, Jim," said Jon. "They're bettern' the ones I make."

"That goes fer me too," said Bob.

"I like 'em too Jim," said Sean. "If you wasn't a deputy now, I could get you a job helpin' Cookie. Now let's finish up and put that fire out. Jon, when you get done eatin', take the horses, and find a spot just over the rise where we can keep 'em, not far, just so they can't be seen from this side. I don't want any horses getting shot. I figure we won't see anyone till just before noon, but we'll keep watch anyway startin' now. I'll go first, and you men can sleep if you want. I'll wake one of you in an hour, then you can wake another one in a hour. Use my spyglass. We can see a long way, but so can they on this open plain. Stay low and try not to let the glass glare in the sunlight. When we know they're comin', we'll take positions behind these few trees and brush. Hopefully, they won't spot us, and we'll let them get as close as we can before we open up. I could get a few of them a good ways off with my Sharps, but that might scare them off. I'll save the Sharps for when they're tryin' to get away after we open up. Now get yourself some rest."

They had each taken a turn and it was back around to Sean. Sean took a look over the other side of the rise to make sure the cattle were all right. The dogs were doing a fine job, plus a lot of the cows were bedded down. Sean went back to the other side of the rise, took the spyglass from Jim, and found a good spot to watch. It was almost high noon now and Sean was convinced that they would be showing up soon. In a few minutes he spotted some dust maybe a mile away. They would be there shortly. Sean woke up the other men, and they went to their positions. "Stay low now, Let 'em get close," Sean said. As they got closer, Sean could see that there were nine riders. They were five hundred yards away now and still coming fast. As they neared the bottom of the rise, they slowed down, but kept coming. At two hundred yards, they had still not spotted Sean or his men. When they were within fifty yards of Sean, they stopped. Sean heard one of them say, "I don't like this. This is too good a spot for an ambush." As soon as he finished talking, Sean opened up. Then the others opened up. Four men fell out of the saddle. The other five turned and headed back down the rise, firing their pistols as they went. Sean and his men fired again, and three more men fell. The last two were really moving now. The other men kept firing at them, but they kept going. Sean grabbed his Sharps, got down in the prone position, and took a bead on the lead rider. The Sharps bellowed, and after what seemed like a few seconds, but wasn't, the lead rider was knocked off his horse. Sean reloaded and began to sight in on the last man. "Save your lead," Bob said. "He must be seven hundred yards out by now."

"Quiet now," said Sean. "I'm workin'." Sean grabbed a little dirt to check the wind, and went back to sighting in. The Sharps barked once more. Bob was sure Sean had missed, and just as he was turning his head to look at Sean, the rider was thrown out of the saddle. "Son of a bitch," said Bob, "I'm sure as hell glad that yer on my side."

The nine riders were all down now. Sean told his deputies to check them all out and see if any were still alive, then he went to make sure the herd was all right. It was. Either the shooting hadn't spooked them, or the dogs had held them if they had tried to run.

All but one of the riders was dead. The last one that Sean had shot was not dead, but his wound was definitely mortal. Sean patched him up as best he could hoping to get any information out of him that he could before he died. "Yer that damn Marshal, aren't you?" the man said. "How the hell can you shoot like that? I musta been over eight hundred yards away from you. It was you that shot me, wasn't it?"

"Yes, it was me, now look Mister," Sean began. "You're gonna die. You're bleedin' bad and you got a hole in a lung. Is there anything you wanna tell me before you die?"

"Yes, there is, lawman," he said. "You can go to hell, and I'll tell you this just so you can go around and always be lookin' over yer shoulder. Anderson has hired several professional gunmen to get you. He put two thousand dollars on your head. It goes up a hundred dollars a month till yer dead. These men don't mind if they shoot you in the back or not. Don't know their names, but two thousand dollars is a lot to think about. Now let me die in peace."

"Don't be dyin' just yet," said Sean. "Is there any more men back at the houses? I counted eleven last night."

"There's two left, but they're not full growed yet. One's sixteen, and the other's seventeen," he answered. "I wouldn't go there if I was you. The women'll shoot you on sight, especially my Grammaw. She's meaner than a snake. She won't like you killin' her famly. There's still more of us. Others are with Anderson right now."

"Did Anderson head south like I think he did?" asked Sean.

"Yes, he did," he answered. "He's not worried about you now. He knows them gunmen will get you sooner or later." When he was finished speaking, he gasped for air a couple of times, then died.

"Well, it's not over yet," said Sean, "but we've cutem down some more. Maybe we can find out from Grammaw how many are left."

"Don't forget what I said about that ugly woman on the front porch of the big house," said Bob. "I swear she had a shotgun on her lap. I bet that's Grammaw. Wouldn't surprise me if she runs the whole show. Them two boys that are still there are big enough to carry guns. If we go there, we gotta be careful."

"We'll be careful," said Sean. "Now I wanna do somethin' I don't usually do for outlaws. I wanna pack 'em up and take 'em back so the others can get 'em buried. Maybe seein' dead bodies will make 'em think some about whether to shoot at us or not. Now let's round up their horses and strap 'em on. Bob, how do you wanna handle this herd? I think we should drive 'em back to near town and see if we can get some hands hired to help you drive them to Kansas City."

"That's what I had in mind too," said Bob. "We just gotta make sure that they're not tied up with the Hawks or Anderson. I figure they got eyes everywhere."

"I'm sure they do," said Sean. "That's why I would like it if Jon and Jim went with you. You can watch each other's back. How about it boys, will you go with Bob?"

"Yeh, I'll go," said Jim. "When I shot Ethan Hawk, I saw a cousin of his, and I would recognize the men who helped load Hawk on that buckboard. Those three are not here with these dead."

"I'll go too," said Jon. "Always wanted to see Kansas City."

~~~~

They got the bodies strapped to the horses, and Sean tied all nine horses together. "I'll ride drag and trail these horses behind me," said Sean. "We can move out whenever you all are ready."

Bob rounded up the same lead cow they had used at the start, and put her in the lead. She moved out and the herd followed. The dogs took care of any that couldn't make up their mind. When they got near the Hawk place, Sean went up to the lead to speak with Bob. "You and Jim and the dogs take the herd back close to town," Sean said. "Me and Jon will visit the Hawk place."

"You be careful Sean," said Bob. "Remember Grammaw and what that man said about the women. He said they'd shoot us on sight."

"We'll have a look-see before we go in," replied Sean. "I don't intend to get shot by anyone. I'll be in town soon as I can. Now get 'em movin'." Bob took off at a slow pace again, and Sean and Jon headed to the Hawk place. When they got around five hundred yards from the place, Sean took out his spy glass and checked out the place. A few women were outside washing clothes and some small children were with them. The old ugly woman was sitting in a rocking chair on the front porch of the big house. There was a blanket across her lap, but Sean couldn't tell if she had a shotgun or not. "Let's go on in," said Sean. "Be alert and ready for anything."

They moved slowly and cautiously. When they got closer to the small houses, they went even slower and eyed each house as best they could. Grammaw's eyes never left them. They stopped about twenty five yards from the front porch of the big house. Sean dropped the rope he had been holding to lead the horses with the dead bodies. "I'll talk to Grammaw," Sean said to Jon. "You watch our backs as best you can." Sean stayed on his horse and was about to speak when the old woman spoke. "So yer that sombitchin' Marshal that's been killin' my boys."

"Your boys kill and steal ma'am," replied Sean.

"They were good boys. They did what I toldem," she said.

"So you're the boss, huh," said Sean. "There's not many left for you to boss around now, is there?" Just as Sean had finished talking, two boys came out the front door of the main house. Sean figured these must be the young boys that dyin' outlaw told them about. They looked full grown to Sean, and they were both armed. One had a pistol stuck in his belt, and the other one had a tied down Colt. The one with the tied down Colt was a good bit taller than the other one.

"I'm gonna kill you lawman," the taller one said.

"Don't you pull on him," said Grammaw. "He'll kill ya. Don't you remember that he killed three of your uncles in a gunfight. They say he's really fast."

"Well me and Joe here can take 'em," the tall one said. "Me and him both are faster than my uncles ever were."

"Don't pull on me son," said Sean. "I've killed enough men today. I don't wanna kill you."

"I'm not yer damn son," said the tall one. When he finished talking he started to draw his Colt. When the other boy saw him starting to draw, he started to draw, too. Sean waited until the boy's Colt was almost clear the holster, then pulled a pistol and put holes in both the boys chests. As soon as he had shot the second boy, he heard the shotgun blast and felt the buckshot slam into his right shoulder and arm as he was being knocked backwards out of the saddle. The pistol fell from his right hand. As he was falling, he managed to grab the pistol on his left side with his left hand. Before he hit the ground, he fired at shot at Grammaw. The bullet struck her in the forehead and she was knocked backwards, still holding the shotgun that had been under the blanket. More shots were fired, but these were coming from behind them. Jon's horse had been hit and was falling. Jon laid behind it now for cover. Then he spotted where the shooting was coming from. There was one woman standing beside one of the houses. She had a Henry rifle and was firing it as fast as she could. Jon's horse was hit several more times. Sean crawled over to the down horse for cover too. She emptied the Henry and was trying to reload. Jon yelled to her. "Put down that rifle lady, I don't wanna kill you," Jon said.

"I'm gonna kill you, you sombitch," she said as she kept reloading. When she had finished reloading and was ready to fire again, Jon shot her through the head. Then he looked at Sean. "We've had us a bad day, Sean," he said. "Didn't think I'd ever have to shoot me a woman."

"Well I never thought I'd have to shoot someone's Grammaw either," replied Sean. "Now would you find somethin' we could use to wrap me up? I'm not bleedin' too bad, but it hurts like hell. I'll need a sling too."

"You got five pieces of buckshot in your shoulder, three in your upper arm, and two in your lower arm," Jon said after he examined Sean. " They'll have to be dug out when we get to town. You're lucky Grammaw wasn't that good a shot. That shotgun was sawed off some too. If it hadn't been, it would have been a tighter pattern and maybe would have torn your arm clear off."

"You're a bundle of joy to talk too right now," said Sean. "Quit talkin' what ifs, and patch me up and get yourself another horse. I'll be able to ride all right. We can send someone else out later to clean up this mess."

~~~~

It didn't take long to get back to town. They took the horses to the livery and then made their way to Maggie's place. As they went in the front doors, Michael was there. He saw that Sean was wounded and ran over to him to see what he could do. "Get me some whiskey," Sean said. "I'll be needin' it when they go to diggin' this buckshot outta me. There is a doctor in this town, isn't there?"

"Yes, there is one now," Michael said. "I'll go see if he's in." Sean was setting at a table sipping his whiskey when Maggie showed up.

"Oh Sean, is it bad?" Maggie asked.

"No, I've had a lot worse," Sean answered.

"Who shot you?" Maggie asked,

" Grammaw Hawk," answered Sean.

"Are you serious?" asked Maggie. "Someone's Grammaw shot you?"

"Yes, Maggie," Sean answered. "I'm dead serious, and she's dead."

"So you had to shoot her?" asked Maggie.

"Well I wasn't gonna let her shoot me again," answered Sean. "Jon had to kill a woman today too, no choice. Grammaw was the boss of the whole gang."

"How do you know that?" asked Maggie.

"Because she told me," replied Sean. Just then Michael returned with the doctor. He was a very young fella. Sean thought he looked like someone who had just got out of school. "Are you old enough to be a doctor?" Sean asked him.

"I'm older than I look, my good man," the doctor said. "I spent three years with the Army of the Potomac. This here is nothing compared to what I've done before. My name is Rawlins, Dr. Joseph Rawlins, and you are?"

"Sean O'Rourke, Federal Marshal Sean O'Rourke," Sean answered. "Pleased to meet you. Now let's get started."

"I don't have a good office yet," the doctor said. "He'll need to be lying down, on a bed preferably."

"Get him up to my room," said Maggie.

"It could be bloody, and I'll need plenty of whiskey," the doctor said. "I don't have all my drugs here yet."

"I have plenty of sheets," said Maggie. "Don't worry about the blood."

~~~~

Sean got into the bed and drank some more whiskey, then told the doctor to get started. Michael and Jon were there to help hold Sean down if it was needed. The doctor started on Sean's lower arm and worked his way up. Sean took the pain very well, but when the doctor started on the shoulder, Michael and Jon had to hold him down. After the first piece was pulled from the shoulder, Sean passed out, and stayed out as the other four were removed. No stitching was necessary, so the doctor bandaged him up, and told Maggie he'd come back tomorrow and check on him. "He'll be fine," the doctor said. "Make him stay in bed till I come back. The only thing to worry about now is infection. Just gotta keep things clean. Since he's a lawman, I hope he can shoot with his left hand. It'll be a little while before his right shoulder and arm are in good shape."

"He can shoot left handed," said Jon. "He shot Grammaw Hawk with his left hand today."

The doctor didn't say anything else. He nodded his head to Maggie and left. "You two can go now," said Maggie to Michael and Jon. "I'll set here with him for a while." The two of them left the room. Maggie sat there in a rocking chair just looking at Sean and thinking. "That's my man laying there all shot up," she said to herself. "If I'm going to be his woman, this is what our life might be like from time to time. I better learn to accept it, because I will love this man as long as I live." After maybe an hour, Maggie nodded off. Another hour later Sean woke up. He saw Maggie asleep in the rocker. "That woman is so beautiful that it hurts," Sean said to himself. "I can look at her forever and not get tired looking." Maggie must have sensed that she was being watched, because she woke up. "Are you in pain?" she asked.

"No, I feel fine," Sean said. "I just need you now."

"We can't be doing that now," Maggie said. "You've been shot, you need to keep still and rest."

"I'm just shot, Maggie," said Sean. "I'm not dead. Now come over here. I've missed you."

Maggie shook her head, undressed, and climbed into bed with Sean. "I missed you too, darlin'," she said. "Now you take it easy, I'll do the moving." When they were finished, Maggie laid there with him for what seemed like hours. There was a knock at the door.

"Maggie, it's me Bob. I came to see how Sean's doin'. Jim and me been worried," he said.

"He's fine," said Maggie. "I'll be out in a minute and you can come in and talk to him." Maggie got herself dressed, gave Sean a kiss on the cheek, and opened the door. "You can have him now," Maggie said as she was leaving.

"Jon told us what happened," Bob said. "Glad yer not too bad off. We got the herd just outside of town. We'll get the word out that we need some hands."

"That's good," said Sean. "At least you didn't have any trouble gettin' back here. Is anything else goin' on that I need to know about?"

"Well there is," Bob started. "For some reason there's a troop of cavalry out here, and their officer wants to talk to you. He wouldn't say why."

"Well, send him up," said Sean. "Maybe I know him or somethin'."

Bob left the room and a few minutes later, a middle aged Captain came into the room. "My name is Maxwell, Captain Edward Maxwell," he began. "I heard that a Federal Marshal named O'Rourke was out here somewhere, and when I heard that you were in Abilene, I took my patrol over this way so I could meet you."

"Well my name's O'Rourke, Sean O'Rourke," Sean said. "Why do you want to meet me?"

"I heard about you from when you were with the Sharpshooters," he said. "We were in some of the same scrapes. I always appreciated what you men did. I just wanted to shake your hand. I hear you have a reputation out here too." Then he extended his hand to Sean and they shook, Sean with his left hand. "If you ever have a need for the cavalry, don't hesitate to get ahold of me," the Captain said. " We will be at Fort Wallace."

"Captain, I do have a favor to ask of you if you could spare the men," said Sean.

"Sure, how may I help you?" asked the Captain.

"About two miles west of town, is the Hawk spread," began Sean. "They are a family of rustlers and killers. My deputies and I killed nine of them earlier today. Me and a deputy were taking the bodies back home when we had to kill some more of them. We even had to kill their Grammaw and another woman. Grammaw's the one that shot me. Could you spare some men to go out there and bury them? I don't think there's any more men out there right now, but there should be some women and small children. If you do send some men, they better be careful. I don't know if those women would shoot at soldiers or not. If there are any men out there, arrest them. All the Hawk men have a one hundred dollar price on their head. The Hawks are workin' with the Anderson bunch too, and I'm sure you've heard of them. One of the Hawks told me, before he died, that Anderson put a two thousand dollar price on my head, and he's hired some professional gunmen."

"I'll be glad to send some men out to bury those folks," said the Captain. "I'll send enough so they can stand guard while the graves are being dug. We'll arrest any men we see out there, if they'll let us. If not, we'll do what's necessary. In the future, if I hear about anyone asking about you and your whereabouts, I'll detain them for you. Now I'll get my men bivouacked just at the edge of town and get that detail sent out. We have all heard about that red haired beauty. I'm hoping to meet her myself."

"Well turn around Captain," said Sean. "She's right behind you." Maggie had slipped upstairs to make sure Sean was still in bed and not getting dressed to go out and do some lawman stuff.

"Oh my, you are even more beautiful than I have heard. It is an extreme honor to meet you," the Captain said.

"Thank you, Captain," said Maggie. "You are a true gentleman. I hope you are here long enough for you and your men to visit my establishment."

"Yes, Captain, I'd be pleased if you would allow me to buy some drinks for you and your men," added Sean.

"You both are most kind," replied the Captain. "I'll arrange it so all of my men will have a chance to visit your place. Now I must see to my troop. Good day."

"Captain, Jon O'Brien, one of my deputies will go with your detail out to the Hawks. He was with me out there when I got shot, so he knows the layout," said Sean.

"Thank you, Mr. O'Rourke," said the Captain. "Now I will take my leave."

"That soldier has very good manners, doesn't he." Maggie said to Sean.

"Yes he does," said Sean. "It's nice to see an officer who is a gentleman. During the war, I knew so many that were snobbish, spoiled little rich kids, and treated their men badly. Men like that don't usually last very long once the shootin' starts."

"Well, darlin', one of these days, I expect you to tell me all about your life up to this point," said Maggie. "I intend to be with you always so I want to know everything there is about you. I will tell you all about myself too."

"We'll have all kinds of time while I'm healing up," said Sean. "Now I need to send a telegram to Judge Simmons in St. Louis. Would you get some paper and write it down for me?"

Of course, darlin', I have paper and pencil in the closet," answered Maggie. "I'll get it, and you just tell me what to write." Maggie got the paper and pencil and told Sean she was ready.

"All right, here we go," said Sean.

Judge David Simmons
Federal court House
St. Louis

Nine more Hawks killed getting back stolen Texas herd
<stop> four more Hawks killed at Hawk place <stop> two
were women <stop> no choice <stop> Grammaw Hawk
was boss of gang <stop> Grammaw Hawk dead <stop>
more Hawks still with Anderson <stop> Anderson went
south to Texas or Mexico <stop> Anderson hired professional gunmen to kill me <stop> Anderson put two thousand dollar bounty on my head <stop> three deputies
will help get Texas herd to Kansas City <stop> wounded
at Hawk place not serious <stop> will pursue Hawk when
healed <stop>

O'Rourke

~~~~

"Now would you get that sent for me darlin'?" Sean asked. "And
would you tell Bob I need to talk to him again?"

"Of course I will," Maggie said. "If you need anything while
I'm gone, Michael and Tom are downstairs. Just give a yell. They'll
hear you." Maggie left the room, and a few minutes later, Bob was
there.

"What do you need, Sean?" Bob asked.

"If I remember right, you said that you would be a deputy
until we got the herd back and those men killed," began Sean.
"Well it looks like we got some a that done. I'm not gonna ask you

to stay on forever, but I'd like for you to stay a deputy at least till you get the herd shipped. Does that sound all right with you?"

"Sure, I'll stay a deputy till the herd is shipped and Anderson is dead," replied Bob. "Bein' a lawman on a drive just might just help things. Maybe a rustler would think twice before messin' with a Federal Deputy."

"Maybe so," said Sean. "Who's lookin' after the herd now?"

"Jim and the dogs are out there," said Bob. "Them are good dogs. I might just keep one of 'em after we get done. I also got two new men hired. Two drifters came into town beggin' for any kind of work. I talked to them a good while before I hired them. I also made them show me all their gear. Neither one of them has a pistol. They both got rifles, Sharps carbines."

"That's a good start," said Sean. "Keep me posted on things. We'll telegraph that cattle buyer when you're ready to leave. I want one of them dogs for that boy at the livery too. He'd probably take 'em all if no one else wanted any."

"All right, I'll keep you posted," said Bob. "And I'll make sure that boy gets his dog."

"Thanks, now would you tell Michael I'd like to talk to him?" asked Sean.

"Sure," said Bob as he was leaving.

~~~~

Michael entered the room. "What is it you need, Sean darlin'?" asked Michael.

"As you can see," Sean began. "My right shoulder and arm will be out of action for a while. I need you to find me some left handed holsters. I want one for a cross draw, and one for a straight left handed draw."

"I'll see what I can find, young Sean," said Michael. "Sometimes they have some at the General Store. I also hear that a man is coming to town and opening up a leather goods store. I've heard all kinds of rumors about businesses coming to town."

"They won't be rumors if that McCoy fella does what he says," said Sean. "Now I got somethin' else to talk about. I don't know if the other men told you or not, but one of the Hawks, before he died, told me that Anderson has put a price of two thousand dollars on my head and has hired some professional gunmen. I don't know what they mean by professional. They might be just somebody who is willing to shoot me in the back, or maybe they are hired killers. Anyway, we need to be alert at all times. Watch out for strangers and such. You never know what these people might look like. They could look like a well dressed business man, or they could look like a saddle tramp. Wear your pistol at all times and keep it close at night. If word gets out that I'm laid up, they could show up any time. I'll make sure Maggie has a pistol on her too."

"We'll do whatever it takes, my friend," said Michael. "Now I'll be off and see if I can round up some holsters. If I do find something, I'll bring it here so we can make sure it fits your pistol." As Michael left the room, Sean nodded off to sleep. It seemed as though he had slept for hours, but it was only a hour. Maggie was whispering in his ear trying to wake him up. "Wake up darlin'," she said. "We need to get some food in you. You haven't eaten since you've been back."

"What's Cookie made this time?" asked Sean.

"Looks like he made you a good stew," said Maggie. "He figured you'd need something that was easy to eat."

"He's right about that," said Sean as he was tearing into his food. "That man can cook. This is really good. His wife is one lucky woman. Do you suppose he cooks at home too?"

"I hear he does all the cooking," said Maggie. "She can cook too. She helps out here when we get really busy, which is what we'll be when those soldier boys start showing up."

"I bet Captain Maxwell told them they better darn well behave too," said Sean.

"I imagine he did," said Maggie. "Now you finish up and get some rest. If you need anything, just yell. I'm going downstairs now. I think I hear some of those soldiers now."

~~~~

Captain Maxwell had sent twenty men out with Jon to get the Hawks buried. The rest of the men he turned loosed to come to Maggie's Place. "You men will behave like gentlemen, or I'll have you shoveling shit till you're dead," he told them. "I will personally make your life a living hell if you get out of line. Now Marshal O'Rourke has been kind enough to buy our drinks, but we will not abuse his generosity. Now you are dismissed. Act like the good men that I know you all are."

As the soldiers began entering Maggie's Place, they all got jammed up at the doors. The first few soldiers through the doors had spotted Maggie's painting, and were standing there looking at it as if they were petrified. This caused the jam up. Seeing the problem, Maggie went to the lead soldiers. "Welcome to my place," she said. "I'm Maggie and I'd be glad to show you to a table." The soldiers acted like young shy school boys, but they followed Maggie to their tables. They were speechless. Finally, one of the soldiers spoke. "Ma'am, are you for real? You can't be. Are you one of them angels?" he asked.

"Yes, young man, I am for real, and please call me Maggie," she said. "My girls are on their way here. Please have a pleasant evening." Then she went to the bar to speak with Michael. "Sean is buying drinks for the soldiers while they're in town," she said. "Please make sure they are taken care of. I'm sure their captain has ordered them to behave."

"That's what Captains do, darlin'," Michael said. "Doesn't always work out. Speakin' from experience of course. Tom and I will make sure the boys are taken care of."

~~~~

Jon and the burial detail had no incidents as they went to the Hawk place. When they arrived, there were some women loading wagons and hitching up horses to the wagons. A Sergeant was in charge of the detail, and he asked the women what they were doing and where they were going. "We're getting' outta here," one of them said. "That damn lawman has done killed our men."

"Where are you headed?" asked the Sergeant.

"That's none of your damn business," said the woman. "But it don't matter. We're goin' back to Missouri to our kin."

"Is there any more men around here?" asked the Sergeant.

"Do you see any?" said the woman. "Now leave us alone so we can get goin'."

The soldiers rounded up the bodies, and took them to the edge of the settlement. They took turns digging and standing guard. By the time they were finished, the women and their children had already left. "We should check out each house and the barns and buildings before we leave," Jon told the Sergeant. "Don't want to get someone shot in the back as we're leavin'. We know there are more Hawks. We just don't know where they all are. Some are with Anderson, but there could still be some around."

"Good idea," said the Sergeant. "We'll do a house to house check. This'll be good practice for the men. Most of them are green."

"Whatever you do or however you do it, do it so your men don't accidentally shoot each other," said Jon.

The Sergeant gave the orders to his men, and the search began. There was no one anywhere. Jon gave the Sergeant a compliment on how his men did the search. Then they headed back to town. The young soldiers were all getting excited about going to Maggie's Place. When they got back to their bivouac area, the Sergeant gave his report, and the men went about their duties. The troop was staying there for two nights and the burial detail would get their turn at Maggie's the next day.

Jon took his horse to the livery and then went to Maggie's to tell Sean about the detail. Sean was awake when he entered the room. "Well we got 'em all buried," Jon said. "We searched the place and we didn't find any more men. The women who were there when we got there were packin' up to leave. They said they were goin' back to Missouri to their kin."

"That's good," said Sean. "When we get a chance, we should check out there from time to time and see if anyone comes back or if any men show up. Now you go on downstairs and have a drink on me. I'm gonna try to sleep some."

Sean fell asleep and he slept the whole night through. He didn't even wake up when Maggie slipped into bed a few hours before daylight. They both woke up around noon. "I'll get us some coffee, darlin'," Maggie said as she put on a robe and headed downstairs. When she got downstairs, Doc Rawlins was there.

"I came to see my patient," he said. "Is he awake?"

"Yes, go on up Doc. Could you use a cup of coffee?" asked Maggie.

"Sounds good," Doc said as he headed upstairs.

"How are you feeling, Marshal?" Doc asked. "Is there much pain? Did you sleep well?"

"No pain unless I move too much, and I slept like a baby," said Sean.

"Good, now let's have a look," he said as he was undoing the bandages. "Look's good. You've begun to heal already, but I must tell you. It will take longer than what you might think. The muscles will heal quickly, but some bones were chipped in your shoulder. You may look good outside, but you cannot see the bones. They will take longer to mend, but you will be good as new in less than two months."

Maggie came into the room bringing the coffee. "How's my man doing, Doctor?" Maggie asked.

"He's doing very good. You just need to make sure he doesn't rush things. Hey, that's good coffee. Who made this?" he asked.

"That would be Cookie, my cook," answered Maggie. "And I'll make sure my man doesn't rush things."

"I'll put on some fresh bandages, and I'll be back in three days," said the doctor. "Maggie, would you mind if I sent my wife over so Cookie can show her how to make coffee? I don't know what she does, but she needs help."

"Sure, she can stop by anytime Cookie's here," said Maggie. "He's a very good cook too if your wife needs help there too."

"I better watch what I say," Doc said. "But she could stand to learn a few things. Not that I'm losing any weight from lack of food. Now you keep this man from moving around too much. See you in three days."

"How'd those soldier boys behave last night?" Sean asked Maggie.

"They did good," answered Maggie. "They seemed so young. I'd say some of them got their first drink last night, and some of them had their first you know what. I hope the one's coming tonight act as well as the others did."

"That's good," said Sean. "Some of those boys may only be seventeen. I was only seventeen when I joined up. Seems so long ago now. Can I get somethin' to eat, darlin'? I'm starved."

"I'll have Cookie make you a good breakfast." said Maggie. "Be back when it's done."

Sean really enjoyed his breakfast. Cookie had made him ham, eggs, taters, and biscuits. Maggie cut up the ham for him. He fell back to sleep and when he woke up, the young soldiers were starting to arrive at Maggie's. Captain Maxwell was with them. He had not been there when the first group of soldiers were there. He asked Maggie if it was all right for him to go up and see Sean. Maggie assured him that it was all right.

The Captain knocked on the door easily and waited for Sean to answer. "Is that you Captain?" Sean asked. "I didn't figure anyone else would knock like that."

"It's me," he answered. "I just wanted to thank you again for what you've done for the men and myself. Soldiers don't usually get this type of treatment from the public."

"Glad to do it, Captain," Sean said. "You helped me out too. So why are they sending you to Fort Wallace?"

"I don't know," he answered. "All I can do is speculate. But you and I both know it's probably got something to with Indians. I have heard that the Cheyenne and Sioux have been raiding."

"Captain, I lived with the Cheyenne for five to six years, and I can tell you that if they are raiding, they feel it's justified," said Sean. "Black Kettle was our main Chief and that man never fought unless he was really forced into it. I heard about that Sand Creek massacre when I was with Sherman. Black Kettle was there. I don't know if my people were there or not."

"What do you mean, by your people?" the Captain asked.

"When I was with the Cheyenne," began Sean, "I lived with an Indian woman named Blue Swan and her husband, John Braddock. He had been a mountain man. I was twelve when I went to be with them. They had a daughter, Katie. We were married when we were both fifteen. We had a daughter, Maggie, and she was pregnant again when they were taken by the cholera. I joined the army a little after that when the war started. I never was able to find out if my in-laws were at Sand creek or not. Anyway, Captain, you need to understand that most of the Indians out here just want to be left alone to live their lives the way they always have. If you can understand that, you'll do better if you ever have to deal with them."

"So how did you get to be with the Cheyenne in the first place?" Captain Maxwell asked.

"Our small wagon train was massacred by white outlaws," Sean began. "I was out hunting at the time. Some Cheyenne happened by and took me in."

"You've had a full life it seems," said the Captain. "I thank you for sharing some knowledge with me. If there is ever anything I can do for you, please don't hesitate to ask."

"Well there might be, Captain," Sean said. "If you do ever have any dealings with the Cheyenne, ask them if they know of a woman named Blue Swan and John Braddock. Tell them that the Shooter wants to know. Sometimes I was known as the "one who kills with the long gun and the big pistol." That's because I had a Sharps rifle and a Colt Walker. If you would hear something, send me a telegram."

"I will remember to ask about them for you," said Captain Maxwell. "Now I'll leave you so you can rest. Thank you again for your kindness." The he extended his hand to Sean and they shook hands, Sean using his left hand.

"You take care Captain," said Sean. "Don't let some glory hunting fool get you into trouble."

"Sound wisdom, sound wisdom," Captain Maxwell said as he was leaving.

~~~~

Maggie came back in the room after the Captain left. "I need you now," she said. Then she undressed and slipped in bed with Sean. After they were finished and laying there holding each other, Sean reminded Maggie that Anderson had put a price on his head.

"I want you to make sure that you have a pistol on you at all times," he began. "Even when we're making love, I want you to have a pistol within reach. I'm not tryin' to scare you, but you never know what that type of person will try. Could get bad since I'm laid up."

"We will do whatever it takes to make sure you stay alive, darlin'," said Maggie. "I will not let some hired scum take my man from me. Now I'm going to get dressed and go back downstairs. That next batch of soldier boys will be getting here anytime."

Maggie then gave Sean a long hard kiss, and then went down-stairs. "I'll bring you up some food later when Cookie gets some-thing done for supper," Maggie said as she was going out the door.

~~~~

The second group of soldiers behaved very well and had the time of their life. Maggie was sure again that some of them had just gotten their first drink and had their first time with a woman. When the last of the soldiers went out the door, Michael and Tom straightened up the place, and Maggie went upstairs and slipped into bed with Sean. She kissed him on the cheek hoping to not wake him, but it woke him and soon they were making love.

CHAPTER EIGHT

Jack Snow was born sometime around 1840 in Missouri, in a small town that was near the Kansas border. His mother was a soiled dove, and he never knew his father. He spent his infant years being passed back and forth by the other women when his mother was with customers. When he was six years old, he helped clean the rooms, helped with the laundry, and cleaned and emptied the chamber pots and spittoons. He never attended school, but his mother taught him how to read and do his sums.

When Jack was ten years old, his mother took up with a business man named Bob Wilson, who said he would give her a good life and she would never have to be a whore again. It started out well, but it didn't take long to find out he was a thief and a drunk. He beat Jack and his mother on a regular basis.

This was the year that Jack killed his first man. One afternoon, Bob came home drunk, and was at the well in the back yard getting a drink. While he was leaning over the well, Jack snuck up on him and hit him in the back of the head with a shovel. Of course he fell into the well and drowned. No one questioned what had happened. He was just another drunk who fell into a well and drowned.

When he was twelve, Jack's mother took up with a farmer named Jacob Haas. This man was hell fire and brimstone. He thought it was his duty to beat Jack. He told Jack he was beating the devil out of him. Being a farmer, they had a team of mules they used for plowing and such. They were good mules, but Jack learned how to aggravate them easily. All he had to do was barely swat them on the nose, and they would kick and buck. One day, after working the fields, Jack was leading the mules into the barn, and Jacob got careless. He got behind the mules and Jack saw his chance. Jack swatted the mules on the nose and they went to kicking and bucking. The very first kick split Jacob's skull wide open. His death was not questioned. The local sheriff just said, "Well he musta done somethin' sometime to get that mule mad at him. You know those mules can hold a grudge forever. They can get you when you least expect it." Jack's mother never questioned his death either. If she was suspicious, she never let Jack know it. The farmer had no other kin so Jack's mother got the farm, and then she sold everything. Jack didn't know how she did it, but all that money was gone in no time.

That same year, Jack's mother took up with a gambler named Clark Adams. Jack found out later he was just a card cheat, but he was good at it. They would go from place to place, win a little, then move on. "Don't get too greedy," he told Jack. "If you win too much, people get to wonderin' if you're cheatin' or not. Win small, and people will say it's just luck." He taught Jack how to play poker and cheat, and he also taught him how to use a knife. "If you have to stick someone, don't go through the ribs," Clark would say. "The blade might get stuck. Don't cut someone's throat. They will die, but they'll lay there and gurgle for a good while. If you cut the jugular, they'll die fairly quick. I always go for the gut at an angle and run the blade up to the heart. That's about the fastest way."

Two years later, Jack's mother died from consumption. When she died, Adams took off and Jack never saw him again. Jack survived by becoming a very good thief. He remembered what Clark had told him about not being greedy. He never stole anything in large amounts, just enough so things wouldn't get missed for a while. He also got himself a job that made him look respectable. He washed dishes and helped in the kitchen at a small eatery. The owner and his wife were very nice to him and they let him stay in a small shack that was behind the place. It wasn't much, but Jack fixed it up and made it liveable. When he wasn't at the eatery, he was out stealing or scouting for another theft. Another boy in town got suspicious of Jack and confronted him one day. That boy was found dead the next day from a knife wound. His killer was never found.

Jack was able to unload his stolen goods because he had made friends with a trader. This man had a wagon, and he went all over the place selling anything to anyone who would buy it. He handled clothing, leather goods, food, cookware, silverware, and guns. You name it, he'd get it sold. He just didn't sell in the same place where the items were stolen. Jack kept him well supplied, so he gave Jack a bigger cut than he used to give others. Having the job at the eatery and being well liked by the owners, Jack was well above suspicion. He now thought it was time for bigger and better things. The day he left, the only thing he had with him that wasn't stolen, was the horse he was riding. It had been a gift from the owners of the eatery. They had liked him so well that they gave him the horse. Jack never knew when his birthday was, but they all pretended that it was his birthday. The horse was an eighteen year old mare, but she'd do for now.

For the next two years, Jack was a horse thief. He became very good at it too, but several times he came close to getting caught, and had to shoot somebody. He didn't mind shooting anyone, but he got to thinking that if he was going to shoot people, maybe he could get paid for it.

Things were really heating up along the Kansas and Missouri border in the years before the Civil war. Jack had no trouble finding someone who wanted someone else dead for a price. He worked both sides of the border. When the war did come, people he knew, tried to get him to join Quantrill, but he said he worked better alone. He did work for Quantrill doing things where it was easier for one man to do than it was to send in a squad. He did jobs for the Jayhawkers too. Who he worked for didn't matter, as long as he got paid. Sometimes he worked with women, mostly whores. He found that it was about money for them too. If there was the slightest chance that he didn't trust them after the job was done, he would kill them too. At times, Jack used men for partners on a job, but more than once, he killed them too so he wouldn't have to share the money.

Jack had never met George Anderson, but he had heard about that crazy son of a bitch who rode with Quantrill and Bloody Bill. When he heard that Anderson had put a bounty of two thousand dollars on a lawman's head, Jack tracked Anderson down, finally finding him in Dallas, Texas. Anderson was spending some time there before going to Mexico. Jack asked Anderson why he would put a bounty on a lawman's head, especially a Federal Marshal. "I've hated that son of a bitch since we were kids back in Tennessee,"

Anderson said. "I have just never had the chance to get him myself. Make no mistake about him. He's good with his fists, and there's probably no one better than him with a rifle or a pistol. I hear he lived with the Cheyenne for a while too. He can track, and he can sneak up on about anything. You got your work cut out for you."

"He's just a man," said Jack. "He can die just like anyone else. I'll kill him for you." Then Anderson gave him five hundred dollars and said he would pay the rest when the job was done. The price would go up one hundred dollars a month till O'Rourke was dead. Jack didn't know it, but Anderson had also talked to several other hired killers. Once word got out about the bounty, every idiot with a gun would be out trying to collect the bounty anyway. Jack wasn't worried about those people. From what he had heard about this lawman, those people wouldn't have a chance anyway. "They're already dead and don't know it," Jack said to himself.

Finding the lawman would not be a problem. Everyone out there had heard of his reputation and knew where he could be found. It would take a little time to get from Dallas to Abilene Kansas, but Jack didn't mind, as the bounty went up a hundred dollars a month till the job was done. Besides, there were enough fools up in Kansas already who would try their luck. After that lawman killed several of them, maybe he would relax a bit, and Jack could get him with his guard down.

Jack was spending the night in Dallas, and was taking the first stage out the next morning. That evening he spent some time at a local brothel, then went to a saloon that was close to his hotel. He was at the bar sipping his whiskey, when he overheard two men talking about some lawman up in Kansas getting shot by someone's Grammaw. Jack went over to them and asked them what they were talking about. One of them spoke right up. "That new Federal Marshal, O'Rourke I think is his name, well he took a shotgun blast from Grammaw Hawk," he said. "I hear he had just shot some of the Hawk boys and she pulled out a shotgun she had hidden under a blanket as she was sitting on the porch and shot him. He ended up killin' Grammaw. Turns out, she was the leader of the Hawk bunch. Anyway, he got hit in the right shoulder and arm. I hear it wasn't bad, but he's laid up some."

"When did this happen?" asked Jack.

"Only two or three days ago from what I hear," the man said. "Do you know him or somethin', mister?"

"No, never met the man," said Jack. "I've just heard rumors about that new lawman, same as everybody else."

"Well from what I hear, his shootin's no rumor," said the man. "I hear he's killed men from over eight hunnerd yards, and there's nobody faster than him with a pistol. He's damn good with his fists too."

"Well it was nice talkin' with you," said Jack. "I'm gonna turn in early tonight. Leavin' on the early stage in the mornin'. Good evenin' to you."

When Jack got back to his hotel room, he decided that he better not take too much time to get up to Kansas. Getting to Kansas while that lawman was still laid up some seemed like it would make things a little easier. That night Jack slept like a baby and was on the early stage as planned.

CHAPTER NINE

Sean was really starting to get restless. Staying in bed all the time was very hard for him to do. It was finally time for the doctor to come back. Maggie was there while the doctor checked him out. After he examined him thoroughly, he told Sean that he could get out of bed now and do pretty much whatever he wanted except riding and using his right arm. "You're healing really well," Doc said. "The buckshot holes have scabbed over well, so I will not bandage you anymore. You will wear a sling at all times, except when you are in bed. Now I know you love this beautiful woman here, and you can't wait to grab her with both arms, but try to keep from using your right arm as much as possible when you are with her. I'll be back in about a week unless something happens and you need me sooner. By then, you should be able to start using your arm."

"All right, Doc, I'll see you in a week or so," replied Sean.

~~~~

As soon as the doctor was out the door, Maggie and Sean were all over each other. It didn't take Sean long to find out why the Doc told him to take it easy with his right arm. It hurt like hell when he moved it too quickly, so he used it gently, and Maggie really liked gentle. When they were finished, they laid there in each other's arms just looking into each other's eyes. Maggie spoke after a few minutes. "I don't have to be downstairs for a while yet," she began. "So I want you to start telling me all about yourself. I want to know everything there is about you. A woman should know about her man."

"Surely you've heard things about me from Michael and others," said Sean.

"I want to hear everything from you," replied Maggie. "I don't want to hear things second hand."

"This may take some time," said Sean. "There's been a lot happen in my life."

"We have all the time in the world, darlin', all the time in the world," said Maggie.

~~~~

Sean began by telling Maggie about his parents coming from Ireland, and how they got their land in Tennessee. "When my Pa won the wager, there was a slave family that came with the property," Sean started. "First thing Pa did was free them. They stayed on the place and worked for wages. There was Big Jim, Betsy, and Little Jim. Little Jim's my deputy now. Only I don't call him little anymore. His Ma died of pneumonia and his Pa was killed when we had a gun battle at our place."

"Just why was there a gun battle at your place?" asked Maggie.

"Some local trash picked a fight one day with my Pa and Big Jim when they were in town after supplies," said Sean. "My Pa and Big Jim beat the hell out of 'em. A bunch of 'em, eight all told, came out one night after that, and was gonna burn us out and hang Pa and Big Jim. Big Jim got killed, and Little Jim was wounded. We killed all eight of 'em. I killed three men that night. My Pa killed two, and my Ma killed one. Big Jim killed the other two. I was twelve years old then. I never said, but my Pa's name was John, and my Ma's name was Margaret, but no one ever called her Maggie."

"So Little Jim healed up all right then, or he wouldn't be out here, would he?" asked Maggie.

"No, he wouldn't," said Sean. "After he healed up, he wanted to go up north to live, so my Pa took him. I never heard from him again till he showed up out here. He said he ended up in the Union Army with the 54th Massachusetts, and then the cavalry. He heard I was out here, so he came to see me. He also heard that they were gonna form up a couple of colored cavalry regiments out here, so he says he's gonna join up when they do."

"So how did you get out here?" asked Maggie.

"My Pa and Ma knew a war was comin' sooner or later," answered Sean. "So we sold out and in the spring of '55 we headed west. When we got to Missouri, the wagon train had left just before we got there, so us and two other families decided that we could catch up to the main train in a week or two. After a few days, we were attacked by some white outlaws. There were ten of them. I was out huntin' for some fresh meat when they attacked. When I got to where I could see what had happened, some outlaws were goin' through the wagons and everyone else was dead. I killed five men that day. My Pa and the others killed the other five before they got killed. I was still just twelve."

"Did it bother you to kill all those men?" asked Maggie.

"No, not one bit," answered Sean. "They needed to die and I helped em out. Some Cheyenne happened by and they took me in." Just as Sean had finished talking, he thought he heard someone outside the door. He looked over at Maggie and motioned for her to be still and quiet. "Get your pistol," Sean whispered. "There's at least two people outside the door. I heard a board creak. Hold your pistol under your pillow and cock the hammer so it don't make any noise." Sean got one of his pistols and did the same. "Now real gentle like, slide out of bed onto the floor, then take your pillow and put it under the covers," Sean told her. Then Sean did the same. "Now as easy as you can, get yourself on that side of the door and I'll get on the other," said Sean. "When they come through the door, they'll be shootin'. After they get done, we'll kill them." Maggie never whispered a word. She just nodded her head yes.

Sean was right. They came through the door shooting. Both men had sawed off double barrel shotguns. They both fired both barrels into the bed as they came through the door. It looked like a snow storm with all those feathers going everywhere. The two men stood there, waiting for the feathers to quit moving around, when Sean spoke. "Are you lookin' for us?" said Sean. Before they could get turned all the way around, Sean and Maggie both fired. Both men were struck in the head. After they fell, Sean shot both of them again just to make sure they were dead. Then he looked over at Maggie. He had forgotten that they were both naked. Maggie went to him, wrapped her arms around him and started crying. Then they heard Tom's voice.

"Maggie, Sean, are you all right?" he yelled. "What happened?" Then they could hear him running up the stairs. "Holy shit," Tom said as he came through the door. "Who are they?"

Then Tom grabbed a blanket out of a closet and wrapped it around both of them.

Michael came running up the stairs next. When he saw the two dead men on the floor, he knew what had happened. "I just stepped out for a minute to go the leather goods store and see about getting your holsters made," Michael said. "I wasn't gone five minutes."

"I must've been in the storage room when they slipped in," added Tom. "There was no one in the place when I went to the storage room."

"Don't worry, you two," said Sean. "These two were just hoping to make some easy money. They shoulda found a different line of work. Maggie, you know that this is just the beginning. Word's got out, and there'll be all kinds of 'em tryin' to get that bounty."

"We'll take care of any that come," said Maggie. "Nobody's going to kill my man, nobody."

"You're a good woman, Maggie. Damn, you're a good woman," said Sean. "Tom, would you and Michael get these bodies outta here? Take 'em to the barber shop. Maybe we'll luck out, and someone will recognize them, but I doubt it. Tell the barber I'll get him paid."

"If this keeps up around here, the town'll need to get a regular undertaker," said Tom. "That barber won't have time to cut hair or shave anyone, he'll be busy buryin' folks."

~~~~

After the bodies were removed from the room, Maggie and Sean got dressed. Maggie helped Sean with his sling, and then for the first time in several days, Sean walked down the stairs to the saloon below. Sean stuffed a pistol into his belt so it could be drawn with his left hand. Tom helped Maggie clean up the room and bring in another mattress and some pillows. The frame of the bed had not been damaged badly. Tom fixed or replaced the boards that had been damaged. Sean sat at a table and asked Michael to have a drink with him. "Let's have a toast, my friend," said Sean. "Here's to not getting killed."

Michael repeated the words. "Here's to not getting killed." Just as they put their glasses down, Bob and Jon walked in to the saloon.

"We heard some shots," said Jon. "Is everybody all right?"

"We are, but them two at the barber shop are not," said Sean.

"Probly someone lookin' to get that bounty I 'spect," said Jon.

"That's what I figure," said Sean. "How's the herd? Have you got enough men hired yet?"

"We got enough to drive the cattle," said Bob. "But I'm expectin' to hear from a cook. S'pose to hear from him yet today. If he says all right, we'll start 'em in the mornin'."

"I got a few things to go over before you leave," said Sean. "We can go over them right now if you're not needed at the herd for a while."

"Jim's out there with them dogs. Them are good dogs. I think I'll keep one when we get done," said Bob. "The new men are out there too."

"Well try to remember what I tell you today," started Sean. "We can write it all down if you want."

"I'll remember," said Bob. "Jon's here. He'll remember too."

"All right, here we go," started Sean. "It's not that far up to Kansas City. It's all open range with very little cover except high grass. There will be some rolling hills but they won't be much.

There are still some border gangs out there. The Anderson bunch are not the only ones out there. Bob, you were a Ranger. I know you'll use good judgment if a situation comes up. Don't trust anyone farther than you can see them. Use nighthawks every night. There might be some bands of Indians out there too, but they are not usually this far east. If you run into any Kiowa, tell them you work for me, and I am a friend of Flying Eagle, one of their Chiefs. Let 'em have a few head of cattle if they look like they're hungry. If you don't, they might steal them anyway. If you come across any Cheyenne, same thing. Tell them you work for me. Ask them if they know Black Wolf. He was my brother-in-law. Give 'em some cattle if they look hungry. I doubt this, but if you did run into some Comanche, they'll steal your horses. They are very good at this. They hate me too, so if you do meet some of them, don't mention my name. Pawnee will steal you blind. Now, back to border gangs. If you do get into it with a border gang, and the shootin' starts, you kill 'em, kill 'em all. If you don't, they might hit you again later. Watch each other's back. You don't really know these men you hired. Anderson and Hawk have eyes and ears everywhere."

"That's not too much to remember, is it Jon?" said Bob.

"No problem," Jon replied. "We'll get there before you know it."

"There's one last thing," said Sean. "Don't be lettin' any of them dogs get killed. I never seen any dogs like these before. I might just keep one myself."

"Well let's see," said Bob. "One for the boy, one for you, and one for me. That leaves one left. Jim won't want no dog since he's goin' back in the army.

"We'll find him a home," said Jon. "I might take one too. I might need some company when I go back to see that Cherokee woman one of these days." Then Bob and Jon went back to the herd leaving Michael and Sean still at the table.

~~~~

"So did those young soldier boys behave themselves while they were here?" Sean asked Michael.

"They were like a bunch of shy school boys," answered Michael. "I can't remember ever being like that, but I suppose I was. I'd say they all left here with a good headache and a good story to tell. It was good of you to buy them their drinks. That Captain of theirs seemed like a good man too. Hope some glory huntin' fool don't get him killed."

"I told him almost the same thing, my friend," said Sean. "And I gave him a little advice about Indians too. I hope he remembers it. So how is it goin' with you and Betty? Is she tired of you yet?"

"No, she likes having me around," answered Michael. "But sometimes she worries that I won't want to be with her because of her profession. I told her that what she does is her business, not mine. I did mention it to her that I hope she keeps a good eye on the men she's with so we won't get something we don't want. Now that we have this doctor in town, I think all the girls should take advantage of him bein' here."

"Sound wisdom, Michael, sound wisdom," said Sean. "So are you happy workin' at the saloon? Do you think you still want to own a saloon?"

"Young Sean, I can't think of anything I'd rather do," Michael said.

"That's good," replied Sean. "If things work out, and that McCoy fella gets the railroad and the cattle pens here, I'm gonna ask Maggie if we can all be partners. We should know by next spring if this will happen. If it does, we should make the place bigger, more rooms upstairs, bigger bar, more tables, and maybe get a piano player."

"Look no farther, my young friend," said Michael. "I learned to play the piano back in Ireland. I haven't played since because I haven't even seen a piano since I've been in America. I heard one once at some bar before I got mustered out. Anyway, I'm out of practice, but I'm sure I didn't forget how. Maybe Maggie can sing too. Wouldn't that be somethin'."

"Yes, it surely would," said Sean. "I do have a concern though, if all this happens."

"And what would that be, my friend?" asked Michael.

"Those Texas boys all carry guns," answered Sean. "They get to drinkin' and carryin' on, anything could happen. I don't think they'd like it if we told them they couldn't wear a gun in here."

"That's probably true," said Michael. "I guess we'll worry about it when all this happens. Maybe if they know about your reputation, that'll help keep them in line. Before I forget it, the man at the leather goods store needs to see one of your pistols so he can make a proper fit."

"I'll walk over there as soon as we get done here," said Sean. "Doc says I can do about anything except ride and use my right arm. Now I think I'll have another drink of this fine bourbon. While I'm out, I'll ask around and see if anybody recognizes those two men at the barber shop."

~~~~

Sean finished his drink and headed out the front door of the saloon. A pistol was stuffed in his belt. As he was coming out, Jim rode up. "Thought I'd come in and get me a drink," said Jim. "Bob wanted me to look around and see if that cook showed and the boys told me you had some excitement too."

"Sure did," said Sean. "Let's go over to the barber shop. Maybe you've seen them two somewhere." As they got closer to the bodies, Jim spoke right up.

"That fella on the right was there when I shot Ethan Hawk," Jim said. "There was another fella that was gonna pull on me but he backed down. After he backed down, two other fellas helped him load Hawk on a buckboard. That fella on the right is one of the fellas that helped load up Hawk. Never seen the other one before."

"They're probably Hawks or cousins. Just how many damn Hawks are there anyway?" said Sean. "Them Hawk women musta been very fertile. We've already killed a bunch of 'em. Jim, after you have your drink and see about the cook, I want you and Jon to ride out to the Hawk place and see if anyone's out there. Just look. Don't get into a shootin' match. Just get back and let me know what you saw."

"All right, Sean, I'll get Jon and get out there as soon as I get done here," said Jim.

~~~~

Sean then headed over to the leather goods store. A short bald headed man and young boy were just inside the door stacking supplies on some shelves. "You must be Marshal O'Rourke. I'm

Jason Hunter, and this is my son, Greg," Jason said as he extended his hand to Sean.

"Yes, I'm Sean O'Rourke," replied Sean as he shook Jason's hand. "Pleased to meet you. I came to see about that left handed holster my friend and deputy asked you about."

I got started on one for you," Jason said. "Let's see your pistol there and make sure we have a good fit." Jason took the pistol and slid it into the holster. "Looks good to me. See what you think."

~~~~

Sean took the holster, slid his belt through its loop, and strapped it on. Then he slid the pistol into the holster. He took his left hand and drew. Then he slid the pistol back into the holster and drew again. He did this ten more times. "Feels good to me." said Sean. "I'll need a tab that'll slip over the hammer and can be flipped off with my thumb, and I need a strap at the bottom so it can be tied down. I need it fastened to a belt that fits me perfectly, and I want two pouches on the belt so I can put two extra cylinders in them."

"We'll measure you right now for the belt," Jason said as he was wrapping a tape measure around Sean's waist. "I'll have everything done by noon tomorrow. Will that be all right?"

"That'll be just fine," said Sean. "Now I have something else I would like for you to make for me if you can."

"If it's made outta leather, I can make it," said Jason. "Now what do you need?"

"I've been wanting a leather vest," answered Sean. "I want it made of the thickest leather you can get, but will still look good and be comfortable."

"I can do that for you," said Jason. "I can make one so thick, a knife will have trouble getting through it. It'll still look good too."

"I think you know what I'm after," said Sean. "Do you know anything about the old armor that knights wore centuries back, like chain mail, or this other stuff that was pieces of steel fastened together, then fastened to clothing?"

"I've seen pictures," Jason said. "I think I know what you're talking about."

"Good," replied Sean, "I'm gonna make up some of that flat steel stuff, and I'll have you fasten it on the inside of the vest. It'll be for my back and front, not the sides. Then once it's fastened, put a lining inside the vest, flannel or anything will do. I'll make the steel so it's small and can't be noticed when I wear the vest.

"Sounds to me like you don't wanna get yourself stabbed, Marshal," said Jason, "This will sure help with that."

"Well get me measured and please get started on this soon as you get done with my holster," said Sean. "One more thing, Word better not get out that you're doin' this for me. Only you and your son know about this, so I'll know who to come after if this would leak out. I'm sure you've heard about my reputation."

"Don't worry Marshal, no one'll ever hear anything from us," said Jason. "Now let's get you measured. You know, I just had an idea about how to fasten the steel in the vest."

"What's your idea?" asked Sean. "Anything that would make it quicker and easier would be a big help."

"All right, here's what I was thinking," said Jason. "After we got the leather part of the vest done, we make pockets on the inside of the material we use for the liner. If you could make the pieces of steel, say two inches by two inches, and as thin as you can, we can put the steel pieces in the pockets. The pockets will only be a quarter of an inch apart. The pockets will be all over the back, and on both sides of the front. We can put them as close as we can to the buttons in the front, or maybe I can make some kind of ties for the front instead of buttons. We'll need a strong material for lining. I'll come up with something. How does this sound to you, Marshal?"

"Sounds good to me," answered Sean. "I'll go see about getting the steel right now." Then Sean shook Jason's hand and left.

When Sean was out the door, Greg looked at his father and said, "Pa, you saw the Marshal drawing his pistol, didn't you?"

"Yes son, I did," Jason answered. "Why?"

"Because he was just trying the holster out," Greg said. "He was just trying it out and he was just so fast. Imagine how fast he would be if he wasn't just trying it out. That wasn't even his good hand either."

"He's a Federal Marshal," said Jason. "If he wasn't fast, he'd be dead. They say he's a killer, "A Killer For The Common Good." I've heard about some of the men he's had to kill, and those men needed to be dead. It's men like Marshal O'Rourke who are gonna make this land out here a safe place to live. Always remember that. If it ever happens that he needs my help, I will do my best for him."

"You mean you would kill someone, Pa?" Greg asked.

"I would if I had to," Jason answered. "You know I had to kill when I was in the war?"

"I know you did, Pa, but you never talk about it," Greg said.

"And I'm never gonna talk about it. Now let's get ourselves back to work," said Jason. "We gotta make sure we get the Marshal's things done."

~~~~

There was a blacksmith at the livery, so Sean went over there to see if he had any supplies of steel there. Most blacksmiths kept a supply of steel for making horse shoes and wagon wheel rims. Steel for wagon wheel rims could easily be pounded down and cut into smaller pieces. When he got to the livery, Billy was scooping up manure. "Hey Marshal, how's my dog doin'?" Billy asked.

"He's doin' good, Billy," Sean replied. "Where's the blacksmith? I need him for a minute."

"He's in the outhouse," answered Billy. "Should be back anytime." Just as Billy finished talking, the blacksmith returned.

"Can I help you with somethin', Marshal?" he asked.

"Yes, I need some thin steel, like you use for wagon wheel rims, or thinner if you have something," said Sean.

"I got some pieces of flat steel maybe a quarter inch thick or thinner that I use for makin' braces and patchin' things," he said. "Will that do?"

"That'll do just fine," started Sean. "Now here's what I want you to do for me. I want it pounded down as thin as you can get it, and cut it into pieces that are two inches by two inches, or as close to that as you can get."

"Just how many pieces do you need?" the blacksmith asked.

"Fifty, maybe more, but we'll start with fifty," answered Sean.

"You know that'll take a lot of time and won't be cheap," the blacksmith said.

"You'll be well paid," replied Sean. "I'll give you a good bonus for gettin' it done quicker, and I'll insist that you don't tell anyone you're doin' this for me."

"I won't tell anyone," the blacksmith said. "If I did, they'd probably wonder what in the hell I was doin' anyway. No, I won't say anything."

"I thank you, sir," said Sean. "I'll check back in a few days."

"If I get done before you get back, Marshal, I'll send Billy after you." the blacksmith said. Before Sean could thank him, he grabbed a hot shoe from the forge and

began pounding on it. Sean headed back to Maggie's place. There was a wagon in front of the saloon, and a rough looking older man was going through the doors. When he got inside, he saw Michael and Jim and announced, "I'm Sam Waters, and I'm lookin' for whoever is in charge of this cattle drive that's gonna start soon."

"Come on over to the bar and I'll give you a drink," said Michael. "This other fella here is Jim O'Rourke, and he's goin' on that drive. He'll take you out to the herd after you've had your drink."

"So this here colored man is goin' on this here drive?" Sam asked.

"Mister, them cows don't care what color I am," said Jim. "And that's Deputy Federal Marshal Jim O'Rourke to you."

"Don't go gettin' yerself in a tizzy there, young man," said Sam. "I just never seen any colored folks pushin' cows. Never seen a colored deputy either."

"Just finish your drink, and I'll take you out to the herd," said Jim.

Sean came up to the bar just as Sam had finished his drink. Jim spoke up. "This is our cook and I'm takin' him out to the herd," said Jim. "Soon as I introduce him to Bob, I'll get Jon and we'll slip over to the Hawk place."

"All right, remember, don't get yourself into a shootin' match unless there's no other way," said Sean. "Get back here and tell me if anything's goin' on. I reckon you all will be leavin' at daylight. Get yourself some good rest when you get back. You won't get much on the trail." When Jim and the cook were gone, Sean got a bottle and sat down at a table where he could see all that was going on. Michael came over and joined him. There were only two other men in the saloon and they were regular customers, so Michael and Sean were not worried about them.

"Is your holster gonna be all right?" Michael asked.

"Yes, it'll be ready tomorrow," answered Sean. "Jason seems like a good man."

"I think so too," Michael said. "He was in Sherman's army too. He told me that when I told him about you and me bein' friends and livin' through the war."

"Well I'm glad he made it through the war too," said Sean. "What's Cookie makin' today? I'm getting' mighty hungry."

"I think he's cookin' some ham today, smells like it to me," said Michael.

"Good, I'll get some shortly," Sean said. Then he just sat there and scratched his head for a few seconds. "I sure hope Jim and Jon don't have trouble out at the Hawk place. Don't want anyone shot up or anything right before the drive starts."

"They'll be fine," said Michael. "Remember, Jon is half Cherokee. He'll know if somethins' not right or somethins' goin' on. He'll get back here and let us know."

"You're right, he's a good man," Sean said. "I'm gonna go see if Cookie's got that ham ready and get me a plate."

"I'll be havin' a plate too," said Michael. "You know that ham goes really good with this bourbon, don't you?"

"Good bourbon goes with almost everything," said Sean as he grabbed his plate from Cookie and headed back out to their table.

"Cookie's outdone himself again," Sean said as he tore into his food. "I hope he can cook a turkey. I sure would like some turkey for Thanksgiving."

"I'm sure he can do a fine job with a turkey," said Michael. "We might just have to go out and get one for him though. When is Thanksgiving anyway?"

"I think it's in about a week or two," answered Sean. "I bet Maggie'll know."

Just as Sean and Michael had finished their meal, Maggie came over to their table. "Maggie darlin', do you know when Thanksgiving is?" asked Sean. "I know it's in the last week or two of this month."

"I'm pretty sure it's next Thursday," Maggie answered. "Why do you want to know that?"

"I got the urge to eat some turkey," said Sean. "I can't remember the last time I ate turkey. Do any of the farmers around here raise turkeys? I'll give 'em a good price if they do."

"I'll ask Cookie," said Maggie. "He knows the farmers around here. He gets his chickens from them. Maybe one of them would have turkeys. Are you feeling thankful, darlin'?"

"Maggie darlin', every time I look at you I'm thankful," said Sean.

"Maybe we better go upstairs," said Maggie. "I'm feeling pretty thankful myself."

A good while later, they were still wrapped in each other's arms and kissing. "Let's get back to you telling me all about yourself," said Maggie. "We were up to the Cheyenne taking you in before we were interrupted."

"All right, but I forgot to tell you about my first sweetheart," said Sean.

"So I'm not your first girl," Maggie said jokingly.

"Maggie, you were not my first girl, but you're sure as hell were my first woman," said Sean. After Sean said that, things got heated up again, and after a good while, they lay there in each other's arms exhausted.

"Now, let's get back to your first girl," said Maggie.

"Her name was Sarah Anderson," started Sean. "Her brother is George Anderson."

"You mean that outlaw is your first girl's brother?" asked Maggie.

"Yep, he sure is," said Sean. "Our farm used to be part of the Anderson Plantation in Tennessee. I told you about that. Anderson's grandpa, owned the plantation, and when he died later, George II got it. That happened after we had gone west. Anyway, George III, Sarah, and I all went to school together. George was a trouble maker. One day he was hittin' on his sister. At the time, I didn't know she was his sister. Anyway, I asked to quit hittin' on her, and he got mouthy with me and I beat him up. He was a year older than me too. Sarah and I became good friends after that, and it grew from there. I butted heads with George a couple times after that. It was hard tellin' her goodbye."

" Do you have any idea where she is now or anything?" asked Maggie.

"She's dead," answered Sean. "Her family and her were killed by Union deserters. We had been fighting over around Chattanooga, and I was out scouting, and I stopped in to see if she was around. She was there and was so happy to see me. Later on, I was given a ten day furlough. My unit was still in that area, and we made arrangements to see each other. We fell in love and were going to get married after the war. After my furlough and some time later, I was out scouting again in the same area when another scout and me heard some shots. We went to her place, and deserters were there. They had killed her folks and her and was raping her after she was dead. I blew their brains out. When I took the deserters bodies back to camp, I met Judge Simmons. He's my boss now. Anyway, that was hard to get over."

"I'm sure it was," said Maggie. "You don't need to tell me anymore right now if you don't feel like it."

"I'm all right," replied Sean. "I'll go on. When I went to live with the Cheyenne. I lived with a woman named Blue swan. Her husband was a white man. Used to be a mountain man. He taught me how to track and hunt and how to stay alive. They had a daughter, Katie. We married when we were both fifteen. We were so young, but we loved each other so much. While I was with the Cheyenne, we had some scrapes with the Comanche and Pawnee. I even had a scrape with a grizzly bear. He came chargin' at me. I shot him three times in the head with my pistol and he fell dead on top of me. Had a heck of a time getting' him off of me. Anyway, Katie and I had a daughter, Maggie."

"You're not serious, are you?" asked Maggie. "Your mother was named Margaret, your daughter was Maggie, and I'm Maggie. What do you know?"

"Remember now, no one ever called my mother Maggie," said Sean. "It was always Margaret. Anyway, Katie was pregnant again, and Braddock, that was her Pa's name, said we should go to a town and get somethin' nice for the women. We were gone about a week. When we got back, the cholera had come. Katie and Maggie died. Someone from every lodge died. After that, I took off by myself to do some thinkin'. That's when I ran into Michael. His cavalry troop was out on patrol. We became friends, and when his unit was sent back east for the war, I scouted for them, and joined the army on the way there."

"So you and Michael were in the same outfit during the war?" asked Maggie.

"No, I joined a Sharpshooter unit before our first engagement," said Sean. "Michael was in the cavalry the whole time, but we were still in the same army most of the time. We were in the same hospital after we got shot at Shiloh. We started a tradition. We always drink this toast. "Here's to not getting killed." We still have that toast. I imagine we'll have that toast several more times before we're dead."

"Well don't be talking about being dead," said Maggie. "I intend for you to live a long time. Now I think it's time I got downstairs. How about helping me get dressed?"

"I love to dress and undress you," replied Sean. "I'm jealous of your clothes when you are dressed. They are always touching you."

"Goodness," said Maggie, "I didn't expect that. I liked hearing it. You should probably get some sleep now. Remember, you've been shot." Then she gave him a passionate kiss and headed down to the saloon.

"I'll go to sleep as soon as I hear from Jon or Jim," said Sean. "They should be back anytime." Sean had just finished his words when he heard Jon's voice as he was coming up the stairs. Jon greeted Maggie and then went into the room to talk with Sean. "We went all over the place and didn't see no one," said Jon. "But there was fresh tracks all over the place, especially over by the graves where them soldiers buried em. I counted five sets of tracks. Looks like they came in from the southwest, had a look-see, and then headed back the same way."

"Thanks, I'll get out there myself in a few more days after I heal up some," said Sean. "You best get back to the herd and get some rest. I'm sure Bob'll have you movin' before daylight."

"I'm sure he will," replied Jon. "Now you keep yourself outta trouble while we're gone. I'll see you in three weeks if we're lucky."

Sean was glad that there was no trouble at the Hawk place, but the five sets of tracks got him wondering. Whose tracks were they? How many more Hawks are there? Did Anderson send some men to the Hawk place? Were they made by rustlers who were going after the herd? "My deputies are good men," Sean said to himself. "They'll take care of things."

Sean slept like a baby that night. He didn't even wake up when Maggie slipped back into bed with him after the saloon closed. He woke up just after daylight, got dressed and went downstairs. Michael was already there sipping some coffee. "Pull up a chair, my friend," Michael said. "I'll get you some coffee."

"Sounds good, Michael," replied Sean. "Why are you up this early?"

"I got plenty of sleep last night," said Michael. "Things were slow, and Tom said he didn't need me so I went to bed. I slept well too. I didn't even wake up when Betty climbed into bed."

"Same for me," said Sean. "I didn't wake up when Maggie came to bed."

"When I was coming over here this morning, I saw four strangers ride into town," said Michael. "I was gonna keep an eye on them after I got some coffee, but I haven't seen them since. I went to the livery to see if their horses were over there, but they weren't. I think we better be alert today, young Sean."

"I'd say you're right, Michael," said Sean. "Somethins' not right. I doubt if they would just ride right through town that early in the mornin'. Could you tell if they were armed or not?"

"They were armed all right," said Michael. "They all had pistols, and two of them had rifles on their saddles. Looked like Henrys."

"Well, I'll stay here for a while and drink some coffee and get some breakfast," said Sean. "Then I'll do some lookin' around. I'll be goin' out the back door. Maybe they got their horses tied somewhere behind one of the buildings."

~~~~

Sean took his time eating breakfast. After he had finished, he had one more cup of coffee, then went back upstairs. He already had a pistol stuck in his belt, but he took another pistol and stuck it in his sling. Maggie didn't wake up while he was in the room. He went back downstairs and told Michael to keep watch out front, and try not to look too obvious doing it. Then he slipped out the back door. He worked his way from building to building and there was nothing on his side of the street. The livery was on the same side of the street and Sean saw that young Billy was out front with a team of mules. Sean worked his way over behind the mules. He was between the mules and the livery. Billy hadn't seen him at all. He was a little startled when he heard Sean's voice. "Billy, it's me, Marshal O'Rourke," said Sean. "I want you to walk these mules to the other side of the street and make it look like you're just walking them. Don't say anything. I'll be on the other side of the mules. I need to get around the buildings on the other side of the street without being seen. After you see me slip away, you get back to the livery, and stay inside. There might be some shootin'."

Billy did as instructed, and Sean slipped behind the buildings. Four horses were tied behind the General Store. Their riders were nowhere to be seen. Then Sean saw the boards leaning against the back of the store. Someone had used them to get to the roof, but how many of them were up there? They all wouldn't be up there. "Maybe two up there at the most," Sean said to himself. "Now where would the other two be?" Sean stayed close to the buildings while he checked them out, but no luck. He decided to work his way back to the saloon and wait. A freight wagon was pulling into town, and Sean slipped over behind it and when it was beside the saloon, he just calmly walked in the front doors. Michael and Maggie were both there waiting.

"Are you out there trying to get shot again?" asked Maggie. "Michael told me what was going on."

"I love you too," Sean said to Maggie. "Let's have some more coffee." They sat at a table saying nothing. Finally, Sean spoke. "Some of them are on the roof of the General Store. Not sure, but I would say only two. I never saw anyone, but I saw where someone had climbed onto the roof. Four horses are tied behind the General Store. I'm goin' to the leather goods store in a few minutes. Let's go up to our room and see if we can spot whoever's on the roof over there."

The curtains were still closed in the room, so they could move around without being seen. Maggie's room was a corner room so it had two windows. After about five minutes, two men were spotted. One was right behind the G in general, and the other one was behind the R in store. Sean showed Michael and Maggie where they were. He grabbed his Sharps and some shells and handed them to Michael. Then he took his Henry and handed it to Maggie. "There's fifteen rounds in this rifle," Sean told Maggie.

"Now I'm goin' to the leather goods store. I'll stay under the porches so they won't have a clear shot. You two give me ten minutes. That'll give me time to talk a bit to Jason. Those two on the roof will get tired of waitin' for me to come back out and get careless. When they show themselves good enough for a shot, kill them. The other two will probably show themselves about the time I come back out of the leather goods store. I'll have two pistols with me. I'll be fine."

Maggie and Michael never said a word as Sean started down the stairs. They opened the curtains a few inches and opened the windows just enough to shoot out of. Five minutes went by and the men of the roof had not shown themselves. Inside the leather goods store, Sean tried on his new gun belt. "Fine job Jason. You do good work," said Sean. "Now I want you and your son to stay inside and get behind something big. There might be some shootin' when I go back outside. Now do what I told you. Don't want you two gettin' hit."

"Marshal, better look out the window," said Greg. "There's two men out there in the street looking this way. They both have tied down guns."

"Do like I said now," said Sean as he headed out the door. As soon as Sean cleared the door, two shots were fired. Two men fell from the roof of the general store. One of the men moved a little after he hit the ground and two more rounds were put into his body. The two men in the street turned to see their friends hit the ground, but then turned back around to face Sean.

"Looks like your friends are dead," said Sean. "Do you want shot or hung?" The two never said a word. After what seemed like a few minutes, they both started to draw. Before they had even touched their pistols, they were falling backwards with holes in their chests, dead before they hit the ground.

Young Greg had not done what Sean had said and was watching the whole time. "Pa, did you see that?" he said. "How can someone do that? Those two never even got their hands to their guns."

"I saw it too, son," Jason replied. "It don't seem possible. If someone told me, I wouldn't believe them. That wasn't even his good hand."

~~~~

Sean went over to the bodies and made sure they were all dead. Maggie and Michael came out into the street carrying their rifles. Sean walked up to Maggie and gave her a big hug. "You put two more rounds in that fella, didn't you," said Sean to Maggie.

"Yes I did," she replied. "He wasn't dead when he hit the ground, so I helped him out. I hope this doesn't go on much longer. I don't want to kill anyone else."

"I'm sure there'll be more of 'em," said Sean. "But when words gets out that we killed four of 'em today, maybe some of 'em will change their mind about comin' after me. I gotta get Anderson and end this thing. If he don't come back here in the spring, I'm goin' after 'em, and when I get 'em, I'm gonna hang 'em."

Michael walked up to his friend and said, "I think it's time for another toast. I'll have someone get these bodies over to the barber shop, then we'll have our toast."

When Michael got back to the saloon, Sean and Maggie were already at a table and had a bottle there with three glasses. Michael filled the glasses, raised his glass, then said, "Here's to not getting killed." Maggie and Sean each repeated the toast, then

Michael said. "Sean darlin', I've seen you shoot, and you are so very fast, but I think maybe you're as fast or faster with your left hand than you are with your right. Just how can that be?"

"I don't know, my friend," said Sean. "I guess it's just somethin' I'm good at with either hand. Michael, after we get done here, we best go see if anybody knows those men. They probably don't, but we better see anyway."

~~~~

No one in town claimed to know the four dead men. Sean checked their gear and pockets and found nothing that would help identify them. He did find some money on them and gave it to the barber to pay for burying them. Then Sean sold their horses and saddles to the livery. Their pistols and rifles and ammunition, he sold to the General Store. He took all the money to the bank and told the banker that he wanted to start a new account. "I wanna call it the "Buryin" fund," Sean told the banker. "I just as well use outlaws' money to bury outlaws instead of usin' my own like I been doin'."

CHAPTER TEN

One of the dogs really took a liking to Bob, and Bob liked him too. He started calling him Jeb. When Jeb wasn't out helping move the herd, he was with Bob. Jeb was the leader of the pack too. The other dogs knew where they stood with Jeb. Bob didn't know how dogs talked to each other, but Jeb seemed to be giving the orders. If a steer wondered away from the herd, Jeb made sure another dog brought it back. Bob never had to tell Jeb what to do. It seemed like he already knew. They had some bulls mixed in with the herd, and every once in a while, one of them would get a little mean. Jeb knew just what to do and always got the bull back in line.

The cook wasn't much on personality, but he was a good cook. He always had the meals ready on time and kept his coffee hot. Even though his name was Sam, the men just called him Cook, and he didn't mind.

The first few days of the drive, Bob, Jon, and Jim, kept a close eye on the new men. They seemed to know what they were doing and never complained about anything. The afternoon of the second day, there was a thunderstorm with plenty of lightning.

Between the dogs, and the new men, they kept the herd settled down. Bob thought for sure they would stampede.

They moved along as fast as they could without running too much fat off the cows. On the fourth day, Bob saw a rider in the distance. He told Jim and Jon to be alert. The rider followed, but never got closer. One time, Jon acted like he was going after the rider. When he did, the rider took off out of sight. Jon didn't pursue him. As the days went on, more riders were spotted, but they never got close. Bob and the others knew something was going to happen, but they didn't know when.

One afternoon, they came to a small stream and there was also plenty of grass. Bob decided they would let the cows have a drink, but not cross till the next morning. The cows would like the sweet grass anyway and not go wondering. That evening Bob had three men out for nighthawks and made sure all the other men had their guns on them or near. Jim was one of the nighthawks so he could keep an eye on the other two. The rest of the men were setting around a fire by the wagon eating their evening meal. Jeb was next to Bob, when Jeb started growling. "What is it Jeb?" said Bob. "Are we gettin' company?" Then someone yelled out. "Hello in the camp," he said. "I'm not armed, can I come in?"

"You come in, mister," Bob said, "But you keep them hands where I can see em." The man did as instructed. When he got close to the fire, he asked if he could get off his horse and talk.

"Go ahead and get down, mister," Bob replied. "Now just what are your intentions? You gotta name?"

"Name's don't count for much," the man said. "My boss there on the other side of the creek says that's his land over there, and if you wanna cross it, it's gonna cost you."

"Well you go back across that creek and tell your boss to come over here in the mornin', and we'll talk," said Bob. "Tell him we won't be sleepin' over here tonight, so he better not try anything." The man never said a word. He just got back on his horse and left.

"Well what are we gonna do in the mornin'?" Jon asked Bob.

"We're gonna kill as many of 'em as we can," said Bob.

"Sounds all right to me," said Jon. "Just hope they don't try somethin' tonight. I'll go tell Jim what's goin' on. We'll need to keep any eye on these new boys just in case too."

No one slept that night. The next morning, the cook served breakfast like always. After breakfast, Bob put two of the new men out to watch the herd, and kept everyone else at the campsite. It wasn't too long before Jeb let out a growl. Five men were coming across the creek. One man was a little ahead of the others. Bob figured he was the boss. There was maybe eight more men across the creek, but Bob couldn't tell for sure. Bob, Jon, and Jim stood out front to meet them, and Bob had the others take cover behind the wagon and some trees. Jeb was right beside Bob. He kept growling as the men approached. When they got close, it was evident that they were all well armed. The one who seemed to be the leader spoke. "Tell that dog a yours to be quiet so I can talk," he said.

"Jeb, you be quiet now and don't kill anyone till I tell you," said Bob. Jeb quieted right down. "All right mister, say your piece, and I'm tellin' you right now. The three of us here are Deputy Federal Marshals."

"That don't mean shit to us. Across that creek is my land," he started. "If you wanna cross it, it'll cost you two dollars a head. I'll give you fifteen minutes to make up your mind."

"That's open range over there, and we don't need fifteen minutes," Bob said. "Are you the boss?"

"Yes, I'm the boss. Name's don't matter," he said. "Why do you want to know if I'm the boss?"

"Because I need to make sure I kill you," said Bob.

Just as Bob finished talking, the five men started reaching for their pistols. Bob, Jon, and Jim drew their pistols and opened fire. Three of the riders fell. Jeb jumped up and grabbed the boss by the throat and knocked him off his horse. Jeb kept ahold of his throat and wouldn't let go. The man lay there screaming and tried to reach for a pistol, but it was too late. Gunfire erupted from across the creek. The only one left from the five riders tried to get back across the creek. Jim took careful aim with his pistol and dropped him. The new men behind the wagon and the trees were firing too. After several minutes, the firing from the other side of the creek started to slow down. Then it stopped.

"Get the horses," said Bob. "We're goin' after 'em. Cook, you're in charge here. Me, Jon, and Jim's goin' after 'em." Jeb went too.

When they got to the other side of the creek, they found three more dead bodies. Two other men were laying there, mortally wounded.

"Looks like your friends done left you," said Bob to the wounded men. "You're gonna die anyway. Got anything to tell me before you die?"

"How about you go to hell," one of the wounded men said.

"You got a name, mister?" asked Bob. "So we can put it on a marker for you."

"Name's don't mean much, mister," he answered.

"Who was your boss?" Bob asked. "Tellin' us that won't hurt anything. You'll be dead anyway."

"Never knew his name," the wounded man said. "He just wanted to be called boss. I do know he's had dealins' with Anderson in the past. I'm sure you know who Anderson is." Those were his last words. The other man died shortly after he did.

"We gonna bury them fellas?" asked Jim.

"No, we're not," answered Bob. "We got a herd to get movin'." Not takin' time to dig graves for a bunch of thieves. We're not goin' after them others. We'll have no trouble from them."

When they got back to the camp, Bob thanked the other men for helping out. "We killed four of 'em between me, Jon, and Jim. Jeb killed the boss. One a you boys must be a good shot. We found three more dead bodies over there and two more that were mortally wounded. Which one a you boys can shoot that good. I know I'm not that good a shot with this pistol to hit them men clear over there."

One of the men spoke up. "I reckon it was me. I always been a pretty fair shot with this carbine. Never was much count with a pistol. That's why I don't carry one. Name's Charlie Johnson," he said.

"Were those the first men you killed, Charlie?" asked Bob.

"No," answered Charlie, "I had to kill some Comanche sometime back. I didn't want to, but they killed my folks and wanted to kill me."

"Well glad to have you with us Charlie," said Bob. "Now let's get ready and get movin'. Damn, Jeb, where you been all my life? I never even heard of a dog like you." Then Bob got down on the ground and wrestled with Jeb like he was a little boy. Jeb loved it.

They moved along for several more days without seeing a living soul or even a fresh track. There was another rain storm, and it started getting cold. "Sure feels like a snow is comin'," said Bob. "Does this a lot in Texas before it snows. Sure hope it don't snow." The next day, it did snow. It snowed so hard, they couldn't see to move the herd, so they set up camp. The next morning, the sun came out and things warmed up just like it was a spring morning. Jim was out checking on the herd and the nighthawk when he spotted some tracks. They were unshod. There were three sets of tracks. Jim followed for a short distance, but quit when they went behind a big rise. He didn't want to ride into an ambush. Jim went back to camp and told Bob about the tracks.

"Well boys, we got some Indians around," Bob said. "Stay alert and don't be shootin' if you see one unless he's shootin' at you. Could be, they just want somethin' to eat. If any of you see any of them, get over to me. I'll go see what they want."

They got the herd moving. By noon, the sun was really bright, and all the snow that had fallen, had melted. Just after noon, three Indians came riding up to the herd. Bob had seen them, and rode out to meet them. Bob spoke first. "Do any of you boys speak our language?" asked Bob. The three of them just looked at each other, but did not speak. Then Bob asked them if they knew a man name Black Wolf. Apparently they did. They motioned for Bob to follow them. Bob yelled back to the men telling them he'd be back shortly and not to worry. Of course the men weren't quite sure what to think.

On the other side of a big rise, was a small Indian village. There was no more than fifteen lodges. When Bob and the three Indians entered the village, an Indian with a bad limp came out of one of the teepees. "I am Black Wolf," he said. "Please accept our hospitality and set with me."

"Be glad to," said Bob. "Name's Bob Wallace. I understand you are Sean O'Rourke's brother-in-law."

"The "One Who Kills With The Long Gun and the Big Pistol" was married to my sister," Black Wolf said. "How do you know him?"

"He's my boss," said Bob. "He's a Federal Marshal, and I'm one of his deputies."

"What does a Marshal do?" asked Black Wolf.

"He enforces the law. He spends most of his time catching and killing bad white men," said Bob.

"He doesn't go after Indians, does he?" asked Black Wolf.

"No," answered Bob. "Sean will never, and I mean never, chase or kill any Indians unless they're tryin' to kill him. He would like to know if you know what happened to Blue Swan and Braddock. He never told me to ask you if I met you, but I've heard from others that he would like to know if they were alive after what happened at Sand Creek."

"Sand Creek was what you white people call a massacre," Black Wolf said. "Most of the men were out hunting when the blue soldiers came. They killed most of the women and children. Some of the women were raped before they killed them. Then they cut off body parts and danced around with the body parts on their sabers. Blue Swan was killed there. She was my mother as you know. I saw Braddock kill some of the blue soldiers with the long gun that Sean gave him when he was with us. Braddock left us after that and went back to the mountains."

"I suppose the blue soldiers will be givin' you a hard time before too long," said Bob. "Soon as they get that mess back east cleaned up some, there'll be more blue soldiers out here. I'm sure you already know that."

"Yes, we know that," said Black Wolf. "They have already broken treaty after treaty. There are just too many white men, and they want everything."

"So where are you headed now?" asked Bob.

"We are headed to the land of ours friends, the Lakota," said Black Wolf.

"May I give you some cattle, so you can have some fresh meat now and jerk some for your trip?" asked Bob.

"We will accept your gift," said Black Wolf. "The buffalo herds have not come over this way as they usually do this time of year."

"Will fifty head be enough?" asked Bob.

"We do not need that many. We are a small band," said Black Wolf. "Twenty head will be enough. When we get to Lakota land, the buffalo will be plenty. Now let's smoke to our friendship." They sat down and passed a pipe back and worth. Then Black Wolf thanked Bob again, and told him to let Sean know where they were and how they were doing.

~~~~

When Bob got back to the herd, he told the men to cut out twenty five head. No one asked why, they just did as instructed. After the cattle were cut out and the herd was moving, Jim rode up to Bob and asked him who he talked to and why they cut out the cattle.

"The man I talked to was Black Wolf. He used to be Sean's brother-in-law," said Bob. "What else do you need to know?"

"So Sean was married to that Cheyenne's sister, right?" asked Jim.

"Yes, he was," answered Bob. "And that man is now a chief. They needed some meat to help them get by while they go to Lakota territory."

"So you say his name is Black Wolf?" asked Jim.

"Yep, that's his name." said Bob.

"That'll be a good name for me to remember once I get back in the army," said Jim. "You never know where the army's gonna be or who they're gonna be fightin' with."

~~~~

There were no more problems or bad weather for the rest of the drive. When they finally got to Kansas City, Bob was able to find Bill Thompson, the cattle buyer, and get the deal made. The men drove the herd to the holding pens, and then helped load them on the rail cars. "I counted twenty one hundred head even," said Bill. "Does that sound about right to you?"

"That should be about right," answered Bob. "We had a few more than that when we left, but I gave twenty five to some Cheyenne."

"Why'd you give some to the Cheyenne?" asked Bill.

"The Chief of the clan that we saw, used to be Marshal O'Rourke's brother-in-law," said Bob.

"Oh," said Bill, "maybe I'll see the Marshal again sometime and ask him about that. Now, how would you like to be paid? I can give you a bank draft that you can take to that bank right across the street there, or I can pay you cash."

"I'll take cash," answered Bob. "That way I can pay the men quickly. I think some of them are ready for a drink and a woman."

"All right, cash it is," said Bill. "Anytime you get some more cows, you get ahold of me. I'll buy 'em. Those slaughter houses up in Chicago are desperate for beef.

Twenty one hundred times thirty five is $73,500. That's a lot of money Bob, be careful with it. There's plenty of thieves in this city."

"I'll be fine," said Bob. "After I pay the men, I'll be puttin' a good bit of this money in the bank. Can you recommend a good hotel and saloon in town?"

"Just stay close to the center of town and you'll be all right," said Bill. "If you get close to the edge of town, you'll be in the shady area."

"Thanks Bill," said Bob as he extended his hand to Bill. "Pleasure doin' business with you. Hope we can do more in the future."

"Likewise," said Bill. "You have a safe trip back to Abilene or wherever you're goin'."

~~~~

Bob gave each of the men, except the cook $100. He gave the cook $125. Charlie couldn't believe it. "I never knew there was that much money in the world," he said.

"Well don't expect to make that much money if you ever go on a drive again," said Bob. "I've heard Texas boys sayin' they only made thirty a month and found. We were paid very well for the herd, so I figure you men deserve it. Besides, you coulda got yourself killed in that gunfight we had a ways back. Now don't go gettin' drunk and gettin' your money stole. There's always thieves in big towns. I'll be spendin' one night here, then I'm goin' back to

Abilene. Anyone wants to ride with me, meet me and Jeb by the cattle pens just after daylight." The men all went their separate ways. Bob went straight to the bank. Someone from behind a counter said, "That dog can't come in here."

"Don't tell him that," said Bob. "He might take it the wrong way." Then Bob told Jeb to stay by the door. "I want to see your boss," Bob said to a teller.

"I can help you right here," said the teller.

"Look mister, I asked you for the boss and if you're not the boss, get him for me," said Bob. The teller gave a look of disgust, but he went to an office in the back of the bank and came back with a tall well dressed man.

"I'm Alfred Brown, I'm the bank President," he said. "May I help you?"

"Yes you can, Mr. Brown," said Bob. "Name's Bob Wallace. I'm a Deputy Federal Marshal, and I'd appreciate it we could go to your office and talk."

"Of course," he said, "right this way." When they got to his office, he showed Bob to a chair and asked how he could help him.

"All right," started Bob, "I need to open up two accounts. One for myself, and another one also in my name, but it needs to have some type of other name."

"Would you explain what you think you need?" the banker asked.

"I just brought a herd of cattle here from Abilene," started Bob. "Some of the cattle were mine, but the rest of them were from men who are now dead. I'll be tryin' to track down their kin, so I can get their money to them. That's why I want two separate accounts."

"That will not be a problem," said the banker. "We'll just put one in your name, and the other will be in your name also. One will be called no. 1 and the other one no. 2."

"That's simple enough," said Bob. "So if I cannot track down anyone kin to the deceased, I can come back and draw out that money, no problem."

"Yes, you can, Mr. Wallace," the banker said. "It's already in your name, no one else's. Now how much would you like to deposit today?"

"$10,000 in the no. 1 account and $55,000 in the no. 2 account," said Bob.

"That's good," said the banker. "We'll take good care of it for you. Must be good money in the cattle business right now."

"I guess there is," said Bob. "My cattle buyer told me that the slaughter houses in Chicago were desperate for beef."

"Sounds like a good investment to me," said the banker as he extended his had to Bob. Bob shook his hand, then left the banker's office.

"C'mon Jeb, let's go find us a hotel for the night. I'm ready to sleep in a bed tonight," Bob said. Bob found the nearest livery and got his horse taken care of. Then he went to the center of town and picked out a nice looking place. It was a hotel with a bar downstairs.

"Need a room for one night," Bob said as he walked up to the counter. The clerk gave a nasty stare at Jeb. "The dog goes with me," said Bob.

"But it's against our—"

Before he could get his words out, Bob opened up his jacket so the clerk could see his gun and badge. "I said the dog goes with me," Bob said forcefully.

"Yes sir," the clerk said, "one night. That'll be two dollars now, or you can pay when you check out. Bob went ahead and paid the clerk.

When Bob got to the room, the first thing he did was flop down on the bed. "I don't know about this," Bob said to Jeb. "That things too comfortable. I might not be able to sleep." After enjoying the bed for a few minutes, Bob decided to go downstairs to the saloon. The bartender gave a strange look at the dog, but didn't seem too concerned. "What'll you have, sir?" he said. "I'll bring it over to you."

"Got any good bourbon?" asked Bob.

"Sure do, straight from Kentucky," he said. He brought a bottle and a glass to Bob's table. "That's some dog you got there mister. What kind is he?"

"He's probly just a big mutt, but he's one hell of a cow dog, and he really likes me, so I hope no one hassles me in here," Bob said. "Jeb would take it real personal like."

"How bout I get him a pan of water?" said the bartender.

"That'd be nice," Bob said. "Can a fella get somethin' to eat in here too?"

"Sure can," the bartender said. "We got a real good cook. We even got a menu. I'll get you one."

Bob was amazed. They had all kinds of things on the menu. There was steak, stew, fried chicken, ham, and venison. "I'll just have a steak," said Bob. "Make sure it's red in the middle, and I'll take whatever trimmins' you got. I don't like my meat all cooked to hell."

"All right, sir, comin' right up," said the bartender.

"The dog'll have a steak too," said Bob, "but don't cook his."

~~~~

Bob and Jeb ate their steaks, and Bob was enjoying his bourbon when some fella came over and made a comment about Jeb. "That's about the ugliest dog I ever did see," the man said. "Yep, he's sure ugly." Jeb was starting a low growl.

"Mister," started Bob, "you better apologize to my dog here, or I might just turn him loose on you."

"I'll shoot that dog before he makes one move," said the man as he started reaching for a pistol.

When his hand touched his pistol, Bob drew his pistol and stuck it in the man's face. "Now I think you better tell Jeb you're sorry, and I mean right now," said Bob.

The man was shaking, but he got out the words. Bob thanked him and told him to be on his way. He left, and it wasn't five minutes later that a man with a badge pinned on, came in the saloon and walked over to Bob's table. "I'm Deputy Town Marshal George Watkins," he began. "I gotta fella come and tell me you pulled a gun on him."

"Sure did," Bob said as he opened his jacket so the deputy could see his badge. "That idiot started for his pistol and I pulled mine. If he says different, he's a damn liar. Now is there anything else I can do for you?"

"Yes, you can tell me your name and who your boss is." George said.

"I'm Bob Wallace, and my boss is Sean O'Rourke," said Bob.

"I sure as hell know who your boss is. Everybody around has heard about him," said George. "Is he really as good with a rifle or a pistol as they say?"

"No, George," Bob said. "He's better."

"So why are you up here?" asked George.

"Just drove up a herd from Abilene," said Bob. "Some of the herd was mine, and some of it was stolen. The Hawk bunch stole them, and we got 'em back. A bunch of Hawks are dead now."

"So do you ever have dealins' with the Anderson bunch?" asked George.

"Yep, that bunch is first on the list to get themselves shot or hung," said Bob. "Does that bunch ever get up this far?"

"They operated around here right at the end of the war for a few months," said George, " but I heard they went down to the Nations. That way, any local law couldn't go after them."

"Well us federal boys can go anywhere, and sooner or later, we're gonna hang that son of a bitch. Even if we shoot him dead, we're still gonna hang 'em," said Bob.

"Well it's been nice jawin' with you," said George. "Better go make my rounds. If I see that fool that said you pulled a gun on him, I'll smack him upside the head for you."

"Thanks, George, you be careful out there," said Bob.

Bob enjoyed another glass of bourbon, and then decided it was time to go to bed. First he took Jeb outside so he could do his necessaries. Then he went to his room and was asleep in no time. Jeb slept at the foot of the bed. He was having a real good dream when he was awakened by Jeb. Jeb had a low growl going. Someone was outside the door. "Quiet now, Jeb," Bob whispered as he grabbed his pistol and slid out of the bed. Jeb obeyed. Bob motioned for Jeb to follow him, and they got down beside a big fancy chair that was in the room. Just as they got there, two men came busting through the door. Bob could see pistols in their hands and he opened fire. He shot the one closest to him and he fell dead. Jeb had ahold of the other one. Jeb had him by his right arm and his pistol was in his right hand. He kept trying to get the pistol to his left hand so he could shoot Jeb, but Jeb wouldn't let him. Bob walked over to them, and shot the man through the head. Bob could hear someone else running towards his room. "You better identify yourself," said Bob, "or I'll start shootin'."

"It's me, the hotel clerk," the man said. "What is going on here?"

"Mister, you just go get the Town Marshal. Go on now," Bob said.

It wasn't five minutes later and George showed up. "What happened Bob?" he asked.

"These two fellas come bustin' through my door, and I killed em. They still got their pistols in their hands," answered Bob. "They musta heard about me gettin' a herd sold today and figured I was carryin' a buncha money. Do you know who they are?"

"I never laid eyes on 'em," said George. "I'll ask around. Somebody's bound to know them. I'll check their pockets right now." There was nothing in either man's pockets that would help identify them. One man had fifty cents, and the other had a dollar. "I'll get these bodies outta here, and you can get back to sleep. Hell, it's only 2am."

"Well I'll be leavin' at daylight, George," said Bob. "If you find out anything about them two after I'm gone, send a telegram to Abilene."

"Sure will," said George. "Have a safe trip back."

~~~~

The next morning, Bob, Jon, and Jim met at the livery. The only other one to be there was Charlie. "Well let's get movin'," said Bob. "You all can tell me about your stay here on the way back."

"Yep, and I heard somethin' about a Federal Deputy killin' two fellas last night," said Jon. "Can't wait to hear about that. I know it wasn't me."

"I'll tell you about it on the ride back," said Bob. "I'm gonna slip over to the telegraph office and let Sean know we're on our way back."

Sean wrote out the message and handed it to the operator. It went as follows:

Marshal O'Rourke
Abilene

drive done <stop> cattle sold <stop> should be back in a week <stop>

Bob

CHAPTER ELEVEN

Two days after the shootout with the would be killers, Jason from the leather goods store told Sean the leather part of his vest was done. Sean went over and tried it on and was impressed with Jason's work. "Jason," Sean began, "if this town does become a cow town, you're gonna be one rich man. Those Texas boys are gonna want all kinds of stuff from you. I'll go check on my steel now. Maybe some of it will be done, and you can get a good start on the liner."

"Already got some material picked out for the liner," said Jason. "If you can get me a few pieces, we can get started with the pockets."

"I'll be back over shortly and let you know," said Sean.

~~~~

When Sean got to the livery, the blacksmith was banging away on a wagon wheel rim. "Be right with you, Marshal," he said when he saw Sean walk in. "Wheel's almost done." After a few more bangs on the wheel, the blacksmith gave it a good look, and then set it aside. "I got some of that steel done for you," he said as he handed a piece of it to Sean. "How's that look to you?"

"Look's good," said Sean. "You got it really thin like I wanted, and the size looks good. I'll take a few pieces with me and make sure they're gonna be all right. Be back shortly." Sean took some of the steel and went back to the leather goods store. "I got some pieces of the steel here," Sean said as he handed them to Jason. "Now you know what you got to work with. Blacksmith did a good job gettin' them really thin. The vest won't be way too heavy when it's done."

"I'll measure everything as best I can so we'll know how much steel we actually need," said Jason. "Then you can let the blacksmith know for sure." Jason got out some paper and a pencil and began some calculations. After a few minutes, he scratched his head, and said to Sean. "If we have a quarter inch between pockets, we should need twenty five for the back and twenty for the front. You're a strong man. After a little while, you won't even notice the extra weight."

"All right," said Sean. "I'll go let the blacksmith know right now." Sean went straight to the blacksmith and told him what was needed.

"I could possibly have that done before the end of the day," the blacksmith said. "If not, they'll be done in the mornin'. If I get 'em done, I'll send Billy to get you."

"Thanks," said Sean. "I'll give you a good bonus for gettin' em done so quick. If you stop over at Maggie's later, drinks are on me."

~~~~

After five days of wearing the sling for his right arm, Sean had had enough. His arm and shoulder did not hurt anymore, and he started using his right arm. He was very careful at first, but now he was doing almost everything. He decided that he would keep the sling on when he was out among folks, but when no one was around, he did whatever he wanted. He also thought that if he kept using the sling when he was around folks, maybe a fella looking to collect the bounty on him might think he was still laid up some. He even took a ride out to the Hawk place to see if there had been any activity. There was not.

~~~~

Sean's vest was done now and he wore it wherever he went. Everyone gave him good compliments on it too. "Jason made it for me," Sean always said. "I'm sure he'd be glad to make you one too." The extra weight was almost unnoticeable. The fit was so good, no one could tell that it was lined with steel. Jason had put sheepskin on the inside making it warm and very comfortable.

~~~~

Jack Snow rode into town when Sean had two more days to wear his sling. He found a farmer just out of town that let him rent an extra room for a few days. He gave his name as Hank Carter. Jack told the farmer that he was a business man, and he had come to town to look around for business locations. He told the farmer that he had heard that Abilene could become a cow town, and he was figuring on investing in different businesses like hotels, restaurants, and saloons. The farmer knew that Abilene might become a cow town, so he was glad to have the business man at his place. Jack dressed himself like a business man too. When he first rode into town, he went around to all the businesses and introduced himself. Everyone was pleased to meet him and glad that he might bring more businesses to town. He was especially interested in meeting the Federal Marshal who had such a big reputation. He also made sure all Maggie's girls knew who he was. Maggie's beauty amazed him, but he seemed more interested in Betty. He and Betty were about to head upstairs, when Sean came down the stairs to the saloon. "That's Marshal O'Rourke," said Betty. "I'll bring him over here to meet you."

Betty walked over to Sean, grabbed his good arm, and led him to the table where Jack was setting. "Marshal, this is Hank Carter," she said. "Says he's a business man and he's here lookin' things over for when this place turns into a cow town." Jack stood and extended his hand to Sean. Sean shook with his left hand.

"Pleased to meet you, Hank," said Sean. "This town'll sure need more businesses if we do become a cow town. So who do you work for? Are you in a firm, or do you have partners?"

"I work alone," said Jack. "That way I don't have to please anyone but me. Partners just get in the way sometimes, and someone's always arguing over money. I see you've been hurt some. Will you be healing up soon?"

"Doc says I gotta wear this thing for a month longer," said Sean. "Don't ever let someone's Grammaw blast you with a shotgun. Lucky I still got my arm. Can't do spit with my left arm." Sean saw how the expression on Hank's face had changed when he lied about how long he needed to wear the sling, so he made the lie even bigger by saying his left arm was no good. "I've gotta go over to the livery now," Sean said. "Enjoy your stay." As Sean was heading out the door, he motioned for Maggie to meet him just outside the doors. "Maggie, you and Michael keep an eye on that Hank fella," Sean said. "I don't trust him. He seemed too interested in my right arm. See if you can tell if he's armed or not. I didn't see a gun on him, but he could have a shoulder holster or a pocket gun. Or he could have a knife. Probably won't spot it if he does."

Maggie went back in and told Michael what Sean had said. They didn't get a chance to watch him for long because Betty was taking him upstairs. "I'll ask Betty about him when she comes back downstairs," said Michael. "She's got a good eye, and she's a good listener. Maybe he'll say somethin' that she'll remember."

A half hour later, Betty and Jack made their way back downstairs. "I'm done for the evening," said Jack, "I'll be back tomorrow and look around town more for locations and such. Nice meeting everyone. Betty, thank you for a pleasant time."

Sean had been outside the whole time. When Jack came out of the saloon, Sean ducked behind the corner of the building so he wouldn't be seen. When Jack was out of sight, Sean went back inside the saloon. Michael escorted Betty to a table and they were joined by Maggie and Sean. "What's goin' on?" asked Betty. "Did I do somethin' wrong or somethin'?"

"No, darlin'," answered Michael. "We just wanted to ask you some questions about your last customer."

"Well he was a gentlemen and didn't mistreat me any," said Betty.

"Did you notice if he was armed or not?" asked Sean.

"I never noticed any guns," said Betty. "Didn't see a knife either."

"Did he talk much?" asked Maggie.

"You're not serious, are you," said Betty. "He didn't go upstairs to talk."

"Probably not, but do you remember him saying anything at all?" asked Maggie.

"Well, when we first got upstairs, he asked me some questions about the Marshal," Betty said. "I told him to concentrate on me. Told him he could talk to the Marshal later."

"Well what did he ask you?" asked Sean.

"He asked me about your arm and if I knew anything about how long you'd be laid up," she began. "He wanted to know if Maggie was your woman too, and where you two were staying. Then he asked if I was interested in making some good money. I told him to shut up and get down to business. I told him if he liked what I was doing, he could pay me some good money when we were done. He seemed to like what I did because he gave me another dollar."

"So you really didn't answer his questions about Sean, right?" asked Michael.

"I told you exactly what I said. I told him to shut up and get down to business. That was it," replied Betty.

"Thank you, Betty darlin'," said Michael. "You go on back to business now. I'll see you later."

"I don't think this fella is any business man," said Sean. "We'll all keep our eyes on him as best we can. Michael, let Tom know about this fella. One more pair of eyes won't hurt."

Business was slow that night, so Maggie closed up earlier than usual. She didn't mind. She wanted some time with Sean, and she could tell he wanted the same thing. After they got untangled from each other, Maggie asked Sean to continue his life story.

"There's not much left now, darlin'," said Sean. "We made it up to the war. I lived through the war and resigned my commission as soon as I heard Lee surrendered."

"So you were an officer?" asked Maggie.

"I was at the end," said Sean. "I started out as a private, but kept getting promoted. I made Corporal when they found out I could shoot. Then General Sherman himself made me a Sergeant."

"Stop right there," said Maggie. "You're telling me that General William Tecumseh Sherman promoted you?"

"Yes, darlin', he did," said Sean. "I was about to give some Quartermaster Captain the butt of my rifle when the General happened by. This was at Shiloh. That Captain didn't want to give me ammunition for my Sharps and I was gonna brain him. I got my ammunition, and the Captain got his ass tore. The General promoted me right there on the spot. Later on when our Captain got wounded badly, they made me a Captain. Later on, General Sherman made me his aide, and I was promoted to Major."

"So not getting killed is a good way to get promoted," said Maggie.

"That's how it works sometimes, darlin'," said Sean. "When someone gets killed, someone's gotta take their place."

"So where were you from right after the war till you came here?" asked Maggie.

"I went to St. Louis to wait on Judge Simmons to get back from the war," started Sean. "While I was waiting, I worked at a nice saloon called "The Palace.""

"I've heard about that place," said Maggie. "I hear it's really nice."

"Yes it is," said Sean. "Sam Draper's the owner. I learned what I could about the saloon business from him because Michael and I always wanted to have our own saloon."

"I've heard he has the most beautiful women working there too," said Maggie.

"He surely does," replied Sean, "and I won't lie to you, darlin'. I got to know all of them, but they can't hold a candle to you, darlin'."

"I wouldn't expect you to say otherwise darlin'," said Maggie. "You're a very handsome, healthy man. I bet they wouldn't leave you alone."

"This didn't go on too long," said Sean. "Judge Simmons came back, swore me in as Federal Marshal, and here I am. Now you know all there is about me. Next time it's your turn."

"My life will sound boring after hearing about yours," said Maggie. "But next time, you'll hear all about my life."

When they woke the next morning, they were all over each other. When they were finished and dressed, Sean looked at Maggie and said, "You should remember to take it easy on me darlin', I've been shot." Maggie let out a laugh as they both headed downstairs.

Michael was already there at a table sipping some coffee. "I'll get you both a cup, darlins'," Michael said as he got up and went into the kitchen. "Cookie's in there already and says he's gonna make us all some steak and eggs and biscuits for breakfast. I'll not stand in his way."

"That sounds really good," said Sean. "That man is one cookin' fool. Maggie, you did good when you found him."

"Yes, I did," said Maggie. "I surely did."

"Sean," said Michael, "I never said anything more to Betty about that business man. She asked me why I was asking questions about him, and I just said we were all anxious to know about new businesses coming to town. I did ask her not to mention that we had asked about him. She said that she wouldn't."

"That's good, Michael," said Sean. "We'll keep an eye on him when he comes back to town today. I'm gonna eat this wonderful breakfast, then walk around town, and every once in a while, act like my right arm is hurtin' me. Maybe even have the Doc come over and have him act like he's givin' me somethin' for the pain." Sean finished his breakfast, gave Maggie a kiss, and then walked around town. Every once in a while, he would stop and act like he was in terrible pain. He went to the Doc's office, and a few minutes later, he came out carrying some kind of bottle. It was just a bottle of water, but no one knew that but Sean and the Doc. Sean had let Doc know his plan, but he did not mention anything about the new business man in town.

~~~~

Jack went to Maggie's Place about mid morning. He got himself some breakfast, and then went all around town talking to all the businesses. The land office was at the bank, so he went there and was asking who owned what property, and what property could be purchased. Then he went around acting like he was measuring out lots. He sure looked like he was a business man to most of the folks in town. He was very convincing. He even opened up some small accounts at the bank. Sean decided he was wasting his time watching this man. "If he's here for me," Sean muttered, "he'll come after me. I'll just wait on him." Sean sat around Maggie's place most of the day playing poker with anyone who would play. He took a table where he could see everything going on. He ate supper with Maggie and Michael. Maggie told them that Cookie was getting some turkeys from a local farmer and was going to make a big feast for Thanksgiving. They sat around and wondered what Cookie would make to go with the turkey. "I just ate," said Sean, "and I'm getting' hungry just thinkin' about what Cookie will make. I feel like a little kid. I can't wait." Just as he finished speaking, Jack Snow walked into the saloon.

Jack had spent most of the day trying to look like a business man, but he was actually thinking about the best way to stick a knife into Sean. Clark Adams had always told him to go for the gut, and thrust the knife upward to the heart. If Jack did it that way, he would have to be facing Sean. Jack was not convinced that Sean was as laid up as he was letting on. The knife he had used on several occasions, had an eight inch thin blade, and was double edged. He had stuck several men through the ribs with no problems. This knife was razor sharp, and the tip was very pointy. Any time he had ever hit ribs, it always made it's way between them, no problem. Jack convinced himself he could get Sean in the back through his ribs and into his heart. He had the knife up his right sleeve fastened to his lower arm. It was rigged so that if he flicked his wrist just a little, the knife would drop out blade first. He could grab the handle as it dropped down.

"Next round's on Hank Carter," Jack said as he made his way inside. "We'll all be wealthy when the railroad comes. Mind if I join you, Marshal?"

"Sit right down," said Sean. "We're all drinking bourbon here. I'll get you a glass." Sean went to the bar and got another glass for Hank. When he returned to the table, he refilled everyone's glass.

"What should we drink to?" said Sean. "Oh, I know. Here's to stayin' alive."

Maggie left the table saying she had to get to work, and Michael did the same. After a little talk about building hotels and such, Jack took his leave, and asked one of Maggie's girls if she was available. She was, and they both went upstairs to one of the rooms. Jack was very careful when he undressed so the knife wasn't seen. When he was finished, he dressed himself, paid the girl, and made his way downstairs. He then went to the outhouse so he could make sure his knife was situated properly. It was pitch dark outside now, and his horse was tied out back for a quick getaway. He went back inside and found Sean. Sean was still at the same table with a glass of bourbon in front of him.

"Mind if I sit back down here, Marshal?" Jack asked. "I always like a good drink after, well you know, after."

"Yep. I know about after," said Sean. "Sometimes, even before, but not too much."

Jack finished his drink and told Sean he was stepping outside for some fresh air and to have a smoke. "Would you care to join me, Marshal?" he asked Sean.

"I'll be out after I finish this drink," Sean said. Sean was wearing his left handed holster and he had another pistol stuck in his belt. No one had noticed, but the pistol in his belt was positioned for a right hand draw. He felt certain that this man was going to try something. He finished his drink and headed toward the doors. The saloon doors were the double swinging kind that some saloons used. Sean did not see the man anywhere near the doors. "He must be to either side where I can't see him," Sean said to himself. "May as well find out if this vest is any good." Sean went out the doors and looked around. Then Jack spoke.

"It's dark as hell tonight," he said. "Can't hardly see my hand in front of my face."

"There's no moon tonight," said Sean as he stepped forward a little. Jack was on his left side. He moved over closer to Sean while looking up in the sky as if he was star watching. He took a drag off his cigar, then flicked it into the street with his right hand. He held his arm low when he did this, and when he did, the knife slid down into his hand. Sean had not seen the knife. Jack saw his chance, and made his move with the knife. Something was not right. The knife wouldn't penetrate Sean's vest. When Sean felt the knife against his back, he quickly drew the pistol from his belt with his right hand and stuck it right under Jack's chin. The hammer was cocked. With his left hand, he grabbed Jack's right arm and told Jack to drop the knife. Just as calmly as could be, he looked Jack right in the eyes and said, "You want shot or hung?" Jack attempted to get his right arm free, and Sean said, "All right, shot it is." He pulled the trigger on the pistol, and Jack's head exploded.

When the shot was heard, almost everyone in the saloon came running out to see what had happened. "I'm sorry, Maggie," Sean said as she came out the doors. "I made a terrible mess out here. I'll get it cleaned up before it starts dryin' too much. Michael, help me get this man over to the barber shop." As they were dragging the body to the barber shop, Michael asked what had happened. "He tried to stick a knife in me," said Sean. "He would have got me if I hadn't been wearin' my vest."

"What's your vest got to do with anything?" asked Michael.

"It's a special made vest," answered Sean. "Got it lined on the inside with steel plates. He couldn't get the blade through it. I never told anyone I had this vest. Jason made it for me, and I got the steel done over at the livery. Anyway, it worked. I'm alive, and this fella isn't. It'd be nice if we could find out who he is."

"Maybe someone'll recognize him tomorrow before the barber gets him in the ground," said Michael.

"I hope so," replied Sean. "I'm goin' through his pockets now." There was nothing to identify the man, but he had over three hundred dollars on him. "Maybe that was part of a down payment from Anderson. I'll put it in my buryin' fund at the bank tomorrow. Let's get back to the saloon. I know Maggie's not too happy about the mess."

"I'll have to agree with her this time," said Michael. "You could have shot him somewhere that was less messy."

Sean did his best to clean up the place. "I'll do some more tomorrow when it's daylight," he told Maggie.

She gave him a firm look, but said, "I'm just happy you are still with me. It's time for a toast." She went to the bar and got a bottle and three glasses, and the three of them, Maggie, Sean, and Michael, sat down at a table and had their toast. "Here's to not getting killed," toasted Maggie. Sean and Michael each repeated the toast.

~~~~

That night, Maggie made love to Sean like she had never done before. After they were finished and laying in each other's arms, Maggie looked into Sean's eyes and said, "I will love you forever."

"Maggie, I will love you as long as I'm alive, and even after that," Sean said. "I am sorry for what you've had to go through the last several days. One day, it will end."

"Darlin', you are a lawman," said Maggie. "You are very good at what you do. There will always be someone trying to get you. Even if you were to quit, you have made some enemies that will not forget you. Together, we will take care of anything or anyone who means to do us harm. By us, I mean that if they harm you, they are harming me, and I will not allow it."

"Maggie, you ARE my woman," Sean proclaimed. "You will always be MY woman."

Maggie began kissing Sean again. Each kiss more passionate than the one before. They made love well into the night.

~~~~

Doc Rawlins came in exactly seven days to examine Sean. "You can get rid of that sling," he said. "If I know you, you've only been wearing it for show anyway. Everything looks really good, but like I said before. We can't see the bones. You may still get a little pain once in a while. Take it fairly easy, and you'll be fine. And before I forget to tell you, that man you had to shoot the other night, well I think his name was Jack Snow. I saw a drawing of him back in Kansas City a while back. It was on a wanted poster, $1500 reward dead or alive."

"What did the poster say he was wanted for?" asked Sean.

"Several counts of murder, I believe," said Doc. "I can't be positive that's him, but it sure looked like him to me."

"Well thanks Doc," said Sean. "I'll tell the barber he can go ahead and put him in the ground today. And thanks for takin' care of me. I guess if I have any problems, I'll look you up."

"Let's hope you never need me again," said Doc. "Have a pleasant day, and I'll take my leave now. Tell that beautiful woman of yours that I said hello."

"I'll tell her, and thanks again," said Sean.

Sean went to Maggie and told her that Doc said he looked good and he wouldn't need to see him anymore. Then he told her that Doc thought the man he killed the other night was Jack Snow.

"I've heard of Jack Snow," said Maggie. "I've heard he'd kill anyone for a price. I hear he's been doing it for years."

"Well if that's him, he won't kill anyone else," said Sean. "I'm gonna get my pistols and go tell the barber he can get that man in the ground now." Sean put on his left handed gun belt and put another pistol in his belt for his right hand. While he was putting on his gun belt, the stage pulled in and two dirty looking men got off. They wore long coats, but Sean could tell they were armed. They stood in the street for a few minutes looking around, then one of them noticed the dead body beside the barber shop. They went over to look at it. "Son of a bitch," one of them said, "that's Jack Snow. Never figured anyone'd ever git him."

Sean had eased up behind the two men without them noticing. They were startled a little when Sean spoke. "So you say that man there is Jack Snow," said Sean.

"Sure is," one of them said. "I seen him some time back. He was working both sides of the border betwixt Missouri and Kansas, killin' for whoever paid him. And who are you?"

"Name's O'Rourke, Marshal Sean O'Rourke," said Sean. "And who might you two be?"

"So yer that famous Marshal that's got a price on his head," one of them asked.

"I'll ask you again, who might you two be?" Sean asked again.

"Names won't matter, Marshal," one of them said as he was pulling his coat back exposing his pistol. The other man did the same. "My brother and me are gonna kill you right now."

As soon as the man finished saying the word now, Sean had the pistol from his belt out and both men were dead in the street. Next thing Sean knew, the barber came running over and said, "Marshal, was that fair?" he said. "Them two never had a chance."

"What do you mean, never had a chance?" Sean said. "They had pistols. I had pistols. They're dead. I'm not. What do you think this is, a game or somethin'? Didn't you hear them say they were gonna kill me?"

"I did, but maybe you could have taken their guns and locked them up," the barber said.

"And then what?" asked Sean. "Ask them to promise to behave, and then turn them loose in a few days. We don't have any judges or courts out here. So would it have been better if they had killed me and just rode off?"

"I don't mean it like that, Marshal," the barber answered. "I guess all the business you're giving me is getting' a little upsettin'."

"Well I hope business slows down some," said Sean. "Wouldn't want you upset, especially if you were giving me a shave."

Maggie and Michael came running out into the street when they heard the shots. "Not already, the last one's not even in the ground yet," said Maggie.

"Well at least these two told me that other fella was Jack Snow before they got themselves killed," said Sean. "Wouldn't tell me who they were. I'm goin' through their pockets and see if there's anything that will identify them."

Sean checked their pockets, and they had five dollars between them, nothing else. "I'll take their guns over to the General Store and see if they'll buy 'em. I'll put the money in the buryin' fund. Barber's gettin' upset over all the extra business he's been gettin'."

"We'll probably get a regular undertaker in town when the place grows," said Michael. "Then watch that barber complain about losing business."

"I'm goin' to the telegraph office and send a telegram to the judge," said Sean. "I'll meet you back at the saloon for a drink shortly."

Sean's telegram went as follows:

Judge David Simmons
Federal Court House
St. Louis

Jack Snow dead <stop> other attempts on me failed <stop> arm and shoulder healed <stop>

O'Rourke

Sean had two more telegrams to send.

Sam Draper
The Palace
St. Louis

Sam <stop> need help <stop> need biggest fanciest bath-tub you can find <stop> send here <stop> will send bank draft <stop> money in bank St. Louis <stop> many thanks <stop>

Sean O'Rourke

Walter Black
Gunsmith
St. Louis

Walter <stop> need four pistol conversions <stop> .44 same as before <stop> four hundred rounds ammunition <stop> will send bank draft <stop>

Marshal Sean O'Rourke

~~~~

Sean was getting Christmas gifts for Maggie and his deputies. He hadn't thought about Christmas but maybe one time during the war, but with Thanksgiving a day or so away, it got him thinking about Christmas. He remembered when he was back in Tennessee and how much Christmas had meant to his folks. Now he had a family again.

CHAPTER TWELVE

Cookie made a tremendous feast for Thanksgiving. Sean ate so much, he didn't think he would be able to move for a week. "That man can sure cook," said Sean after he had stuffed himself. "I hope he never leaves this place." Everyone there felt the same. All of Maggie's girls were there. Tom and his wife were there too. There were a few other folks there, but most of the other people were home with their families.

Before Cookie had everything ready, Sean asked if everyone would say what they were thankful for. Maggie's girls went first. They all said that they were thankful for having such a great boss and a great place to work. Then Betty added that she was also thankful for that big handsome Irishman, Michael. Tom said he was thankful for his wife and Maggie and everyone there. Maggie said she was thankful that she had the best man in the world and the best people to work with. Michael said that he was thankful for all the new friends he had made, especially Betty, and that he and Sean could still have their toast, "Here's to not getting killed."

When it came Sean's turn, he said he was thankful that the most beautiful creature on this earth loved him and he loved her. Maggie almost cried. Cookie was still in the kitchen with his wife, but he heard what was going on, so when Sean was finished, he came out and said that he was thankful that Maggie allowed him to work there and that everyone always like his food.

Bob, Jon, and Jim were not back yet, so Sean asked Cookie if he would make a feast like this for them when they got back. Cookie said he would be glad to.

~~~~

Business was slow on Thanksgiving day, so Maggie closed down early. All the girls went to their homes. Michael went with Betty. Tom and his wife went home as did Cookie and his wife. Sean and Maggie sat at a table in the saloon by themselves sipping bourbon. "So you're really thankful for me?" asked Maggie.

"Yes I am," said Sean. "I surely am. Let's sit here awhile and you can tell me your life story. Then we can go upstairs, and I can be thankful properly."

"I told you that my life will seem boring compared to yours," said Maggie.

"How could anything with you in it, be boring?" said Sean. "That just wouldn't be possible."

"All right, darlin', here goes," started Maggie. "I was born in New Orleans. My father was a very good gambler, and my mother was a Madam. She ran a very high class place and the customers were high class too. Foreign dignitaries frequented the place when they were in town. As far as I know, my mother was never a whore, but she knew how to run her business. She had her own security people, and if there were ever any problems, they were taken care of very quickly and very discreetly. My father only gambled with the very rich, so he was well known by them and well liked. I worked in the place doing whatever was necessary. I developed at an early age, and at times, some of the customers thought that I might be one of my mother's girls. She assured them that I was not on the menu. My father died one day when he and my mother were making love. I think they said it was his heart. My mother did not take another husband or lover after that."

"When did you meet your husband?" asked Sean.

"It was three years after my father died," answered Maggie. "I was doing some shopping one day, and I actually bumped into him and almost knocked him over. My packages went all over. He helped me pick everything up, and walked me home. He was a perfect gentleman. He courted me for a short while, and I fell in love with him. He was an artist then, and he made good money at it. He did this painting of me when we were first married. I think it's pretty good, don't you?"

"Maggie, it's beautiful, and I love it, but it still doesn't do you justice," said Sean.

"You're a good man, darlin'," said Maggie. "Back to my husband, somewhere along the line, he started gambling, and it got worse all the time. It wasn't that he was losing or anything like that. It was just that he felt constantly compelled to do it. We lived in New Orleans the whole time we were together. One day a local constable came to the house and told me my husband had been killed. He said it was during a poker game and someone had accused him of cheating. The man pulled a pistol and shot him. My husband never carried a gun or a knife. The killer fled and was never caught. We were only together for three years. My mother died from influenza the next year. She left me the business, and I sold it."

"So how did you end up out here?" asked Sean.

"I wanted to get away from New Orleans, and I had heard about this new town out here that was just getting started," Maggie began. "I figured it would be a good place to have a new start, so I took the money from the sale of my mother's place and what my husband had, and here I am. I had also heard that this town could become a cow town."

"I know it's not polite to ask a woman her age," said Sean, "but you and I must be about the same age. I just turned twenty two last month."

"I'm a little older than you, darlin'," said Maggie. "I'll be twenty three in February."

"That's great," said Sean. "I believe I really like being with older women. Let's get upstairs."

"I like my men young," said Maggie. "Let's go."

They made love well into the night. Next morning they woke up in each other's arms. Sean kissed Maggie several times then told her he wanted to talk a little business. "Business first thing in the morning," said Maggie. "Even before I have some coffee. This must be important. What is it, darlin'?"

"Well, darlin', you have heard me say the Michael and I always wanted to own a saloon," began Sean. "We both have plenty of money now. I propose that you, Michael, and I become partners. I think we should make the place bigger, more saloon space, more rooms upstairs, get that ice house built, and whatever else we would need. Michael even says he can play the piano. Maybe you could sing. You know that if this does become a cow town, you will need to get bigger. What do you think about all this? I haven't scared you, have I?"

"No, my darlin'," said Maggie, "I was going to make this same suggestion sometime in the future. I was not sure about your financial situation."

"I still have money that my parents had, my army pay, my Marshal's pay, and all the reward money I have collected." said Sean. "When the boys get back, I need to get them their share of the reward money. I don't like killin' anyone, but it sure pays good on some people. I s'pose that someday, they won't let a lawman collect reward money, but I don't figure that's gonna be till they get judges, lawyers, and courts out here."

"I never knew you could collect reward money," said Maggie. "What's Jack Snow worth?"

"Jack's worth $1500, and I think Anderson is worth $2000," said Sean. "I don't care if I collect on Anderson or not. He just needs to be dead."

"You'll get him," said Maggie. "I have no doubts."

"I have one more thing to bring up," said Sean. "How would you feel about spending the rest of your life with me?"

"Nothing could stop me," said Maggie. "I'll be with you as long as there is breath in my body."

Sean pulled her close and kissed her and kissed her and kissed her. "You just say when, and we'll have the ceremony," said Sean. "If we don't have a preacher near here, I'll go get one, or we can go somewhere and get married, and have a big honeymoon. Is there any place special you'd like to go, Chicago, New York, St. Louis?"

"I'll think about the honeymoon trip," said Maggie. "Anywhere we go, as long as we're together, it will be all right. There is one thing I think we should consider."

"And what would that be, darlin'? asked Sean.

"I think we should wait until we get Anderson before we go on a honeymoon," said Maggie. "I'll feel better knowing that he's dead, so we won't need to worry about him showing up when we least expect it. If he's dead, his bounty hunters will stop coming after you too because there will be no one to pay them."

"I liked it when you said we," replied Sean.

"I meant it. I'll kill him if it comes down to it," said Maggie. "Anyone trying to hurt my man is going to pay."

"You've already proven that two times, darlin'," said Sean. "Let's get some coffee and breakfast. If Michael is downstairs, can we go ahead and tell him about the partnership?"

"Yes, we can," answered Maggie. "I imagine he'll be excited."

~~~~

Michael was already downstairs sipping on some coffee when Maggie and Sean went downstairs. Maggie went to his table and Sean went to the kitchen to get them some coffee. "Morning, Michael," Maggie said. "Sean and I have some news that we think you will like."

"You mean that you two are gonna get married?" said Michael. "Hell, everybody knows that."

"No, that's not the news we were going to tell you about," said Maggie. "When Sean gets here with the coffee, we'll tell you."

Sean came to the table carrying a full pot of coffee and two cups. Then he filled his and Maggie's cup, and refilled Michael's. "All right," said Michael, "what's this great news I'm s'posed to hear?"

"Michael, my friend," began Sean, "Maggie, you, and me are going to be partners."

"That's great, a man couldn't ask for anything better," said Michael. "We'll be getting' a piano, right? I can't wait to start playin' again. It's been years."

"Yes, we'll get a piano," said Maggie. "I might even give singing a try."

"Maggie darlin', when people look at you, they won't care if you can sing or not," said Sean.

"I'll take that as a compliment," said Maggie.

The three of them spent a good part of the rest of the day talking about changes they would like to make, and things they would like to add. "I think we should go ahead and get some lumber ordered," said Sean. "When the boys get back, maybe they wouldn't mind doing some construction work and take a break from playing lawman for a spell. I think we should build an ice house first. It should be big enough so that when business gets bigger, we won't need to add on to it."

"Yes, and if we get the ice house done first," said Michael, "we might be able to have some cold beer while we're working on the other additions or changes."

"I would say that come next spring," started Maggie, "there will be all kinds of buildings going up around here. If we have our things done before anyone else does, we will make plenty off the people who are building the other businesses. When we get more rooms added on, some people might rent them until hotels are built. Who knows, maybe we'll build a hotel too."

"You know," started Sean, "even if this place don't become a cow town, sooner or later, it will grow. We may as well get started growing. I think I'll send a telegram to that cattle buyer, Bill Thompson, and see if he's heard anything new about the railroad coming. He should be in Kansas City. He bought that herd that

Bob and the boys took up there. Bob and them should be back any day now."

~~~~

Two days later, Bob, Jon, Jim, and Charlie Johnson made it back to Abilene. Sean was out in front of the saloon when they rode in. The four dogs were with them. "Good to see you boys," said Sean. "After you get rid of your horses, come on back, and we'll have a drink or two, and you can tell me all about the drive. Billy will look after them dogs."

"We'll be right back," said Bob. "I am a little thirsty."

"Jim and me are too," said Jon. "I reckon Charlie here could use a drink too."

~~~~

When the boys got back to the saloon, Jeb stayed with Bob. Sean already had a table ready with a couple of bottles and enough glasses for all of them. Michael was there too. "Would anyone like a beer too?" asked Sean.

"I'll have a beer," said Charlie. "I drink whiskey, but sometimes it goes down really good if you have some beer with it."

"Sure thing, young fella," said Sean. "Bob, when I get back with his beer, you'll have to introduce me to this young fella." Sean returned with the beer, and Bob introduced Charlie.

"Sean and Michael, this is Charlie Johnson," said Bob. "He was a good man to have on the drive. Good with the cows and a darn good shot with that carbine of his." Sean and Michael both shook hands with Charlie.

"Well Charlie, if Bob says you're a good man to have around," said Sean, "consider yourself a friend of mine. Have you got any plans, Charlie?"

"No, not really," said Charlie. "I was just gonna work my way back down to Texas and see if I could find some work."

"Well, Charlie, if you know how to saw a board and drive a nail, I can give you some work right here," said Sean. "We're gonna be buildin' an ice house and addin' on to the saloon as soon as we get the lumber. What do you say?"

"I can do that, and thanks," said Charlie.

"Now tell me all about the drive, Bob," said Sean. "Somethin' musta happened if you know that Charlie here is a good shot."

"We had a run in with a fella who said we had to pay a tax to cross his land," said Bob. "He wanted two dollars a head. He had maybe twelve or thirteen men. We killed ten of them, and the others run off. Jeb here killed their leader. Ripped out his throat."

"Good dog to have around," said Michael.

"Don't forget, young Billy gets one of the other dogs," said Sean. "Is anyone else wantin' one of these dogs?"

"I was thinkin' about takin' one," said Jon. "I thought he might keep me company when I go back down to the Nations and look up that Cherokee beauty I met a while back. That is, if you can spare me for a spell, Sean."

"That'll be all right," said Sean. "I'd like for you to be back by Christmas if you wouldn't mind."

"That'll give me plenty of time," said Jon. "I'll be back sooner if I find out she got herself married or something."

"I doubt this'll happen," said Sean, "but if you would happen to come across some of Anderson's gang, or some of the Hawks,

I'd expect you to get back up here and let us know, or get word to us."

"That goes without sayin'," replied Jon. "Law comes first."

"I also have some bad news for you, Sean," said Bob. "We met your former brother-in-law while we on the drive."

"You mean you met Black Wolf?" asked Sean.

"Yep, we met up with him after we had that fight with them other fellas," answered Bob. "He was with a small band, and we gave him twenty five head to help him out on his trip to Lakota land. He said the buffalo were not plentiful where they were, but they would be plentiful when they got to Lakota land. That man has a bad limp."

"Yes, that happened on a buffalo hunt several years ago," said Sean. "We had several men hurt and several horses killed that day. Did he have anything else to say?"

"He said that white people keep breakin' treaties," said Bob. "Then I asked him if he knew anything about Blue Swan and Braddock."

"Well, what did he say?" asked Sean.

"I hate to be the one tellin' you," said Bob. "He said Blue Swan was killed at Sand Creek and Braddock went back to the mountains."

"Did he give you any details?" asked Sean.

"Are you sure you wanna hear this?" asked Bob.

"I already heard rumors," said Sean. "Tell me what he said."

"He said the soldiers killed women and children, and raped many of the women," replied Bob. "Then they cut off body parts and danced around with them stuck on their sabers. Braddock killed some of the soldiers with the Sharps you gave him. Then he went back to the mountains."

Sean was quiet for a minute, then he spoke. "I hope I never run into any soldier or ex-soldier and they're braggin' about what they did that day. I will beat them till they can't stand."

"Don't you think maybe they were just followin' orders?" asked Bob.

"Doesn't matter," said Sean. "If there was an order to kill women and children, it was not a legitimate order and any decent man should not have followed it. Let's talk about somethin' else now. I can't bring Blue Swan back."

"Well, I'm gonna stick around till we get Anderson," said Bob. "I'll get that son of a bitch if it's the last thing I do."

"Well Cookie's gonna make a big feast again tomorrow," said Sean. "You boys missed the Thanksgiving feast, so he's gonna make you one tomorrow. Jon, I hope you wait till after you eat before you take off after that woman."

"I never turn down good food," said Jon.

"In the mornin', I'll give you men your pay and share of reward money," said Sean. "And speakin' of money, Bob, how are you gonna handle findin' the kin from those stolen brands and get them their money?"

"I opened up an account for them in Kansas City," said Bob. "It's in my name, and I'm sendin' a telegram to Austin, Texas, and it'll have a list of the brands, and how many head there was from each brand. If they can prove that their kin had that brand, they can get aholda me, and I'll make sure they get their money."

"That much money can make some folks lie a bit," said Sean. "You did get $35 a head didn't you?"

"Yep, that's what we got," said Bob. "And I'm pretty good at spottin' a liar. They won't touch that money till I'm one hundred percent convinced they are kin."

"Did any of your former Rangers have any kin?" asked Sean.

"No, they were like me," said Bob. "No family at all. The one's they did have, either got killed or died during the war."

"Not to sound nasty," said Michael, "but don't that leave you with a lot of money for yourself. You and your men had five hundred head to start with, didn't you?"

"Yes, we started out with five hundred head and ten extra horses," said Bob. "I have no idea what I might do with that much money. It'll just set there till I make up my mind. Could take twenty years."

"Jim, are you still goin' back in the army if they form those colored cavalry regiments?" asked Sean.

"I believe so," said Jim, "but I'd like to be around when we get Anderson."

"Whatsa a fella gotta do to become a deputy around here?" asked Charlie. "I've never had a run in with Anderson, but I heard of 'em, and I can help get 'em. If we get down to Texas, I know my way around pretty good."

"Consider yourself sworn in, Charlie," said Sean. "But I do have one condition."

"You name it, I'll do it," replied Charlie.

"Well I see you don't pack a pistol," said Sean. "I want you to start packin' a pistol and become a decent shot with it. Is that all right with you?"

"I never packed a pistol cause I was never any good with one," said Charlie. "But I'll sure try to get better. Nothin' wrong with more firepower, is there?"

"No, there isn't," said Sean. "I'll make sure you improve, and we'll get you somethin' that shoots faster than that carbine. Not that I have anything against your carbine. I carry a Sharps rifle myself, but I also carry a Henry too. We'll get you a Spencer or a Henry. We never want to be out gunned."

~~~~

The next day, Cookie prepared another feast, and everyone stuffed themselves. Jon was so full, he considered waiting till the next day to leave, but decided to go anyway. "Still got some daylight left," said Jon as he was mounting his horse. "I won't need to stop and eat, so I can ride till dark, or even longer if there's much moon tonight."

"What're you gonna do if you get down there and find out that girl got herself married or engaged or somethin'?" asked Sean.

"I reckon if she got married, I'll be right back," answered Jon. "If she just got engaged, I'll hafta find out just how engaged she is."

"Well you be careful," said Sean. "I don't know about Cherokee, but men in some tribes can be pretty darn jealous when it comes to their women. If she got herself engaged, you best get to know her intended before you get in his way."

"I'll be all right," said Jon. "You be careful yourself while I'm gone. Could be more men out there lookin' to get that bounty. Let's get goin', Dog. See you all sometime before Christmas."

As Jon was riding away, Michael, Bob, Jim, and Charlie were taking lumber out behind the saloon. There was enough lumber for the ice house, so they intended to start on it the next morning. The rest of the lumber for the saloon additions would arrive in a couple of weeks.

CHAPTER THIRTEEN

Ethan Hawk was the father of six children. The oldest was a boy, Jake. He was fifteen now and almost as big as his father was. He had a full beard, but his facial features were more like his mother's than his father's. When he was only thirteen, he tried to join Quantrill and Bloody Bill, but they found out he was only thirteen, and wouldn't take him. This really upset Jake, so he went out on a killing spree just to prove to them that he was capable. He ambushed and shot several "Redlegs". His weapon of choice was a sawed off double barrel shotgun at close range, but he also carried a Colt revolver. He also killed several runaway slaves. Ethan never cared what his oldest son did as long as he was there when it came time to rustle some cows or horses. Even though he was only thirteen, Ethan knew his son could take care of himself.

When he turned fourteen, they finally let him join up with Bloody Bill. He got to know George Anderson, and was even with him on some of the raids they did. When the war ended, Jake went back to rustling cows with his father. Jake was with Anderson when they rustled the Texas herd that Bob Wallace and his men were driving. When Anderson headed back south, Jake went with him. He stayed in Texas when Anderson left for Mexico and spent his time drinking and whoring. He was in Dallas when he got word that his father had been killed. He had always expected that sooner or later, his father would get himself killed. But shot by a nigger, and that nigger was a Federal Deputy too. That stuck in his craw, and wouldn't get out. He was going back to Kansas and kill that nigger, lawman, or no lawman.

When Ethan got killed, his wife loaded up all the other children, and headed back to Missouri to be with her kin. Grammaw Hawk tried to get her to stay, but she'd had enough and left. On his way back to Kansas, Jake heard about the lawmen getting that herd back and killing his kin, and then killing his Grammaw. Every saloon he stopped in on the way back, that was all people talked about. Everyone had heard about that fast and accurate lawman and his deputies. Jake decided he had better come up with a good plan. He couldn't just ride into Abilene, kill that nigger, and just ride out.

Jake wasn't well known in Abilene, so he could ride in without any trouble. When he finally got close to town, he stopped out at the Hawk place just to see if anything or anyone had been there. There were no fresh tracks, but he decided he best not stay there in case these lawmen were checking on the place from time to time. He made camp about a mile from town and would ride in the next morning. He made himself some biscuits and beans for supper, and also a pot of coffee. He tried to sleep, but anger was overtaking him. "I'm gonna just ride in there, find that damn nigger, and blow his damn head off," he kept saying to himself. Finally, he fell asleep. When he woke up, the sun had already been up for a couple of hours. His anger had subsided, and now he was thinking about a plan. He made himself some coffee, bacon, and biscuits for breakfast, and then saddled up and headed to town. On the way to town, Jake made up his mind he would call himself Jethro White, and he was just a Texas boy looking for work. There were always Texas boys looking for work.

When Jake rode into Abilene, the few people he saw on the street seemed to look him over pretty good. "Maybe they know who I am," he thought to himself. "Or maybe they just looked at me that way cause I'm a stranger to them." Jake found the livery and left his horse there. He left his shotgun in the scabbard, and took off his Colt and put it in his saddle bag. Young Billy was there and asked if there was anything special he wanted for his horse. "Just give him a good rub down and a full order of oats, young fella," said Jake. "We've had a long ride. Don't know how long I'll be here. Tryin' to find some work. You wouldn't know where a fella could find some work, do ya?"

"Just ask around at the saloon," said Billy. "If there's work to be found, someone there should know somethin'. They got a good cook there too if you're hungry. I hear he cooks better than most women."

"Well thank you, young fella," said Jake. "I'll go over there and see what I can see." Jake went around to every business in town and introduced himself as Jethro White, and said that he was a Texas boy looking for work. Everyone told him the same thing. There wasn't much going on now, but maybe next spring things would boom if the railroad came to town and the cattle pens were built. Jake went to Maggie's Place last. When he walked in, he was mesmerized by the painting on the wall. He stood there for what seemed like several minutes acting totally amazed. Then he heard a voice from behind the bar.

"What can I get for you there, young fella?" asked Michael. "Have a seat and I'll bring it to you."

"I'll take a shota rye," Jake said as he was still staring at the painting. "Is that Maggie in that painting there?"

"Sure is, breath takin', isn't she?" answered Michael.

"Yep, it is," replied Jake. "By the way, I'm Jethro White. I'm here lookin' fer work, any kinda work. Already talked to every other place in town. They all said the same thing. Seems like everyone's justa waitin' to see if the railroad comes or not."

"That's right, young fella," said Michael. "We're doin' some work here, but we got plenty of help, plus we're waitin' on lumber too."

"Well thanks anyway," said Jake. "I'll finish this drink, then take a stroll, and maybe come back later and get somethin' ta eat. By the way, is this where that new Federal Marshal hangs out? I heard about him all the way down in Texas."

"Yes, he's here sometimes," said Michael. "Allow me to introduce myself. I'm Michael O'Connor, Deputy Federal Marshal Michael O'Connor." Michael extended his hand and Jake accepted the hand shake. Just as they finished shaking hands, Jim came in the saloon. When Jake saw him, it was all he could do to control himself, but then he remembered. His Colt was in his saddle bag at the livery. Michael motioned for Jim to come over to him. When Jim got to the table, Michael introduced him to Jake. "Jim, this is Jethro White from Texas, and he's lookin' for work," said Michael. "And Jethro, this Deputy Federal Marshal Jim O'Rourke."

Jake did a good job controlling his anger and his hatred and extended his hand to Jim. "Pleased to meet both of you, I've heard about you deputies and your boss," he said as he shook

Jim's hand. "That's what all the talk is in every saloon I went to on my way up here from Texas. Is that Marshal as fast as they say?"

"No, he's faster," said Michael. "And he can shoot with either hand. I've seen him shoot countless times, and you don't dare blink, or you won't see him draw. Even if you think you see it, you're not sure. But you know that he did draw, because someone'll be layin' there dead." Michael was starting to wonder if this fella wasn't a bounty hunter after Sean. It seemed like he was asking too many questions. He wasn't armed that Michael could see, but Michael decided to keep an eye on this young man. Sean and Bob had gone out to the Hawk place just to have a look and wouldn't be back for a while. Charlie was out back sawing a few boards for the ice house. Between himself, Jim, and Charlie, they should be able to keep an eye on this fella.

Jake finished his drink, excused himself, and went out to take the stroll he had mentioned. He had controlled his anger very well up to now, but he was losing the battle. He went straight to the livery and saddled his horse, strapped on his Colt, and made sure his shotgun was loaded and ready. The shotgun was on the right side of the horse. Jake paid Billy, then walked his horse over in front of Maggie's place. He stopped in the middle of the street, and positioned his horse between himself and Maggie's Place. He just stood there in the street staring at the saloon doors.

After a few minutes, Michael noticed him out there and told Jim that one of them better see what he was doing out there. Jim said he would go out and see if the fella wanted something. "You be careful," Michael said. "You can't see his hands. He could have a pistol or somethin' on the other side of that horse." Michael was right. Jake had already taken the shotgun from the scabbard and was ready to slip it up over the saddle and fire. Jim went out the saloon doors with his hand already on his Colt. "Is there somethin' we___." He couldn't finish. Jake had slipped the shotgun up over the saddle and cut loose with both barrels. The blast caught Jim full in the chest and threw him backwards on the sidewalk. When the shotgun fired, Jake's horse reared up, and Jake was knocked down. He quickly got up and began firing his Colt into Jim's dead body. "Damn nigger, you killed my Pa," he kept saying.

Michael was behind the bar when Jake fired the shotgun. He drew his pistol and went running out the door. He fired, and Jake was struck in the chest. As Jake was falling, he fired at Michael. The ball caught Michael in his left thigh, and he went down. Jake somehow got himself up and was trying to get on his horse.

Maggie was upstairs in her room sleeping when the shooting started. When the shotgun blast woke her, she ran to the window overlooking the street. She saw the man firing his pistol at Jim. She saw Jake fall backwards from the shot to his chest. Sean had left her the Henry, so she grabbed it, opened the window, chambered a round, and waited for a good shot. When Jake finally got himself mounted, Maggie squeezed off a round. Jake was struck in the head and thrown from the saddle. Then she chambered another round, threw on a robe and headed downstairs. When she got downstairs, Charlie was there with Michael trying to get the bleeding in his leg stopped. He had been out back when the shooting started and came running, but it was too late. "Jim's dead," said Charlie. "Darn near cut in two. Michael'll be all right. Ball passed through without hittin' bone."

"Just what in the hell went on here?" said Maggie. "Who was that man?"

"I heard him sayin' that Jim killed his Pa," said Michael. "If that's what he said, that fella there was Ethan Hawk's son."

"Son of a bitch," said Maggie. "Just how many more Hawks are there? Charlie, I'll look after Michael. You go get the doctor."

Sean and Bob weren't far from town when the shooting started. When they heard the shotgun blast, they came back to town at a fast gallop. "Just what in the hell?" exclaimed Sean. "That's Jim layin' there dead. Why? And who's this other fella?"

"That, young Sean, is Ethan Hawk's son," said Michael.

"Son of a bitch," said Sean. "There can't be too many more of them left, can there? Michael, are you all right?"

"I'm all right, my friend," said Michael. "Ball passed through without hittin' bone. You better talk to Maggie. She killed that fella. I hit him in the chest, and he got me in the leg. Maggie finished him off."

Sean went over to Maggie. She was wrapping Michael's leg, but she still had the Henry across her lap with the hammer cocked. Sean knelt down and took the rifle from her lap, released the hammer, and laid the rifle on the nearest table. Then he knelt back down and hugged Maggie. He could tell that she wanted to cry, but the tears didn't come.

Doc Rawlins showed up and went to work on Michael. "Good clean wound," he said. "Sorry, I didn't mean to say that a wound is good. Anyway, you'll be fine in no time. Just don't go dancing for a week or two. Keep an eye on it, and keep it clean. I'll see you in a week unless there is a problem."

"Thanks Doc, hope no one else needs you for a gunshot wound for a good while," said Michael.

"Charlie, you go get a buckboard and some boards for a marker," said Sean. "I'm gonna go bury Jim. I'd appreciate some help with the diggin'."

Tom was at the saloon now, so he stayed there while everyone went out to bury Jim. Charlie, Bob, and Sean got the grave dug, six full feet, and Sean carved on the marker, Jim O'Rourke, Deputy Federal Marshal, born 1840, killed 1865, a good man. Sean said some words about Jim and their childhood, and then the Lord's Prayer. Maggie cried a little, and then it was over.

That night, Sean and Maggie didn't make love. They just held onto each other and never let go until the next morning.

CHAPTER FOURTEEN

It didn't take Jon long to get to Cherokee Territory. He was able to find the woman he was looking for with no problems. Leah Roundtree was her name, and she was beautiful. Jon played the perfect gentleman and asked her father if he could court her. "You can court her, young man," her father said. "But if I was you, I wouldn't take too long doing it. One other young man has convinced himself that she is going to marry him. My daughter does not want this man. He is a good man and a good worker, but she does not love him, and the choice is hers."

"I'll do my best, and if it works out," said Jon, "you'll get a son-in-law. If it doesn't, I'll be on my way."

"I see you wear a badge," said her father. "That can be dangerous work. I have heard that not too many white lawmen live very long."

"The war was dangerous, and I lived through that," said Jon. "If your daughter and I end up together, I will do my best to stay safe for her."

"That's good to hear," her father said. "Now you best get busy with her. You didn't come this far to spend too much time with me. Does that dog go everywhere you go?" Sean nodded his head yes, then went to Leah.

"You know I've come down here so you will fall in love with me, don't you?" said Jon.

"I know," said Leah. "I knew we were attracted to each other when I first saw you. I have thought of you a lot, and I hope you have thought of me."

"I will not lie to you, Leah," said Jon. "I am no saint, but I have thought of you a lot, and once I'm with someone, I am with no one else. Let's take a ride, and we can talk some more."

"Is that your dog?" asked Leah.

"I reckon he is," said Jon. "Me and the boys ended up gettin' four dogs from some rustlers. They're good cow dogs, and this one seems to like me now."

Leah got her horse, and she and Jon rode at a slow walk talking the whole time. "Tell me about your family," said Leah. "Are your parents still alive?"

"My folks are gone now," said Jon. "My father was full blooded Cherokee and my mother was white. When they were married, my mother kept her maiden name. That's why my last name is O'Brien. Things didn't go well at times because my father was Cherokee. Some white folks hate Indians no matter what. Anyway, as far as I know, all my kin is dead. I had no brothers or sisters. How about your folks?"

"My father and most of the elders were forced here on the 'Trail of Tears'," said Leah. "I was born here. My mother died two years ago from the coughing sickness. My father is a good man and a tribe elder. We don't have too much trouble here. Sometimes a few white outlaws will come through and cause a little trouble, but they usually move on. They seem to like it better over in Osage land. We have our own tribal police, and they take care of any problems. We had a murder last year, and they hanged the murderer."

"Did they have a trial?" asked Jon.

"Yes, they did," answered Leah. "But it wasn't big and fancy like I hear the white folks trials are. Two different people saw him kill someone. They told this to the tribe elders, and he was hanged."

"Sounds fair to me," said Jon. "I've never been, but I hear some of those big trials can get pretty stupid. It seems like it don't matter if someone is right or wrong, it's who's got the better lawyer."

"So tell me why you went to fight in the war over the black men," said Leah.

"Just plain stupid, I guess," said Jon. "I never had no slave ever. I just had this idea that I had to go along with my state. As I said, stupid. The longer it went on, the stupider it got. I met my boss at a battle around Chattanooga. He actually shot me, got me patched up, and then helped me escape."

"He sounds like a good man," said Leah.

"He is," said Jon. "None better. I ran into him in Abilene after the war, and now I'm his deputy. If you ever have trouble, and I'm not around, remember this name, Sean O'Rourke. He will help you. He helped the Osage rid themselves of the Anderson gang."

At times, they dismounted to rest the horses and talked. Finally it was getting late, and they headed back to Leah's house. As they neared the village, a man was standing at the edge of the village giving Leah and Jon a very nasty stare. "Who is that nice lookin' fella?" asked Jon. The dog let out a low growl.

"That is Sam Blackhorse," said Leah. "He thinks that I should be his. He knows I don't want him, but he is convinced that once we are together, I will learn to love him."

"Why don't you introduce me, Leah?" said Jon. "That way he'll at least know my name." They dismounted and walked over to Sam.

"Sam Blackhorse, this is Jon O'Brien," said Leah. "He has come here to court me."

Jon extended his hand, but Sam would not shake hands with him. "Leah was meant for me," Sam said. "You will see. She will be mine in the end."

"Pleased to meet you too," said Jon. "I believe the choice will be hers, not yours." Sam didn't say another word. He just let out some sort of groan and walked off.

"We need to watch out for him," Leah said. "I think he is a little crazy."

"Well, Leah, you are very beautiful," said Jon. "That could make many a man a little crazy." Leah didn't expect to hear that, but she liked hearing it. No one had ever told her that she was beautiful.

She invited Jon for supper that evening. He found out right away that Leah was a very good cook. After the meal, her father invited Jon to spend the night in their house, but Jon declined. He told him that it didn't seem proper, and he would fend for himself. When it was time to leave, Leah and he went outside, and Jon pulled her to him and kissed her. Not long and hard, but long enough so she knew she had been kissed. He could feel her body responding to his. "I'll be back in the morning," said Jon. "Don't wanna waste any time."

"Goodnight," said Leah. "I will lie awake and count the hours till we are together again."

~~~~

That night, Jon camped about a mile from Leah's house. He built a small shelter to keep off any wind and had plenty of good blankets. It was early December, but it was not cold yet. He picked a spot that gave him a good view of everything, just in case ole Sam Blackhorse tried something. He figured Dog would wake him too.

It took Jon a good while to get to sleep. Thoughts of Leah kept him awake. When he did fall asleep, he slept as he hadn't slept in a long time. The warmth of the morning sun woke him, that and Dog letting out a low growl. Jon had his Henry next to him, and he sat up with it laying across his lap. Dog kept growling, and Jon spotted movement about a hundred yards away from the direction Dog was looking. It was Sam Blackhorse. He was just standing there beside a tree staring at Jon. "You want some coffee?" yelled Jon. "I'm getting' ready to make some." Sam just stood there. Jon could tell that he was carrying a '63 springfield rifle. He'd seen enough of those during the war. "You sure you don't want some coffee?" asked Jon. "Be done in no time. I don't mind sharin'."

Blackhorse stared even harder at Jon, and Jon thought for sure he was going to take a shot at him. Jon chambered a round on the Henry. When Blackhorse heard Jon work the lever on the Henry, he ran off. "That's good," Jon said to himself. "I didn't wanna kill him today anyway."

After breakfast, Jon went straight to Leah's house. He didn't see Blackhorse on the way there. Leah heard him coming and ran out to meet him. She wanted a hug and a kiss, and Jon was happy to oblige her. "How did you sleep?" she asked Jon.

"After my thoughts of nothing but you slowed down," started Jon, "I slept like a baby."

"I did not sleep much," said Leah, "but I am not tired at all. Thoughts of you kept me awake most of the night."

"Sam Blackhorse paid me a visit this morning," said Jon. "He had a rifle with him, but he stayed a ways off and just stared at me. I invited him for coffee, but he wouldn't come over. I thought he was gonna take a shot at me. When I chambered a round in my rifle, he ran off."

"I told you I thought he was a little crazy," said Leah. "I will tell my father, and he can tell the tribal police."

"There's no law against staring at a man," said Jon. "We can't arrest him for that, but we will keep a watch for him. Dog here is very good. I think he don't like folks that don't like me."

"Why don't you give that dog a name?" asked Leah.

"I been callin' him Dog, and that's what he answers to," said Jon. "Dog is his name."

"All right," said Leah, "I'll call him Dog too. Now I'm going to pack us some food, and we'll take a ride, and stop at a nice place for a meal. I know a very good spot."

Leah packed the food and they took off on the horses at a nice slow walk. Three hours later, they came to the spot she wanted. It was beside a small stream. There was a deep pool in the stream, and the bank of the stream was lined with big sycamore trees. It was beautiful. There was no wind, and the sun was shining brightly. It was too warm to be early December. Jon unsaddled the horses and tied them off. Leah laid out a blanket and the food. She gave Dog an old ham bone and he laid by the blanket chewing on it.

"I need to bathe," said Leah. "I want you to bathe with me."

"Are you sure this is what you want?" asked Jon.

~~~~

"Yes, this is what I want," said Leah as she undressed and went to the water. Jon laid his rifle beside the water, and then undressed and went to Leah. Neither one of them noticed the water temperature as they wrapped themselves together. After what seemed like hours, they came out of the water and got dressed. Jon helped her get dressed and was kissing every part of her body as he was helping her. "Hurry," said Leah, "I am starting to get cold now." Jon did as instructed, and then Leah laid out the meal. "You know I'll have to marry you now," she said as they started eating.

"Well when we get back, we'll talk to your father," said Jon. "I know he'll be happy for us. You do understand about what I am don't you.?"

"Yes, I do," said Leah. "You are a lawman. What you do is dangerous, and you can be gone for long periods at times. Did I leave anything out?"

"No, that about covers everything," said Jon. "Let's eat and get back."

~~~~

When they got back, Jon went straight to Leah's father and asked for her hand. He was happy for them. "We can have the ceremony as early as tomorrow," he said. "You can use this house as your bridal chamber. I will stay at my brother's house for a while so you two can have time alone. As an elder, I will do the ceremony myself. Now I must go and tell everyone the news. They will want to come to the wedding. That is everyone except Sam Blackhorse."

~~~~

The next day there was a feast and some dancing, and then they had the ceremony. When it was over, Jon picked up Leah and carried her into the house. Dog laid by the door. They were not seen for two days. On the third day, they let Dog into the house. Jon told him he had to sleep by the door and he obeyed. On the fourth night, after they had made love and were in each other's arms, Dog started a low growl. Jon heard someone outside. "Get over behind the stove," he told Leah as he rolled out of bed and grabbed his Colt. He had been keeping it right beside the bed. Slowly he cocked the hammer so it wouldn't make any noise. Jon stayed low beside the bed.

The door burst open, and a man came charging in and he fired two shots from a double barreled shotgun into the bed. "If I can't have you, no one else will have you," he yelled as he stood there. It was Sam Blackhorse. Dog was on him as soon as he finished talking. Dog had him by his right arm and was dragging him around the floor. Jon went over and struck him in the head with the butt of his pistol. When he quit moving, Dog let go.

When the shots were fired, the village came alive. Leah's father was the first to get there. He knew what had happened when he saw Blackhorse laying on the floor. "I never thought he would go that far," he said. "I will get the police. If the elders don't hang him, I will kill him myself."

The police and the elders were there in no time. They did not waste any time. They woke Blackhorse and took him out and hanged him. No questions were asked, and Sam didn't say one word before he was hanged.

"I guess that's what you call swift justice," said Jon.

"Sometimes it's the best," said Leah's father. "When there is no doubt about guilt, why waste time?"

After a week of what Jon thought was pure heaven, he told Leah that he was supposed to be in Abilene by Christmas. "That is all right," said Leah. "We are not Christians here so we don't celebrate like the white people do. There is a small town to the north that borders our land. It is only a half day's ride. They have a telegraph there. Maybe you can go there and telegraph your boss. Maybe he will not need you for a while, and you can stay here. But if he needs you, I will be here when you get back."

"You are a good woman, Leah," said Jon. "In two more days I'll go there and send a telegram to Sean."

Jon went to the small town in two days as planned and sent the following telegram to Sean.

Marshal Sean O'Rourke Abilene

Got married <stop> do you need me by Christmas <stop> will wait for reply <stop> village half day ride from telegraph <stop>

O'Brien

~~~~

Jon told the operator that he was a Federal Deputy and would stay in town waiting for a reply. He told the operator to find him when it came in. Then Jon went exploring the town. It was small, but they had a General Store, a saloon of course, a livery, and a few other shops. Jon went to the saloon first. It was a small place, only three tables, and a bar that was just a big board across a couple of wooden crates. The place was empty when Jon walked in. The bartender was an older, tall man with a short beard and bushy eyebrows. "I only got whiskey," he said to Jon. "Beer ran out last week."

"Whiskey it is," said Jon. "It's not somethin' you made, is it?"

"No," the bartender answered. "This stuff is good sour mash from Tennessee. I see that badge. What are you doin' here? Is there somthin' I need to know about?"

"No," said Jon. "I'm just here usin' the telegraph. That is good whiskey, believe I'll have another."

"Are you one a them deputies for that O'Rourke fella everyone talks about?" the bartender asked.

"Yes I am," answered Jon. "Why do you ask?"

"Well about a week ago, a bunch of hard lookin' riders came through here," he said. "They weren't none too friendly. When they found out there weren't any workin' girls here, they left, but they shot up the place a bit first. You can see some of the bullet holes."

"So you don't know who they were, or you didn't hear any names mentioned, did you?" asked Jon.

"I did hear one of them say somethin' about that Marshal a yours killin' Jack Snow sometime back," the bartender said. "I heard a Jack Snow. He's a hired killer."

"I know about Jack Snow," said Jon. "I was on a cattle drive when that happened. So which way did they go when they left and how many of them was there?"

"They headed northwest, and there was eight of 'em," the bartender answered. Just as he finished talking, the telegraph operator came into the saloon and handed Jon a telegram. It went as follows:

O'Brien

Stay with new wife <stop> you are not needed now <stop> Jim killed by Ethan Hawk's son <stop> son is dead <stop> Michael shot in leg but all right <stop> quiet here now <stop> check telegraph weekly in case I need you <stop> congratulations <stop>

O'Rourke

Jon went back to the telegraph office and sent the following:

Marshal O'Rourke Abilene

Thanks <stop> will check weekly <stop> eight riders through here week ago headed northwest <stop> no idea who they were <stop>

O'Brien

As soon as Jon was sure the telegram was sent, he mounted his horse and headed back to Leah. On the way back, he thought about Jim and wondered how many more Hawks there were.

CHAPTER FIFTEEN

Things were pretty quiet in Abilene after Jim was killed. Michael's leg was healing well, and the other men had gotten the ice house finished. Sean had given Jim's Henry and pistol to Charlie, and whenever they had some spare time, Sean worked with Charlie on his pistol shooting. Charlie was not fast, but he could now hit a man sized target dead center at over fifty yards, and did well while firing on horseback. "Don't go gettin' yourself killed on me, and I'll get you a new pistol, one of those new conversions like I got," said Sean.

~~~~

When Sean read the last telegram from Jon, he realized that if those eight riders were headed northwest a week ago, they could be in town any day now. That is, if they were actually headed to Abilene. "Jon wouldn't have mentioned this at all unless they were a rough lookin' bunch," Sean said to himself. "I best let the men know to keep an eye open. Course eight riders comin' in would be hard to miss. Maybe they won't come in all together. Maybe they'll be two or three at a time. Maybe they're not comin' here at all. Maybe I'm worryin' too much, maybe not. Think I'll tell some of the businesses to keep an eye open too."

Sean went back to the saloon after reading the telegram. Michael and Maggie were at a table sipping coffee. "I need to find Bob and Charlie, are they out back?" Sean asked them.

"They were out there cutting some boards a little while ago," answered Maggie.

"Thanks," said Sean. "You two stay here while I go round them up. We need to have a little talk." Sean went out back and asked Bob and Charlie to come to the saloon. When everyone was there, Sean got everyone some coffee, and then began.

"In Jon's telegram, he said there were eight riders headed northwest from where he was. This was a week ago. I don't think Jon would have said anything unless there was cause for some concern," Sean said. "If those eight were comin' here, they could be here any day. I don't mean to sound jumpy, but we all should be on the lookout. Maybe they won't come here at all, but let's be ready just in case. Soon as we're done here, I'm goin' to some of the businesses and ask them to let me know if they see any strangers in town. More eyes can't hurt."

"I sure hope they're not headed this way," said Maggie. "There's been enough killing. Maybe they are just a bunch of boys looking for work."

"Just make sure you got that pistol on you," said Sean as he headed out the saloon doors.

The first place Sean visited was the leather goods store. Jason was in the back room, so Sean knocked on the door frame to let him know someone was there. "Hey, Marshal," Jason began, "what can I do for you today?"

"Just need a favor," said Sean. "My deputy was down in Cherokee Territory, and he sent me a telegram that there could be eight riders headed this way. If those eight are comin' here, they could be here any day. I would just like for you to let me know if you see any strangers in town. Don't know for sure if those eight are up to somethin' or even comin' here, but the way things have been around here, I need to be ready."

"Sure Sean," said Jason. "I'll keep my eyes open, and if you need my help, I'll be there."

"Thanks Jason," replied Sean. "I hope it don't come to that. Take care now."

Sean went to the barber shop next. The barber didn't have any customers and was setting in the barber chair reading a newspaper that looked very old. "What do you need today?" he asked Sean.

"I just want you to let me know if you notice any strangers in town," said Sean. "Especially if they are in groups."

"You're not figurin' on givin' me some more business, are you?" he asked Sean.

"I hope not," answered Sean, "but it could happen. My deputy told me there were eight riders headed this way and they could be here any day. Just let me know if you see anything, all right."

"I sure will, Marshal," he said. "I better enjoy the extra business while I can. Soon as that railroad gets here, some regular undertaker fella'll probably come here and set up a business."

"Probly will," said Sean. "If I was you, I'd make your bathhouse bigger and get a partner and another chair. Some of those Texas boys will want to clean up before they visit the ladies."

"Already thought of that," the barber said. "Just waitin' to make sure the railroad is comin' before I spend a dollar on things."

"Wise choice," said Sean. "See you later."

~~~~

Sean went to the bank next. The banker was concerned that maybe the bank would be robbed, but Sean told him that was unlikely. "If these men do come to town, chances are, they are after that bounty that Anderson put on me," said Sean. "That bounty might be more than what you have in your bank."

"You may be right about that," said the banker. "You're my biggest account here, especially since you started that buryin' fund. I'll let you know if I notice anything, Marshal. Take care of yourself."

~~~~

Next stop was the General Store. The owner and his wife assured Sean that they would let him know of any strangers they saw. Sean also asked them to put any ammunition they had in stock, somewhere where it wasn't easy to find. The store did not have any repeating rifles or pistols in stock, so Sean didn't have to worry about that.

~~~~

Billy was at the livery when Sean arrived there. His two dogs were moving some horses over to another corral. "Billy," said Sean, "if you're not careful, they'll be cuttin' your pay in half and givin' the other half to them dogs."

"They're good dogs," said Billy. "I named them Suzie and Sam. The way they been actin' lately, I'd say Suzie'll be havin' pups afore too long."

"Well if the pups take after their folks and can move stock like their folks, maybe you can start a business. I'd say some folks'd pay good money for a good cow dog, or a dog that can move horses like these two," said Sean. "Now is that blacksmith here today?"

"He's out back takin' inventory on his steel," said Billy. "He said it was time to get some ordered."

"Well come with me," said Sean. "I want to tell you and him at the same time."

They went out back, and the blacksmith was there mumbling to himself.

"What can I do for you today, Marshal?" the blacksmith asked.

"I just want you to let me know of any strangers in town," said Sean. "Could be eight riders here any day now. Don't know for sure if they're comin' here or not, or if they're up to somethin', or not. I just wanna be ready after all that's been goin' on here. I'd appreciate any set of eyes I can get."

"Sure thing Marshal," the blacksmith said. "If they want their horses took care of, they'll come here. Me and Billy'll let you know."

~~~~

Sean went back to the saloon after he finished talking to the businesses. Michael was still at the same table. There was a bottle with two glasses there and both glasses were empty. As Sean neared the table, Michael spoke. "I think it's time we had another toast, my friend," said Michael. "I think it's a little over due."

"I was gonna say the same thing," said Sean as he took the bottle and filled the glasses. "Here's to not getting killed."

"Here's to not getting killed," repeated Michael. When they finished their glasses, Michael grabbed the bottle and refilled them. "Here's to Jim, a good man, may he rest in peace."

"May he rest in peace," repeated Sean. "Jim, we're sorry we didn't toast to you sooner. We'll talk again when we get this mess cleaned up."

~~~~

No strangers showed up in town the next morning, so about noon, Sean decided he would take Charlie and check out the Hawk place. They did not see any fresh tracks on the way there, but when they got closer they could see some horses in the corral, and smoke was coming from a chimney on one of the small houses. There was not much cover, but Sean and Charlie moved behind a low rise and tied the horses to some brush and crawled to the top. Sean took his spyglass and began his search of the place, being careful not to let the sun glare off the glass. There were eight horses in the corral, but no men had been spotted yet. After maybe a half hour, one man came out of the house with the smoking chimney and went to an outhouse. "That fella's not out here for a picnic," said Sean. "He's wearin' two pistols, and he's got two bandoliers of ammunition on him. A few minutes later, another man came out of the same house and headed to the corral. He only had on one pistol, but he also had two bandoliers of ammunition. He took one of the horses, tied him, and began brushing him down. Two more men came out of the same house and sat down on the front porch and passed a bottle of whiskey back and forth. One of them had two pistols, and the other one had two pistols and a sawed off shotgun strapped across his back. No more men were spotted. "Charlie," said Sean, "if the other four are armed like the first four, they're packin' some firepower. I'm gonna stay here and watch for a while. You head back to town and tell the boys what we've seen here. Tell them to stay there, and I'll be back directly. Tell them to be ready for anything."

Charlie hadn't been gone for more than a few minutes when the rest of the men were spotted. They were all heavily armed. All eight of them were enjoying some whiskey now and showed no sign of going anywhere for the time being. Sean watched them till almost dark, then decided to get back to town. When he got back to town, his deputies were waiting in front of Maggie's Place.

"What do you think they're up to?" asked Michael. "If they're armed as well as Charlie said, they mean business."

"They surely do," said Sean. "I'm figurin' that they're after that bounty. Two thousand split eight ways is still a good bit a money for one man. Maybe they're thinkin' that some of them will get themself killed and make the shares bigger. Anyway, we don't want eight men comin' to town with all that firepower. We don't want no bystanders killed."

"So you got a plan?" asked Bob.

"Yep," started Sean, "we're gonna go out there and surround them and ask them to surrender."

"Let's see," said Charlie. "There's eight of them and four of us, and we're gonna surround them. That's what I call ambitious thinkin'."

"Just kiddin', Charlie," said Sean. "Here's what we're gonna do. We're gonna slip out there well before daylight. I'm gonna borrow them two dogs we give young Billy, and with Jeb here, we're gonna run off their horses. They will probably have a man on watch. I'll knock him out and pin a note on him. Hopefully, we can do this on the quiet. Then we'll see how they act when they find their man with the note on him. We got a half moon tonight so we'll be able to see good, but so will they. While I'm there, I'll see if I can figure out which house or houses these men are in. Shouldn't be hard. It's cold enough for them to have a fire in the stoves or fireplaces. Now we'll take turns standin' watch here in town. We don't want them slippin' in on us. The rest can get some rest. I'm gonna go see Billy about them dogs. Charlie you take first watch. Go two hours, then Bob, then Michael. I'll go last."

Billy was still at the livery and was glad to let Sean borrow the dogs. "Remember, she's Suzie and he's Sam," said Billy. "Please don't let nothin' bad happen to them."

"I'll make sure nothin' bad happens to them," said Sean. "Leave em tied up here somewhere, and I'll be gettin' them a couple hours before daylight. They'll probably be glad to see Jeb too. I'll get 'em some scraps from Cookie when we get back too."

Sean knew he had better talk with Maggie and let her know what was going on. When he got to the saloon, there weren't many customers, so Sean took Maggie by the hand and led her upstairs to their room. "Maggie darlin'," Sean began, "I've gotta go out early mornin'. There's eight heavily armed men out at the Hawk place. Gotta find out what they're up to. Better to tangle with 'em out there than in town where innocent folk could get hurt."

"You know what they're after," replied Maggie. "It's gotta be that bounty money Anderson has on you. Wasn't it supposed to go up a hundred a month till you're dead?"

"Yes, darlin', it goes up a hundred a month till I'm dead," said Sean. "Now I want you to make sure you keep your pistol on you, and I'm gonna give you my pistol that I put in my shoulder holster. You figure out a way to hide them, or strap on a holster."

"I know how to hide a gun," said Maggie. "Two will be no problem. Now you help me get undressed. I need you now."

"It's nice to be needed. I need you too," Sean said as he helped Maggie undress.

~~~~

When they were finished, Sean pulled Maggie to him again, kissed her passionately, and got out of bed. "I'm gonna stay up all night, darlin'," said Sean. "I got the men taking turns on watch, but I'll feel better if I'm watching too. We'll be leaving a couple hours before daylight. I'll feel even better if you stay awake while we're gone. I don't want one of them slippin' in on you while we're gone. They might wanna grab you to get at me."

"Sounds like you love me, darlin'," said Maggie. "I'll go ahead and sleep now, and you can wake me when you're ready to leave."

"I do love you, Maggie darlin'," said Sean. "And I'll wake you when we're ready to leave. See you in a few hours."

Sean went downstairs to the saloon. Michael and Bob were setting at a table drinking coffee. "Come over and join us," said Bob. "I need to tell you somethin' anyway."

"I'll get some coffee and join you," said Sean as he headed to the kitchen. He came to the table with a full pot, refilled the men's cups, filled his own, and sat down. "Not a good night for whiskey, is it?" said Sean.

"No, it isn't," said Bob. "I don't like drinkin' when I know there's gonna be some gunplay. And sure as hell, there's gonna be some."

"I hope you're wrong, but I know you're not," said Sean. "Now what did you need to tell me?"

"Well," started Bob, "I got no kin, and there's all that money in that bank at Kansas City. If somethin' was to happen to me, I want you to take care of that money. There's two accounts. One's mine, and the other is in my name, but it's for the kin of those brands we drove. I already sent a telegram to that banker."

"Well first off, Bob," started Sean, "nothin's gonna happen to you. Don't even think that. I won't allow it. Second, that dog a yours won't let nothin' happen to you either. Now if you get throwed from a horse and die, or somethin' like that, I'll look after that money for you. You will not get yourself killed in the line a duty. That's an order."

"All right boss, I'll just hafta stay alive," said Bob. "Wouldn't wanna go against orders."

Michael never said a word when the other two were talking. When they finished, he spoke. "Sean darlin', do you think someone should stay here and look out for Maggie?" he asked.

"I thought about that," said Sean, "but we got someone on watch now, and when we leave, we'll fan out some so no one can get past us. Maggie'll be awake when we leave, and she'll be packin' two pistols. She's smart. If someone would get around us, I have faith that Maggie can take care of them. She's a strong woman."

~~~~

Nothing happened during the night, and it came time for them to go. Sean woke Maggie. "Remember what I said now," said Sean. "You keep them two pistols on you. It wouldn't hurt if a shotgun was close too. And you got those shotguns behind the bar."

"Don't you worry, lover," replied Maggie. "I have no intention of letting myself be taken or killed. You hurry up and get back to me. I'll be missing you while you're gone." Sean pulled her to him and kissed her hard.

"If you weren't my woman, I'd make you a deputy," said Sean.

"You just make sure you get back to me," said Maggie. "Now get going."

~~~~

When Sean got downstairs, the men were already mounted and ready to go. "Everyone got plenty of water and ammunition?" asked Sean.

"We got enough ammunition to wipe out two divisions," said Michael. "Let's get it done."

"All right, let's fan out good," said Sean. "I don't want anyone gettin' around us. When we get closer, we'll get back together. Then I'll slip in with the dogs, take care of any guards, and run off the horses. I'll find out which houses they're in, then I'll come back to you."

With the half moon that night, they were able to see good. When they were about five hundred yards from the Hawk place, they could see smoke coming from the chimneys of two of the small houses. One man was outside on guard. He gave himself away when he lit a cigar. Sean took them behind the low rise that he used when he and Charlie first spotted the eight horses in the corral. "You all just stay here till I get back," said Sean. "Me and the dogs'll be back shortly."

Sean moved like a cat and got up to the corral without being seen. He opened the gate to the corral, and then spoke to Jeb. "All right boy, you go in there and get those horses back to the others," said Sean. "Don't make no noise." Jeb did as instructed. He and Sam and Suzie moved the horses like they were going to a church social. They were just as calm as could be. Sean got behind the shelter and watched. There were only six horses. "Where's the other two?" he asked himself. "Did they get around us?" About that time, the guard heard the horses moving and came to see what was going on. Sean stood behind the shelter to the corral and waited. When the man got closer, he sprang out and hit the man in the head with the butt of one of his pistols, knocking him out. Then he drug him to the porch of one of the houses where the men appeared to be staying, and pinned a note to his chest. He had written the note in town before they had left. The note read: "This is Marshal O'Rourke, you are surrounded. We have your horses. Throw out your guns and state your business here. You have till a half hour after daylight. If we don't see guns on the ground, we'll send you straight to hell. Those houses should burn pretty good."

Sean worked his way back to the others. The dogs had done their job, and the men had the horses all hobbled. "Those are the best dogs I ever saw," said Sean. "It's just amazin' to watch them work. Got a problem though. You know what it is. Two horses are missin'. They got around us somehow."

"Don't worry, Sean darlin'," said Michael. "Maggie can take care of herself. I wouldn't want to be the one or two tryin' to get her."

"Thanks, friend," said Sean. "I'm still gonna worry."

"So what's the plan now?" asked Michael.

"I put a note on the guard I knocked out sayin' they was sur-rounded," started Sean. "I said they had till a half hour after day-light to throw out their guns or we'd send them to hell. Oh yeh, I also said those houses should burn pretty good."

"Sounds like a good note," said Michael. "What if none of them can read?"

"I'll volunteer to read it for them," said Sean. "Now let's slip up and take positions around the two houses they're stayin' in. It'll be daylight in bout an hour. Let's close in and wait. Just one thing men, I would like to take one of them alive if possible."

The two houses were next to each other and the men took positions around them as best they could and waited. Jeb stayed with Bob and Suzie and Sam were with Sean. Daylight would come in a half hour.

Right at daylight, a man came out of the house where Sean had dragged the man who was on guard. He came out the door yawning, then rubbed his eyes and tripped over the man. "What in the hell?" he said as he fell. After he got his senses back, he noticed the note on the man's chest. The man with the note on his chest was starting to come to. "Zeke, you better get out here," the man who tripped over the unconscious man yelled. "Some-thin's not right. There's a note pinned to Bill here. You better get out here."

"All right, all right," Zeke replied, "comin' out now." Zeke came out the door still half asleep, and yawning when he saw the note. "What in the hell? This damn thing says we're surrounded and the horses are gone. We got a half hour after daylight to throw down our guns or we're goin' to hell. Son of a bitch, git yer guns boys and get ready. We got company."

As soon as he finished talking, Sean fired his Henry. Zeke was hit dead center in the chest, dead before he hit the ground. When Sean fired, the rest of the outlaws woke up and scrambled for their guns. Two more of them ran out the door of the house to see what was going on. Bob, Michael, and Charlie fired as they came out. Two more men fell dead.

The man who had been the guard, was trying to get himself up and get out of the field of fire. "Stay where you are, or we'll kill you," yelled Sean. The man didn't pay attention to Sean and tried to get inside the house. He was cut down before he got to the door. The man who had tripped over him had got back inside and was now firing as fast as he could. "He's got a Henry," said Sean. "Stay low and let him waste ammunition. Now where is that last fella?" Sean didn't need to wait long to find out. Shots started coming from the other house. Sean and the men then let loose with everything they had. When all the men were reloading, Sean spoke. "Just stay low," Sean yelled, "We'll burn them out shortly if we can't talk them into givin' up. Probably shoulda burned this whole place to the ground when we had that shootout a while back. One hour, and we start burnin'."

One hour later, Sean yelled, "We're burnin' you out. Come out now and we won't kill you."

"We got your woman by now, Marshal," one of the outlaws yelled. "You best back off if you want to see her alive."

"She's already killed your two fellas," said Sean. "You best give up now." Sean had no idea if Maggie was all right or not, but what he said, worked. The two outlaws threw their guns out and surrendered. One of the outlaws was gut shot and could barely stand. He begged Sean to kill him, saying he couldn't take the pain, and he was going to die anyway. "How bout I give you back your pistol with one bullet, and you do it yourself." said Sean.

"All right," the man said, "I'll do it myself." Sean took the man's pistol and made sure there was one shot left in it and handed it to the man. The man took the pistol in his right hand, and raised it up to shoot himself in the head. When the muzzle of the pistol touched the side of his head, he cocked the hammer. He stood there for a moment. It seemed as if he wasn't sure he could do it. He was facing Sean and was looking straight at him. "I can't, I can't," he said and started lowering the pistol towards Sean. Before the pistol was low enough for him to fire, Sean put a bullet in his forehead.

"I believe that's what the man wanted, Sean darlin'," said Michael.

"I believe you're right," said Sean as he approached the other outlaw. "Now who are you? Why are you here? And who's your boss?"

"My name's Fred Brown," the outlaw started. "You done kilt my boss. It was Zeke there. And we was after that bounty money. Anderson's boss put up another two thousand dollars on you."

"What's that you just said?" asked Sean. "Anderson's boss put up another two thousand on me. You mean to tell me Anderson's got a boss."

"That's just what I heard," the man replied. "Zeke there worked for Anderson, and he's the one told us about more money from Anderson's boss. You're worth over $4000 now."

"You wouldn't lie to me would you mister, would you?" asked Sean.

"Why should I lie," he answered. "Yer gonna kill me anyway."

"I oughta kill you, mister," said Sean, "but I think I'll let you live so you can go back and tell Anderson what happened here. You know where Anderson is, don't you?"

"I know where he was headed," the man said. "I reckon I can find him."

"Is he in Mexico?" asked Sean.

"He was, but it was gettin' too tough down there with those Frenchmen and the Mexicans fightin' all over the place," he answered. "So he came back to Texas. I heard a rumor he was thinkin' bout ranchin'."

"Do you know the names of those other two that went after the woman?" Sean asked.

"Not their real names. One calls himself Cracker, and the other calls himself Froggy," he answered. "They're not too smart, but they shoot good."

"Well Fred Brown, if Maggie hasn't killed Cracker and Froggy by now, I'll be killin' em shortly," said Sean. "Now I'm gonna give you back your pistol and a horse, and you're gonna get outta here and get down to Texas. If I see you even touchin' that pistol before you get outta sight, I'll get out my Sharps and blow you outta the saddle. Is that clear, Fred?"

"Clear as a bell," replied Fred. "I'll be sure to get to Anderson." Fred mounted the horse, gave him a kick, and took off. Sean watched him till he was out of sight.

"Bob, you and Charlie gather up all their guns and belongings, and strap the bodies and stuff to their horses, then head to town. Me and Michael are headin' back right now."

"All right," said Bob, "we'll be in shortly."

~~~~

Michael and Sean had ridden for just a few minutes when Michael spoke. "Do you really think Anderson's got a boss?" Michael asked.

"I can't think about that right now," Sean said. "Gotta get back and make sure Maggie's all right. We'll talk about Anderson later."

~~~~

After Sean had left, Maggie got up and put on a big warm robe. It was thick and had very big pockets on each side. The pockets were perfect for keeping pistols hidden. A person would have to look very hard to see if anything was in the pockets. She placed a pistol in each pocket and went downstairs and made some coffee. When it was done, she sat at the table that Sean always used so he could see everything going on and no one could get behind him. She sat there thinking about Sean and hoped he and the others would be all right. Right about daylight, she could hear a couple of people walking on the sidewalk towards the saloon. When the walkers stopped right in front of the saloon doors, Maggie slipped over behind the bar. She stood at one end, with her hands in her pockets, and the shotgun in front of her. Since it was almost winter, and getting colder, the main big doors were closed, but were not locked. She cocked the hammers on the pistols.

The doors opened and two dirty looking men walked in. "I told ya she was a looker," said the one called Cracker. "I sure do hope we don't gotta kill her later. I wanna get me some a that."

"Me too," said Froggy, "she surely is a looker. Yer a goin' with us now missy." Cracker and Froggy both drew their pistols. "You step out from behind that bar now and get over here. We gotta be movin'."

Maggie could see that Froggy and Cracker did not have their hammers cocked. She kept her hands in her pockets, and when she cleared the end of the bar, she pulled both pistols. She could see a look of amazement on both of them as she squeezed both triggers. That look was still on their faces as the bullets struck them in the forehead. They hit the floor dead.

Maggie then went back to drinking her coffee. She heard someone running on the sidewalk toward the saloon. Jason from the leather goods store came rushing in. "What happened? Are you all right? Are there any more of them?" he asked.

"I'm all right," Maggie answered, "but they're not. They wanted to take me to get to Sean. They won't be taking anybody ever again."

"Do you want me to get them bodies out of here?" asked Jason.

"Just leave them for now," answered Maggie. "Sean'll need to see them before they get moved. He and the boys'll be back shortly."

"All right, Maggie," said Jason. "If you need anything, anything at all, just yell."

"Thank you, Jason," said Maggie. "You're a perfect gentleman."

"Well I don't know about perfect, but I try to be a gentleman," said Jason.

"Your wife is a lucky woman Jason. I hope she knows that," said Maggie.

"Thank you Maggie. Sean's got himself one hell of a woman in you," said Jason. "I'll be sure to tell him when I see him again. Now I'll be off."

Maggie was still drinking coffee when Cookie showed up. "How about some breakfast?" said Cookie. "Looks like you been busy."

"I am kinda hungry," said Maggie. "I'll have some of whatever you're making today."

"How bout some flapjacks and eggs?" said Cookie.

"Sounds good," said Maggie. "I expect the boys'll be back shortly, so you might want to make up some extra batter. I imagine they'll be hungry too."

~~~~

When Maggie finished eating, she made up her mind to give Cookie a raise. Cookie came out of the kitchen to see if she needed anything else, and Maggie asked him to sit down for a minute. "Cookie," she began, "you are the best cook I have ever known. I'm going to give a you a pay raise. How about fifteen more dollars a month?"

"You'll get no argument from me," said Cookie. "I do love being here. I hope it's always that way."

"I hope so too," said Maggie. "I am concerned about what it'll be like when the railroad gets here, and all those Texas boys get here after those long drives. I guess we'll find out when that happens."

"I guess we will, Maggie," said Cookie. "I reckon those boys will be a rowdy bunch. Might have to take their guns from them while they're in here. You're a wise woman, Maggie. You'll know what to do."

~~~~

Maggie had just started on another cup of coffee when Sean and Michael came through the doors. "I see you been busy," said Sean.

"Nothing I couldn't handle," said Maggie. "How was your day?"

"The boys are bringin' in five dead bodies," said Sean. "None of us got hurt. I turned one loose to get back to Anderson and tell him what happened. What's Cookie got for breakfast this mornin'? I'm starvin'."

"Flapjacks and eggs," said Maggie. "I've already had mine. I'll have him make some for you and Michael. I'll bring you two some coffee."

"Thank you, darlin'" said Sean. "The others should be here shortly."

"Well young Sean," said Michael. "Let's get back to that question I asked you earlier. Do you think Anderson does have a boss?"

"I woulda never thought that," said Sean. "Maybe he's not as smart as we think. Maybe someone else is givin' the orders. If we don't find out this winter, we'll find out come spring cause I'm gonna get on his trail and not get off till he's dead. I don't care how far it is or how long it takes. I do know one other thing. When we get a good snow, I'm goin' out to the Hawk place and burn everything to the ground. That way, I won't worry about startin' a prairie fire."

"And why do you want to burn the place?" asked Michael.

"We've had two shootouts out there, and there won't be anymore," answered Sean. "If any Hawks or anyone else shows up, they'll hafta find themselves another place to hole up."

Just as Sean and Michael finished their breakfast, Bob and Charlie arrived. "Come on over and get some breakfast," said

Sean. "Then we'll get rid of them bodies and the rest of the business."

"What happened to these two in here?" asked Charlie.

"Maggie took care of them," answered Sean.

"Good woman," said Charlie, "good woman."

~~~~

After everyone had their breakfast, they took all the bodies over to the barber shop. When they went through their pockets, they found a gold watch and fifty dollars total. They took the horses to the livery to be sold, and Sean took their guns to the General Store. Each of the outlaws had a fairly new Henry rifle, and there was the shotgun, and all the pistols. "The buryin' fund sure is gonna make a lot of money today," Sean said to himself as he headed to the bank. After he deposited the money at the bank, Sean went back to the saloon and got some scraps for Billy's dogs. "Got yourself some good dogs there Billy," said Sean as he gave them the scraps. "I still say you should start a business when them pups come."

"We'll see how many pups she has," said Billy. "If she has a bunch, I'll need to get rid of some of them. My folks'd never let me keep a pack a dogs, no matter how good they were. Thanks fer makin' sure nothin' bad happened to em. If ya need em again, just let me know."

"Sure thing Billy," replied Sean. "See you later."

~~~~

When Sean got back to the saloon, he rounded up Maggie and the men and had them set at their regular table. He went behind the bar and got two bottles and glasses for everyone. "It's time for a toast," said Sean as he filled all the glasses. "Here's to not getting killed." Each of them repeated the toast.

"Now, Maggie darlin'," said Sean. "Would you tell us how you took care of those two men?"

"Sure," began Maggie, "I had a pistol in each pocket. When I heard them coming on the sidewalk, I got behind the bar and cocked the hammers. They came in and pulled their pistols and told me I was going with them. They did not have their hammers cocked. When I saw that, I pulled my pistols and shot them. They had a total look of amazement on their faces even as the bullets hit them."

"Remember that boys," said Sean. "When you pull your pistols, make sure you cock your hammers. When someone pulls on you, remember to see if they cocked their hammers."

~~~~

That night Maggie and Sean made love till they were completely exhausted, and then fell asleep in each other's arms.

CHAPTER SIXTEEN

Three days before Christmas, a huge freight wagon pulled into town and stopped in front of the leather goods store. Sean was in the saloon drinking coffee when he saw the wagon. "I'm goin' over and see what's on that wagon," Sean said to Michael. "That just might be the biggest wagon I ever did see." When Sean got over to the store, Jason and the driver were going over the manifest sheet.

"There's some stuff on this wagon for you," Jason said to Sean. "It's buried some. Should be right under my stuff."

"If it's the stuff I ordered," said Sean, "I'd appreciate it if you let me keep it here for a couple days. That one thing's too big to hide from Maggie."

"What'd you get her that's so big?" asked Jason.

"A bathtub," answered Sean. "I had a friend a mine order me the biggest prettiest tub he could find. And I got the men some new pistols."

"I'm sure she'll like that tub," said Jason. "Any woman would like that."

"Yep, and I'll hafta help her try it out," said Sean.

"You two'll be the best smellin' folks in town," said Jason.

~~~~

Sean helped them unload the wagon, and when they got to the crate that held the tub, Jason and Sean carried it to the back of the store. The shipment from the gunsmith was there too. "I'll help you get the rest of this stuff unloaded, then I wanna open these crates up and make sure everything is all right," said Sean.

After Jason's things were unloaded, the rest of the load was for the General Store. Sean went over there and helped them unload too. After everything was off the wagon, he went back to Jason's store, grabbed a hammer and a crowbar, and opened the two crates. Sean and Jason just stood there and stared when the bathtub was uncrated. "Oh my," started Sean. "Have you ever seen anything like that? There's only one thing in the world more beautiful than that, and that's Maggie."

"You may be right," said Jason. "That's gotta be gold and ivory, and all those designs had to be hand carved. That's definitely big enough for two people."

Sean had never used a good bathtub before. Most bath houses just had some wooden thing that wasn't much more than a big wooden barrel cut in half, and most of the time, the water would leak out before a person could get done. This tub was made out of some type of reddish looking wood. Sean didn't know if it was cherry or oak, but whoever had made it, had it smoothed down and finished to perfection. The top edge was lined with brass, and there were four pieces of brass that went from the top down to the floor for the legs. All over the brass were carvings. Most of them were the shape of naked women. The outside of the tub was white. It had some type of finish to it that Sean had never seen. There were some gold carvings attached to the sides. There were eight of them. Two were eagles in fight, two were of doves, and four of them were of female lions. It was oval shaped, and at the ends, there was an ivory carving of a buffalo. "Someone sure put a hell of a lot of work into this thing," said Sean. "I suppose all these carvings have some kind of meaning. I'm sure Maggie will let me know what they are."

"I'm sure she will," said Jason. "I better not tell my wife about this thing. She'll be wantin' to see and tell the whole town."

"She can see it all she wants," said Sean. "As long as she keeps quiet."

"I doubt if she could keep quiet about something like this," said Jason. "Maybe sometime after you and Maggie get it broke in, she could come over and have a look."

"That'd be just fine," said Sean. "Now I better get this other crate open and make sure everything is there and all right." Everything Sean had ordered was there, the four pistols, and the ammunition. Since Jim had been killed, Sean would give his pistol to Charlie. Jon would not be there for Christmas, so Sean would keep his pistol till they saw each other again. Sean had been sending weekly telegrams to Jon letting him know he was not needed. He did let Jon know about the incident with the eight riders, and thanked him for letting him know about them. He thought that Jon might be upset that he was not there to help out with the eight riders, but Sean tried to assure him that he could not have gotten to Abilene in time to help out.

~~~~

When Sean went back to the saloon, he went straight to Maggie and gave her a big kiss. "Why don't we see if we can find us a

Christmas tree to set up," said Sean. "It's been a lot of years since I've seen one. Gotta be a pine tree somewhere around here."

"I've never set up a tree since I opened the place," said Maggie. "I think it would be nice if we set one up. If we can't find a pine tree, then we'll use something else."

Bob was in the saloon drinking coffee and he heard the conversation. "I think there might be some pine trees just northa here a little ways," Bob said. "If I recollect right, I seen some by a small stream when we took the herd that way. I'll get Charlie, and we'll get us a buckboard and see if we can't get us one."

"Make sure you take your weapons with you," said Sean. "Wouldn't want you two gettin' bushwacked out there. Lotsa folks know that you are my deputy."

"Jeb'll be with us," said Bob. "Anybody gets within a quarter mile a us, and Jeb'll let us know."

~~~~

Bob and Charlie were back in less than three hours. They had a spruce tree that was around eight feet tall. Charlie cut some boards and made a stand for it. They took it inside and put it in one of the front corners. "It's just beautiful," said Maggie. "Now we need to get some decorations for it. I've got some ribbon and things, and I'm sure the girls have a few things. Everyone pitched in and the tree was decorated in no time. "It's too bad that we don't have one of those photographers in town," said Maggie. "We could have a picture with all of us setting in front of the tree. That would be beautiful."

"Maggie, any picture with you in it would be beautiful," said Sean.

"You always have the right thing to say to me, don't you dar-lin'?" said Maggie.

"I try," said Sean. "I surely try. Now I think we should have ourselves a toast. Let's round up the boys, Tom, all the girls, and Cookie. When everyone was there, Sean filled each person's glass with the best bourbon in the house and asked all of them to join him for a toast. "Here's to all of us," he said. "May we always be as happy as we are right now." Everyone repeated his words.

~~~~

Sean felt like a little kid. He just couldn't wait for Christmas to come. He had to figure a way to get the bathtub over to the saloon and keep it hidden from Maggie till Christmas. He decided that he would get the men to carry it to the back room on the morning of Christmas Eve. He would keep Maggie occupied while the men did this. Then on Christmas morning, he would just have Maggie cover her eyes, and he and the men would carry it into the saloon.

~~~~

Christmas morning came, and Sean kept Maggie occupied while the men put the bathtub in the back room. When Maggie and Sean finally came downstairs, everyone was already in the saloon drinking coffee. "Merry Christmas," they all yelled as the two of them came downstairs. Michael, Bob, Charlie, Tom and his wife, Cookie and his wife, and all the girls were there. "Merry Christmas," Maggie and Sean said as they made their way downstairs.

Cookie had made some kind of fancy pastry for the occasion. No one knew what it was called, but it sure was good. For the big feast, he was going to cook a huge ham and all kinds of trimmings. They had several tables pulled together already, and Maggie and Sean sat down next to Michael and Betty. "Merry Christmas, darlin'," Sean said to Maggie, "now cover your eyes. I've got a surprise for you. Maggie covered her eyes as requested, and the men brought the bathtub out to the saloon. "Open your eyes now, darlin'," said Sean.

Maggie opened her eyes, and when she saw the bathtub, she almost cried. "Oh my," she said. "It's beautiful, and it's huge. Never in my wildest dreams could I even imagine something like this. How in the world did you get this? Everything on it looks to be handmade. Oh my, I'm going to cry." Maggie cried for a few minutes, and then said to Sean, "You know you'll have to help me try this thing out."

"I was countin' on that darlin'," replied Sean. "I do think we'll need to build us a bath house out back so we don't need to haul all that water upstairs."

"We can use the ice house till we get one built," said Maggie. "We don't have ice yet anyway. We'll put us a stove in there to heat the water, and we'll be all set. I intend to try it out tonight."

"As you wish, darlin'," said Sean. "Now I've got somethin' for the men. All you deputies get up to the bar." The men went up to the bar as instructed, and Sean went behind the bar and pulled a small wooden crate from behind the bar. He reached into the crate and pulled out a brand new pistol for each of his men. "These are brand new conversions, boys," Sean said. "Got plenty of ammunition too. No more cap and ball for you now." Each man handled his weapon, working the action and such.

"This is great," said Bob. "No more worryin' too much about getting your powder wet. All of us thank you. Now we have somethin' for you."

Maggie walked up to Sean and handed him a folded handkerchief. "Unfold it," said Maggie. "There's something in it for you." Sean unfolded the handkerchief, and he almost cried when he saw what was in it. "It's solid silver," said Maggie. "We had it made up special in St. Louis."

It was a Marshal's badge. "I'll wear it with pride, and I'll do my best to make sure it doesn't get dented or get a hole in it," said Sean. "Thank you all."

They sat around and sang a few Christmas carols that they all knew. Then Cookie said he needed to get started cooking and headed to the kitchen. Sean and the boys took the tub to the ice house and rounded up one of the stoves that wasn't being used and set it up. Sean brought in two water barrels and filled them so they would have water, and also wood and pans to heat the water.

Betty was feeling a little amorous, and she took Michael by the arm and led him back to her place. Martha took Charlie by the arm and led him to a room, and Sally did the same with Bob. Tom was feeling that way too, and he took his wife by the arm, and told Maggie that he'd be back in an hour or so. Maggie didn't want to look, but she was sure she could hear Cookie and his wife having a good time in the kitchen. As soon as Sean got done with his chores, she took him upstairs too.

~~~~

Cookie's Christmas feast was spectacular. Everyone stuffed themselves till they thought they wouldn't be able to move. After everyone had finished, Sean asked everyone to raise their glasses, and then he wished everyone a very Merry Christmas. "Now if you all will excuse me," he said. "I'm goin' out and get a fire started so this gorgeous woman of mine and I can try out that beautiful bathtub."

Sean had a good fire going and the water was heated in no time. When Maggie first got down into the tub, she was silent for a moment, then she spoke. "If heaven feels like this, I guess I wouldn't mind going," she said. "We didn't have anything like this back in New Orleans. Now get in here with me," she told Sean.

Sean didn't need any coaxing. "This is amazing," he said. "We might be in here for hours. I got plenty more water to heat up when this cools down. Now, darlin', I'm gonna scrub you all over, and I expect you to do the same to me."

"It'll be a pleasure, lover," said Maggie. "This could take hours."

They were right. It did take hours. When they finally got upstairs to their room, they were almost completely exhausted. "I can't wait to take another bath," said Maggie as she was falling asleep. They fell asleep in each other's arms and did not wake till late the next morning. When they both went downstairs the next morning, Michael was at their usual table with coffee and cups ready for them. "Nice day we had yesterday," said Michael. "It's been a long time since I've even thought about Christmas. I hope we see many more."

"We will, Michael," said Sean. "We will. Now I think I'm gonna do absolutely nothin' today. I need to get my strength back after yesterday."

"Go ahead and get your rest," said Maggie. "I might feel the need to bath every day now since we have that beautiful new bathtub. I will need you to help me stay clean."

"Glad to, darlin'," said Sean. "Glad to."

~~~~

A few days after Christmas, several loads of lumber arrived, and the men got busy working on the bathhouse, and the changes and additions to the saloon. It was almost New Year's, and it was still not very cold, so the men did not mind the outside work. They had the bathhouse finished in two days. If the lumber kept arriving as expected, all the additions and changes would be done by spring. On January 3rd, it started snowing. It snowed for two days, but it was a wet snow and wouldn't be around long.

The day after it quit snowing, Sean got a buckboard, loaded up a bunch of kerosene, and took Bob and Charlie with him out to the Hawk place. They drenched every house, building, and shelter as best they could, and started burning. When the buildings were burning good, they took the wood from the corral fences and burned it too. They stayed and watched till everything was destroyed. "Like I said before," said Sean. "There's been two shootouts out here already. There won't be another. I actually did some checkin', and those Hawks really didn't own this land. They were just here on it, and no one would say different. Now let's go home."

~~~~

The winter of 1865 – 1866 was not a bad winter. There were times when it was extremely cold, and there was some snow; but overall, it was tolerable. Sean sent telegrams to Judge Simmons from time to time just to make sure nothing required his immediate attention. He also told the Judge that come spring, he would be going to Texas for George Anderson, and he wasn't going to stop till Anderson was dead.

CHAPTER SEVENTEEN

When George Anderson left Texas for Mexico in the fall, he had every intention of spending the winter down there. But when he crossed the border into Mexico, he found that it was very different than it was the year before. There was constant fighting between the Mexicans and the French. Several times, he almost got himself shot because each side accused him of helping the other side. He finally decided enough was enough and went back to Texas. He met a beautiful whore while he was in Mexico. She begged him to take her with him. The Mexicans hated her, not because she was a whore, but because she had been with French officers. Her name was Lolita Gomez. She did not love Anderson, but she pleased him, so he brought her to Texas with him. When he got back to Texas, he decided to quit wearing the Confederate jacket and hat and shove the saber into the scabbard on his saddle.

All the way down through Texas on his way to Mexico, he noticed that there were thousands and thousands of longhorns everywhere. George knew that sooner or later, Abilene would be a cow town. If not Abilene, then another town in Kansas. Cattle were free for the taking, and if you could get them to market, the slaughter houses in Chicago were paying premium prices. In the meantime, if he had the cattle, he could most likely get contracts to supply beef for the army posts in Texas and western Kansas. Anderson made up his mind right then that he was going into the ranching business. All he needed was a ranch and several good men. He also started going by a different name. He was now Thomas Sanderson.

Finding a ranch after the war was not a problem. They were everywhere. The war bankrupted most of them, and most of the men had run off to fight and gotten themselves killed. George settled on a place just three days ride west of Ft. Worth. Carpet baggers were selling it for back taxes, and George bought it. Finding men was no problem, but he needed men who were not afraid to use their guns, either against Indians or rustlers. His ranch bordered the Comanche to the west and the Kiowa to the north. He finally settled on twenty men. Not one of these men knew who he really was. He interviewed each man personally, and the man who knew the most about cattle, he made foreman. His name was Jug Carter. George took the men out to the ranch, showed them what he wanted done, and then he and Lolita took off for some army posts hoping to get contracts. Jug was told that after things were readied at the ranch, he was to take the men and start rounding up cattle. The brand would be a simple TS. George told him that two thousand head would be a good start. George also gave Jug some money and told him to get a cook hired and get him some supplies.

It didn't take long to get the cattle rounded up as they were everywhere. Some were wild, and some had gone wild after not being attended to during the war. None of them were branded. Jug hired a good cook too, and it wasn't long for the men to start getting excited about what he was going to fix next. "He's a better cook than any woman in my family," Jug said.

Five days later, Lolita and George came back to the ranch. George had gotten contracts for every army post in central Texas and western Kansas. He didn't even need to visit most of them. The army was so glad that someone could get them their beef, that after the first few posts, telegrams were just sent to the others. The army didn't pay as well as the slaughter houses in Chicago, but Anderson was on his way to being a rich, legitimate cattle rancher.

Jug was a good foremen and knew how to treat the men and the cattle. Every drive they made to an army post was successful. Sometimes they had trouble with the Comanche, but Anderson made sure his men were well armed with repeating rifles and the newest conversion pistols. Sometimes the Comanche would steal a few head, but other times, all they got was dead.

Lolita was enjoying herself playing the dutiful wife, even though she and Anderson were not married and she knew he would never love her. He was not mean to her, but most of the time, he paid no attention to her unless he wanted to release his urges. George hired a woman to cook and clean the house, and she lived in her own room beside the kitchen. Her name was Barbara Sanchez. She was half Mexican, and at times, Lolita was glad to have her company, and they could speak Spanish and George had no idea what they were saying. He did know a few words, but they were not complimentary words. At times, George took Lolita with him on trips to Ft. Worth. It was mostly to make appearances, but Lolita was happy to get out of the house once in a while.

On one the trips to Ft. Worth while Lolita was shopping, a man on the sidewalk came up to Anderson. "George Anderson," he said. "Is that you?"

"Name's Thomas Sanderson," said George. "Who in the hell are you?"

"You sure look like Anderson some. My name's Fred Brown," he said. "I was with Zeke awhile back."

When George heard the name Zeke, he grabbed Fred by the arm and pulled him into a nearby alley. "Just what are you doin' here?" asked George. "And where's Zeke?"

"Zeke and the rest of 'em got kilt," said Fred. "That Marshal and his deputies kilt em. He turnt me loose to let you know that they was kilt."

"Well shit, that damn Marshal sure is gonna take a lota killin'," said George. "I go by the name of Thomas Sanderson now. I own a good cattle ranch west a here. I can give you a job if you want, but if you open your mouth at all about me, I will kill you and feed you to the hogs. Do you understand me?"

"I surely do, and I'll take that job," said Fred. "I just hope that Marshal don't come down here alookin' fer ya. He'll remember me fer sure."

"Well if he ever does come down here and you spot him, you get yourself lost real quick," said George. "Now I've got to get back to my woman. You head out to the ranch. It's due west and you can't miss it. It's the only workin' ranch over that way. The foreman's name is Jug Carter. You tell him I knew you from sometime back, and I hired you on. Now get goin'."

~~~~

Two thousand cattle need plenty of grazing space, and more and more, they would wander onto Comanche or Kiowa land. The Kiowa mostly just tried to steal cattle, but the Comanche wanted to kill all the whites on their land that they could. They started raiding on a regular basis. George lost five men in a single week. Typically, the Comanche would send out a small raiding party, usually only two or three men, and ambush a lone rider. Then they would move on and look for another lone rider. They were so good at it that most of the time, the riders never got a chance to fire their weapons. This also meant that now those Comanche had repeating rifles and good pistols. George asked for help from the army and the Rangers, but they were always busy themselves and couldn't spare the manpower. George was told to deal with the problem himself.

He decided to go Ft. Worth and spread the word that he needed help, experienced help that had fought Indians and were not afraid of them. He also sent out telegrams to other cities and placed ads in newspapers. He even stated that he would be glad to have anyone who had ridden with Quantrill and Bloody Bill and wanted to make a new start. He realized that by doing this, any man who rode with Quantrill or Bloody Bill would recognize him, but he knew his secret would be safe with them as they once were comrades in arms. He spent two days in Ft. Worth before heading back home.

While he was gone, Jug was in charge. The men went out in groups of three, and they kept the cattle from wondering too far onto Indian land. There was only one incident while George was gone. One man had taken an arrow in his right shoulder, but they had killed two Comanche. There had been three Comanche, and none of them were armed with rifles.

Jug figured that since Lolita was the bosses wife, he should always let her know what was going on. Every evening he went to the big house, had a cup of coffee with Lolita, and told her what had happened that day. Lolita enjoyed his visits. She was glad for the attention, and was impressed that Jug thought enough of her to tell her the day's happenings. Jug was not a handsome man, but he was a big powerful man and was a perfect gentleman. Surely he knew that Lolita had been a whore, but that didn't seem to bother him.

On the fourth day, while giving her the day's happenings, Lolita stopped him, and asked. "You do like me, don't you Jug?" she asked.

"Of course I do ma'am, you're the bosses woman," he answered.

"That's not the answer I wanted," said Lolita. "Do you like being with me? Do you want to be with me?"

"I'm not sure what you want me to say, ma'am," said Jug. "You're a handsome woman and most men would want to be with you."

"That's a better answer," said Lolita. "Now I know that you come to see me, not just to tell me about what happened each day."

"You're a might forward ma'am," said Jug. "You are the boss's woman."

"First off, you will quit calling me ma'am. My name is Lolita," she said. "And you are right, I am the bosses woman, but I will never be his wife. He just uses me when he has the urge."

"That's a shame for a woman with your looks and as nice as you are, Lolita," said Jug. "Another time or another place, I would be after you."

"You know that I was a whore in Mexico, don't you?" said Lolita.

"I was not always an upstanding person myself," said Jug. "I figure the past is the past. Live for now and the future. Let the past go."

"You are a good man, Jug," said Lolita. "I will look forward to our meetings everyday till George gets back."

"I look forward to seeing you again tomorrow, Lolita," said Jug as he was leaving.

Fred Brown was standing in front of the bunk house when Jug was leaving the main house. "That Lolita, she's a looker," said Fred. "I heard she was a whore down Mexico way."

"She's the boss's woman, and she's a lady, and around me, you will address her as such," said Jug.

"Didn't mean nothin' by that," said Fred. "But you gotta admit, she is a looker."

"She surely is," said Jug. "Shouldn't you be out to the east range now?"

"I just come in to tell ya that we saw some Kiowa out there," said Fred. "It looked like they was gonna try and steal some cows, and we ran em off. We shot at em, but we never hit none. The other two boys are still out there. I'll be goin' back out now."

"Well be careful," said Jug. "Them Kiowa might come back."

~~~~

The next day at the same time as always, Jug went to the main house. "The boys on the east range saw some Kiowa yesterday, and ran them off," said Jug. "That's about all that's happened to right now."

"I was thinking, Jug," started Lolita. "Why don't we go for a ride tomorrow? It's been a long time since I've ridden."

"That would be nice," said Jug, "but it could be dangerous. Could be some Comanche or Kiowa anywhere out there. They'd love to get their hands on you."

"Well, Jug Carter," she said. "I believe you care about me."

"Yes, I do," said Jug. "And it would just about do me in if I was the one responsible for gettin' you hurt or took." As soon as Jug had finished his words, Lolita got up from her chair, went over to Jug, sat down on his lap, and kissed him full on the mouth. "This isn't right," said Jug. "We shouldn't be doin' this."

"Maybe we shouldn't," said Lolita. "You can tell me to stop if you don't like it."

Then she kissed him again and again. He did not pull away.

"I think we should quit now before things get out of hand," said Jug.

"I suppose you're right," Lolita said, "but you did like it. I know you did."

"I'm not dead," said Jug. "Of course I liked it."

"I fully intend to do this again," she said. "I want to be with you, Jug. You are a good man. I know I could make you happy."

"You surely could," said Jug, "but this could also make us dead. Most men don't cotton to their women bein' with someone else."

"He calls me his woman, but he has no affection for me, and I am just here for his urges," said Lolita. "I'm going to tell you something, and you must promise that you will not tell a soul."

"I can keep a secret as good as anyone can," said Jug. "What is it?"

"Your boss's real name is not Thomas Sanderson," she started. "It's George Anderson."

"Are you serious?" said Jug. "You mean he's George Anderson the outlaw and gang leader?"

"Yes, that's him," she said. "You and I are the only ones who know and he would kill us if he found out I told you. He is trying to become a legitimate rancher and staying low for a while. No one recognizes him when he's not wearing his Confederate coat and hat and not carrying his saber. He probably figures I wouldn't tell anyone since I was just a whore and should be thankful for him taking me away from Mexico. You must never let on that you know until you know for sure what you will do."

"That won't take much thinkin'," said Jug. "I'll be leavin' when I figure out the best time. He should be back any day now. Maybe the next time he goes to Ft. Worth."

"Would you take me with you?" asked Lolita. "I do not want to be here anymore. I want to be with someone who really wants to be with me."

"I can take you with me," said Jug. "But we could be on the run for a long time. Men like him live on hate, and even though he doesn't love you, he will hate me for taking you."

"Maybe we could find that Marshal that everyone always talks about," said Lolita. "I'm sure he'd like to know where George Anderson is. I hear he and his deputies have killed many outlaws up in Kansas and the Nations."

"I heard that Anderson put a bounty on that Marshal's head, and several have tried to collect on it and gotten theirself killed," said Jug. "Now let's you and me try to act normal, and I'll figure out a plan. I'll be getting' back to the men now. See you tomorrow the same time."

"I look forward to it," she said.

~~~~

The next two days, Jug went to the big house and gave his report to Lolita. Nothing had happened either day, so the visits were short. Jug could tell that she wanted to hold him, but he kept his distance. He wanted no suspicions from anyone.

On the eighth day, George returned home. The first thing he did was take Lolita by the arm and take her to bed. There was no passion, just one of his urges. After he finished, he went to speak with Jug. Jug filled him in on what had happened in his absence, and also informed him that he had been telling Lolita the day's happenings."

"Why would she need to know anything?" said Anderson. "She don't know nothin' about nothin'."

"Sorry boss," said Jug. "I won't bother to tell her anything next time you leave."

"Should be going back to Ft. Worth in a month or less," George said. "I put the word out all over that we need help here. Might even get some men that used to ride with Quantrill or Bloody Bill. I put ads in newspapers sayin' I would take them and give them a chance at a new start. Could be a rough bunch if some of them come. Do you think you could handle them, Jug?"

"As long as they can handle cows and are willin' to fight Indians, there shouldn't be no problems," said Jug.

"Good, now I think I'll get me a horse and ride out and check on the men," said George.

"I'll go with you boss," said Jug. "It's not really safe to go out by yourself. I been havin' the men go out in threes. I think it's been helpin' to keep them Comanche from ambushin' us. They like it when there's only one rider."

It took some time, but they found several of the men. They were doing their jobs and nothing had been going on. Jug did spot several tracks from unshod horses though, and some of them were not too far from the big house. "You don't s'pose they got eyes on your woman, do you?" asked Jug. "They'd love to get their hands on her."

"I'm sure they would," said George. "I reckon if they did, I'd just go get me another one. There's lotsa them Mex women who'd just love to come here and live in this big house."

"Wouldn't you miss her any boss?" asked Jug.

"Only when I get one a them urges," George said. "Sure she's a looker, but there's lotsa other lookers out there. I like a woman when I want a woman. Other than that, they just get in the way."

Jug could see why Lolita was ready to leave. A nice house and clothes and money, doesn't mean you'll be happy.

The next two weeks were uneventful. The men saw unshod horse tracks, but no one was ambushed, and no Indians were spotted. At the end of the second week, two riders showed up. Jug had been out with the men, and he saw the riders with Anderson when he got back. He could tell by the way they were talking that they knew each other. "Come on over here, Jug," said George. "We got two good men here. This one here is Jed Hawk, and the other one is his cousin Matt."

Jug extended his hand to both of them, shook, then told George he would show them to the bunkhouse and get their horses taken care of. Jug noticed right off that these men were very well armed. Both of them had two pistols, a shotgun, and a repeating rifle. "These two are not regular cow men," Jug said to himself. "I wonder what will show up next."

Jug spent the next week trying to come up with a plan to get him and Lolita out of there. He decided it would be good if he could make it look like the Comanche took Lolita and he went after them, and got himself killed. But how could he do this? Early the next week, he figured it out. He needed some unshod horses for making tracks to appear that Comanche had been there, and something to make tracks that looked like moccasin tracks, and some blood. He would have two unshod horses leave tracks all around the area, and wear the moccasins, and go up to the house, and make it look like Lolita had been taken. Any horse in the corral would be turned loose to make it look like they had been stolen. He would ride off on his horse, and Lolita would ride one of the two unshod horses. They would also take three other horses with them. Once away from the house a good ways, he would pour blood all over his horse and saddle, and pick a spot and make it look like there had been a struggle, and his body was drug off. He and Lolita would then ride off on the two unshod horses leaving his horse there. It would most likely go back to the ranch. The other three horses would be used for trading or anything necessary.

When he got the chance, he told Lolita his plan. She was all for it, even though he explained to her the dangers. "We'll be in Comanche and Kiowa territory for a good while," he told her. "When we can, we'll swing up through the Nations and into Kansas. There's a good chance we'll get ourselves killed, at least me anyway. They'll want you."

"We'll make it Jug," she said. "You are a good man. We'll be all right."

~~~~

Jug started collecting all the food they would need, extra canteens and plenty of ammunition. The day before Anderson was to leave for Ft. Worth, Jug went out hunting and dropped an antelope. He hung it from a tree to gut it, collected the blood, and poured it into a canteen. He brought back the antelope for the cook to fix for the men. Next morning after Anderson left, Jug sent all the men out to the farthest western range. That would give him plenty of time for the plan. The cook had been up to fix breakfast for George, but as soon as he was gone, she went back to bed.

Jug wrapped some leather around his feet to make it look like moccasin tracks, and walked to the house. He and Lolita knocked a few things around in the house to make it look like there had been a struggle. Then Jug mounted his horse and Lolita mounted one of the unshod horses. They went to the corral and let all the horses out, then drove the horses to the northwest. Jug was leading the second unshod horse and the other three horses. When they got about a mile from the house, Jug got off his horse and poured blood all over the saddle and the horse's neck. Then he turned the horse back toward the house and gave it a swat. He poured some more blood on the ground and tried to make it look like there had been a big struggle. Then he and Lolita took off heading north. Every so often, Jug would pour out some more blood so it could be easily trailed.

When the men got back that evening, Jug's horse was standing in the corral. Fred spotted it first. "Just what in the hell?" he said. "That's blood. That's Jug's horse. What happened here?" They all looked around, but didn't find Jug. They went up to the big house to see if Lolita had seen anything. When they knocked on the front door, the cook answered.

"Have you seen Jug, ma'am?" asked Fred. "His horse is out here with blood all over it and he's nowhere to be found."

"I haven't seen him, and I can't find Lolita," she said. "Something has happened here. There's been a fight or something. Several things have been knocked over and broken. I can't believe I didn't hear anything. I took a nap after the boss left this morning, but only for an hour or two. I didn't think anything was wrong till I saw all the broken things. I've been all through the house and I can't find Lolita."

"She's been took," one of the men yelled. "There's tracks out here, moccasin tracks. They musta took her and the horses and Jug went after 'em. I bet he's killed for sure. There's some unshod tracks out here. We can track them a little while till it gets dark."

They followed the tracks and came to the place where Jug had tried to make it look like there had been a struggle. There was blood all over the place, but no Jug. "They drug him off," one of the men said. "Probably gonna skin him alive or somethin' if he's not dead yet."

"I'd say he's already dead," said Fred. "That's a lotta blood. We best head back. Don't wanna be caught out here after dark. Injuns don't usual fight at night, but don't wanna run into some that don't know that."

~~~~

Next morning right at daylight, five of the men went out to follow the trail. No one was in charge now, so the men voted and decided five would be enough to go out. The others would stay there and wait till they got back and then decide what to do. After they got to where the struggle had happened, they followed the trail for two hours. One of them had dismounted and was looking for more blood when an arrow slammed into his chest. Then a shot rang out, and another man was hit in the shoulder. One of the men shouted, "Let's get the hell outta here!" The man who had been hit with the arrow managed to mount his horse, but as he turned to ride away, another arrow hit him in the back. Another shot was fired, but no one was hit that time.

When they got back to the ranch house, the man who had been arrowed, fell off his horse and died. The man who had been shot in the shoulder was cussing at the top of his lungs. "Dirty damn red devils," he kept shouting. All the men came out to see what had happened.

"We better fort up here for awhile," said Fred. "No tellin' how many's out there and what they're up to. One a you take a look at that shoulder and see what you can do fer him." Men were stationed all over so every avenue of approach was covered. Nothing happened the rest of that day and the next morning. "We better get word to the boss on what's goin' on here," said Fred. "Any volunteers?" Jed Hawk said he'd go.

"Take plenty a ammunition and food and water," said Fred. "Mebbe you should take two horses so you can trade off and ride harder."

It was a three day ride to Ft. Worth, but with two horses, a man could make it in two. Jed Hawk made it to town in two days, but he wasn't sure where to look for Anderson. He visited several saloons and a couple of hotels before he found him. Anderson was having a drink in a saloon when Jed found him. "Just what in the hell are you doin' here?" asked George.

"I got some terrible news boss," Jed started. "Your woman's been took. The Comanche took her. Jug went after 'em and got himself kilt. We trailed em and one man got kilt and another got shot in the shoulder. The boys are forted up back at the place. I volunteered to come let you know."

"Are you sure it was Comanche?" George asked. "Tell me everything that happened."

"Well the day you left, all us men were out with the cows as usual," Jed started. "When we came back in that evenin', Jug's horse was in the corral and there was blood all over it. The horses in the corral had been took. We looked around and couldn't find Jug. Then we went to the big house and the cook said she couldn't find yer woman, and it looked like there had been some trouble in the house. Things were knocked down and busted. She said she took a nap for a couple hours after you left that mornin'. We found some moccasin tracks by the house, and some unshod horse tracks. We followed them till we came to a place where there was a lotta blood and it looked like there had been a fight. It was getting' dark, so we went back. The next mornin' five men went out trackin'. They went about two hours past where all the blood was. There was more blood on the trail. One of the men was on the ground lookin' fer more blood when they stuck an arrow in him. Another man got shot. We got the hell outta there. As we was leavin', that fella that got the arrow in him, took another arrow in the back. That's what I know."

"Damn Injuns," said George. "When my boys get here, we're gonna kill us some Comanche. I got ten or more boys comin' that I used to ride with. We'll make 'em pay. They should be here to-morrow according to the telegram I got. I want you to rest tonight, then get back there. The boys need to get out there some or them Comanche and Kiowa will run off all them cows. Tellem to be well armed and have at least five in each group. I'll be back soon as the boys get here. Here's some money. Go get a hotel room and get goin' early."

"Sure thing boss," Jed said. "I'll have a couple drinks, then get myself right to sleep." Jed slammed down his drinks than went to get a hotel. "See you back at the ranch, boss," Jed said as he was leaving.

CHAPTER EIGHTEEN

Jug and Lolita headed north deeper into Comanche territory. He figured it would take two full days to get from Comanche land into Kiowa land. He'd always heard that the Kiowa were not as blood thirsty as the Comanche. There had been eight horses in the corral when they let them loose. Since he took three of them with him for their trip, Jug was hoping that the Comanche would spend their time rounding up the other five, and give him more time to get away. Jug knew they could not have a fire for several days. That would be like saying to the Comanche, "Here I am, come and get me." He and Lolita packed several blankets and plenty of food and water. Jug had a strip of canvas so they could build a shelter. It was a good thing because towards the end of the first day, it got colder, and was snowing before dark. They traveled as far as they could, then stopped to set up. Jug set up a shelter, and they had jerky and water for supper. After two hours, the snow quit, but it had snowed enough to cover their tracks.

"Since it snowed," Jug said, "I think we'll be safe not keepin' watch tonight. But we'll hafta stay close together so we won't freeze. We'll be all right. We got plenty a blankets."

"Yes we do," said Lolita. "I intend to keep you very warm to-night. Now get under these blankets and I'll warm you up." Jug did as instructed. He'd been so busy worrying about the snow and whether to keep watch or not, that he had not noticed Lolita getting undressed under the blankets.

"Oh my, you are a beautiful woman," Jug said as he slipped under the blankets.

~~~~

A couple of hours later, they fell fast asleep in each other's arms. At daylight, Jug woke up, got dressed, and went to check the horses and make sure they did not have any visitors. Just as he was coming back to the shelter, it started snowing again. "That's good," he said to himself. "Hope it snows enough to keep our tracks covered."

They got mounted and headed north again. They chewed on some jerky as they were moving. They came to a small stream, and there was a cut out on one side and it overhung the stream some. Jug decided it would be safe to build a small fire and have some coffee. He tied the horses and got the fire started. When the coffee was done, they sat around the fire enjoying each other's company. "I really like being with you last night," said Lolita. "I would like to do that very often. You are a good man. You know how to please a woman."

"I'm glad you like to be with me," said Jug. "I fully intend to be your man. Now all we gotta do is not get killed or captured."

"You are a good man, Jug," Lolita said. "You will not let that happen, and I am your woman."

With talk like that, Jug was getting worked up again. He grabbed some blankets and they were soon making love again. After they were finished, they had another cup of coffee and then headed north. They followed the stream for a good while. When it bended heading northwest, they continued to follow it. The snow had stopped now, so they moved in the stream to keep their tracks concealed. Right before dark, Jug spotted a fire in the distance. "Gotta be Indians," said Jug. "No white man with any sense would build a fire like that. We'll stop here for the night, then see what things look like in the morning. Maybe we can get around em without being spotted." Jug tied the horses to some trees by the stream and set up the shelter.

"You'll have to keep me warm again tonight," said Lolita.

"I'll do my best," Jug said as he wrapped himself up with her.

When they woke up at daylight, Jug thought he saw some movement on the other side of the stream. He and Lolita got dressed and started taking the shelter down. Then he saw them. There were five Indians starting to move toward them. Jug didn't really know his Indians, other than these had to be either Comanche or Kiowa. He knew about war paint and these Indians were not wearing paint. As they got closer, Jug motioned for them to come in to his camp. "Anybody here speak American?" he asked. They just stared at each other.

"Habla Espanol?" said Lolita.

One of the Indians answered her. "Ask them if they would like to sit down and have some coffee." Jug said to Lolita. "Tell them I'll have it ready in no time."

To Jug's surprise, they agreed. Jug gathered some wood and got the fire going. After he had the coffee started, he told Lolita to ask them if they were Comanche or Kiowa. She asked them, and they said they were Kiowa. They said they were going hunting when they spotted them. "Why are you here, and where are you going?" the brave asked them.

"Tell them we need to find Marshal O'Rourke up in Kansas and tell him that there is a very bad outlaw in Texas," he said to Lolita. "Tell them that this outlaw will kill us and many Kiowa if we do not get word to the Marshal." Lolita said what Jug told her to say.

As soon as the brave heard the word O'Rourke again, he spoke. "Our Chief knows O'Rourke. He is the one who kills with the long gun and the big pistol. He helped our people once. I will take you to our village." Lolita translated the words for Jug, and they mounted up and followed the Kiowa to their village. They took them straight to Flying Eagle's lodge. The brave who spoke Spanish, went into his lodge, spoke a few words, and Flying Eagle came outside. He spoke English almost perfectly.

"I am Flying Eagle," he said. "O'Rourke is my friend. He is always welcome in our village. I have not seen him for a good while. Now why do you need to see him?"

"There is a very bad outlaw in Texas," started Jug. "He has already killed many whites and Indians alike. The whites have been searching for him since the big war ended. When they catch him, he will be hung. He has many men now, and he is getting even more men. If I can get to O'Rourke, he and his deputies will catch him. My name is Jug Carter."

"What is this bad man's name?" asked Flying Eagle.

"It's George Anderson," answered Jug. "He has a ranch now and goes by the name of Thomas Sanderson. No one knows who he is except some of the men he rode with during the big war."

"I've heard of this man," said Flying Eagle. "We have stolen some of his cattle, but no one got hurt. I have heard about him killing many Osage and some of the other people who live on the big reservation that you white people call the Nations. You will rest here today, and then some of my braves will get you as close to O'Rourke as we can. There are some soldier forts along the way so we must be careful. I will send Bear Claw with you. He is the brave who speaks Spanish. That way, he will able to speak with you through your woman. She is your woman, isn't she?"

"Yes, she is my woman," said Jug. "You may have three of these horses as a gift for your hospitality."

"You are a wise man, Jug Carter," said the Chief. "Get your rest and my braves will be ready to lead you at daylight. You may stay in my lodge tonight. My wife is old like me, but she is still a good cook. You may mount your woman all you want. It will not bother me or my wife. We will be asleep anyway."

That night, Lolita and Jug wrapped themselves in each other's arms, but did not make love. Both of them were a little uneasy about having company in the same room. In the morning after breakfast, they were on their way.

They moved at a fast pace, and stopped only to rest or water the horses. Jug figured they had gone maybe forty miles the first day. One of the braves had killed a small deer, and that night for supper they had venison, biscuits, beans, and coffee. They moved like this every day. During the day, they chewed on jerky while moving and only stopped to rest and water the horses. When they got anywhere near an army post, they were very careful and made sure that no patrols were out. After eight days, Bear Claw told them he could take them no farther. They were only a day and a half ride from O'Rourke. Jug thanked them for their help. He gave them some of the food they had left and a couple of blankets. Bear Claw thanked them and was on his way.

~~~~

Back in Texas, the men who had ridden with Anderson, were now with him again, and back at the ranch. The men were back to tending the cattle and some of them kept looking for any sign as to what had happened to Lolita and Jug. Any evidence that might have been there, was lost when it snowed. There was no more Indian activity either. Anderson and his men went out from time to time hoping to find a village and kill as many as they could. But none could be found. "They musta got tired of eatin' my cows and followed the buffalo herds, or went to their winter camp," said George. "They musta headed west or northwest. They'll be back in the spring, and then we'll kill as many as we can." Anderson let the Rangers and the Army know what had happened, but they said they couldn't, or wouldn't, help till spring. Anderson never did like the blue bellies. It was all right for his men to drive cattle to their posts in the winter, but they wouldn't get off their asses and go out to look for his woman or his foreman.

Anderson had started with nineteen men and a foreman. Fred Brown made it twenty men. Five men had been killed earlier. One was killed after Jug was killed and Lolita taken. The man who had been shot in the shoulder while looking for Jug and Lolita, died of his wound. When the ones he had ridden with during the war showed up, he was up to twenty four men. Out of the twenty four, there was still a bunch of them who didn't know who their boss really was.

One snowy day when it was bitter cold and the men didn't go out, a big fight broke out in the bunkhouse. Someone said something bad about Quantrill and Bloody Bill, and fists went to flying. After a while, the guns came out. Several shots were fired before George left the big house to see what was happening. Five men were on the floor either dead or dying. "Just what in the hell is going on here?" said George as he stormed into the bunkhouse.

"Them sons a bitches said Quantrill and Bloody Bill weren't no soldiers, just some murderers and thieves," said Jed Hawk. "We won't stand fer that, and we kilt em."

"Did any more of them say that?" George asked Jed.

"Them two there on the left did," said Jed.

"Did you two say that?" asked George.

"Yes we did," they both said. "We rode with John Bell Hood and was in the real Confederate Army, not that buncha riff raff."

George didn't say one word. He just pulled his pistol, and shot both of them in the head. "Now is there anyone else here who's got something to say about Quantrill and Bloody Bill." No one said a word. "Well git this scum outta here," said George. "Take 'em out a ways and leave em for the wolves and coyotes. You can have any of their things that you want." The bunkhouse was quiet that night, but the next morning, it was discovered that two men had run off. George was now down to fifteen men. "Anybody else gonna run off?" said George when he found out.

"I doubt it boss," said Jed. "If they was gonna git, they'da went with them others. You want me to trackem down fer ya."

"No, mebbe the Comanche'll get 'em," said George. "We'll get us some more men come spring."

"You think that damn Marshal'll ever find out yer down here?" asked Jed.

"I figure he will sooner or later," said George. "He won't go lookin' too far from Kansas till spring anyway. We'll be ready for him when he does show up. I hope to kill him myself. I heard Ethan's boy killed that nigger deputy he had before they killed him. One less lawman for us to kill."

"I heard that lawman kilt Jack Snow too," said Jed. "Jack was s'posed to be real good with a knife."

"Jack was good with a knife," said George. "You gotta get close to use a knife. That's where he messed up. You don't wanna get close to that man. He's too fast. Jack probly coulda shot him in the back several times, but no, he wanted to use a knife. He got himself dead. I shouldn't have given that man a down payment."

CHAPTER NINETEEN

Jug and Lolita made it to Abilene in a day and a half without any problems. When they got into town, they went to the livery and boarded the horses. Billy was there with his dogs. "Them are some good lookin' dogs there," Jug said to Billy. "Could you tell us where we can find that Marshal O'Rourke?"

"Yer not one a them fellas tryin' to get that bounty money that outlaw put up fer the Marshal, are ya?" asked Billy.

"If I was, do ya reckon I'd tell ya," said Jug.

"I reckon not," said Billy. "Ya probly wouldn't have that woman with ya neither."

"Nope," said Jug. "Now I got some news for the Marshal about that outlaw."

"Well, you can find him over at the saloon," said Billy. "If he's not there, someone'll know his whereabouts."

"Thank you, young man," said Jug. "Take good care a them horses. Ask the smithy if he could get some shoes on em."

Jug and Lolita went to the saloon. When they entered, there was a group of men at a table back to the side. Jug saw the badges on the men. He went straight over to the table. "Name's Jug

Carter, this here is my woman Lolita," he started. "We know right where George Anderson is. Which a you is Marshal O'Rourke?"

Sean stood up and introduced himself. "I'm Sean O'Rourke and these are my deputies," he said. "This is Michael, Bob, and Charlie, and that red headed beauty is Maggie. I got another deputy over in Cherokee territory. Just got himself married. Take a seat. I'll get us a bottle and some glasses." Sean returned with everything and poured everyone a drink. "Would you like a drink too, Lolita?" asked Sean.

"Yes, thank you," she said. "It's been a long trail."

"All right Jug, tell me what you know about Anderson," said Sean.

"He has a ranch down in Texas now," started Jug. "It's three days ride west of Ft. Worth. He's goin' by the name of Thomas Sanderson. I was his foreman. I never found out who he was till Lolita told me. I decided I best get outta there. I brought Lolita with me. Everyone down there thinks he's an upstanding citizen. He's got beef contracts for most of army posts in central Texas and western Kansas."

"How'd you get away from them with her with you?" asked Sean.

"I made this plan where I made it look like she was took by the Comanche and I was killed," Jug said. "I reckon it worked. Anderson was getting more men because we did have some Indian trouble. We had some get killed while I was still there. These new men were s'posed to be men he rode with during the war. Don't know exactly how many, ten or more. He could have more'n twenty men now."

"How'd you get through the Comanche and the Kiowa?" asked Sean.

"It only took two days to get out of Comanche land," started Jug. "The first day we left, there was snow and it covered our tracks. When we got in Kiowa land, we met some braves, and said we had to find O'Rourke. When they heard the name O'Rourke, they said they were taking us to their village. We met Flying Eagle. He speaks highly of you. We told him about Anderson. He let us rest that night, and the next day, some of his braves gave us an escort till we were only a day and a half away. And here we are."

"That's good news Jug," said Sean. "I wanna thank you for bringin' it to us. Anderson has been killin' and such for way too long. We'll be goin' after him soon as I can round up my other deputy. You and Lolita can have a room upstairs. I reckon you're a little tired. We got a real good cook here too. You can eat all you want and stay here as long as you need to, no charge."

"What I'd like to do is get myself married," said Jug.

"I'd like to get myself married too, Jug," said Sean. "But we don't have no men of the cloth in this town yet. I got an idea though. I'll send a telegram to my boss. I'll ask him that since I'm a Federal Marshal, would it be legal if I appointed someone as a Justice of the Peace. Won't hurt to ask. I gotta go to the telegraph office anyway and send a telegram to my deputy."

"Is there a place in town where a person can get a bath?" asked Jug. "Me'n Lolita are getting' a little ripe."

Maggie spoke right. "Follow me, you two," she said. "I got just the place." She took them out to her bath house. Lolita took a look at that tub and started crying. Jug was in total amazement.

"There's water and wood and buckets," said Maggie. "I'll get some towels. Have you got any other clothes with you?"

"No," answered Jug. "We packed only what we needed to get outta there."

"Well I can find a dress for Lolita, and I'll find you some clothes somewhere, Jug," said Maggie. "Now you two take your time and have a good bath. First time I got in there with Sean, we didn't come out for hours. You can use the robes that are hanging there. The one will fit Lolita, but the other one might be tight on you, Jug. Now enjoy yourself. If you need anything, let out a yell."

Around three hours later, Lolita and Jug came out of the bath house. Maggie had found a nice dress for Lolita and some clothes for Jug. They didn't fit Jug real well, but they got the job done. "Why don't you come and sit with me a while," said Maggie. "Jug can sit with the men while we talk." Jug went over and sat with the men, and Lolita and Maggie sat at a table on the other side of the room.

"I thought you might just like to have some female company for a change," said Maggie. "If you were down there with that bunch, you probably didn't get much company."

"You are most kind, Maggie," Lolita said. "Jug and I are so glad to meet you. You know that I was a whore, don't you?"

"All I see here is a brave woman who had the guts to finally get away from that piece of trash," said Maggie. "This country needs more people like you and Jug who are not afraid to do the right thing. Jug must be a very good man."

"He is," said Lolita. "He's the only man I've ever known who treated me like a lady and like I was somebody."

"I've got a good man too," said Maggie. "I worry a lot about him a lot though. There's more outlaws than there is lawmen. Once he gets Anderson, this whole area will be a lot better. How about we go join the men and get something to eat." They both got up and went to the men's table. Jug got up and pulled out a chair for Lolita. Maggie was impressed. "I'll go let Cookie know we'll be eating shortly."

Sean got to the telegraph office and sent the telegram to Jon telling him to return immediately and where they would be headed. Then he sent one to Judge Simmons. It read as follows:

Judge David Simmons
Federal Courthouse, St. Louis

Do I have power to appoint a justice of the peace <stop> if not can you appoint one by telegram <stop> want to get married <stop> Anderson known to be in Texas just west of Ft. Worth <stop >will purse within the week <stop>

O'Rourke

~~~~

Sean told the operator that he needed replies to both telegrams and he was to find him as soon as they came in. On the way back to the saloon, he stopped off at the leather goods store. Jason was just inside doing some straightening up. "What can I do for you today, Sean?" asked Jason.

"Well, I might have a favor to ask of you," said Sean.

"Anything you need, Sean," said Jason. "I'm your man."

"I'll bet you would never expect this," said Sean. "You know that Maggie and me want to get married, but we have no preachers around here. I sent a telegram to the Judge asking if I could appoint a Justice of the Peace. If I can't, could he appoint one by telegram."

"Let me guess," said Jason. "You want me to be the Justice of the Peace."

"Yep, that's about it," said Sean.

"Sure," said Jason, "I can do that for you."

"I'll let you know the minute I get a reply back from the Judge," said Sean. "Could hear back today."

"I'll get my suit out and brushed off," said Jason.

"If you do get appointed," said Sean, "there's another fella here who wants to get married. He just got here from Texas. He told us where Anderson is holed up, and soon as Jon gets back, we're goin' after 'em."

"That's good news," said Jason. "Let's hope you get him."

~~~~

Sean went back to the saloon, and all of them had their meal. They had just finished when the telegraph operator came into the saloon. "I got your answers, Marshal," he said. "Both of 'em." Then he handed them to Sean, and Sean read them almost aloud. The first one was from Jon and it said he would be back as fast as he could. The second one was from the Judge. It read as follows:

O'Rourke

Justice of Peace must be elected or appointed by local citizens <stop> find someone willing <stop> besides weddings they are responsible for minor local law <stop> they can refer cases to higher court <stop> good luck on Anderson <stop> God speed <stop>

Judge David Simmons
Federal Court House St. Louis

When Sean finished reading the telegram, he looked straight at Maggie. "Maggie, darlin'," he started, "If I can get us a Justice of the Peace, would you wanna go ahead and get married?"

"Yes, I would," said Maggie. "Have you got someone in mind?"

"Jason at the leather goods store said that he would," said Sean. "How bout you, Jug? Do you and Lolita wanna go ahead and get married too?" Jug didn't know exactly what to say. He looked over at Lolita.

"Yes, we will get married too," said Lolita. "The sooner, the better."

"Will tomorrow be all right with you ladies?" Sean asked.

"That'd be just fine," said Maggie. Lolita shook her head yes.

"Well I'll go tell Jason the news," said Sean. "Then I gotta make sure the local citizenry is all right with that." Sean went straight to the store and told Jason the news. "I gotta make sure everyone in town is all right with this as you are s'posed to be elected or appointed. One other thing, as a Justice of the Peace, you will be responsible for minor local law enforcement. Anything you think you can't handle, you can refer it to a higher court. Not sure where that would be, but if somethin' comes up, we'll find out. Are you still all right with this?"

"Yes, I'll get you married, and I'll take care of the other things if something comes up," he said. "If things get too much for me, I can always resign."

"Yes, you can," said Sean. "Now I'll go all over and get you appointed."

~~~~

Sean went to every business in town, and everyone was in favor of Jason's appointment. "Just tell us what time for the wedding," almost everyone of them said. Sean told everyone the news, and then went back to the saloon and asked the ladies what time they wanted to get married.

"I think noon would be fine," said Maggie. "Is that all right with you, Lolita?"

"Yes, that is wonderful," she said. "I wish I had a new dress for the wedding."

"I'll find you something," said Maggie. "We need to find something for Jug, he's a big man. Sean, why don't you take Jug over to the General Store and see if they have something nice for him."

"Yes darlin'," said Sean, "I might see if there's somethin' for me too, and I need to tell everyone what time the wedding is." They found some nice suits at the store, but Jug's was a little tight in the shoulders. They assured Jug they would have it altered and ready to go in time. As they were walking back to the saloon, Jug spoke.

"When you go after Anderson," he started, "I should go with you. I know that place and all around it very well. I know every ditch and tree and bush and building at that place. I know the whole area for miles around. You could use me."

"That would be a great help," said Sean. "Maybe you should talk this over with your intended. Don't wanna make her a widow just yet. Have you ever been shot at before besides Indians?"

"I fought in the war, Sean," said Jug. "I seen plenty a killin' and done plenty."

"Well you talk with your woman and see what she says," said Sean. "If she's against you goin', I could sure use you here to keep an eye on things. There's been a few outlaws that tried to take Maggie to get at me. I figure there'll be more of 'em. Are you fast with that pistol?"

"Not really, but I hit what I shoot at," said Jug. "I was in the cavalry, and I was a pretty good shot on horseback too. Pretty good with a long gun too."

"Well talk to your woman, and let me know," said Sean. "I know I'd feel better with you back here. Deputy pay is forty a month. Consider yourself sworn in."

~~~~

That evening, everyone celebrated the upcoming nuptials. Sean got a little drunk, as did Michael and the boys. Jug didn't drink as much. Sean knew why. He wanted to have a serious talk with Lolita. Maggie and Lolita also kept their wits about them.

That night when they went to bed, Jug told Lolita that they needed to have a serious talk. "Lolita, I talked with Sean, and I told him that I should go with him when he goes after Anderson," Jug said. "I told him I know the whole area down there for miles around and such and that would be a great help. I need to know what you think."

"Jug," she started, "I just found you, and I do not want to take a chance on losing you. I have an idea. Can't you draw Sean a map of the ranch and the surrounding area? He knows Anderson and the type of men who'll be with him. He'll be all right without you. I hope you understand."

"I do, Lolita," said Jug. "I would hate to get myself killed and leave you alone. I'll draw Sean a good map and tell him I'll stay here and look after things while he's gone. He already swore me in as a deputy."

"Well now you have a job," said Lolita. "Let's hope you don't need to do much deputy work while they're gone. Now come over here and kiss me, and then kiss me some more." They made love well into the night.

~~~~

The next morning, Sean and Maggie took a turn in the bathtub, so they would smell nice and sweet for the wedding. After they were done, Lolita and Jug took a turn. Then the women went their separate ways from the men. "You won't see us again till the wedding," Maggie told Sean and Jug. "It's bad luck. Now if you'll excuse us."

Jug went to the General Store and his suit was ready. "We'll see you at the wedding," the store owner said. When he went back to the saloon, Sean was setting there at his regular table drinking coffee. Jug got himself some coffee and joined him. "Lolita and me had that talk last night," said Jug. "She really doesn't want me goin' with you."

"I understand," said Sean. "Like I said earlier, I could sure use you stayin' here keepin' watch over things."

"Well Lolita said I can draw you a map of the whole place down there," said Jug. "That's what I'll do. When I get done, you'll know exactly where everything is. I'll even make a drawing of the house showin' where all the rooms are and the cellar too. Now what are we gonna do till it's weddin' time?"

"Well let's get a little breakfast, and when time gets closer, we'll get ourselves dressed in them suits and set around and wait," said Sean. "Don't eat a whole lot for breakfast. Cookie's gonna make us a big feast for the weddin'."

Michael was there as was Charlie and Bob, and they were starting to arrange the tables for the ceremony. They made a big opening, so the women could be walked down the aisle. The women would come down the stairs, and then Michael would walk Maggie to Sean, and Bob would walk Lolita to Jug. Jason would then do the ceremony. Someone found out that the blacksmith could play the fiddle, so they were hoping to have some dancing afterwards.

~~~~

It finally came time for the wedding. Practically the whole town was there. Sean, Jug, and Jason took their positions at exactly twelve o'clock, and the blacksmith played the wedding march on his fiddle. Maggie came down the stairs first. She was wearing the beautiful blue dress that she had been wearing when she and Sean first met. Sean was still amazed by her beauty as she came down the stairs and Michael walked her to him. When Lolita came down the stairs, Jug was beside himself. She was absolutely beautiful. Maggie had given her a light green dress that was the same style as the blue dress she was wearing. It fit her perfectly, showing every curve of her body.

Jason went back and forth between the couples on their vows. When he got to the part where he said, "Do you Sean, take Maggie, and do you Jug, take Lolita, as your lawful wedded wife, to have and to hold, for richer, for poorer, in sickness and in health, as long as ye both shall live?" Both of them answered, "We sure as hell do." When Jason told them that they could kiss the bride, both couples kissed for what seemed like five minutes.

Then everyone let out a cheer, and the blacksmith started playing his fiddle. No one recognized what the blacksmith was playing, but it sounded like a waltz to some of the people.

"Maggie, I have never danced," said Sean. "I sure wish you would teach me."

"I will darlin'," she said. "You just relax, and we'll be waltzing in no time."

Jug knew how to dance, and he and Lolita were all over the place with their moves. "You watch Jug," Maggie said to Sean. "He's very good. Try to move like he does." It took a while, but between Maggie and Jug, Sean was getting better. After the first song, the townspeople joined in.

Cookie announced that the meal was ready, and everyone sat down to eat. There were several toasts first, then Cookie's fine feast was enjoyed. After the meal, there was more dancing, and drinking. It went on well into the evening. After the crowd had left, Jug led Lolita up the stairs to their room. He opened the door, then picked her up and carried her inside. They were not seen for two days. Sean did the same with Maggie, and they were also not seen for two days.

Michael and Betty stayed for a while after the couples went to their rooms. "Is all of this giving you any ideas?" Betty said to Michael.

"And just what do you mean, Betty darlin'?" asked Michael.

"You know exactly what I mean," replied Betty. "I know you love me, and you know I love you. I always figured that one day we would get married. You are a good man Michael. You have never said one word about my work."

"I always figured that one day we would get married too," said Michael. "Your work does not bother me, as long as I know that you love me. When we do get married, I would expect you to quit your work."

"Of course I'll quit my work, in fact, I'll quit it right now," said Betty. "I'll let Maggie know when I see her again."

"Well then we'll get married after we get Anderson," said Michael. "We'll be leavin' in a week or so. It'll take us eight or nine days to get down and there and that many to get back. If Anderson is where Jug says he is, it might take a day or two to get him. Betty darlin', you should be married in a month."

"All you gotta do is not get yourself killed," said Betty. "Now let's go back home. I intend to wear you out tonight."

"That'll be fine, Betty darlin'," said Michael. "I'm feelin' that way myself."

~~~~

Two days after the wedding, Jug and Lolita did come out for meals and such, but they did not stay out long. On the fifth day, Jug decided he would get with Sean and draw the map of Anderson's ranch and the surrounding area. Sean rounded up Michael, Bob, and Charlie, and they all sat down at their regular table in the saloon. Jug got started.

"The ranch is three days ride west of Ft. Worth," said Jug. "You can see the main house from way off. The road looks like it leads right up to the front door. It's a huge two story house. The front door is dead center. Inside to the right is a huge room. I think he called it the entertaining room. On the far corner of it, there was a small room that he called his study. To the left is the dining room. It's toward the front, and the kitchen is on the back corner. There is a small room off of the kitchen where his cook and housekeeper lives. Across from the front door, are the stairs that lead to four big bedrooms upstairs. He sleeps in the one that is to the left front. The only other door that leads in or out of the house is on the backside of the kitchen. The outhouse for the big house is about thirty yards behind the kitchen to the left. Directly behind the house, maybe twenty yards, is a small hill. It's just a small hump. Whoever was there first, built a root cellar into it." Jug was drawing the whole time he was talking so everyone would understand what he was saying. "About a hundred yards to the left of the house, is a big barn, and there is a huge corral and some horse shelters attached to it. Fifty yards from the barn, and to the east, is the cook shack. The bunkhouse is maybe twenty yards to the east of the cook shack. There are two outhouses behind the bunkhouse. There are a few big trees near the big house, and there are two big trees not far from the bunkhouse. I'll put them on the drawing."

"You do good drawings," said Sean. "We'll know as much about that place as Anderson does when we get down there. Now tell us about the surrounding area."

"Most of the land there is open plains with rolling hills," started Jug. "About two miles to the west there is a small stream, and there are some small trees and brush along the banks. There are a lot of rises to the northwest and the north. It's the same to the east as you will see if you take the road from Ft. Worth to the ranch. Some of these rises are just the right size. A whole platoon of soldiers could hide behind some of them and not be seen from the house." Jug had his pencil and paper and was drawing the map showing everything that Sean needed to know.

"This is good," said Sean. "I'd like for you to make several copies so each of us can have one. I want every man to know that place like it was his own home. Don't forget to make one for Jon. He'll be here any day now."

"I'll get them done," said Jug.

~~~~

Lolita asked Maggie if she could help out in the kitchen while they were there. "I don't care if Cookie doesn't," said Maggie. "His wife helps at times when we're busy. I bet she won't mind not helping." Lolita went to Cookie and asked if she could help in the kitchen.

"Why you sure can," said Cookie. "Maybe you can show me how to make some Mexican type food. I've never made any. I bet when them boys get up here from Texas, they'd like some of that food."

"I'll show you what I know how to do," said Lolita. "My mother was a good cook and always kept my father happy. Both of them died when I was fifteen, but I learned well from her."

"That'll be fine," said Cookie. "You let me know what you need, and I'll get it. Maybe we can try something new tomorrow. For now, you start cuttin' up that piece of beef over there. Just gonna make some stew today."

~~~~

Betty told Maggie about her plans, and Maggie told her she was happy for her. "If you would like," said Maggie, "you can help tend the bar when the men are gone."

"I'd like that," said Betty. "That'd be a good time to let some of my regulars know that I'm out of the business. I don't think they'll be any trouble."

"Well if there is," said Maggie, "Jug'll be here, he can throw them out."

~~~~

Two days later, Jon rode into town. Dog was with him. Jeb and Dog were happy to see each other again. "How's that wife a yours?" asked Sean when Jon came into the saloon. Jon went to Sean and they shook hands. "She didn't say," started Jon, "but I'd say I'm gonna be a father in the summer."

"That's great," said Sean. "Me'n Maggie got married a few days ago, and I hear Michael's gonna get married when we get back."

"All of us best not get ourself killed then," said Jon. "Don't wanna make our women widows just yet."

"No we don't," said Sean. "Now you get yourself fed and get some rest. We'll get together tomorrow mornin' and go over what we're gonna do." Just then, Jug came over to them. "This big fella here is Jug Carter." Jug and Jon shook hands. "That good lookin' woman in the kitchen is his wife Lolita. Jug's up from Texas. He was foreman on Anderson's ranch. He'll be lookin' after things here while we're gone."

"So Anderson is tryin' to look like a respectable rancher," said Jon. "We'll respectable him right to his own hangin'. We gotta get him this time."

"We'll get 'em," said Sean. "We'll get 'em. Now go get fed and rested. We'll meet here after breakfast in the morning."

~~~~

After breakfast, Sean made sure each man had a copy of the drawings Jug had made. "I want you men to study these drawings over and over till you have them memorized," Sean started. "We'll be leavin' in the mornin'. Anderson will not expect us in the winter. We must pack plenty of food and warm clothes. Each man will take a pack horse. We'll take some canvas so we can build shelters. It might just snow on us. Take all the ammunition you can pack. We'll take a few spare horses too. We might do some tradin'. I'm hopin' we run into Flying Eagle on the way. I'd like to talk him into helpin' us a little."

"Do you think he would?" asked Michael. "It would be nice if he did. We'll be outnumbered as usual."

"If he would lend us some men," started Sean, "we could get them surrounded. I figure his men can run off their horses, and then lay back. We'll go in and kill as many as we can. Any tries to run off, the Kiowas can get them. We'll do some more figurin' on the way down, and after we get there. But whatever happens, Anderson gets hung. Even if he gets shot or is dead, he gets hung."

"There still might be some men down there who don't know who Anderson is," said Jug. "You should try to get word to them somehow, so they don't shoot at you thinkin' you're just someone who come to the place to do some killin'. And you don't wanna kill men that don't need killin'."

"I'll do some thinkin' on that on the way down," said Sean. "It'd be nice if they already found out, and took off. Jug, while we're gone, you keep yourself armed at all times. Keep a loaded gun next to your bed. There are two shotguns behind the bar, one at each end. Maggie always keeps a pistol on her. We got a jail with one cell here. Between you and Jason, use it if you hafta. Hopefully, it will be quiet while we're gone. Now everyone get their gear rounded up, and try to get some rest. We'll be leavin' right after breakfast."

CHAPTER TWENTY

Next morning after breakfast, the men mounted up and headed for Texas. Jeb and Dog were eager to go. Sean made sure each man had his proper gear and weapons. Michael had his new pistol and the old army revolver, plus a Spencer that he had gotten recently. Jon had his two pistols and his Henry. Charlie also had his new pistol and the Henry that had been Jim's, plus Jim's old army revolver. Bob had his new pistol, his old revolver, and his Spencer. Sean was packing two pistols, a Henry, his sharp's, and his ten gauge double barrel shotgun. His other pistol that he normally wore in his shoulder holster, he left with Maggie. He could still feel Maggie's goodbye kiss on his lips as they got out of sight of town.

"We'll head down through Osage land and see John Littletree and make sure everything is all right there," said Sean when they had been on the trail for an hour or so. "Then we'll go through Creek territory, and then Choctaw land. We shouldn't have any trouble with the Creek or Choctaw. I'd say once we tellem we're after Anderson, they'll be happy to let us pass through. They've probably had trouble with outlaws before."

~~~~

The weather was fairly good until they got to Osage land. It started snowing. It wasn't a hard snow, but it was wet. They set up shelters when they camped that night. Next morning, the snow quit and it warmed up. By the time they got to Littletree's village, it seemed like a spring day. The sun was shining and there wasn't a cloud in the sky.

Littletree was standing in front of his cabin when the men rode into the village. "You're after Anderson, aren't you?" John said. "We haven't had any trouble since you were here last time. Is he in Texas now?"

"Yes, he is," said Sean. "We know right where he is this time, and we're gonna get him."

"You will spend the night here," said John. "I'll find a place for all your men so no one will sleep outside tonight. I'll have some of the women make us a fine meal."

"Many thanks, my friend," said Sean. "When we leave here, we'll go through Creek land, and then Choctaw land. We shouldn't have any trouble with them, should we?"

"You shouldn't," said John, "but I will travel with you. I speak Creek and Choctaw. Most of them speak English, but not all of them. I am not sure who their Chiefs are now. They did have some young men who talked about the old ways. Why, I don't know. They aren't old enough to know about the old ways."

"I know sign," said Sean. "If they know sign, I can talk with them."

"I will go with you anyway, my friend," said John. "It's good to get out once in a while and see your neighbors."

That night, the women cooked a very good meal, and the men were glad to sleep under a roof for a change. A few days later, they were in Creek land. The men they met all spoke English, and led them to their village. The Chief was an older man, but still looked strong and healthy. He was glad that Sean and his men were going after Anderson. Anderson had stolen a lot of horses from them last year.

Choctaw land was a different story. They spoke English, and the Chief was a nice person, but there was a young hothead who didn't want Sean to pass through. "This is our land," he kept yelling. "No white man has any business on our land, no matter what the reason." He had an old sharp's carbine and he kept acting like he was going to cock the hammer and shoot one of them. Finally, Sean had enough.

"Young fella," started Sean, "I do not kill Indians unless they're tryin' to kill me, but if you touch the hammer on that rifle one more time, I'll blow your damn head off. Now we're Federal Officers, and we're goin' through here whether you like it or not." Sean saw the man's thumb move toward the hammer, and Sean had a pistol out and pointed at the man's head before he even touched the hammer. "Are you ready to die?" Sean asked him. "If you are, I'll oblige you. If not, put that rifle down right now, and I mean now!" The young man was embarrassed and apparently didn't want to lose face, and he tried to cock the hammer on his rifle. When he did, Sean squeezed the trigger on his pistol, and the man flew backwards. Blood went everywhere.

Sean felt really bad about this, and apologized to the Chief. "I am very sorry about this, but I won't stand around and let some young hothead shoot me or my men," said Sean. "Are there any more like this that I need to worry about?"

"No," said the Chief, "he was the one who tried to lead the young men. They have no one to follow now. You will not have any more trouble in our land. I hope you get Anderson. That would be one less white man to worry about."

~~~~

A few days later, they crossed into Texas, and John Littletree headed back home. The closer they got to Ft. Worth, the quieter the men became. They knew a big fight was coming soon. When they finally got close to Ft. Worth, Sean decided they should send a man to town and see if Anderson might be there. That had to be Bob. He could identify Anderson, but it was very doubtful Anderson could identify him. Bob had seen Anderson when his herd was rustled, but Anderson had most likely not noticed Bob. "He won't be wearin' that reb coat and that hat with the big plume on it," said Sean. "He'll probably be wearin' nice clothes and tryin' to look respectable."

"I'll know his face," said Bob. "Won't matter what kinda clothes he's awearin'."

"Well you be careful in there," said Sean. "Somebody might just remember you from your Ranger days, maybe somebody you don't want to remember you."

"I'll be careful boss," said Bob. "Be back shortly."

~~~~

Bob took his badge off, then rode into town, and visited every saloon and hotel. He did not see Anderson. While he was in one of the saloons, he overheard two men talking about some ranch that was hiring. Bob went over and asked them where the ranch was, and who was the boss. One of the men he had overheard, spoke right up. "Man's name is Sanderson," he said. "Place is three days ride westa here. I hear he needs men who know how to fight Comanche. Who might you be?"

"Name's Ed Smith," said Bob. "Been lookin' fer work for a while."

"Well good luck to you, if you go out there Ed," the man said. "Me, I don't want nothin' to do with no Comanche." Bob thanked the man, and left. Then he decided to take a chance and go to the town Marshal's office, and see what he knew about Anderson.

The Marshal was setting behind his desk drinking coffee when Bob walked in. "Name's Ed Smith," said Bob. "Some boys in town told me bout a man named Sanderson who's doin' some hirin' for his ranch. Would you know anything about it?"

" Sure do," said the Marshal. "I'm Mark Sims. Sanderson's got a ranch three days westa here. He's had Comanche trouble. Needs men who know how to fight Injuns. His woman got took, and his foreman got kilt. He should be out there. He comes to town about once a month, and he was here not long ago. Are you a Injun fighter?"

"I done some," said Bob. "I reckon I can help Sanderson if it's a payin' job. I'm flat broke."

"Well good luck to you," said Mark. "Keep yer hair."

~~~~

Bob got back to the others and told what he had heard. "Well we'll head west till we find the ranch," started Sean. "Then Jon can scout out the place, while I go lookin' for Flying Eagle. He should be to the north just a bit in his winter camp. We need to watch for Comanche too. They could be in the area. If I find Flying Eagle, maybe I could ask him if he would tell the Comanche what we're doin' and ask them to leave us alone."

When they got close to the ranch, they could see that Jug was right. The road looked like it went straight up to the front door. They backed off some and found a good spot to lay low. "Now I'll go find the Kiowa," said Sean, "and Jon can start scoutin' the place. You need to be very careful. They might have someone on watch all the time since they've had Comanche trouble. If some of those men rode with Anderson during the war, they'll shoot first and ask questions later. I'm still thinkin' about what to do about any men who might not know who Anderson is. I'll be back in two or three days."

~~~~

Sean rode north and then northwest. He saw plenty of unshod tracks so he knew he would find the Kiowa soon. On the second day, he was watering his horse at a small stream when he saw two Indians in the distance. They saw him too and were coming toward him. When they got closer, he signed, and they answered. He mounted his horse and they took him to the village. Flying Eagle was setting in front of his lodge when Sean rode in. "It's good to see you again, my friend," said the Chief. "I know you are after Anderson. What do you want from me?"

"It is good to see you too, my friend," started Sean. "My deputies and I are down here to kill Anderson and his men. There are only five of us. We would like your help. We would like for you to tell the Comanche what we are doing so they will leave us alone. I would like for your men to help us steal their horses, and then surround the place. My deputies and I will go in amongst them and kill them. Your men can kill anyone who gets past us. When it is done, you and the Comanche can have all the horses and cattle you want. You can even have the guns from the men we kill."

"There is only five of you, and you expect to kill all of them," said the Chief. "You and your men must be very good warriors. Anderson may have twenty men."

"He just might have that many men," replied Sean. "But we intend to kill 'em."

"We will help you," said the Chief. "I will send a brave to the Comanche, and I will give you fifteen warriors. I will send my best horse stealers. They will stay back from the fight and kill any men that get past you and your men. Now you will spend the night with us, and my warriors will go with you in the morning."

~~~~

Jon scouted the ranch with no problems. There were eighteen men, the cook, and Anderson. The cleaning lady was there too. They went out in groups of five to tend the cattle. The three that didn't go stayed back and kept watch around the big house and the buildings. Anderson didn't go out with them, at least when Jon was watching. No nighthawks were sent out, but they kept one man on watch at night.

~~~~

On the ride back to the men, Sean thought about what do about the men who didn't know about Anderson. He couldn't come up with a plan.

When Sean got back with the Kiowa braves, all the men seemed to be relieved. "What'd you find out, Jon?" asked Sean.

"They got eighteen men, the cook, and Anderson," said Jon. "There's that cleaning lady there too. In the mornin' they send out the men in groups of five, and three stay behind to keep watch. Anderson did not go out with the men. At night, they keep one man on watch. They trade off every three hours."

"All right, any a you got an idea?" asked Sean.

"We could wait till the men go out in the morning, then take Anderson and the rest," said Charlie.

"We could do that, but if there's shootin'," said Sean, "some of 'em might come back and some might skedaddle. I don't want any of 'em gettin' away. I want to end this thing. We'll only have fifteen braves out there. They're coverin' a lotta ground. Some could get paste 'em. Anybody else got an idea?" No one else did.

"Well here's what I was thinkin'," started Sean. "Bout two hours before daylight, Me and Jon'll slip in there and take care of the man on watch, and the cook. The cook should be in the cook shack. Then the Kiowa can take the horses. When this is done, the rest will slip in. Four of us will take the bunkhouse, and one of us will get the woman outta the house, and then take Anderson."

"This all sounds good as long as we get the guard, the cook, the woman, and the rest of them are still asleep," said Bob.

"We could just set the bunkhouse on fire, and get the drop on them when they run out," said Michael. "I doubt if they would take the time to get their guns and such when the place is burning."

"That might be true," said Sean, "but I'd hate to burn an innocent man if someone didn't get out on time."

"I guess it's too late to call in the army," said Michael.

"Yes it is," said Sean. "They think he's Thomas Sanderson and a respectable rancher. It'd take forever gettin' them to believe us,

Marshals or not. He'd get word and be long gone before they got off their asses. Now let's end this thing."

Bob said he wanted to be the one who went for Anderson, so Sean, Michael, Jon, and Charlie would take the bunkhouse. The men didn't talk much that evening. They didn't get much sleep either.

When the time came, Sean and Jon moved toward their targets. All of their horses were tied behind a low rise about a hundred yards to the north of the house. Bob and Jon told Jeb and Dog to stay and watch the horses.

The man on watch was standing in front of the barn. He was smoking, and every drag gave away his position. Jon slipped up on him with ease, knocked him cold, tied and gagged him, and dragged him into the barn. Inside the barn, he tied the man to the side of a stall. When Sean got to the cook shack, the cook was already up, starting work on the morning meal. He was singin' to himself. Sean just walked in and stuck a pistol in the man's face. "I'm Federal Marshal O'Rourke," said Sean. "We're here after Anderson."

"I heard a you," said the cook. "Who the hell is Anderson?"

"You never heard a George Anderson?" asked Sean.

"Sure I heard a him," said the cook. "Everybody's heard a that son of a bitch. I never seen him though."

"Well your boss is George Anderson," said Sean. "I've known him since we was kids back in Tennessee. Now there could be a lota shootin' shortly. If you don't want to git yourself shot, you best stay low and stay put. If I find out you're lyin' to me, I will shoot you dead."

"I'm not lyin' Marshal, I'll stay low," the cook said.

"Some a his men are about as bad as he is," said Sean. "If they would see you, and you weren't helpin' them, they'd shoot you too."

"Like I said, Marshal, I'll stay low," said the cook.

"You got any guns here?" asked Sean.

"There's a shotgun over there in the corner," he said. "It's not loaded. I take it with me when we drive cows to the army posts. I got mebbe four shells for it."

"Well you use them if you hafta," said Sean. "I'm trustin' you mister. If I didn't, I'd knock you out and tie you up. Don't let me down."

"You can trust me, Marshal," he said. "I'll be so low in here, they'll hafta dig me up ta bury me."

~~~~

Some of the Kiowa slipped in and took all the horses. Once the horses were taken, Bob slipped around the big house and into the kitchen. He could hear the woman in her room snoring. Bob snuck in, and put his hand over the woman's mouth. When she looked up at him in terror, he whispered to her. "I'm a Federal Deputy," he said. "If you promise not to scream, I'll take my hand from your mouth. If you do scream, I will knock you out and gag you." The woman shook her head no telling Bob that she wouldn't scream. He removed his hand, and she did not scream. "I am Deputy Bob Wallace," Bob said. "Your boss is really George Anderson, the bad outlaw and gang leader. We're here to arrest him." The woman looked at Bob in disbelief. "Whether you believe me or not, there could be a lotta shootin' shortly," said Bob. "I want you to take yourself to that root cellar out back, close the door, and stay put. Don't come out till me or another deputy comes and gets you." The woman put on a robe, and ran out to the root cellar.

Sean, Michael, Jon, and Charlie were ready to take the bunk-house now. Sean had his ten gauge in one hand and a pistol in the other. The hammers were cocked on the shotgun and his pistol. Michael had his rifle in one hand, and a pistol in the other. Jon had a pistol in each hand. Charlie was armed with his new pistol and a Henry. All of them had their hammers cocked. The only door to the bunkhouse was on the end that was toward the big house. They could hear the men inside snoring. Sean went through the door first, then Michael, Jon, and Charlie. There were ten bunks on each side. Three of them were empty. After a few seconds, Sean let out a loud whistle. The men started waking up. "Good morning sweethearts," said Sean. "Move slow or we'll kill you."

The man in the first bunk on the right made a move for his pistol that was in a holster at the head of his bunk. Sean pistol whipped him, knocking him cold.

"Next one that tries something like that'll get this ten gauge in the face," said Sean. "Well look who's here. It's Fred Brown. I see you made it down to Anderson." Fred was in the first bunk on the left side.

"Yep, I made it, Marshal," Fred said. "Been working here ever since."

"Well Fred, you're gonna help me out," said Sean. "You're gonna tell us which a these fellas don't know that the boss is really George Anderson."

"How would I know that?" said Fred.

Sean got in Fred's face and stuck the shotgun on his throat. "Now who don't know?" asked Sean.

"The last three on this side and the last two on the other side," answered Fred as he was shaking. "Now would you get that thing away from me?"

Sean took the shotgun away from Fred's throat. "You five, git yourself outta here," said Sean. "Just go down the road aways. When this is over, we'll get your gear and horses back to you." The five men did as instructed.

~~~~

After Bob made sure the woman was in the root cellar, he started making his way upstairs to Anderson's bedroom. He tried to be as quiet as he could, but one of the steps squeaked a little. When it did, Bob stopped for a while before moving again.

George Anderson always kept a pistol under his pillow and a Henry beside his bed. He trusted no one. He had been a light sleeper his whole life and when he heard the step squeak, he grabbed his pistol and cocked the hammer. He laid flat on his back pretending to be asleep with the pistol in his right hand and down to his side. The door to his bedroom was open, and when he saw Bob in the doorway, he raised the pistol and fired from under the sheets. Bob was struck in the chest and thrown backwards. The sheets caught on fire, and George got up and put out the fire. Then he grabbed his Henry and ran to a window so he could see if anything was going on below.

When the shot was fired, Charlie looked out the door of the bunkhouse to see if he could see anything. When he did, a bullet struck him in the chest. He fell backwards, bleeding from his mouth. When Sean turned his head for a second to see Charlie falling backwards, the men in the bunkhouse all scrambled for their guns. Sean had only looked at Charlie for a split second.

When he looked back, he saw what was happening and cut loose with the ten gauge. Michael and Jon cut loose with their pistols. Blood went flying everywhere. Several of Anderson's men had gotten their guns and the firing was getting very intense in the bunkhouse. There was so much smoke, Sean, Michael, and Jon were having a hard time seeing them. George was still up in his bedroom and was firing at the bunkhouse hoping to hit Sean and his deputies. He could see a little of what was happening through the small windows on the bunkhouse, but there was so much smoke, he couldn't be sure of his targets. He kept firing anyway.

Sean emptied both of his pistols and reloaded the ten gauge. He could hardly see because of the smoke, but fired at the muzzle flashes he saw. Michael was lying on the floor trying to reload his pistol and the Spencer. He had blood all over him, but Sean could not tell where he was hit. He may have been hit several times. Jon was still standing and firing when Sean saw him go down. He couldn't tell if he was alive or not. Sean felt a bullet rip through his right side. He went down, but was able to reload the shotgun. After he fired one barrel, another bullet ripped into his left shoulder. He managed to fire the other barrel. He reloaded again, but before he could fire again, he had a strange feeling come over him. It was quiet. He waited a few seconds. It was still quiet. He sat on the floor and waited for the smoke to clear. After a few minutes, he was able to see enough to tell what had happened. Michael had been hit in his left arm, his right leg, and a bullet had creased his skull. Jon had been hit two times, once in each shoulder. There were twelve dead men in the bunkhouse. They were ripped to pieces. Sean was amazed. How could that many men have a shootout for that long a time in such a small place. It looked like the man that Sean had pistol whipped when they first came into the bunkhouse, had not regained consciousness before he was shot to pieces. Sean went to Michael and Jon and checked their wounds. Their bleeding had slowed down some, so Sean decided to go outside for a look.

When the shooting in the bunkhouse ceased, George decided to go have a look. He kicked Bob's body when he left his room, making sure he was dead. He made his way downstairs and worked his way to the bunkhouse. He spotted Sean before Sean spotted him. He took aim with his rifle and was squeezing the trigger when a bullet ripped into his back. He fell forward, bleeding from his mouth. Sean heard a voice and looked toward the house. It was Bob. He wasn't dead yet. "I said I'd get that son of a bitch if it's the last thing I do." Then he slumped over in Anderson's bedroom window.

Sean went over to Anderson. He was not dead. Sean took George's rifle and checked him for other weapons. There were none. Sean went back to the bunkhouse, found some rope, then came back and tied Anderson's hands behind his back, and tied his legs together. Then he went to Michael and Jon. "My friends," said Sean, "I'll get the cook and that woman, and see if they can't find something to bandage us up with."

"I'll be all right, young Sean," said Michael. "Bullets just bounce off my head."

~~~~

Sean went to the cook shack. The cook was still hiding. "C'mon out," said Sean. "You any good on bullet wounds? Got some men who need some patchin' up."

"Looks like you could use some patchin' too, Marshal," the cook said.

"My friends are over at the bunkhouse," said Sean. "Look after them first." Then Sean went to the root cellar for the woman. She was curled up in a ball when Sean opened the cellar door. "I'm Marshal O'Rourke, ma'am," said Sean. "It's all over now. You can come out. We need some bandages. We been shot up some." The woman finally quit shaking.

"I'll go in the house and get some linen," she said. "I'll start boiling some water. Get the wounded men into the kitchen and I'll do what I can."

~~~~

When the cook got to the bunkhouse to see about Michael and Jon, he looked at the carnage for a good while. "God almighty," he said, "haven't seen men ripped up like that since the war." Sean was coming back to the bunkhouse now.

"Bring Michael and Jon over to the kitchen," said Sean. "That woman's heatin' up some water and has bandages. Don't worry bout Anderson. I'm gonna hang him soon as we get patched up. Just leave him lay where he is."

Sean and his two deputies were lucky. Every bullet that had hit them, had passed through and not taken much bone with it. The bullet that hit Sean in his left shoulder had missed his new badge by only an inch. It missed his lung too. Both of the bullets that had struck him, passed between the pieces of metal that were in his vest. Sean was glad that they did not hit the metal directly, or it might have slowed the bullets down enough that they wouldn't have passed through, and would have to be dug out. He decided right there that he would remove all the metal plates from the vest. The woman cleaned the wounds and patched them up like she had done it several times before.

Sean told the cook where their horses were tied, and told him to get down the road and bring those five men back. "Take the other horses with you," said Sean. "There's two dogs there watchin' the horses. Their names are Jeb and Dog. Talk nice to them and call them by name, and they'll leave you alone. Tell those men they best not even think about takin' off. We got the place surrounded by some Kiowa." The cook did as instructed, and the five men were back in no time. They had actually started walking back when the shooting had ceased. "You men can go get your gear now," said Sean. "I'll have the Kiowa bring in your horses shortly. I need you men to do some buryin'. I got two dead deputies, and there's twelve dead men in the bunkhouse. Hell, I almost forgot. I got one of 'em tied up in the barn. Some a you go get 'em outta there, but leave his hands tied. I don't know who he is yet." Two of the five went to get the man out of the barn and the other three went into the bunkhouse. The three of them that went into the bunkhouse, ran out and threw up after they saw the carnage. The other two men brought the tied man to Sean. "Who might you be?" asked Sean.

"Go to hell, lawman," he shouted and spit at Sean.

"I'd just about say your name is Hawk," said Sean. "Is it, young fella?" He didn't answer. One of the two men who had retrieved him from the barn spoke.

"That's Jed Hawk," he said. "His cousin Matt was in the bunkhouse."

"So, Jed Hawk, how many men you killed?" asked Sean.

"Not near enough," he answered. "Yer still breathin'."

"Well, you're not gonna be shortly," said Sean. "I'm gonna hang you right after I hang Anderson there." Jed turned a little pale and didn't say a word. "One a you boys get me a couple a good ropes." One of them brought Sean the ropes. "Now get two horses. Untie Anderson's legs and throw him up on a horse. Go over to that oak tree by the house. Sean put the rope around Anderson's neck and threw it up over a big limb. Then he tied it off to the trunk of the tree. Anderson was bleeding from his mouth a lot and could barely set up.

"You got anything to say before I send you to hell?" asked Sean.

"I shoulda killed your ass back in Tennessee," George gasped. Sean slapped the horses rump and George was hanged. He must have been almost dead because he didn't kick at all.

"Now throw this Hawk fella on a horse," said Sean. They did as instructed. Sean placed the rope around his neck and threw the rope up over the same tree limb and tied it off to the trunk of the tree. "You got anything to say, Hawk?" asked Sean.

"Yeh, I do," Hawk said. "Anderson's boss won't like you killin' all a us."

"Well if Anderson did have a boss, which I doubt," said Sean, "sooner or later I'll catch him and hang him too. Now you can go straight to hell too." Then Sean slapped the horse's rump and Jed Hawk was hanged.

"Now one a you boys help me up on a horse," said Sean. "I'll go tell them Kiowa to come in and bring your horses back. You men get to buryin'. When you get done, I want the names of those men we killed, if you know them. Don't be afraid when them Kiowa come in. They're my friends."

~~~~

The five men started dragging the bodies out of the bunkhouse. When Sean and the Kiowa got there with the horses, they rounded up a couple of buckboards so they could take the bodies where it was easier digging. "Bury my two deputies separate from them others," said Sean. "I'll be puttin' up some markers and sayin' some words." Then Sean went to the house and talked to the woman. "Ma'am," started Sean, "my deputies and me will be stayin' here for a spell so we can heal up some. I'd like for you to stay while we're here. You seem to know about wounds, and you can cook for us. I'll pay you for your time."

"I would be glad to stay," she said. "My name is Barbara Sanchez. I'll need to get all the money I can since I just lost my job and place to stay."

"I'm sorry about that, Miss Sanchez," said Sean. "Anderson had a lotta people fooled."

"Well, it will be good to talk with someone again," said Barbara. "Mr. Sanderson, or Anderson, or whatever his name is, never talked to me at all after Lolita was taken."

"I got some news for you, Miss Sanchez," said Sean. "Lolita was not taken and Jug Carter is still alive."

"How would you know that?" asked Barbara.

"Because Lolita and Jug are up in Kansas right now," said Sean. "They came up there to get away from Anderson. Jug was the one who told us that Anderson was here. Him and Lolita got married. In fact, we had a double wedding. Jug married Lolita, and I married my Maggie."

"I am so glad," said Barbara. "I was having nightmares thinking about Lolita being with the Comanche."

~~~~

It took several hours, but all the dead men got buried. Sean put up markers for Bob and Charlie. They had a small service and Sean,

Michael, and Jon, each said a few good words about them. They said the Lord's Prayer, then Sean thanked both of the dead men for being his deputies, and gave Bob an extra special thanks for saving his life. Jeb laid on Bob's grave the whole time.

Then Sean handed a piece of paper and a pencil to one of the five men, and told them to write down the names of the men killed. Some of them, they only knew by nicknames, but they were written down. "Now, boys, I want you to write your names down," said Sean.

"Why do you need our names, Marshal?" one of them asked.

"Because, young fella," started Sean. "We're gonna stay out here for a spell and heal up some. All five a you are gonna promise me that you will not tell a livin' soul that we're here and what happened for two weeks. If you do, and I find out, I'll be huntin' you down. We don't want nobody else out here gunnin' for us. I'm gonna give one a you a couple a telegrams to get sent too. I'll give you some money. In fact, since you all just lost your jobs, I'll give you all a month's pay, forty dollars. That sound all right?"

"Sounds good to us," most of them said.

"Another thing, when you give them telegrams to the operator, you tell him that if he runs his mouth, I'll be huntin' him down," said Sean. Then Sean got some more paper and wrote the two telegrams. The first one went as follows:

Judge David Simmons Federal Courthouse St. Louis

Anderson and twelve of his men dead <stop> two deputies killed <stop> Myself and two deputies wounded not badly <stop> back to Abilene when healed some <stop> O'Rourke

The second one went as follows:

Maggie O'Rourke Abilene Kansas

Anderson dead <stop> Bob and Charlie killed <stop> me Michael Jon all wounded not badly <stop> home in two or three weeks <stop>

Love
Sean

Here ends The Sean O'Rourke Series, Book 2, *A Killer For The Common Good—LAWMAN*. Continue reading for a preview of The Sean O'Rourke Series, Book 3, *O'Rourke's Revenge*.

The Sean O'Rourke Series
Book 3

O'Rourke's Revenge

by

Michael E. Cook

CHAPTER 1

After the five men left for Ft. Worth, Sean went to the bunk-house to take a count of the twelve dead men's weapons. He had told Flying Eagle that the Kiowa could have all the weapons. It was still pretty messy in the bunkhouse. Besides all the blood, there were pieces of skull and brain all over the place. Sean rounded up every weapon and all the ammunition and took it outside. There were ten rifles total not counting Anderson's Henry. Eight of them were Henrys and the other two were Spencers. Of the eight Henrys, six of them were damaged so badly that they couldn't be used. Four of those had their stocks shot off next to the receivers, plus their magazines shot off. Two of them had been hit on the receiver and were bent so much that the action wouldn't work. The other two just had the magazines bent a little, and holes in their stocks, but could probably still be used. One of the Spencers was missing a hammer. The other one had been hit two times on the receiver and the action wouldn't work. There were twelve pistols and only two of them were conversions. One of the conversions was missing a hammer and one of the other pistols had its' loading rod missing. There was not as much ammunition as Sean had expected. He figured that anyone working for Anderson would be well supplied. Maybe there was more ammunition in the house, but he wouldn't worry about that now.

The Kiowa picked out the weapons they wanted and with the extra horses, were on their way. Sean could tell that they were disappointed about the weapons but were glad to get what they could. Sean told them that he and his men would be staying at the place for a week. Then they would go to Ft. Worth. He told the Kiowa that it would be all right with him if they burned the place down after he left.

Sean and his men were pretty shot up, and he needed someone to take care of their horses, so he went to the cook shack to ask the cook if he would stay for a week. "We need someone to look after the horses for us," said Sean. "Would you be willing to stay? I'll pay you for your time. I'll also give you a month's pay like I did those other men."

"Sure, I'll do that for you," he said. "I got nowheres to be right now anyhow. I can help with the cookin' too if that woman needs help. By the way, name's Joe, Joe Taylor."

"Pleased to know you Joe," said Sean. "You got a cook wagon, don't you?"

"Sure do. We can use it to help take you and your boys outta here when you're ready to go," said Joe. "Don't reckon you all will be up ta ridin' for a spell."

"You're right there, Joe," said Sean. "That big geldin' a mine is a smooth ride, but a wagon'll be a might easier on me and the boys. Well I'm gonna go see how the boys are doin'. See you later."

When Sean went back to the house, Michael and Jon were asleep in some big fancy chairs in the entertaining room. Miss

Sanchez was in the kitchen preparing the next meal. Sean went into the kitchen to talk with her. "Miss Sanchez, have you got any relatives around or anywhere to go after we leave here?" Sean asked her.

"My husband and I didn't have any children," she began. "My husband was Mexican, and he got himself killed fighting the French. My parents are long gone, and I have no idea where any of his family would be. I have been taking cooking jobs wherever I could get them. I should be able to find something. And would you please call me Barbara?"

"Sure, I'll call you Barbara," responded Sean. "I was thinkin' that maybe you would come to Kansas with us. Abilene is gonna grow soon, and I'm sure you could find work there. I got a lotta influence there, too. I can help you with a place to live while you're lookin' for work. As good as you are with bullet wounds, you could probably be a nurse anywhere. You're a handsome woman too. Could be you might find yourself a new husband."

"You are embarrassing me, Mr. O'Rourke," Barbara said. "I haven't thought about a man for some time. I suppose if a good one would come along, I could make myself available. I'll think about Kansas. We have plenty of time. I hope you and your men like my cooking."

"I'm sure we will," said Sean. "Now you can call me Sean. I have something to ask you."

"What can I do for you?" she asked.

"Michael was shot in the leg, and it might be too much for him to sleep upstairs," said Sean. "Would you mind letting him sleep in your room and you can have your pick of the rooms upstairs?"

"That will be all right with me," Barbara answered. "I'll get my things out of the room right after we eat."

Michael was awake now, and Sean could hear him saying something and went to the other room to see what he wanted. "Is there anything to drink around here?" Michael asked Sean.

"I'll see what our former host has in the house," said Sean. "I would say that Anderson had only the best." Sean looked around the entertaining room and didn't see evidence of any liquor. Then he went into the study. Sean came back out carrying two bottles and four glasses. "We're well supplied," said Sean. "There's a big cabinet in that room that is just clear full. I brought a bottle of Irish Whiskey and some good bourbon. What'll you have, my friend?"

"I'll have some of that Irish Whiskey," said Michael. "I haven't had any of that for years. You should try some too, my friend. The smoothness of it will amaze you."

"All right, my friend, I'll give it a try." said Sean. "Barbara, would you like a glass of whiskey too?"

"I'll try some of that Irish Whiskey too," she said. "I have heard that it's very smooth."

Jon was still asleep so Sean filled three glasses. "Oh my, that stuff is amazing," said Sean after he took a sip. "A fella could get himself drunk pretty quick drinkin' that stuff. It would go down so quick. How in the hell can they make that stuff so smooth?"

"I don't know," answered Michael. "Sure is good, isn't it? What do you think, Barbara?"

"I think a person could get hooked on this stuff very easily," she answered. "I've never had anything like this before."

Jon was starting to wake up now. "So you all are drinkin' without me," said Jon. "Somebody get me a glass." Sean poured Jon a glass of the Irish Whiskey. "Whoa, this is some good stuff," said Jon after he took a sip. "Let's make sure we take this stuff with us when we leave, if there's any left."

"There's a liquor cabinet in the next room and it's clear full," said Sean. "We'll take all of it with us when we go. We'll try some of this bourbon next. I'm gonna go ask Joe if he would like a drink. Don't wanna be selfish." Sean left the house and returned in a few minutes with Joe. "Try some a this Irish Whiskey," said Sean. "You'll like it for sure." Sean went to the study and got a glass for Joe.

"I never had nothin' like this before," said Joe. "It goes down too good. Are you sure it's whiskey?"

"Yes, I'm sure," said Sean. "We'll have some bourbon next and you can decide which one you like the best."

When everyone was finished with the Irish Whiskey, Sean got everyone a fresh glass and poured the bourbon. "This is some damn good bourbon," said Sean. "Anderson musta liked good liquor." Everyone enjoyed the bourbon, but no one could decide which of the two whiskeys they liked better. "I could drink either one of them any time," said Sean.

"Same for me," said Jon and Michael.

When mealtime came, they all sat at the kitchen table. Barbara had made a stew because it would be easier for the men to eat. Everyone thought the food was great. Joe was asking her what she used for seasonings and such. After the meal, Joe helped Barbara with the dishes. "How bout I hang around and help with the next meal," said Joe. "Mebbe I can learn somethin' from ya. When yer out on a drive, it sure helps if the men are happy about what they're eatin'."

"Sounds good," said Barbara. "After breakfast in the morning, you and I can look around and see what's here, and figure out what we'll have for supper tomorrow."

The next morning after breakfast, Sean had a talk with Jon and Michael in the big room. "I told the Kiowa we'd only be here for a week." started Sean. "Joe's gonna take us outta here in his wagon. We'll use a buckboard too if needed. I figure we'll go to Ft. Worth and catch a stage that can get us to the closest train station. We should be able to take a train all the way to Kansas City, and then take a stage to Abilene. Does that sound all right to you men?"

"What about the horses?" asked Jon. "I'd kinda like to keep my horse."

"We'll take'm with us." said Sean. "I intend to keep that big red a mine too. The railroad should be able to come up with a stock car for us. What about you, Michael? Are you wantin' to keep your horse?"

"I've spent half my life in the cavalry, so I'm used to havin' different horses," said Michael. "Makes no difference to me."

"All right then, we'll take the horses with us," said Sean. "You men keep gettin' your rest. I'm gonna look around this house and see what I can find. I bet Anderson's got a bunch of ammunition stashed somewhere in here."

Sean started his search upstairs with Anderson's bedroom. There were two big closets and a chest of drawers. One of the closets was full of fancy clothes and shoes and boots. The other closet was full of ammunition. Sean figured there must have been 10,000 rounds of Henry ammunition, and another 2000 rounds of Sharps ammunition. There was also a few hundred rounds of .44 pistol ammunition and 1000 rounds of Spencer ammunition. The bottom drawer of the chest of drawers was full of shotgun shells. "Me'n the boys won't hafta buy any ammunition for quite a while," Sean said to himself. "It's a good thing we're usin' Joe's wagon." No more ammunition was found anywhere. The pistol that Anderson had used to shoot Bob was laying on the bed, and his LeMat was under the chest of drawers. The LeMat was loaded, but Sean could not find any other caps or balls for it.

The days went by quickly, and the men tried to rest as much as they could. Sean felt sorry for Jon. He and Michael both had slings for their left arms, but Jon had a sling for each arm. Barbara checked them every day to make sure they were healing well and there was no infection. Sean was impressed with the care she gave them. During this time, Jeb decided that Sean was going to be his new master. Sean didn't mind.

When it was time to leave, they needed the wagon and a buckboard to haul everything. The ammunition and the liquor took up a lot of space. Joe drove his wagon and Michael and Jon rode in the back, while Barbara drove the buckboard and Sean sat beside her. Jeb and Dog followed. It was winter, but it was not cold yet. They took some canvas with them so they could build shelters if necessary. It took them three days to get to Ft. Worth and they had no problems on the journey.

Upon their arrival in Ft. Worth, Sean went straight to the Marshal's office. When he walked in the front door, the Marshal was half asleep at his desk. Sean let out a short whistle to wake him. "Sorry to wake you, Marshal," began Sean. "Name's O'Rourke, Federal Marshal O'Rourke. Got a bit a news for you."

"So yer really him. Yer really that man that shoots so good." said the Marshal. "Pleased to meet you," he said as he extended his hand to Sean. "Name's Mark Sims. What can I do fer you?"

"First off, George Anderson is dead. Me and my deputies killed him and a buncha his men," began Sean. "The fella you knew as Thomas Sanderson was really George Anderson."

"Are you fer real, mister?" Mark said. "He seemed like a nice fella to everone here."

"Well he was not a nice fella," replied Sean. "I knew him from when we were kids back in Tennessee. He was Anderson all right. Now I hear he had beef contracts with a buncha army posts around here. If he did, I'd take it kindly if you'd send a telegram to the army and tell them they better get their beef somewhere else."

"I can do that fer ya," said Mark. "Looks like you and yer boys been shot up some. We got us a good doctor here."

"We got a good nurse with us," said Sean. "Now I need to know when the next stage is leavin'. We need to get a stage that'll get us to the nearest train station so we can get back to Kansas."

"Next stage should be leavin' in bout four hours," said Mark. "That clerk'll know about the closest train station."

"I thank you." said Sean. "Is there a freight office in this town in case our stuff won't all fit on the stage?"

"The stage depot is just down the street and there's a freight office right beside it," said Mark. "Can't miss it."

"I thank you again," said Sean. "Now I got a favor to ask of you, Mark."

"Sure Marshal, what do you need?" Mark asked.

"I'd really appreciate it if you wouldn't tell anyone that me and my boys killed Anderson and some a his bunch till we're outta town," said Sean. "Might cause some gunplay. Me and the boys are shot up some, but we'll hit what we shoot at if we have to."

"I understand," said Mark. "Won't say a word and I won't send that telegram till yer gone."

They all went to the stage depot and Sean showed the clerk everything that they intended to take with them. "All of that stuff will not fit on the stage," the clerk said. "If I was you, I'd talk to the freight office. They do a good job."

"Thank you very much," said Sean. "I'll do that. Now we're gonna need four tickets that'll get us to the closest train station so we can get to Kansas."

"That'll be no problem. You four are the only customers I got for the next stage," the clerk said. "That'll be $16, and the stage should be leavin' in just under four hours." Sean paid the clerk, thanked him, and then went next door to the freight office.

"I got some stuff I need shipped up to Abilene Kansas," said Sean. "It'll need crated up too."

"We can do it for you," the freight clerk said. "Show me what you got, and we'll get started cratin' it up. Sean showed the man what they needed shipped. He could tell that the clerk was astonished by all the ammunition and the liquor.

"Are you a drinkin' man?" Sean asked him.

"I appreciate good whiskey just like any man should," the clerk answered.

"Well we got plenty," said Sean. "You pick yourself out two bottles. Consider it a gift since my men and I can't help you much with the unloadin'."

"I got a man out back," the clerk said. "I'll get him, and we'll get it done. I'll guarantee that no bottles will get broken during shipment unless there would be a natural disaster like a flood or a cyclone or somethin'. By the way, my name is George Claybourne. Pleasure to do business with you."

"I'm Sean O'Rourke," said Sean as he extended his hand. "Pleasure to meet you."

"I've heard that name O'Rourke," said George. "Are you that Marshal that everyone's talkin' about?"

"Yes I am," said Sean. "Could you keep that to yourself till we get outta town shortly."

"I will," said George. "It's an honor to meet you. Hope you get that Anderson son of a bitch soon. He killed some a my kin back in Missouri."

"We'll get him," said Sean. "He's number one on the hangin' list."

After Joe's wagon was unloaded, he said his goodbyes and took off heading south. He was hoping to get hired on at a ranch or whatever he could find. He learned a few things from Barbara and was hoping to try them out soon. Sean found the livery and sold the buckboard and the extra horses. They found a small eatery and had a meal while they waited on the stage.

The stage left on schedule and they were still the only passengers. There would be four horse changes before they got to the nearest train station. On the third change, they picked up another passenger. He looked like a gambler to Sean, but he never said one word after he first boarded the stage. He gave a second look when he saw that all the other men were wearing slings but didn't speak. He slept all the way to the next stop. Their horses were tied to the stage, so every stop, Sean got out and made sure the horses got a drink and a little feed.

The train ride worked out well. They would only change trains once before getting to Kansas City. The train wasn't crowded so they could stretch out and sleep all they wanted. On the train ride, Jon told Sean that he wanted to take some time off and decide what he wanted to do. "I got a baby comin' and I wanna be around to see him grow up," said Jon. "I need to make up mind about this job. I been shot five times in the last three to four years. That's enough for a while."

"You take all the time you need," said Sean. "I'll go along with whatever you decide."

"Thanks Sean," said Jon. "Me and Dog'll get off somewhere before we get to Kansas City. It'll be closer to Cherokee Territory for us. I'll send you a telegram now and again."

~~~~

When it came time for Jon to leave, Sean and Michael gave him a hug and a handshake as best they could. "You take it easy on horseback," said Sean. "You're gonna be sore for a while yet. Stay in touch so I can get your money to you. Dog, you make sure he does all right and keep him outta trouble."

When they got to Kansas City, Sean sent a telegram to Maggie and told her when they should be in Abilene. They would spend the night in Kansas City and leave the next morning. Barbara was amazed in Kansas City. She had never been to a city that was that big. Sean found a livery for the horses, then got each of them a hotel room. Michael went to his room and went to sleep. Sean took Barbara downtown and let her do a little shopping. Sean went to the bank and withdrew some money. There was a saloon downstairs at the hotel that also served food, so when they got back, they got Michael and went downstairs for a meal. Jeb went with them. They took a table, and the bartender came over and asked what they needed. "Bring us a glass of your best whiskey," said Sean. "And what do you have in the way of food in here?"

"We got a good cook here," the bartender said. "I'll bring you a menu when I bring your drinks over. I'll get that dog a pan of water. That dog sure looks familiar. There was a lawman in here a while back that had a dog that looked just like this one."

"Probly same dog," said Sean. "My deputy was here sometime back when he drove a herd here."

"Where's your deputy?" asked the bartender.

"He's dead," answered Sean. "His dog claimed me now."

"I'm sorry for your loss," the bartender said. "He seemed like a good man."

"He was a good man," said Sean. "I'll miss him."

"I'll get those drinks and menus," the bartender said. "How bout I get that dog a steak, uncooked of course?"

"That'll be just fine," said Sean.

They ate their meal, had another drink, and went to their rooms. Sean had a hard time getting to sleep thinking of Maggie. Michael had the same problem with Betty. Barbara couldn't sleep either. She was going to a new place and would meet new people. Hopefully, she would be accepted.

When the stage pulled into Abeline, Maggie, Betty, and Lolita were there waiting. Maggie ran to Sean and they hugged and kissed till they were out of breath. Betty did the same to Michael. Lolita introduced Barbara to Maggie and Betty and then gave Barbara a good hug. Sean instructed Lolita to show Barbara to a room upstairs, or outback if she preferred, and then he and Maggie headed to their room. No one saw them till late the next day. When they got to their room, Sean told her, "I been shot again. Take it a little easy on me."

"I can do easy," said Maggie. "I have missed you, my lover. I can do easy for a long time."

No one saw Michael and Betty till late the next day also. "We gotta get you healed up, you big Irish hunk," said Betty. "We gotta get married soon."

"I'll heal as fast as I can," said Michael. "Don't wanna be limpin' when it's time to dance. Now let's have some more of that healin' you've been givin' me."

The next evening, both couples were at their regular table for the evening meal. "I have some sad news, darlin'," started Maggie. "Right after you left, Cookie's wife caught pneumonia. She hung on for two weeks, but Doc Rawlins couldn't save her. Cookie's not sure what he wants to do now. Lolita's been doing all the cooking. Jug's been helping out wherever he was needed."

"I feel for him," said Sean. "I hope he figures out what he wants to do. Was there any other trouble while we were gone?"

"Nothing serious happened," said Maggie. "One evening, some man saw Lolita and said something out of line and Jug broke his jaw."

"That's how it should be," said Sean. "A man should stand up for his woman. That Barbara Sanchez is a good cook. She was Anderson's cook at his ranch, and she cooked for us for a week while we were healing up some. Her and Lolita can work together in the kitchen till we see what Cookie's gonna do."

"She's already in the kitchen with Lolita," said Maggie.

"That's good," replied Sean. "Once I give Jug his reward money for Anderson, he and Lolita might decide to move on. I was gonna give him the whole $2000. I got plenty of money to give Jon and Michael. Bob left all his money to me. He made a bunch from that cattle drive. We got us a dog now too. Jeb here decided I'm his now. Hope you don't mind."

"I like that dog too," said Maggie. "He can't sleep in the bed with us though."

"No, he won't be in bed with us, but he can sleep at the foot of the bed if that's all right with you," said Sean. "That dog's like you, darlin'. Neither one a you is gonna let anything bad happen to us. Now if it's all right with you, I'd like to get some real sleep now. Didn't sleep much on the stage or the train. "

The next morning when Sean woke up, he felt really good. His wounds weren't hurting at all. "You go ahead and sleep, darlin'," he said to Maggie. "I'm goin' down and get some coffee." Sean and Jeb went downstairs and Jug was setting at the usual table drinking coffee. "Just the man I wanna see," said Sean. "Got somethin' very important to tell you."

"I'll get you some coffee," said Jug as he got up and headed to the kitchen. He brought back a full pot and another cup for Sean. "Now what you got that's so important?" asked Jug.

"I'm gonna give you all the reward money for Anderson, $2000," said Sean.

"What about your men?" said Jug. "They deserve some of it."

"I got plenty of money for them," said Sean. "They'll be fine. Now just what would you do with that kinda money?"

"That gets a man ta thinkin'," said Jug. "I always wanted my own ranch. That might get us a good start."

"Well if all them longhorns in Texas are free for the takin', all you need is a place and some good men," said Sean. "Tell you what. If you're serious about ranchin', I'll stake you. You can pay me back on your first drive. Maybe it'll be to Abilene."

"I know ranches are sellin' for just back taxes," said Jug. "That's how Anderson got his. I'll talk to Lolita and see if she wants to do this. Ranchin' can be lonely for a woman. Reckon we'll hafta have a buncha kids too. You're a good man, Sean

O'Rourke. I'm proud to call you my friend. If I do good, I'll pay you back with interest."

Sean and Jug were enjoying their coffee when three men came into the saloon. All three of them were wearing cavalry hats and one of them had something long and black hanging from his belt. They sat at a table at the other end of the saloon. Tom went over and asked what they needed, and they ordered a bottle of whiskey and three glasses. Sean wasn't too concerned about them, but he still kept an eye on them. Jug could tell that Sean was watching the three men. "Are we gonna expect trouble from those three?" asked Jug.

"I'm not sure," answered Sean. "I'm just keepin' an eye on them. I think one of those fellas has a scalp hangin' from his belt. Let's see how they act when that whiskey bottle is about empty."

Sean and Jug sipped their coffee and talked about ranching and such while still keeping an eye on the three men. As the bottle got emptier, the three men's conversation got louder and louder. One of them sounded like a big braggart. He said something about riding with Chivington and being at Sand Creek. Jug saw a change come over Sean when they heard the man say Sand Creek. The only time he had ever seen a look on a man's face like that was during the war. Jug knew something was going to happen.

Sean had two pistols on him and he checked them to make sure they were fully loaded. Then he got up and walked over to the table where the three men were sitting. Jeb went with him. "Did I hear one a you say somethin' about Sand Creek?" Sean said.

"I did," said the braggart. "I rode with Chivington and proud of it. We killed us a buncha Redsticks that day. Got me a scalp here ta prove it."

Sean was able to see the scalp now. Something shiny with a long chain was hanging from the man's belt with the scalp. Sean knew right away that this was the necklace that he had bought for Katie, and gave to Blue Swan when he had left the Cheyenne. Rage was overtaking him. Jeb had a low growl going. "Where did you get that scalp and that necklace?" Sean asked him.

"It's from a Redstick bitch I kilt," he said. "She was older, but she was a looker."

Sean pulled a pistol and stuck the muzzle of it right in the man's left eye. "You're gonna die mister," said Sean. "I'll give you your choice on how. There's three choices. One, I'll put my pistol back in my holster, and you can try to pull your pistol and kill me. Two, I can beat you to death with my fists. Three, I can take you out to Indian territory and give you to some Cheyenne Dog Soldiers. You got one minute to think about it."

To continue reading, look for The Sean O'Rourke Series, Book 3, *O'Rourke's Revenge* at your favorite online retailer starting in Summer, 2015.

Books by Michael E. Cook

<u>The Sean O'Rourke Series</u>

Book 1: A Killer For The Common Good

Book 2: A Killer For The Common Good—LAWMAN

<u>Coming soon</u>

Book 3: O'Rourke's Revenge

Available in paperback and eBook formats at Internet retailers everywhere.

ABOUT THE AUTHOR

Michael E. Cook was born in 1951 in South Central Ohio. After High School graduation, he served four years in the U.S. Marine Corps and saw service in Vietnam. After military service, Mike attended and graduated from Ohio University, Athens, Ohio, majoring in Psychology. While attending the university, he met his wife of 38 years. After working in maintenance for a short period, he worked as a brakeman, and then a locomotive engineer on the B & O Railroad of the Chessie System. When his division was shut down, Mike became Plant Manager at a snack food production facility and stayed there for almost thirty-one years, retiring in early 2014. He now resides on his mini-farm in Southwest Central Ohio with his wife. They have two children and two grandchildren. Mike's goal is to write Westerns that can be entertaining and believable.

Contact the author at mailto:cookorourkeseries@gmail.com